Prai

"A disturbing, bewilde_ _ _ _ _ _. But its very confusion dazzles rather than dazes; it creates a compulsive effect on the reader. Once caught in Pinget's maze, he will not want to put it down until he has heard the old servant out."

—Thomas Bishop, *Saturday Review*

"Pinget has succeeded in creating a character fit to rank with Joyce's Bloom; for all his illiterate-speech habits, the nameless one is a poet and a philosopher, meditating aloud on the nature of memory, truth and happiness."

—Vivian Mercier, *New York Times*

"A highly unique enterprise."

—John J. Murray, *Best Sellers*

Also by Robert Pinget in English Translation
(Dates indicate original French publication)

Novels

Between Fantoine and Agapa (1951)
Mahu or the Material (1952)
Baga (1958)
Mr. Levert (1959)
No Answer (1961)
Someone (1965)
The Libera Me Domine (1968)
Passacaglia (1969)
Fable (1971)
The Apocrypha (1980)
That Voice (1980)
Monsieur Songe (1982)
The Enemy (1987)
Be Brave (1990)
Théo or the New Era (1991)
Traces of Ink (1997)

Plays

Dead Letter (1959)
The Old Tune (1960)
Architruc (1961)
Clope (1961)
The Hypothesis (1961)
About Mortin (1967)
Abel and Bela (1971)
A Bizarre Will (1986)

THE INQUISITORY

by
Robert Pinget

Translation by Donald Watson

Dalkey Archive Press

Originally published in French as *L'Inquisitoire* by Les Éditions de Minuit, 1962
Copyright © 1962 by Les Éditions de Minuit
Translation © 1966 by Donald Watson

First Dalkey Archive edition, 2003
All rights reserved

        Library of Congress Cataloging-in-Publication Data

Pinget, Robert, 1919-1997.
    [Inquisitoire. English]
    The inquisitory / Robert Pinget ; translated by Donald Watson.
       p. cm.
    ISBN 1-56478-327-8 (alk. paper)
     I. Watson, Donald. II. Title.

PQ2631.I638I513 2003
843'.914—dc21

                                          2003055100

Partially funded by grants from the National Endowment for the Arts, a federal agency,
and the Illinois Arts Council, a state agency.

Dalkey Archive Press books are published by the Center for Book Culture, a nonprofit organization.

www.centerforbookculture.org

Printed on permanent/durable acid-free paper and bound in the United States of America

Yes or no answer

Yes or no yes or no for all I know about it you know, I mean I was only in service to them a man of all work you might say and what I can say about it, anyway I don't know anything people don't confide in a servant, my work all right my work then but how could I have foreseen, every day the same the daily round no I mean to say you'd better ask my gentlemen not me there must be some mistake, when I think that after ten years of loyal service he never said a word to me worse than a dog, you pack up and go you wash your hands of it let other people get on with it after all I mean to say, man of all work yes but who never knew a thing it's enough to turn you sour isn't it, my gentlemen didn't care so long as I did my work, at the start I was sure it couldn't go on like that let's at least try to have a little chat from time to time but in the end you get used to it you get used to it and that's how I've been for the last ten years so don't come asking me, a dog you understand and yet they chat to him there was one they used to take with them on their trips, my gentlemen took him with them on their trips

It's not about the dog it's about him, when did he leave

It must be about ten months ago, yes ten months ago from now or next month about ten months I'd say at half past six on a Monday, I was coming out of my room and going past his and what do I see the door open everything upside down drawers and cupboards all open, I went in and looked around nothing left where the suitcases were on the basin nothing left,

I went downstairs and what did I see the front door wide open, I went into the kitchen nothing not a word a note, I went back upstairs knocked at my gentlemen's door and told them he'd gone they wouldn't believe me, they slipped on their dressing-gowns and came to see for themselves that right through the house he'd left nothing of his behind, but he'd taken nothing gone off with his personal belongings and that's just what they did say straightaway, but what I must say is that they didn't say anything special they never seemed specially upset about it, they almost seemed to find it natural and that I mean to say that gave me a bit of a turn after all after ten years of loyal service I mean ten years

Was he in service there too

In service I wouldn't say he was in service, not a servant but on the whole it came to the same thing, a secretary who did everything fixed everything made all the arrangements for travelling invitations orders bills friends all those little chores, to start with I thought he was someone like me who does what he can to earn his living, I tried I tried to talk to him find out the why and wherefore something about him but not for long not for long, I soon had to admit it's no good, the cold type if you see what I mean, secretary yes everyone had to pass through him he did the work of a dozen people at least but no talking, I used to wonder what on earth can he do his day off on Tuesdays when he never came out of his room, what on earth can he do never a soul to visit him not one friend I never knew of a single one, I'd like to have known just have a chat but nothing doing and in the end you get used to it you get used to it, but there were things he must have known because people who shut themselves up like that on Tuesdays they don't need a chat that's what I always told myself, they know enough already perhaps they're tired and that's why I just put up with it I thought oh leave him be and it's understandable, and yet when you think of it he might have noticed I didn't know what to do with myself on Wednesdays my day off, he might have noticed and said the odd word to me now and again, no always busy in a hurry you'd think he did it on purpose I mean anyone who didn't know, never looking at anyone coming and going yes on purpose and that's something I don't understand instead of taking advantage of a minute's break between two appointments, not even a smile he couldn't stand even the sight of a fly in the house I was the one who had to chase after them, just to show you how it all went a bit too far

Did he stay with your gentlemen the days they entertained

Did he stay with my gentlemen how can I know if he stayed, you mean with my gentlemen and their guests I've no idea, when my work was finished *I* used to go out or up to my room because when they had company there was no question of my waiting on them and I didn't complain I'm not curious by nature, they could have entertained the Pope I wouldn't have known, when my work was finished I used to go out or up to my room noise doesn't bother me I'm deaf as a post you know that as well as I do, these notes with your questions on, well and then the noise no I used to sleep or I'd go out they could have entertained anyone, what I do know is that he saw to everything I'd see him on the phone, I'd see him run and give orders to the other servant they had plenty to do all day getting everything ready I'd do what I had to do and then I'd go out or off to bed, if I'd had to wait on them in the evenings as well I'd never have gone to bed, it was nearly every evening or every other evening if it was one of their good weeks, when I say good I'm not thinking of myself it made no difference to me but of them running all over the place not to mention getting ready for their trips, because that well that was quite a business and preparations would start a week in advance and it wasn't just two people going away sometimes it was ten or twelve, and the whole mob would meet first at our place you can guess the work, I'm not talking about mine it made no difference to me once I'd finished I'd go out or off to bed

You say there was another servant

Better if I hadn't mentioned him, not interesting and no more chatty than the others never a word from him either, we should have got on together after all working for the same folk eating together always run off our feet together, but no nothing it was as much as he could do not to tread on my corns and even if he had and knocked me about I think I'd rather have had that than the silence it's true, I wasn't made for a graveyard like that as a young man I was full of life didn't have to ask me twice to tell a good story I knew some I knew some, but now I can hardly remember any so you see the others didn't do me much good, the flunkey I used to call him the flunkey and that put him against me he'd keep his lips pursed in a vicious circle, for two pins I'd have had a word with my gentlemen but knowing them it wasn't worth it they'd have sent me packing, besides they preferred the other chap always fussing round them he's the one you ought to interrogate but where is he now, it's no wonder if he hasn't joined the other one a couple of blighters like that could be up to anything they ought to get on together, they got on well enough anyway nattering in corners and how could the flunkey have stayed on without someone to chat to, you need a make-up like mine to make-do with things as they were

What good would conversation have done you seeing you're deaf

Conversation I don't say but a word from close up like this very close up I could hear that and that would have been enough, a word can set up a train of thought for quite a while or just you see I'm not hard to please just to watch the lips move without understanding it all helps, when I went to the village or into town I used to watch them all moving and it took the place of conversation, and then there are little notes the little notes he could have passed me from time to time to tell me something or other as my gentlemen did, he knew how to write what he shouldn't on other

8

occasions all right, my gentlemen's notes you know even if they were only orders well I've kept them all I re-read them in the evenings in my room, you'll say it's silly but it keeps me company, no I wasn't made for a graveyard like that and the flunkey I don't want to talk about him, can you imagine living like that side by side with someone who doesn't even look at you, side by side all day long doing the same work or almost and then you see him joking with the others, because I can guarantee he joked with my gentlemen and now I even wonder if he didn't stay with them the evenings they entertained, I say that I'm not sure but sometimes you can't help ideas crossing your mind, come to think of it he wouldn't have had much to say on social occasions, no trace of an education and from the company he kept in town where I met him sometimes by chance I can tell you the sort of type he was, no I mean to say the flunkey

You say he used to natter with the secretary, who wasn't *always* in a hurry then

Yes always you can say, perhaps natter isn't the word I called it natter out of spite it would be chat that's all exchange a few words, anyway they got on together that's certain even someone in a hurry you can see if he quite enjoys a chat but not with me, for a long time I wondered why the other chap was in such favour and then you get used to it I gave up racking my brains, did I make a bad impression at the start did I put my foot in it it's quite likely but at least that gave him a chance to write me a note and tell me about it, ask for an explanation apologies even it's natural enough, I wouldn't have said no I'm sure not at the start, at the start I wouldn't have said no not knowing him but no later on that man you see he had something disagreeable about him something held back something personal which doesn't make you want to know him better, and come to think of it I really wonder if it's not just that that made my gentlemen seem not to miss him much, for as far as I can tell their relationship was perfectly correct and I don't remember any scenes between them like one sees in families I mean ordinary households not one, always correct but I don't know perhaps my gentlemen would have liked him a little more affable, I say that thinking of the flunkey who used to enjoy a joke with them

Why do you say you were the man of all work when there were other servants

Let's say the odd-job man if you like or if there's some other name for a man who does all sorts of general things like putting straight and cleaning and pottering, with looking after the cars in the garage as well the laundry giving a hand to the flunkey and the gardener there was no shortage of jobs, I seem to be there still and in a minute I'll find some order in the hall, and just to show you even now at night I wake up and think I've forgotten to wash the cars or put something away in the attic and it's hard to get to sleep again then all these questions why I don't know, what's to stop you questioning my gentlemen the best source of information I should say and again I may put you on the wrong track, or else in town why not ask the tradesmen the people he was in contact with perhaps they know a darn sight more than I do, perhaps there's someone who knows but don't wait for them to come and confide in you

Why not

Because as soon as there's a risk of people sticking their necks out they sit tight, but now I come to think of it there's the baker's boy I wouldn't mind betting you could get something out of him, every morning he used to call and very often the secretary and very often he used to hang about with the cook, two large loaves to deliver that doesn't take long yes the baker's boy or even the milkman or the gardener

There was a cook too

She was already there when I took up service with my gentlemen it was she who showed me the ropes, the chambermaid we were constantly changing her we called her a chambermaid but that wasn't right the rooms were the flunkey's responsibility, the woman chiefly she used to look after the clothes the footwear the linen of the house the silver and give the cook a hand but my gentlemen are hard to please she never stayed long

Who was the cook

Madame Marthe Pacot the widow of a jeweller who went bankrupt, she had a situation twenty years ago now after her bereavement she had two or three posts before going to my gentlemen's, she's got two sons who have left the country one for Belgium the other for Canada where they're both in agriculture, she gets letters from them about every six months that she let me read and I know quite a bit about them I mean all fair and above board in detail I mean, we used to talk a lot about them Marthe and me

So you used to talk to the cook

At the start yes it was still possible but my condition's got worse, she found it more and more tiring it's understandable but from time to time she'd shout me a word to explain something for example in her letters or about my work, she's a good sort but I was bound to get on her nerves and I gave up trying to spend a moment with her in the evenings, she looked after her own affairs she's kept on a cottage in the country that she let to people named Lacroix Eugène bad payers, she was always having to get some woman neighbour down there to go and see the tenants about her money, yes never-ending letters from this woman called Jeanne I don't know what she used to sign Jeanne or from the Lacroix who were after something and bills she'd had nothing to do with but the dirty brutes would have them sent on to her, just imagine one day a bill for a hundred thousand francs for a washing machine it took three weeks of correspondence with the maker, and in the end she had to go and see the Lacroix and try and talk sense to them and the poor woman fell and broke her leg as she got off the train on the way back, we had a temporary cook in the kitchen for nearly six months it was a bad break in three places it wouldn't mend this temporary help

And the baker's boy

Oh I've no fears for him he'll make his way in life, I saw him born so to speak what can he be now fifteen his father's Robinson the vet he knows the whole district the lad takes advantage of it to extract money from everyone once is enough his father's had some trouble already, he doesn't let the grass grow under his feet he's got in touch with the Boche factories to go as an apprentice, what I mean is he's pushing honesty won't kill him Marthe used to tell me the Robinson boy would go a long way, every morning round about ten he'd turn up with his bread and I'd watch them discussing things every time the boy would ask for his glass of wine which she gave him she likes a chat, I pointed out to her he was too young to drink in the mornings

When used the baker's boy to talk to the secretary

He never did as far as I know

You were about to say before that very often the secretary

I couldn't have said that I never saw them together besides he never came down before eleven o'clock or a quarter past, all he had to do in the mornings he did by telephone from his room and to give out orders for the staff he'd have the flunkey go up, yes eleven o'clock or a quarter past he'd come down and have a talk with my gentlemen the things they had to talk about about half an hour I suppose, then he'd have a stroll round the garden or he'd take the car out or else he'd have some appointment in the small drawing room we'd had fitted up at his request eight years ago, a large period desk my gentlemen had discovered on one of their local excursions, a real bargain it appears a hundred thousand francs and worth somewhere near a million I polished it often enough, he burnt a hole in the leather with his cigarette that I never managed to hide he told my gentlemen I'd done it, and the large bookcase behind we brought down from the attic ten shelves of mahogany weighs a ton full right up to the top with great tomes no-one's ever read, where it joins the ceiling there's an imitation row imitation leather of books with gilded backs he'd ordered six feet the exact width, there were only two armchairs apart from his own all covered in olive green it's in the one on the right as you go in more threadbare than the other that the visitor used to sit facing the light while the other chap had it behind him, it seems it's a special technique above all at night the lampshade was always turned up on the visitor's side, an appointment never went on after half past twelve and I used to ring the bell at a quarter to, the secretary would join my gentlemen in the dining room and the service would begin at one o'clock always with soup even at luncheon it's a tradition it seems in the family of one of my gentlemen

Why do you say honesty won't kill the baker's boy

Because as I say he extracted money or shall we say borrowed it from almost everyone seeing his father was so well-known and his father had to pay it back, the boy didn't have the wherewithal besides he's hardly been at this job more than a couple of years before that he was at school several times he was expelled, he went back again thanks to the Mayor who's a friend of his father's or his mother's, then he got a post with Letournat the cabinet-maker where he only stayed three months because as well as some money business he'd got involved with the daughter just think at thirteen or was it after he'd left Letournat, anyway as regards the other money he borrowed I don't know the names except Pitut who nearly took the father to Court he'd already sent a summons to pay, it seems the boy told them his father had authorised him to collect for the new equipment in the laboratory where Pitut works, he went to see them with an official note from the laboratory where he'd typed out something or other and a forged signature, his father's a man who doesn't mark time you might say he's got all his customers during the week and on Saturdays he goes to this laboratory to do experiments with professors it seems from Paris, he takes his job seriously and people were easily taken in by the lad it seems a bit much and yet he got something like two hundred thousand francs, about this apprentice business with Boche I told Marthe to encourage him a baker's job's no good in our part of the world there's nothing but bakers and I should say the boy's not cut out for it, all in all I don't hold it against him he's trying to make his own way in life

What do you mean when you say your gentlemen talked about the things they had to talk about

As I said before their invitations their excursions all the usual business, I don't know about anything else except there was once some complicated affair with the son of one of their friends which kept them busy for a long time, my gentlemen know a great many people they'd got involved from what I understood I'm not in the know, they talked about it at meal-times too I'd see the flunkey say his piece from time to time which proves he was more or less in the know about at least a part of what they were saying

Why do you say it's a technique to have the visitor facing the light

Because that's what I've been told but I can't think why, I'd say it was rather unpleasant to have the sun or the light shining in your eyes

Did the secretary often receive visitors at night

Often I can't say often, I used to notice sometimes in the morning that the lampshade was turned up

What kind of lampshade

A parchment lampshade, turned up's hardly the word let's say askew but always lower on the bookcase side, and as it sits high on the lamp a visitor sitting down couldn't help having the bulb in his eyes I've experimented with it myself

What gave you the idea of making this experiment

Only because several times I've seen the lampshade all askew and I wondered why seeing it's firmly fixed to the holder and you've got to force it to tip it, and I spoke to the cook about it who told me it's a technique that's used in certain cases for certain people it was then I tried it while I was sitting in the armchair and I noticed
  Why do you say in certain cases for certain people
  Because I don't believe all the cook says and I repeat I find it unpleasant to have the light in my eyes
  What does the cook say about these cases and these people
  She says they're interrogations
  What interrogations
  Criminals
  Who by
  By the police or the judges or I don't know
  Why don't you believe what she tells you
  I said I don't believe it all, I didn't believe it all
  Why
  Because I have my reasons for being suspicious, she used to see the police everywhere with all her tenant trouble she wanted to have everyone shut up all day long she went on about thieves bankers everyone, she always had her nose stuck in a newspaper on the murder page in all the photos she saw a likeness with her tenants, she has a book about the foreheads eyes and ears of maniacs and convicts, in the Lacroix she sees all the stigmatas of her swindlers and what with her detective novels too she makes up such a farrago she can't sleep at nights and upsets the chambermaid so you understand I take it all with a pinch of salt
  What do you mean by forcing the shade in order to tip it up, how was it made
  Just a circle of wire on top and another below and fixed to the upper circle I think three little vertical pieces of wire or four which enclosed the bulb and are joined to a tiny little ring you put

between the socket and the bulb and it all holds firm thanks to the parchment, so to tip it up you have to pull it towards you and that bends the vertical pieces which is what he did and I put it straight, once even one of them got broken with the forcing I had to buy another lampshade and again he said it was me, I said I always found the lampshade tilted but it didn't matter what I said you can imagine, I found it exactly the same again and he went on pulling it about as if it wasn't easier to find a lampshade designed for that or a different shape if he was so keen on his technique

Where did you find another lampshade

At Tripeau's at the Carrefour des Oublies, ten years ago it was a nondescript junkshop now they've enlarged it you should just see, there are two floors and twenty assistants the lampshades are on the first floor on the right at the back a salesman called Masson, he couldn't find the same model as mine we looked at everything and I found one in the end up on one of the shelves, he told me it was the last one a model they don't make any more but I'd been told to find one exactly the same

You did say it was parchment

They call it parchment but I think it's imitation

What colour

Red outside white inside

Was there anything else a red colour in the office

A lot of books high up and all those on the lower shelf hidden by the desk, the carpet was a red and black pattern or rather a red background with a black geometrical design it's oriental like all the carpets in the house except in my gentlemen's bedrooms, and the little chandelier with three red lampshades that was hardly ever lit, and the top of the little table at the back on the left is in red leather I think that's all, yes that's all

What was the little table used for

Nothing

What do you mean

I mean it wasn't used, it could have been used for standing something on flowers for example but he hated flowers and that that was often the cause of argument with my gentlemen who wanted them everywhere, don't I know it every day I had to see to them it used to upset me to throw away flowers not more than two days old but it was an order, very often I'd put them in my own room to keep them longer

How do you know the name of the lampshade salesman

I remember on the counter there was a note addressed to M. Masson, I told him the name reminded me of something and he told me his father was Blaise Masson an old school-friend of mine I'd never seen since anyway now he's dead, we talked about him I mean as much as he could, he didn't dare bawl too much in the shop about things that had nothing to do with business but I've remembered since his father had red hair like him, at the local school I'm talking now about fifty years ago one of us was teasing him on account of its colour, Masson pushed him down the stairs and this other chap was picked up at the bottom with a fractured skull it's a thing that's stayed in my mind

What kind of visitors did the secretary receive in his office

Very good-class gentlemen generally like M. Rufus M. de Longuepie M. Carré M. Antoine I don't know his name unless that was it, M. de Ballaison who owns the Manor of Malatraîne the solicitor, whether he came on business I don't know and M. Chantre who was the most frequent visitor the son not the father *he* quarrelled with my gentlemen more than fifteen years ago he'd extracted some money from the sister of one of my gentlemen, but less distinguished visitors too like Gérard or Fifi as he was called or even Pierre Hottelier who tried to act big giving me tips but you can't fool an old 'un, I saw at once he had no education

Used they to come on business

Now you're asking even the cook didn't know which didn't

stop her guessing comparing and making up farragos as usual I couldn't care less, perhaps in this connection I'm practically sure the chambermaids could give you some information it was they who opened the door and I've caught them I won't say a hundred but a thousand times listening at the office door, which didn't do them much good it seems because of the door curtain inside which muffled most of the sound but they didn't tell us what they heard anyway, it was Marthe who was sure they heard, by the way I forgot to say that the door curtain in the office was red too

Why do you wonder if Ballaison the solicitor came on business

Because I don't know, he might just as well have come as a relative being a distant cousin of one of my gentlemen on his wife's side a Bonne-Mesure who gave him as they say three daughters each one uglier than the last, I've seen these young ladies several times in the town out for a walk, the eldest must be about twenty twenty-two the second one eighteen perhaps and the youngest is sixteen this year because last year for her fifteenth birthday in June my gentlemen gave her a pearl necklace fit for a princess just another of their eccentricities it's so like them, a girl they rarely see her mother quarrelled with them Marthe wouldn't need asking twice about that it's one of her favourite stories, it started twenty years ago I find it was rather good of my gentlemen under the circumstances unless they're making presents to the girls to please their father to grease his palm as they say if he looks after their affairs

Why are there no carpets in your employers' bedrooms

I said no oriental carpets they're fitted carpets but I've no idea why

What kind of fitted carpet

A fitted carpet's a fitted carpet how can I say, a fitted carpet are there fifty different kinds, a pale grey fitted carpet in one dark grey in the other there's nothing better for the housework one go with the vacuum cleaner but with these other carpets they slide about slip out of place all the time turn up at the edges you catch your feet in them, not to speak of the parquet to be polished underneath as fussy as they can be, and what's more once a month take them out in the field at the back to beat them as if the vacuum cleaner wasn't enough

What was this work on physiognomy the cook used to read

I don't understand the question

What book did she read about the foreheads eyes and ears as you say of convicts and maniacs

A book with photos, you can see all these heads front view profile back view not very appetising which means that with anyone she sees she says he's got the nose of someone in her book or the sticking-out ears of someone else enough to put you off we were always being catalogued in that house, me she found I'd the right eye of a clergyman the type that'd steal everything in sight and the left eye of a nymphatic

Why do you say she upsets the chambermaid at night

Because as she can't sleep after her reading she gets up goes back to bed switches the light on switches it off goes into the corridor to eat or for something else, she makes such a noise it gets on the chambermaid's nerves they've all complained about it

Do they both sleep in the same room

No two adjoining rooms but the partitions are thin and the W.C's not far and the light shines from one room to the next because of the glass pane over the doors which lead into the corridor, anyway she always forgot to put out the light in the corridor or she didn't close the door of the W.C. or she slammed the door of the little fridge we had on that floor for our personal use, it'd make for scenes all next day if it wasn't during the night but I'd sleep through it

Why do you say the flunkey was more or less in the know about a part of your employers' discussions, why a part, what do you suspect your gentlemen had to hide from him

It's no more my pigeon than the rest I've never minded other people's business still less my gentlemen's affairs, it seems to me everyone has a right to stand on his own dignity and everyone has some and I don't see why my gentlemen should be an exception and why they should speak about everything in front of the flunkey, I sometimes found their familiarity out of place anyway there are limits to everything

Don't you rather suspect he knew a lot more than you thought he should

I've told you I've no idea all I know is he annoyed me with his airs and graces, when we're all one on top of the other as you might say in our profession we're all in the same boat I've told you before

What guesses did the cook make about the secretary's visitors

She had her own idea about each one I can tell you if it interests you though I'm not the one to take it for gospel any more than all the rest, Monsieur Rufus for example she said he used to come on business about some textile companies in the north according to her he was the owner of several factories or president, he had some problems about his income tax he used to buy land and other factories like the last one at Le Chanchèze in order to cheat the Treasury it seems by placing his capital under different names or abroad I don't understand, he was a great traveller every year he used to order two wigs for his wife from some firm in London they're practising Jews it seems the women have to wear a wig with their heads shaved underneath, once even at one of my gentlemen's soirées she was pretty tight and they'd taken her wig off and it was quite a sight, she goes with him on some of his travels especially to America where some of her family are jewellers, she's a woman about sixty eight years older than her husband still according to Marthe and who spends a fortune getting her wrinkles removed or rolls of fat ironed out all over it appears she's all seams if you can believe such gossip, last year on the way back or two years ago back from America she had three minx coats the best you can get it seems for all I know about furs, which she brought back for one of their friends Jacob Goldshitt someone in trade who couldn't obtain minxes from Canada because of some new customs regulation, she'd managed to get them through thanks to the girl who was travelling with her more than a friend according to Marthe her husband's meant to be in the know but there, they entertain a lot too not anyone as Marthe says when you're not out of the top drawer you have to try and find your way in, they started as small tradespeople it seems or the grandfather did which doesn't stop Monsieur Rufus having a certain class and I know my onions, as for Monsieur de Longuepie he's one of the three oldest families in the district no question of commerce there, he's so tight-fisted he's starving to death gradually selling off the whole Le Rouget mountain they've owned since the Middle Ages and the peasants are always doing him down, they've still got the castle falling in ruins that'd be why he'd come and ask advice to find Spanish workmen without work permits for his repairs it's not so dear, or else for his daughter again according to the cook who's an idiot in some home in Switzerland having treatment that costs the earth, he'd be getting some mortgage loans off my gentlemen he's already sold them the land at Les Vernes which they've sold off to some people who came to our place once or twice, its Madame de Longuepie who looks after the good works in the parish she runs the charity ladies' needlework school collections the poor the jumble-sale everything, every time I got stuck with the chores for the local fête the drinks that had to be fetched from the town the flunkey used to drive me to Bize in the little van and all the decorations to hang and the stands to put up it's no sinecure, no-one wants to give you a hand it's badly paid except for the Spaniards of course but they're not very tough and lazy as lizards, yes I was saying she looks after all that which gives her husband a bit of a break he can't stand her they've been talking for a long time about a judicial separation but their families are against it, by the way five or six years ago from now there was an incident that lasted near on a week, Monsieur de Longuepie was staying with us he was drunk from morning till night my gentlemen didn't mind another excuse to get the same way, Marthe would remember the punch session all right poor old Longuepie but there it can't be helped you can't always control your feelings

How could the cook be sure the chambermaids heard the conversations between the secretary and his visitors

How I've no idea women guess a heap of things, probably a word here a word there and Marthe knew what to make of it at least that's what she said

Why do you think none of the chambermaids ever said a single word to you about these conversations

They were too afraid they'd lose their place they were well paid they didn't trust us old retainers but it made no difference they didn't stay as I said

Do you think it was only their negligence in carrying out their duties that made your employers dismiss them

That was always the reason they did it the slightest thing and that was that, I remember one called Rose who had to pack her bags for not putting a pair of shoes back in their right place and Léonie Dothoit who used to fill in between times up to three years ago, a trustworthy woman who knew the house better than the rest of us was given the sack for not having cleaned the bathroom of a guest although she'd never even been warned there was someone there that day in that part of the house

Did the cook never listen at doors

She was far too busy in her kitchen for that

The people the secretary saw during the day were they the same as those invited in the evenings

Longuepie yes he often came in the evening by that I mean

when he came in the mornings he stayed all day and Monsieur Carré the same though he usually came in the afternoons he stayed on for the evening, Monsieur Rufus too often came in the evening and so did

How do you know

I could see that they stayed couldn't I and Marthe had orders for dinner

And the secretary

What about the secretary

Did he dine with them

Of course where else should he dine

So you know he used to stay with your gentlemen the days they entertained

I said dined I didn't say entertained they're two different things

What do you mean by that

They entertained after dinner

And you never found out from the cook whether the secretary was present

What on earth do you think the cook cared about that, with the washing up done she wasn't going to start checking who stayed in the drawing-room she went up to bed or out for a walk, anyway it was no interest to either of us to know whether the secretary stayed or not you're the one asking the question

Was there no-one to do the waiting when there was company

Always extra personnel

Who

Jean-Pierre Cruchet and Guillaume Luisot usually and when there was a big crowd Poulet as he was called and Cyrille Mauvoisin

What time did they arrive

About nine o'clock half past nine we'd be finishing the washing-up and at times they'd give us a hand, then they'd look after everything the door the cloakroom and the drinks and they'd stay till the end, they had to wash the glasses and put the drawing-room back straight even at six in the morning I could still come down and find them at work

Were you never tempted to ask them who was present among the guests

Sometimes they told me there was this one or that one but what did I care I ask you

The guests or some of them stayed the night

Often yes there are guest rooms

Were they usually the same people

Longuepie as I said and also Chantre and Gérard and Pierre Hottelier

Whereabouts are the guest rooms

Two in the south wing on the first floor, four on the second over the main façade and another next to the secretary's room, the house is like a square horseshoe we're in the north wing under the rafters

What is there below your apartments

That's the second there's only the billiard room and a bathroom, no-one ever stayed long in the billiard room it's very large and uncomfortable but it has to be kept clean all the same, there are show cases full of statues and fragile stuff their collections as my gentlemen call them, they're a real bind to keep dusted they're very proud of them and don't know where to put them they show them off to new visitors but I tell you the billiard room they don't use it it looks good to have one, better if they'd given it up a long time ago with their collections and given us a bit more elbow room by converting it into bedrooms we're very cramped up above

And on the first floor

The library and a bathroom on the corner which communicates with a bedroom, on the ground floor there's a small dining room and the office and a W.C.

The personnel that comes every other evening do you call them extras

I didn't say they came every other evening they weren't needed every time, anyway that's what we called them they weren't boarded and they were paid straightaway

Who is Jean-Pierre Cruchet

Mother Cruchet's son in the past she used to keep the refreshment bar next to the Trois-Abeilles she sold it, Barbatti the *patron* slipped her a nice fat sum at the time to get her out he told her it wasn't doing her any good, now the lads go drinking at Le Cygne which has always kept the same character, just between us Monnard must have made a packet in the twenty-five years he's been there and no alterations that's the idea in my view, they all ruin themselves making alterations thinking they'll attract the customer but the customer here they're not teenagers *they* go into town it's the old 'uns and *they* don't give a damn if they prop up their elbows on plastic or the lights are neon

Say what you know about Jean-Pierre Cruchet

He's Mother Cruchet's son I've told you he's been an extra for my gentlemen for five or six years

Has he no other occupation

He's a tailor by profession he works with Nantet who dresses my gentlemen, he doesn't make more than fifty thousand francs his mother's almost given up work she's more or less dependent

Didn't you say she got a nice fat sum from Barbatti

All blown by her son at the casino he was always stuck in there he's even been borrowing recently

And Guillaume Luisot

He's the Luisots from Le Rouget he and his brother are with Maître de Ballaison, Guillaume perhaps for eight years he's the head clerk's assistant now and the young one for two years as office boy

And Guillaume likes going as an extra to your employers'

Well I told you they pay well and it was a lucky chance his boss being a friend of my gentlemen's it's like keeping it in the family and the work's not backbreaking filling up glasses and washing them no need to study books

And this Poulet and Cyrille Mauvoisin

Poulet I'm not quite sure what he does outside and Cyrille is waiter at Le Cygne, when he's extra at the house he arranges things with his colleague at the café, he's a serious lad his parents came back from Martinique when he was born his mother came from there, as well as his work he's studying arithmetic he'd like to become a chartered accountant but it's long

How many rooms do your employers have

There are ten bedrooms five bathrooms and the large drawing-room the large dining-room the small one the office the billiard room the library which makes twenty-one counting the bathrooms which are as big as bedrooms two in any case, or sixteen rooms without the bathrooms or the kitchen in the basement that is

Why is the kitchen in the basement

Now you're asking

How are all these rooms laid out in the house

On the ground floor overlooking the main courtyard the large drawing-room, in the south-wing the large dining-room in the north wing the small one and the office as I said, on the first floor over the courtyard my gentlemen's two bedrooms, in the south wing a bathroom and a bedroom in the north wing a bathroom and the library, on the second floor over the courtyard four bedrooms, in the south wing two bathrooms one bedroom and the secretary's bedroom, in the north wing the billiard room and a bathroom

Where is the staircase that gives access to these floors

Between the courtyard façade and the south wing in the corner, it's spiral

Describe it
Describe it
Give details

Oh well if you're interested it's a staircase how shall I say a spiral staircase as I said, it's in marble with bannisters in wrought iron they're twisted rails with kinds of snails in between and little gilded flowers, there's a red carpet down the middle with those horrid rods that are always working loose, the wall is of stone light grey pointed white and there are pictures all the way up to the top, four between the ground and first floors and three between the first and second, the fourth one's not been replaced they gave it to one of their friends two years ago, it was a portrait it appears seventeenth century which showed a man in a wig some historical character but my gentlemen said it was a forgery of the same period that's why it wasn't in the drawing-room, a duke I think or a marquis painted by La Vallière the original something like that

The other pictures on the staircase

Coming up from the ground floor first there's a large landscape all dark and gloomy which shows trees and a lake and boats and fishermen with their nets, it seems you couldn't see anything when they bought it they consult an expert about their pictures to clean them or frame them Térence Monnier he's one of their friends too, they often buy pictures the loft's full of them, this landscape then and after that another landscape a light one all yellows you can see a large square with a bell-tower the one at Venice St. Mark's I believe and churches and a crowd of tiny little people such detail you've no idea, there are carriages too and horses it's incredible the patience to do all that and none of it any use, when you look all you can see is the bell-tower and the biggest of the churches you have to be right on top of it to see the crowd, then there's a large Dutch flower-piece of the period roses lilies campanulas and masses of little flowers to set them off the same type as gypsophila, and some other flowers too that don't exist in any case we don't know them like blue marguerites unless they're badly drawn scabious and that's a flower they haven't been forcing long you can't floor me about flowers, then just before the landing a man in hunting gear holding two partridges against a landscape where there's a river and on the right a kind of building like an orangery it's School of Fontainebleau as they say, then of course the landing and then still going up if you're interested some woman with nothing on but a flimsy little veil with a swan that's got his beak against her cheek and his tail half between her legs it's pretty filthy, she's got one arm under his wing to hold him and with the other hand she's stroking his head, one of the swan's feet is resting on her thigh it's a wonder he can keep his balance and then comes the last picture now the portrait's gone

Describe the last picture

With all due respect I'd rather not

Describe it

Well I mean to say it's men stark naked, ten or twelve of them in a room with a swimming-pool having a bath or a rest and so on and the guests always used to have a laugh in front of it looking at the details I felt ashamed of them, it comes from Germany those Boches you know

You say the chambermaid didn't strictly speaking look after the bedrooms, did the flunkey then do six bedrooms all on his own

I gave him a hand when he'd too much to do but generally there were only my gentlemen's bedrooms and those of one or two guests on the first floor, the others weren't always in use

Who did the secretary's room

Himself always he wouldn't have anyone else tidy up for him I used to give him his sheets and his towel every Saturday, I must say it was clean he even used the vacuum cleaner we had one on every floor in a cupboard in one of the bathrooms and the W.C. on the ground floor

Who did they give the portrait of the man in a wig to
To Monsieur Rivière
Who's that
A gentleman who deals in all kinds of business blocks of flats land but chiefly collections, he lives in Amsterdam now he comes back about once every three months very rich but he prefers to lunch or dine out with my gentlemen they go into town to Philippard's or to the Mouton Gras they're the best restaurants, *I've* never eaten there they say the oysters are no good anywhere else and at Philippard's they get a Vosne-Romanée always *première cuvée* because of Philippard's son who has a friend who's a wine-grower there, name of Poisson Monsieur Rivière orders about thirty bottles from him every year what a fuss, it seems in Amsterdam he has one of the finest cellars in Europe where he's had some special equipment installed the climate doesn't suit all the wines, he insisted on buying that picture although my gentlemen said it was a forgery because in Holland he'd discovered a whole series of forgers of that period who'd flooded the market with their paintings and most museums have a number of them without knowing it, Monsieur Rivière was preparing a big exhibition when he'd collected all his forgeries he's got experts he pays specially to see to all that *he's* always travelling, I remember one year he brought me back why me a little Chinese statue showing an actor in tears leading a performing bear, you can turn the actor's head round it's a ball let into the ivory I don't know how and on the other side the face is smiling
   Didn't you say there was a gardener
   Yes Pompom as we called him he was mad about pompom roses those tiny old-fashioned roses he took great care of them, my gentlemen weren't very keen but the gardener they never contradicted him, he has a daughter who also used to help Marthe and who saw to the vegetable garden and once a month gave everything a thorough scrub Gabrielle she's a very good worker,

and his wife Jeannette who hardly ever goes out of doors they live in the lodge at the other end of the park on the Crachon side, she does needlework mending and darning for almost everyone and lace table-mats she sells at a good price, they had a son who died a prisoner they always have his photo on the sideboard handsome lad who it seems used to come to the house as an extra too, Pompom had plenty of work in the garden I gave him a hand every day in the summer with the watering chiefly the flowers I've always liked that, we had a bed of zinnias just above the field at the back which was my preserve as he used to say I cut bunches every day during the season but my gentlemen preferred other flowers on the whole those from the hot-house, we used to grow three varieties of orchids the attention they need and some special ferns too which can't stand the light, they come from tropical forests we had a lot of trouble with them but the rich always have a craze for something

How old is the gardener

Sixty-five he's getting on he tipples a bit I must admit he's got arthritis I feel he won't last much longer, several times my gentlemen have offered to have his arthritis cured far better if they'd offered him a cure for drinking, it can be done it appears you come away unable to stand the smell of alcohol but they said it was the only pleasure he had left and every year at Christmas they gave him ten or twelve bottles and not cheap stuff I can tell you

Used you to go to the gardener's place

No because of old Jeannette who didn't approve, Pompom used to be in a black mood with her by the evening I'd arrange sometimes to take him with me

You used to go drinking

You know what it's like a tot here a tot there at Julot's or at Le Cygne, what did you think we'd do the two of us I can't understand a word he says what's more he's got an Alsatian accent and me and the movies, we'd see his pals two or three chaps his own age they'd talk about the district in their day yarns about people that would really amaze folk nowadays who have forgotten or pretend to

You took part in their conversation

Not any more in the last few years on account of my hearing, in the old days a little though we're not the same age I used to know Pompom before I went to work for my gentlemen

Did they talk about your employers

They talked about people they used to know they had nothing to say about my gentlemen who belong to the gentry it's not the same world

Did they talk about the secretary

He was the last thing they cared about the secretary a fellow who never kept company with anyone and who didn't even come from our part of the world

What does the secretary's window look out on

You mean his bedroom it's got four windows, two over the main courtyard two over the park

What can you see from the windows on the park side

The park

Give details

On the south side the terrace where they often take their aperitifs in the summer it's got oak trees along on the left and on the right a big lawn with a clump of trees in the middle, the terrace leads on to another lawn that goes to the orangery there are fields at the back till you reach the wood of Le Furet which is part of the estate, to the west let's say in front of the house you can see the ornamental lake and the trees as far as the river, the lake is seventy foot by forty long side on as you face it, there's a fountain in the middle with several jets and statues they're mythological gods Neptune and Amphibite I think and sea dolphins and at each corner too the statue of a siren or a triton in bronze, and after that the main drive lined on each side with plane trees and elms very tall and more stone statues a bit like Versailles if you see what I mean, and that leads to a terrace by the river you go down by a semi-circular staircase which cost a lot in Italian marble, they built it five years ago the work went on and on there's always some work in progress somewhere in the park or the house

What can you see from the windows on the courtyard side

You can see the courtyard paved as it was in olden times where you sprain your ankle and the other wing with the glass door of the small dining room on the ground floor and its two windows on either side they're lattice windows the frames painted white, and the two windows on the first floor and the same on the second and our dormer windows in the roof

What is there behind the house

The terrace and a big field gradually rising with two rows of oaks that cut right across it, at the top my zinnias and three other flower-beds the dahlias in the autumn, and the meadows till you get to the Sirancy woods a part belongs to my gentlemen a real forest compared to Le Furet, they have trees cut down from time to time for logs for the chimney-piece they're very fond of that in the winter on top of the central heating which was never allowed to drop below twenty-one degrees, even in summer when we were stifling they'd ask me to light the fire in the drawing-room in the evening it was only for something to look at

How many windows are there at the back of the house

On the ground floor five on either side of the glass door which corresponds to the one on the courtyard but smaller, my gentlemen's friends were always arguing whether to get rid of it or not they couldn't agree some said two doors facing each other as you come in makes it less intimate better to wall it up, there's enough light as it is in the drawing-room too much even and move the chimney-piece over to take its place others thought that when you come in and look right through to a view of the park that's just what was nice about it and that must be what my gentlemen think they're leaving things as they are

What was this work they had done in the park and the house

Last year there was the roof to repair that lasted eight months they reduced the pitch three feet we lived amongst the rubble and the dust while my gentlemen were away on their travels, we had to makeshift in the attic and move around as the work progressed until our bedrooms were straight again, Marthe wanted to leave she said it was a shame to spend those millions all for three feet it was immoral instead of giving us a raise or donating the money to Christian missions or to societies for social work, she was probably thinking about her house she'd have liked my gentlemen to give her something for repairs but they were under no obligation one must be fair, and the year before it was the farm an extra stable and modernising the farmers' quarters, the old ones had left on account of their daughter-in-law who died their son arranged to let them buy his mine-works at Le Canaillou on credit he set himself up in town with his father-in-law the hosier quite a big firm, I don't know the new arrivals doesn't seem to be going well they make one mistake after another, last year the wheat was harvested eight days late completely flattened by storms and then there's the maintenance of the machines and all that, the year before there'd been a fire in the tool shed behind the orangery all the window-panes had blown my gentlemen took the opportunity to have it enlarged, the year before that there'd been what had there been yes the painting of the ground floor and the chimney-piece rebuilt in great stone slabs from Le Trognon, that was the time when the others argued most strongly for moving it in place of the door and the year before that the staircase down to the river and the year

You said the roof was last year, hadn't you left your employers by then

It's true time passes two years already but the roof was just finished when I was leaving, two years so the other work was before that or yes the farm that started at the same time, yes that's it the same year they started on the farm but the painting of the ground floor that's five years ago I'm sure it's every five years, they'll be at it again this year Pompom told me I wonder if the chimney-piece will be left where it is this time

Who are these farmers

I tell you I don't know them

The old ones

Clément Vinage and his wife he's a bit dour she's very sweet always ready to oblige she used to come and help Marthe in emergencies she was paid to be sure but it was the way she did it, specially as that farm-girl was as thick as they come poor Renée had to do all *her* work over again, after all they had ten pigs and twenty cows not counting the horse and the fifty hens, the Slattern as we called her ruined a whole batch of chickens once when Renée was away at her son's for three days she'd been told to see to the incubator and somehow or other she'd switched off the current, another time she forgot to feed the hens another time she marched all over the seed-bed another time

Had the farmers any other helpers

Two farmhands Pipi and Tourniquet they'd never set the Seine on fire either but they were workers especially Pipi that's a nickname always at his machines the equipment's good, they've both stayed with the newcomers mind but the girl's got a job away with some Irish folk near Douves she was more or less meant to be pregnant but people's tongues

Is Tourniquet a nickname too

Yes as a little kid he always had the fidgets I remember his mother couldn't control him even now he's still restless a bundle of nerves

Used he to come to your employers'

A farmhand who do you take them for I mean to say, what would he have been doing over at the house he stinks of cows a mile off no I mean to say

Explain the other one's ridiculous nickname

That was when he was small too for a long time he went on wetting himself and it stuck

Whereabouts is the farm in relation to the house

On the Crachon side near the gardener's lodge just under a mile from the house

Describe the buildings

There's one long building with first the little pigsty almost hidden by the hedge which curves round, then the new stable for ten cows and the horse in place of the old pigsty where they once had about thirty pigs they moved it along to the end, then the old shed for ten cows modernised then the old wine press they sold when they pulled up the vineyard seven years ago that's where they plant the beetroot and the potatoes, over it the hayloft and then the living quarters, in front of the stables there's a new galvanised drinking trough next to the old well that's dried up my gentlemen say it looks picturesque because of the three cypresses round it all dying off, the gardener's house is about say fifteen yards away next to the vegetable garden and on the right there's the farmyard and the shed for the machines, they're always having trouble with the septic tank which is too small there's a flow-back it's between them and the gardener, used by eight people my gentlemen are bound to have it changed the time old Jeannette's been complaining about the stink, you hardly smell the pigsty now since they've had fewer pigs because even when that tank's kept properly clean

What is there behind the farm

Fields on the right the Sirancy woods on the left

What alterations have been made to the farmers' living quarters

They took a bit off the hayloft to make a bedroom for the boys and their old bedroom's used for the girl she had to sleep down below before, and they took a bit off the farmers' bedroom to make a little corridor so you don't have to pass through their room and the staircase has been rebuilt too in concrete the other was worm-eaten, and in the kitchen they made a large window at the back to give more light and installed an electric cooker and repaired half the floor tiles it's more commonsensical as they say apart from the two stables, they caused a bit of argument with Thiéroux they decided to open up only one small door between because that thick wall they'd have needed some small steel girders if they'd made a larger opening and it would have come too expensive, although one large stable was better for the ventilation and easier to modernise the old one at the same time as the new one, by the way the new farmer would have liked electrical equipment for milking the cows he didn't manage to persuade my gentlemen now Tourniquet's got to take on ten more animals unless he gets help from the new Slattern

What do you mean by new Slattern

The girl who's come in place of the old one I told you but the farmer's sure to tackle them again and they'll install it in the end

Why do you say you don't know the new farmers

Because first of all I've hardly had time to get to know them but even apart from that I'm not very keen I mean to go and see them

What are your reasons

Who they are that I do know the wife's a cousin of mine or rather of my poor mother's, our two families had words about a parcel of land near Nutre which should have come to us I'm talking now about fifty years ago, we never made it up her mother never missed a chance of having a dig at us my father always said that the first one of us who had anything to do with that lot he'd shoot him down he was a violent man I've always known him like that my poor mother went through a lot, I think he'd have done it too this business used to get him so worked up whenever he talked about it, I should explain that this parcel of land on top of our legal rights but you know what they are adjoined his field and was more productive being in a better position, not the Quillets I'm just not interested it's not that there's much wrong with him he had his two sons killed in the war but her she's a Mouchin all right gossipy old skinflint and all, to give you an idea three or four years ago she quarrelled with her own sister-in-law who had lent my sister her iron, I suppose she'd heard the party-line in the family same as we did since our parents' day but this sort of thing can get forgotten in time above all with a sister-in-law you've got to be pretty mean to take it as gospel, well that's just to show you it made me even less anxious to get in touch with them seeing things still go on in the same old way, I can do without their company and if it only leads to more family squabbles it's not worth the candle

Apart from your sister have you any other close relatives

My brother Gustave who went to Australia when he was twenty he still writes to my sister occasionally, he's a grandfather he was ten years older than me I could be one too come to think of it

Is your sister married

She'd been a widow for fifteen years she married again last year when she was forty-six he's a tradesman from Agapa she's not sorry and no wonder he's good to my nephews he took Michou into his business that lad will get along nicely it seems he's got a good business sense, in two years' time he does his military service he's plenty of time to learn his trade the little girl too she enjoys it already she's only sixteen but she's just the sort to sell things coax anything out of you, my sister's very happy to see her children settled pity I don't see them more often

Who is Thiéroux

The local builder got to give him some work from time to time he comes from the village but for the work in the house they always send to town, it's Monsieur Ducreux the architect one of their friends who looks after that got his own builders Thiéroux's not too fussy all right for the farm, not that he's without work on the contrary all the locals take their custom to him but my gentlemen want to be well in with everyone it's only the Mayor who can't stand the sight of them, you'll tell me he's the most important but they don't care they can get enough support if they need it and Bottu that's the Mayor is furious he's got a shrewd idea he's losing ground for the next elections, not that my gentlemen go in for politics they can't abide them but it looks bad with the locals he administers when he's often forced to give in over little things like a right of way or a telegraph pole it happened not long ago, a pole my gentlemen were asking him to move it had just been set up slap in the middle of the gap in the woods on the other side of the river it spoilt the landscape, the Mayor had done it on purpose that's sure but my gentlemen soon got him to have it moved thanks to the Sous-Préfet Monsieur Simonot

Do you still see this Pompom

There's no reason for me to drop Pompom because I've left my gentlemen, we meet one or two evenings a week at Julot's he prefers it to Le Cygne

Who is Julot

The Bistro de la Goutte-Blanche he did a turn in the foreign legion, been married three times widower at fifty-three he says it's the best life anyway he's got a barmaid Louisette who lodges upstairs, the tongues wagged at first but with time and they're good sorts the two of them, that kind of parish-pump feather-bed tittle-tattle keeps the scandal-mongers busy all right but I can tell you I've known a few of these so-called paragons who are only too willing to turn a blind eye on other folk when their own interest's at stake, no Julot he's respected and Louisette too even the women forget in the end, when it comes to wheedling bread out of her on a Sunday evening she never says no always chalks up the drinks they're not the sort to pester the customers and as far as I know no-one tries to cheat them, they're a sturdy couple their character I mean they go well together but I don't think he'll marry her on account of a son he has from his second marriage it's almost you might say like a souvenir when he talks about him he says it's sacred and bangs on the table, the boy's no good I think he takes after him when he was young but not so strong a character, he *knows* but he'd never admit it for the world he wants to leave him the bistro it's his idea it will settle him down, if he married Louisette it would risk complications with the inheritance or something like that mind you *he* doesn't say so but I've always thought that must be it unless I'm wrong, perhaps if she pressed him Louisette would manage to get herself married I'd be surprised all the same she looks happy enough as she is he pays her liberally, she's filling her stocking all right they say she's going to buy some shares and she's got a bank account

What do you know about Julot's son

Not much he lives in town he often has a night out from what they say he's a pal of Guillaume Luisot's, they went off together for a trip in the north one year to Amsterdam I believe, he hardly ever comes to see his father he doesn't like Louisette I've no idea what he does but the fact is he was had up in court a few years ago only just escaped prison, his father never breathed a word we heard it from someone else

You say he went to Amsterdam with Luisot

I wouldn't swear to it

Were they expected there

I've no idea they went off on a motor bike and came back about a week later it was in the summer

You don't know if perhaps they were invited by this Monsieur Rivière to Amsterdam

I tell you I've no idea

Why was he had up in court

False pretences or some swindle of that kind, it was a whole gang of them I know my gentlemen were called as witnesses as to his character they were rather peeved as they didn't know the boy well, they did it for Guillaume it probably did the trick he only had a fine to pay

How did you find this out

Through Marthe

Why do you prefer going to Julot's rather than to Le Cygne

Not me it's Pompom who prefers it he says it's not so noisy, at Le Cygne there's always quite a crowd it's true and a fruit machine that makes a racket it doesn't bother me in fact I'd rather have Le Cygne now you've hit on my weakness, their white wine's better they get it from Monachou while Julot gets his from Lantoy who mixes it with the local stuff

Who is this Ducreux

The architect who generally sees to the alterations in the house I told you

Is he often entertained by your employers

He's a friend yes I said so

Why didn't you mention him among the persons they usually entertain

Because I'm not a walking directory

Answer

If you think I can keep in my head the names of all the people who come you're mistaken, you asked me who the secretary's visitors were and if they were the same people as those who were entertained I said yes for those best fixed in my mind having seen them most often but for all the others you'd better ask my gentlemen

Answer, who is this Ducreux

The architect I've told you before

Say what you know about him

He's from Douves I believe or from Vichy been settled here oh perhaps twenty years he married one of the Malévole girls she never comes to the house, he's got two or three children I don't find him very agreeable he hardly says good-day he wears large spectacles and always has a brief-case stuffed with plans to make an impression on my gentlemen, Marthe says he doesn't do all that much work except for us people find him stuck-up but his wife's got money, old man Malévole left her his millions Ducreux did well enough out of it he bought up a small property not far from the castle, he knocked the old house down and built in its place some ghastly horror like three shoe-boxes which spoils the look of the hill, how anyone can live in it you can touch the ceiling with your hand it appears and to get undressed in the evening in your bedroom it must be ever so practical as Marthe says, all the front of the house is glass you can see everything that goes on inside from the road it's the American style, every time he used to make a song and dance about the alterations in the house when my gentlemen used to ask him saying he wasn't interested in patching things up but only in doing something new but my gentlemen know he's happy enough to have something to do

You say he *generally* sees to the work, so there are other architects

There was Monsieur Jumeau who worked with him over the roof he made a second bathroom on the first floor too as though one wasn't enough, Ducreux never missed the chance of bringing up the business about the leaks as if it was all a great joke but he doesn't like him, the other man's younger than he is does a lot of work for the new blocks of flats in town and on the outskirts, he even won a competition out of several architects for Ducreux's hospital that's a subject he doesn't like you to mention, Jumeau wasn't interested in all our affairs quite right too he's a sporty type as they say even when we entertain he doesn't often come he goes away every weekend with his wife mountaineering or ski-ing, Ducreux seems to find even that funny making it look as though fresh air means more than anything to him, he just can't help opening his big mouth but jealousy it's funny how it makes you behave like an idiot

Why was Ducreux in the hospital

I didn't say that I said he was in for the hospital competition

What do you mean he wasn't interested in all our affairs

Ducreux's gossip and my gentlemen's little upsets about their house he does what he's asked and that's that

Why do you think your employers give work to Jumeau

They know he's successful, I sometimes wonder if they wouldn't rather entrust him with all the work perhaps that'll happen gradually, because of Ducreux they can't hand it over all in one go no-one can say they let their friends down, Marthe says they're tied hand and foot by other people it all snowballs they should never spend out so much on folk like that half of them inefficient and no mistake, and yet they'll be mean about small things the secretary had to battle at times for a thousand francs and they're very hard about things that don't interest them like for example some charities they won't support no-one knows why, or people like the Hartbergs or the Foissets who are rolling in money and who'd give their eye-teeth to be on visiting terms as Marthe says they see red when they're mentioned, I remember one day they were invited to the Hartbergs' to the wedding of a niece of theirs who married the son they never went they were off to Italy a week before and wrote that it was urgent, it was their only way out it would have been known if they'd stayed at home it's amazing how complicated they make their lives I think they like it and they've nothing else to do, it's bad enough when it's the Hartbergs or people who don't interest them but when it's their friends it's enough to drive you round the bend the fuss they make usually for no reason at all, they're with them again the week after yes they must like it

Who are the Hartbergs

They own the flour mills at Hottencourt even larger than those at Vériville where my gentlemen take their custom, the wife of the previous farmer Renée is a distant cousin of theirs she's a Kellermayer they all came from Germany with the great-grandfather or great-great-grandfather Hartberg, there are some Kellermayers at Douves who own the machine-tool factory Renée's from the branch that's stagnated as she used to say, yes the Hartbergs live in style they've got three cars an old-fashioned Rolls-Royce with a chauffeur I see him going by in town sometimes with the grandmother always draped in furs even in the summer, she's friendly with the mother of Dame Longuepie a lady called Binet they go and take the waters together, it seems she's even richer than her son she'd placed her capital in America before the war she owns half a town over there some outlandish name and stingy like most of her sort, she bosses everyone around the castle belongs to her the son would love to get hold of it and it would seem still according to Renée that they tried to poison her with her *tisane* jolly family aren't they, Mme Hartberg the daughter-in-law that is had two children by her first marriage everyone knows she's divorced, it so happened they were married in Tunisia so they put out this first marriage was annulled in Rome and they're always stuck in church, she has another daughter by her second husband but no boys she can't have any more had an operation for ovatories it seems, her husband's in a quandary about the flour mills which'll pass on to someone else or to the nephews and they don't get on but you needn't worry they'll always know which side their bread's buttered

Where are Hottencourt and Vériville in relation to Sirancy

Hottencourt's sixteen miles to the north-west and Vériville to the north about twenty-five miles from Fantoine which is six from Sirancy

When you mention the town you mean Agapa

Yes nine and a half miles from my gentlemen's place
When you mention the village you mean Sirancy
We call it the village compared to the town but it's a small town of two thousand inhabitants Sirancy-la-Louve is its real name, people think there were wolves there once upon a time it's possible but the Curé's got some story about it meaning on the left in Latin so nothing to do with wolves instead it would mean on the left of the Roman theatre when you come from Agapa, you know we've got ruins for the tourists from May to September there's a special coach service organised from Douves foreigners chiefly who come for the theatre, at Sirancy there's still a well and some catacombs and at Agapa the whole district of Les Oublies is built on Roman foundations, there was a triumphal arch near the Rue des Casse-Tonnelles and a bath-house beneath the Rue Charles the foundations are still there they were both destroyed during the invasions, at Sirancy the Mayor's been trying for fifteen years to get the Sous-Préfet interested in excavations they made a start eight or nine years ago now near the well but gave up six months later it was impossible, everyone complained at the time and much too costly especially as they'd have to found a Society for it which no-one's interested in, but at Agapa they're going on with it it's coming along slowly they've only got about ten workmen specialists so-called who manage to dig the whole time where they shouldn't, last month they brought down a whole stretch of wall which had some cornice or other the pieces were carted off to the museum, they haven't found any place for them yet they dumped them in the entrance-hall for the time being I don't find that very interesting a cornice they're always the same even if they are Roman, but then in the small room on the left as you go in there's the head of some chap with his hat on meant to be Mercury who had some connection with commerce, and jewellery in the show-case glass-bead necklaces and a gold bracelet that represents a wolf-hunt it's written underneath the

curator doesn't agree with the Curé, and then a lot of stones from the bath-house and the triumphal arch the school-children come and draw them on Thursdays, they copy a bit of the frieze that's been found with soldiers and horses to commemorate some battle I can't remember which, it appears it's one of the most beautiful though the Curé says it was smaller than the one at Orange

Who is this Curé

The Abbé Quinche an old man with a game leg he knows all about history or he did he can't do much reading now except for his breviary, he's as blind as a bat his parishioners are waiting for the diocese to decide what to do they've had more than enough of his sermons always the same and he takes three hours over confession, it's hard mind if you put yourself in their place old boys like that who have spent their lives telling you where you get off for he was far from easy-going, he's a bit more mellow than he was but they won't keep him on, he still goes his rounds and looks after his garden with his maid Phyllis Legouard, I remember he always used to say it was a pagan name and he calls her Marie but she never gave way and if anyone calls her Marie she still gets cross all red-faced and old as she is seventy-six, she has a game leg too but when it comes to good sight she easily beats the Curé at her age she recognises us all and the kiddies for example who go after the cherries near the cemetery or the pears in her kitchen garden she bawls them all out by name, clear off you little scalawag it's a word that's hardly used nowadays the kids have given it her as a nickname

What sort of relations do your employers have with the Curé

As far as that goes they get on very well together once a month they invite the Curé to lunch it's a tradition, they go and fetch him in the car he doesn't need asking twice and each time Marthe has to make up a different menu, she makes a note of it in the engagement book in the kitchen to remember from one time to the next she's too many menus in her head, the Scalawag is jealous to think the Curé can have a go as they say at some ortolans she has to stay at the rectory so Marthe invites her for tea a few days later and they have a good old chinwag that's how we know what goes on in the parish, yes the Curé says in fun that my gentlemen are his best customers although they never go to church but they don't mind giving and a lot more than the rest to his good works, the old boy flatters my gentlemen and they're amused he says Dame Longuepie is very devoted but you can tell he doesn't like her, she always wants her own way bossing everyone as if she was at home and what annoys the Curé she even dares to tell him what to say in his sermon next Sunday, not just like that of course but sweet as honey and in a roundabout way and the Curé's got to do as she says, because one year he didn't take her advice and Dame Longuepie wouldn't run the local fête out of spite using some trip as an excuse or no maybe she had to take the waters with her mother and Mme Hartberg so they didn't make a quarter as much as usual

Why do you think neither Longuepie nor Ballaison nor Ducreux bring their wives to see your employers

I told you about Ballaison his wife quarrelled with my gentlemen a long time ago, as for Longuepie it's because he doesn't want to they nearly got divorced I told you, there's no reason why my gentlemen should insist besides she wouldn't come even if invited she knows my gentlemen take his part and anyway she calls them heathens and all that I don't know what enjoyment they could have with a sanctimonious prude, besides when the Curé talks mildly about her they add their own comments and you can see he enjoys it even if he does say let us be more Christian, and Ducreux I just don't know

What do you mean by heathens and all that

I don't know heathens drunkards wasters God-knows what she's jealous of their money and she's wrong about that, if my gentlemen weren't so generous to the parish she'd have ten times the problems but women are like that and let me say she's never the one to approach them it's always the Curé does that himself, and what's so funny is the annual fête my gentlemen always go and pay it a visit they amuse themselves with the village lads in the shooting galleries and games like that it makes them feel younger and they see Dame Longuepie at the *vin d'honneur*, she can't do anything but play up to them my gentlemen have a good laugh afterwards

Didn't you say the solicitor's wife is related to your employers

To Monsieur Louis his mother was a Bonne-Mesure like La Ballaison I told you they're cousins three or four times removed, my gentlemen often used to talk about Aunt Ariane she was an old maid and half scatty towards the end, she used to walk around in her garden with toilet paper rolled round her head she did the dirty on someone about who should inherit the Château her sister or her brother I don't know, by some manoeuvre she left it to her niece who didn't have as much legal right to it and the quarrel came partly from that I'm talking now of twenty years ago my gentlemen had made some joke about Bonne-Mesure I think which was repeated from one old maid to another, La Ballaison took offence her family probably had an eye on the Château which is the finest in the district and they had to write it off, mind you I'm not sure of all this it's Marthe who knows

Where is Bonne-Mesure situated

Between Fantoine and Agapa off the side road, you can't see it it lies well back and it's screened by the wood

Is it still this niece that lives there

I think so yes but she never goes out she must be crazy too, six or seven years ago when I went or Clément I should say I was going with him to talk about the crops with the farmer at Bonne-Mesure I caught sight of her at her window, she was crossing herself as fast as she could and she closed the window going Shshsh but it wasn't for us she couldn't see us

Why aren't you sure whether she's still there, didn't your employers talk about her

Well yes they did talk about her shortly before I left Marthe said something to me in this connection I can't remember, oh yes I can it's coming back she has a companion who's related to Monsieur Chantre

Say what you know about this Chantre

He often used to come to the house he's a medical student he's generally the one who takes my gentlemen off on their travels he almost always spends his holidays with them, he's very gay sings all the time and says he has to as his name's Chantre the corpse and the crabs and such-like songs, he's a lot of friends he brings along to see my gentlemen doctors and artists, I shall never forget one Sunday afternoon about ten of them turned up in fancy dress and on the Monday morning I found them sleeping all over the place, we made breakfast for them all and they searched everywhere for their clothes silly things please young minds and Chantre made a speech at breakfast and called for champagne, my gentlemen told me to go and get some and they went on drinking all day Marthe and I were given the day off, they cooked their own lunch and dinner and when we came back in the evening they were still there, but luckily not on the Tuesday morning as we had the Sous-Préfet for lunch mind you he wouldn't have been the one to stand on ceremony, the house was in such a state no question of having the extras even though Jean-Pierre and Guillaume were furious not to have been sent for it was improvised without them

Why do you say the Sous-Préfet wouldn't have been the one to stand on ceremony

Because he *knows* my gentlemen I told you he's a friend but for his wife who was coming too everything had to be impeccable, we'd just finished tidying up when they arrived my gentlemen gave us a hand, they must have been anxious to have the good opinion of the Sous-Préfet's wife seems strange people as easy-going as they are

What do you mean by the good opinion of the Sous-Préfet's wife

What do you mean what do I mean

Would it shock her to find his friends' house turned upside down

She's very finicky and you can't say she's really a friend of my gentlemen's it's more her husband and on top of that she's very conscious of her position as Madame la Sous-Préfète, she comes from a family of small shopkeepers my gentlemen would have put their foot in it if it had looked as if they didn't care they couldn't do that to Simonot and get him into trouble, I remember Monsieur Louis had put on his tie in such haste it was all crooked Madame Simonot commented on it when she came in and they laughed and he put it straight

What sort of comment

Something like not knowing how to tie his tie at his age or that sort of thing

What kind of trouble would Simonot have got into because the house was turned upside down

I told you his wife is very middle class she would have told her husband his friends were a bit peculiar that sort of business

What do you mean by a bit peculiar

You know very well

Explain

Well a bit bohemian or artistic which isn't looked on at all well she's bound to have spread it around and my gentlemen

What were you going to add

That my gentlemen wouldn't have liked it

Why

Because I tell you the artistic type isn't at all well looked on in the district

Didn't Madame Simonot know your employers well then

I told you Simonot's their friend, as for her she came maybe three times to the house

Was that in the evening

No lunch-time

How then if she was so little acquainted with your employers could she comment about the tie

So as to appear more relaxed and not look as if she wasn't at home with her husband's friends, when I say three times perhaps it's four or five and she'd probably like to have come more often

Did her husband often come without her

Fairly often yes

Did she know

She probably had an idea

Would she in your view have had any reason to take exception to this

Doesn't a wife have to follow her husband

Why didn't your employers always invite her with him

She's so middle class I told you, and heavens above surely they could do as they liked

What do you mean by easy-going

They didn't like a lot of chichi they weren't fussy about the sort of formalities they make so much of in the backwoods except on special occasions when they had to, not so much for themselves but on account of their friends

What do you know about Pierre Hottelier

He often used to come too I told you during the day or to parties, he tried very hard to look well-bred but it stands out a mile that he's not I don't know his family they're from the West, Marthe says they must have been actors their son looks so much as if he's playing a part she doesn't like actors at all, there were several among my gentlemen's friends

How could you tell he had no education

Various little details always combing his hair or scratching at some spot on his trousers or too much of his handkerchief showing from his top pocket, or talking with his hand in front of his mouth or his way of walking or sitting down things like that

Why did you observe him in particular

I didn't say that

Who were these actors who were friendly with your employers

Douglas Hotcock Michael Donéant Ralf Morgione Sylvie Lacruseille Babette Saint-Foin and also young Jean Duval on one of his flying visits he's almost settled in Hollywood now he's one I almost saw come into the world you might say, his poor mother as good as died of grief when he got in with that cinema crowd she was sure he'd go to the bad

Was Jean Duval a pseudonym

Yes his real name is Martin Coulon the stockbroker's son, his mother was a Parazou Yolande Parazou she worried herself sick over him it's no exaggeration to say it killed her, my sister knew her well she was very pious and she went to Lourdes when Martin made his first film, she used to tell my sister she was praying for him to be cured as if the cinema was a disease my sister's sure that was it but it didn't work and I tell you she didn't last long after that, she used to come and see my sister every day to talk to her about Martin always in tears and three years later she died, my sister was sure she must have had something wrong with her chest grief alone could never have finished her off so quickly anyway she could never understand what poor Yolande found so awful about her son's career, he's never given rise to any scandal in any case not here with us on the contrary we always thought he was more like a shy little girl

Who is Douglas Hotcock

An American in the forties he speaks French badly but he says he only likes French films, he's been in one or two small ones I've seen him with Marthe two or three years ago now he acted with Florence Barclay in that one what was it called something like The Blood of the Roses or The Blood of the Flowers, he acted some chap who gambled at the casino and Florence Barclay was his mistress he deceived her with some other women from the casino it was at Monte Carlo I think, and in the end she kills him you see him lying on the floor beside a vase of flowers that's been knocked over yes they were roses she was always wanting him to buy her some it comes back to me now, she's the actress I've always liked best she never seems to grow any older I don't often go to the cinema it's not my strong point I've said that before I've seen perhaps twenty movies in all

Who is Michel Donéant

He acts for the theatre never has any work he used to belong to a company The Amphitheatre or The Amphitryon they went touring in Morocco, he was sacked by the director I believe he took part in cabarets he had no right to or he'd signed a contract with another theatre, anyhow he must be about thirty the look-at-me type he tries to get by with radio work he says he's often on but Marthe never sees his name in the radio magazine, she knows he borrows from everyone and he does some filing too at his brother-in-law's who has an insurance office, all the time he's in trouble with the police I mean for his income tax and his tailor for example my gentlemen told him to go to Nantet they'd have paid but he doesn't want to, it seems he doesn't like Nantet's cut you can see the sort of bird he is

In trouble with the police you say

I don't mean the police but the authorities and the lawyers

Who is Ralf Morgione

A cinema actor too he's Italian but the only one that's rich, got a lovely Farina car at times there are eight of them in it he races up to the house and shoots the gravel all over the place and on to the lawns again and again his filthy wheels making ruts I had to even out or else the gardener and sow fresh grass, once I was there to open the car door he'd just ruined one of the lawns and they were all killing themselves with laughter, Morgione shouted *scusa scusa* into my ear but he didn't give a damn just like the American with his sorries he'd knock us down or run over our feet he couldn't care less just says sorry but it's as good as saying drop dead

Who came with Morgione in the car

Friends they weren't always the same, rushing about all the time and smashing glasses they got me down

Who is Sylvie Lacruseille

She's on television she's the friend of Mademoiselle Babette they always come together very nice both of them, Mademoiselle Sylvie always has a very strong scent which lingers on till the next day in the drawing-room, Marthe says it's called *Ton Coeur* and Mademoiselle Babette's always smoking cigars it's funny for a woman, they live in a flat in town Rue Gou the new block of flats on the eighth floor I know the concierge he doesn't like them, as if it was any business of his if they live together this tittle-tattle about people it's of no interest to me if they're pleasant they can live with whoever they like, they're very sweet they often used to bring me tobacco

What kind of tobacco

Dutch for my pipe you can't get it here, they often go to Holland for the television or to order tulips, they've got a little place at Rottard-Chizy they've shown me some snaps of their tulips there's a great flower-bed in front of the house with five

Babette Saint-Foin is she also on television

I think so yes

When they go there do they visit Rivière

They don't go to Amsterdam they go to Holland, Amsterdam is the Low Countries

What impression do they make physically

What do you mean

Describe what they look like

Mademoiselle Sylvie is fairly tall she's got rather short brown hair, she's a large hook nose as she says or as she used to say when I could still enjoy a little chat, she almost always wears trousers it's Nantet who makes them for her she has a large green ring and her scent as I said what else she's got a nervous tic lifting her shoulders as if she was hampered by her clothes and Mademoiselle Babette is blonde and small rather plumpish, she has black eyes and earrings at least a dozen different pairs last time I saw her she had some that hang down to the shoulders I don't think much of that, she's got very tiny feet and Italian shoes Marthe says she knows, she's very fond of a chat with these young ladies who always come to the kitchen they bring her chocolate and they've given her several recipes Mademoiselle Sylvie that is, for example let me see yes the Soufflé Baptiste with almonds and rum and a green sauce she's invented tarragon with a pinch of mint and several others, she took a cookery course she doesn't hold with pressure cookers just like Marthe but Mademoiselle Babette says they're both antediluted and you've got to be up-to-date pressure cookers save a lot of time

Describe Douglas Hotcock

He's on the tall side thin with wavy grey hair he must appeal to the women, always an impeccable shirt with a button-down collar and those little suits they have over there you know very fine cloth and tight all over, it's only his shoes that don't go my gentlemen make fun of him but he doesn't like modern shoes, it's true in town you get used to seeing young chaps with elegant shoes he won't have them although he says he's so fond of our fashions, he's got blue eyes I think and his mouth and nose well I can't remember

Why do you say he must appeal to the women

Because he's a handsome man with soft eyes and always well-dressed the best cocks as they say aren't always the fattest
   Do you think he appeals to your young ladies
   How should I know they all lark about together they've been good friends for a long time as for the rest I don't know
   Describe the others
   Morgione always well-dressed too quite tall but rather fat he perspires all the time he has a spare shirt in the boot of his car, he's got black eyes and hair too like all Italians and fat hairy hands and a diamond on his little finger that's said to be worth a couple of million, he's been getting a corporation over the last few years what can he be somewhere about thirty-five
   Michael Donéant
   Pale and weedy with long fair hair and terribly thin hands, the young ladies were fond of him he never stops talking he has a sister who came a few times tall and affected never says a word
   Is she a friend of the young ladies
   I don't know I only know she was engaged to someone called Tolkovitch or Toklovitch who trafficked in drugs he committed suicide in her house they said something in the papers at the time, an article by that Lorpailleur woman I remember
   Did your employers know this Lorpailleur woman
   There was a time when they talked about her they'd gone to a cocktail party at her publishers for one of her novels they found her quite ridiculous with her blue stockings it seems, when you think what some people will do to be famous it really makes you wonder, it's like Morgione if he's the richest it's because he's the biggest show-off all that publicity about his so-called engagement in the illustrated papers even last week an article in the Agapa Echo just imagine, I'm sure it's my gentlemen who were responsible for that
   What do you mean by so-called engagement
   Nothing at all he's never been engaged the girl with him in the

photos is a friend of that Odette or Yvette who needed some publicity too, she's gone off to Mexico or somewhere like that
  Who is this Odette or Yvette
  Donéant's sister
  What do you mean by they all lark about together
  I told you they drink like fishes all night they're lucky not to have any other neighbours but farmers and gardeners, even at that distance Clément used to say he couldn't sleep at times
  Do you know when
  When what
  What times
  You really make me wonder what you're after, how do you expect me to know
  How do you know Morgione had a spare shirt in his car
  Because they used to damn well tell me to go and fetch it and once even I found the boot full of photos all scattered about I had to gather them up before I could find the shirt underneath
  What kind of photos
  Just photos
  Answer
  Dirty photos
  Describe them
  Not on your life it's worse than animals
  Was the boot left open
  No he used to give me the key and that time with the photographs he must have forgotten about them till later, he told me he had a photographer friend who was doing some research and he laughed
  Was Morgione in these photographs
  You couldn't see the faces
  Sylvie and Babette you say you know these young ladies' concierge
  Yes that's Soulevert André an old army pal of Pompom's and

his wife's a Juvy Marguerite Juvy, you can forgive them really for not being very agreeable they've had a lot of trouble that business with Nollet's bank they lost everything in that, they intended to retire to a lodge they had near Crachon but they had to sell up it wasn't worth much and they found this place in the new block of flats, they'll never get over it I mean to say first they found a two-roomed flatlet at 16 Rue Vieille but it was too dear for them and then this job, they're fairly comfortable mind they've two rooms there too and the fridge and not much to do for the staircase there's a woman who comes poor old Margot has aches and pains she can't do much now neither can he, he was quite a handy man once when they were still at Fantoine they had the grocer's next to the Migeotte laundry he used to knock up shelves in the shop and potter about the room at the back where they used to hang out in the end he'd made it quite habitable, he had his son to help him then Philippe young Pipo as they called him he was killed in the war, their daughter Agathe married Sinture the expostman's son she's settled in town now he's in an office some export business I think, she doesn't see her parents any more they quarrelled her husband's not baptised old Sinture's as hard as nails they're bringing their two children up without religion, it made old Margot quite ill and they've never met since but now after all her disappointments she'd like to make it up with her daughter who's not too keen because of her husband

Whereabouts is Rottard-Chizy

It lies to the west about a hundred and twenty-five miles there are springs for the digestion and the liver a luxury hotel where the young ladies go, my gentlemen have been there too two or three times but they prefer Vichy, at Rottard there aren't many amusements apart from walks through the valley, but a little while ago I saw in the paper they'd made a golf course so perhaps that will bring some customers back, the Mayor is related to Mademoiselle Babette that's what gave them the idea of buying something there, a Monsieur Borra or Borro where they get invited there's a swimming pool it seems with water from the springs that cost him a packet specially as he had a long drawn-out law suit but he won, the young ladies said that after the verdict he threw a great banquet at home and a lady fell into the pool

Did your employers know this Borra or Borro

I don't know

Did Ralf Morgione bring his so-called fiancée to see your employers

No I told you it was last week, once he brought a negress Marthe was horrified she said that lot should stay where they were born they called her Boubou she was very smart the Josephine Baker type and not very dark, they'd organised a leopard hunt for her it was all so stupid, the leopard was Gérard with cat's fur sewn all over his clothes he hid in the garden and jumped around and they shot arrows at him that I'd made up out of bamboo with a piece of cloth at the end so as not to hurt him, for two hours they played about at this game then they took the car out with the leopard at the wheel and they all ended up at the Trois-Abeilles, there was a picture in the *Petit Photographe*

What do you know about this Gérard

He's one of my gentlemen's friends I told you

Why do you say you don't put him in the same class as Monsieur de Longuepie and the other gentlemen

Because it's true

What do you mean by that

He's a hooligan from the village I mean a loafer his parents never knew what to make of him, he's twenty-four or five better if he'd stayed in the colonies after his military service, his father is Vélac the coal-merchant he tried to get him interested in commerce but the boy's always junketing in town or at my gentlemen's place, they tried too to get him in with Monnier the picture dealer but that didn't work either when he got out of the army he married one of the Quinche girls the Curé's cousins they're rich, Gérard managed to extract some money out of his wife which he put into the Hottencourt flour mills a good investment just before his divorce, the Quinche family wanted to take him to court for swindling but it was a gift from their daughter she'd signed a paper you can see he knew how to fiddle it, it was to be separate maintenance there was nothing they could do or else they just gave it up, so the dirty work goes on last year he nearly married an English widow he got to know in the coach on the trip to the ruins he often goes as guide in the summer, she stayed three months at Sirancy they put out they were engaged she gave him some money and then she had to go back home for someone who died, Gérard was rid of her but she chased him up it's Louisette who knows all about it, the English woman wrote to her they got to know each other at the bistro she must have been one for the bottle those English women you know, but Gérard dropped her he's on the track of someone else just now always thanks to the ruins where he picks up his foreign women, an old maid who doesn't know what to do with her millions Norwegian or Swedish staying at the same hotel as the English woman it's bound to end the same way, come to think of it these foreign women must all be potty you don't have to look at him twice to see his little game as my mother used to say when a girl wants to stray her wits fly away, all this I know through Marthe we still see each other in town at Gorin's she loves their *petits fours* but now she puts it all down on paper for me

Are you a hopeless case, have you seen a specialist

I saw one a couple of years ago and he prepared me for it so now, but you get used to it you're more observant you see everything that goes on around you at the café for example once upon a time I'd never even have noticed, now I tell myself it's a compensation if I've got a long time ahead of me perhaps I'll acquire an innate gift as they say for observation

Térence Monnier does he sell pictures or restore them

Both he has a studio for restoration and framing Rue Surtout where he has two experts at work and he sells pictures too at his gallery Rue de Biron, that's where they wanted Gérard to go he'd have been quite good at it he's got the gift of the gab

Why did you say your employers took their custom to the flour mills at Vériville

Because they do what else do you think they did with their crops, the farmer has a right to half he keeps what he needs for the chickens and the rest goes to the flour mills at Hottencourt, my gentlemen take their half to Vériville it's one of their arrangements to try and please everyone

Who was the flunkey

Fellow named Randon Eric he joined the household five years after me didn't know a thing I'm the one who showed him everything you'd think he'd never seen a bed or a bath, came straight from his backwoods Lozère and at once started pretending he knew it all one blunder after another and it didn't do to remind him of them later, sometimes Marthe would say to him when he annoyed her why don't you have another go at the parquet he'd washed the whole drawing-room floor with soapy water you can imagine, another time it was black coffee in the breakfast cups another time a whole dish of *quenelles* on the carpet of the large dining-room, another time the office curtains he got them so they wouldn't pull and we had to have the furnisher in, another time he handed Marthe a bottle of *marc* for a sauce instead of cognac she had to start it all over again at the last minute believe me she'd never ask him a favour again, not to speak of his waiting at table three weeks I spent on him nor his behaviour nor his way of opening doors or anything else, so to see my gentlemen make a joke of it got on my nerves they'd easily give a housemaid the sack in a week even less for some nonsense or other, but him they kept him he was cunning he used to flatter them or he'd make his excuses in all the right words but I'm sorry for his accent, Marthe told me he used to say *môchieu* for monsieur and cooberd for cupboard perhaps that's what used to amuse them it wasn't so funny, even Marthe at table though she didn't trust him she'd laugh and correct him she's had some education I told you, when she had her jewellers shop she used to see the right people and she reads books just to show you she writes down in an exercise book every day what interests her and things about people she calls it her diary and it's very well written, about the flunkey for example she'd heard quite a bit all in all from the village or the town amongst other things the time he'd spend in front of the men's clothing shops, he blew everything he earned togging himself up we wondered how he could have bought his suede jacket and his shirts from Jacquot's it's the most expensive shop in Agapa only for tourists, he must have worked some fiddle with someone from the shop and that reminds me his radio set fifty thousand he paid for that in his second month I'd stake my life he didn't have that when he arrived, his parents are muck-rakers in the back of beyond he must have borrowed from someone I don't know, then he got on well with Luisot they used to go out together and you can ask the boss of the Colibri that's the bar in the Rue des Albigeois which leads onto the Quai des Moulins, Servais his name is he only serves whiskies and vodka a thousand francs the glass again I ask you how could they both pay that price, Servais said they were good customers but I don't believe it worked some fiddle with him too probably, still it's a crying shame in our profession the kind of people get handed on to us now a well-trained valet no-one knows what that is any more they used to be classy in my day even the company they kept

You said you used to meet him sometimes in town, who was he with

With Luisot or some of the others a rum lot of lads not even clean about their person a bunch of drunkards and tarts like that redhead she hangs round the Colibri too, girl called Viviane whose bit of pavement is the corner of the Rue des Casse-Tonnelles and the Rue Charles very central her hotel's in a cul-de-sac the Deux-Gros they say she gets up to twenty clients on a good day, the market's not far off plenty of people all through the evening it's a place for tourists I told you

Who is this Jacquot

The posh shirt-maker in the Avenue Dominique-Lapoire next to the Mouton Gras it's on the corner of the Rue Filière which at the far end leads onto the Place des Maures if you understand, he started as a draper quite a tiny shop in the Rue Octave-Serpent it's during the war he made his pile now he's successful you can't even wish him good-day, he's bought a villa on the outskirts too his wife's an old cat always pushing him on one of the Pintonnat girls very ordinary family, her parents both worked for Boche it was the grandmother I knew best she was a washerwoman she slaved away for us all right my mother never did the washing we weren't without means, when I see Mother Jacquot it makes me think of old Ma Pintonnat and I have a good laugh people forget they're not the only ones who have a good memory

What do you mean by working some fiddle with someone from the shop

How do *I* know an assistant or a saleswoman or the boss how can you tell unless

Unless what

Unless Mother Jacquot but that's between ourselves it seems she's not above a little slap and tickle as Renée says, she used to know her well she still went in for it while she was engaged with a chap called Sureau and she's meant to have gone on after the wedding

What do you mean by muck-rakers

Peasants clod-hoppers

What do you know about the boss of the Colibri

Servais oh him no need to worry he'll always fall on his feet you know the kind of bar it's only your backside that counts forgive the expression but it's true, Viviane isn't the only one who goes there she's only there from time to time, there are three or four other tarts and boys too it seems it's disgraceful it's never empty, they close at six in the morning special licence no-one could ever find out why but I suppose it's the Mayor who does it for the town an advertisement like anything else, Servais uses it as a hotel too on the quiet there are bedrooms on the upper floors the building belongs to him, if you like foreigners that's where you go you'd think it was only when they came to us that they let their hair down, men you'd take to be gentlemen and so-called society women you should see them rolling under the table, there are some old regulars women like the Princesse de Hem and the Duchess they've been laid by all the lads in the district and the negro type they know them too, talking about negroes there's often a fight there Servais has threatened to keep them out, you can say what you like about racialism there's a good side to it I'm like Marthe they haven't got our way of thinking, I don't mean their morals we're all tarred with the same brush I mean their sense of humour they're too offensible they don't understand and Bob's your uncle a brawl

Whereabouts is the Quai des Moulins

Along the river on the left bank on the west side of the town it continues to the north along the Quai des Tanneurs to the south along the Quai Henri-Vachon, it's one of the oldest districts after the centre round Les Oublies and the cathedral, that's where I most like to take a walk round Les Moulins there's one mill left on the corner of the Rue des Rats not been used for a hundred years now, all the houses round about are half-timbered going back to the Middle Ages there's an *estaminet* with an inn sign the Pou-qui-rote and a little cobbler who looks as old as his workshop, he wears a skull-cap winter and summer alike old Père Michel as he's called in memory of his wife old Mère Michel because she used to feed all the cats in the district, the roofs are dark brown tiles they use mass-produced tiles to repair them much redder they spoil them, good thing if the Mayor looked into it it's true for the visitors but there are still some who look at the old bits not only the baths and the ruins, not far off there's the Rue du Trou-de-Poil funny name the Curé from Sirancy says it's a deformation of the Latin I remember Marthe had noted it down in her book, it's *troncus* and *politus* that means polished trunk there must have been some cabinet-makers in these parts in Roman times it joins the Rue des Rats to the Rue des Albigeois, a bit further there's the Rue du Son because of the old mills where there's a potter who makes souvenir pots red or black with Agapa written on them, not very modern when you compare them with the shops on the main avenues but they sell all right to the English anyway there are other things in his shop but it's chiefly the pots that go well, I could stay for hours in those streets you can see the windows all crooked I mean the house-fronts all askew full of dents and bulges and tiny little balconies, most of them are being removed they're dangerous but they're restoring the ones at the Maison-Bertrand that belongs to the Archaeological Society the president is Monsieur Carré a friend of my gentlemen's as I said, I often sit on the embankment under the plane trees we have very beautiful plane trees

The name of the river

I was just going to say it's the Manu which runs from east to west but after the forest it bends to the south, then it winds back to the north and again to the west it makes a great curve round the Plateau as it's called, that starts behind my gentlemen's house rises slowly and then falls away again about nine miles further on down to the town so when you're on the embankment the river flows from north to south, in fact in the Rue Octave-Serpent past the

Rue du Son there's the Plumet bookshop on the corner where they have an old map in the window you can see it all, not a map like nowadays the houses are all there and the trees too it's very practical, the Rue Octave-Serpent used to be called the Rue des Chaudrons this Serpent was a town councillor before the fourteen war there's a plaque I've forgotten the dates, the Rue de Broy finishes on the right one of the longest streets that goes on to the Avenue des Africains in front of the hospital, the whole of this area's full of little streets you can easily get muddled if you don't know and on top of that they change their names, for example the Rue du Nid after the Rue Serpent becomes the Rue des Trappes then it joins the Rue de Broy and as it bends round just at that point you might think it still went on the same but after that it's the Rue Chattemite et cetera, it's the history of these streets and houses that's so fascinating they'd do far better to run a regular column in the Echo or the Fantoniard instead of those articles by that Lorpailleur woman on the new novel as she calls it her theories don't interest anyone, yes the old streets in that part as far as Les Oublies there's a book mind at Plumet's but it's an old one not so easy to understand it's worth twenty-thousand francs just imagine that for a book

Where is the site of the old triumphal arch

I told you Les Oublies, from the embankment you can take the Rue Gou near the Rue des Rats you cross the Rue des Marquises and go straight on along the Rue Souper-Trombone you see the name changes, according to Plumet this one comes from *super* and *tropoum* Latin again because of the triumphal arch, so if you follow that road you come out just at the right spot there's a railing in the little square you go down into a kind of cellar and you can see the stones that are left, its like the baths you can find them on the right if you go on up the Rue Edouard-Flan you cross the Rue du Magnificat then Casse-Tonnelles and you're in the Rue Charles, twenty yards along on the left the cul-de-sac of

Deux-Gros with the old baths almost opposite you go down as before, mind you when you leave the embankment it's shorter to go up the Rue des Albigeois, you cross Les Marquises turn to your left and the first on your right is the Rue du Cimetière which takes you straight there it bends round and comes into the Rue Charles, I tell you if I'd known I'd have studied when I was young to become a guide instead of spending my life in other people's houses

You mentioned the main avenues, which are they

Let's just say the avenues there's the Avenue Dominique-Lapoire that goes from Les Oublies to the Place de l'Hôtel-de-Ville and continues south as the Avenue de l'Hôtel-de-Ville, the Avenue Georges-Pompier which runs from the Quai Henri-Vachon and also ends up at the Hôtel-de-Ville, the Avenue Paul-Colonel which starts at the Quai des Tanneurs and leads to the crossroads at Les Oublies, the Avenue des Africains which comes from the Place de l'Hôpital and is continued on the north side by the Avenue Amélie-XXXIII and the Avenue de Douves which shoots off Dominique-Lapoire towards the station

From your Quai des Moulins how do you get to the cathedral

The easiest way is to follow in the direction of the Quai des Tanneurs, you pass the Rue Gou on your right and you take the next turning the Rue Surtout you follow that up to the Rue Croquette on your left go up that street then cross the Rue Bassinoire and straight on till you reach the Avenue Paul-Colonel, you go along there for a while on the right-hand side so you can cross at the crossing and then the Rue des Irlandais which is almost opposite, there's first the Rue Sam then the Rue Suzanne on the left the Rue du Coucou on the right and the narrow Rue du Triet you go straight on till you get to the Rue Jérôme, it's not really worth crossing though you could mind the Rue des Irlandais goes on as the Rue des Omelettes, that comes into the Rue Pisson and there you're quite near the square but you might just as well take the Rue Jérôme for a while on the right it's easier you run straight into the Rue de L'Enfant-Dieu which joins the Rue des Trouble-Fête to the Place Karl-Marx, that's the old cathedral square they've changed its name right in the middle there's a statue of the philosopher holding a dove it's by a sculptor called Surprend such a nice little square it spoils it, before there was a statue of Sainte Fiduce patron saint of the church they've sent that to the museum, in stone all crumbling away she wears a crown but not because she was queen it's the crown of the virgins and martyrs, she didn't want to sleep with some barbarian chieftain I ask you it was during the invasions they threw her in the river with a stone round her neck it's written down in the little guidebook they sell Rue Baga a few doors away, except they say marry instead of sleep with of course, they explain the construction of the cathedral too its length and width all that, and how the Bishop doesn't reside in Agapa as you know they have a Canon you'd have to look up the guide for the details anyway all this part is the oldest you can go for long walks there to Les Moulins for example, and on the other side of the square there's the Rue Saint-Violon which corresponds to the Rue Baga, they join up again in the Rue du Crève-Tombeau which crosses the Rue de la Chèvre and goes on till it reaches the Avenue Amélie-XXXIII passing in front of the castle, it's not bad with a big square keep in the middle and round the curtain wall the Tower Amélie-XXXI, the Jews' Tower on the corner of the Avenue and the Dualie Tower behind the corner of the Avenue and the Rue des Tatoués, the fourth one collapsed that was the Tower of Bois-Suspect the Dukes of Bois-Suspect were once the Lords of Agapa but the castle's belonged to the state for a long time now, you can visit it Wednesdays and Saturdays there's nothing inside everything of interest has gone to the museum, you can climb up the Dualie Tower and have a view of the Avenue with the shops and museum opposite, the Place des Maures on the right and the Rue de Biron which goes to the station the steps are very steep and frighten the ladies there's a notice up warning slippery steps, you cross the main courtyard you can't visit the keep that's where the caretaker lives with his daughter money for jam, all he does is take the visitors to the bottom of the steps he doesn't even go up any more and close the main door after the visit, in the building to the south there's the police-station on the Rue des Tatoués you can go back that way, cross the Rue Magnasse which forks off towards the cathedral leave the Rue des Singes behind on the left then take the Rue du Panier-à-Pain till you get to the Rue des Clous, cross it and take the narrow Rue du Docteur-Tronc which leads into Trouble-Fête, turn to the left and the first on the left is the Rue Duport with the house of Antoine Duport head of the Merchants' Guild the house is intact all carved with garlands and local worthies with its beams and tiny stained-glass windows they had then, there's a boundary stone in front which used to mark the end of the monastery estates I forgot to say that the monastery

Do you know if there are any surviving members of the Bois-Suspect family

Well in a way there's the Duchess Madam Sham we call her too, she's no more a Duchess than I am she's from the Balkans mind Rumanian or Bulgarian who knows, twenty years ago she married the old Duke Alphonse who still had a house near the Hospital he died soon after in narrow straits, this is where they first met she'd already been a bit of a rolling stone, married again straight after Alphonse died married a Greek shipowner chap called Patrocles Frimides then he died too and left her his millions, she insists on being called Duchesse de Bois-Suspect she must be nearly seventy, every year she stays at the Grand Hôtel I mean that before the Grand Hôtel the Hôtel des Bains was the smartest and the Grand Hôtel was completely transformed ten years ago, every year she comes for the season with her friend old fat Hem they meet here for the waters so they say they're more often out than in

There are waters at Agapa you say

I should jolly well think so since Roman times the springs are still running for the circulation rheumatism all that, the old pump room still exists Rue Bitard opposite the ruins but no-one goes there much now it's not well kept up and there are no mud baths like in the new buildings, the local people some of them still go it makes a big difference in the price but visitors go to the new one the S.B.A. runs that too the Society for the Baths of Agapa comes under the Corporation, they don't want for luxury there marble everywhere by that I mean the stone's from Chanchèze and when it's polished it's like a kind of marble, there are little springs in every corridor birds that spit water because of the name of the pump room Les Oiseaux-Baigneurs, it's all fitted up in the latest fashion the mud comes from Malatraîne round that way it's Dumans who sees to the transport

Whereabouts is the new pump room

Not far from the old Rue des Bains as they call it now it used to be the old Rue du Goret-Sifflard between the Rue Charles and the Rue des Marquises, there's a swimming pool and private bathrooms and on the first floor the mud, they've a large staff two doctors masseurs and masseuses servants and waitresses, a bar on every floor where the whisky's as dear as at the Colibri but you should just see how they get through it, that sort of crowd don't need treatment any more than you or I do, behind the pump room they've knocked the old houses down to make a garden with a swimming pool too and an outdoor bar open to non-residents

Who is this Princesse de Hem

The Duchess's friend they go tippling together I told you she lives in Vienna in Austria, a plump blonde about fifty it seems her husband's been in the government she looks more like a housemaid in spite of her pearls and her Cadillac she gets her chauffeur to drive it here Petit-Louis nice fellow, the journey takes him three days you can't say he likes his mistress you know how it is but he's been working for her for fifteen years, he told us she'd made advances to him at the start even if something did happen for a while it's all over now she gets herself a new gigolo every year, last year it was one called Franz a fair boy who came to my gentlemen's with her and Madam Sham

Did he come from Vienna with her

Yes she's brought several with her like that or else she finds one on the spot out of those who come for the season, Gérard's had his turn too but that didn't last a fortnight later she'd found another called Albert which caused a row at the Colibri with Gérard

Why if Gérard visits the Colibri does he chase after women at the ruins

The questions you ask, I suppose he finds they're the real thing as he says besides at the Colibri he's too well-known

The Duchess and this Princess did they often visit your employers

Yes during the season they generally arrive in June and stay a month

What do you mean by the season

That's from May to September they tried one year to keep the baths open in winter with a smaller staff, they only had four or five visitors it wasn't worth the candle they didn't repeat the experiment

Does the old pump room also close in winter

The same, they made a case for opening it once for the local people Doctor Ducuze asked the S.B.A. not to close it his patients are on the spot it would be more advantageous for them not to wait for the season, but they refused on account of the cost

Who is this Doctor Ducuze

One of the doctors here specialist in rheumatism it was he who recommended the waters for my lumbago three years ago they were quite a help, he's responsible for the old pump room during the season he's there every morning they're almost all his patients since the death of Doctor Tronc

Who was Doctor Tronc

The oldest in the town, he died five years ago people have really missed him he wasn't expensive and very good he often used to recommend the baths, they've changed the name of the Rue Crasse in memory of him

So Doctor Ducuze has taken over his patients

What I mean is Tronc's patients have gone over to him for rheumatism he's been in the town a long time too but he's dearer, Tronc was a general practitioner

Are there other doctors in Agapa

There's Mottard from the hospital he takes charge of the Oiseaux-Baigneurs during the season he has a permanent assistant usually an intern, and Doctor Bompain who's also at the hospital on Tuesdays and Saturdays it's he who operated on my sister for pendicitis

Why do you say usually an intern

Because sometimes it's a doctor from Douves who comes it depends

It depends on what

How should I know

Didn't you say that Chantre used to practise medicine

Study I said

Is he an intern yet

No he's finishing his studies at Douves the university, I don't know if he'll be an intern here it's a small hospital there aren't more than two or three

Do you think in view of his contacts in Agapa it would be to his advantage to come here

On the whole I should think not

Why

For professional reasons Douves is much more important and here it will always be the same hectic life, if he did ask for a post here mind I wouldn't be surprised he can't have much ambition except to enjoy himself

Do your employers encourage him to do his hospital training in Agapa

I've no idea

Aren't they very attached to him

They'd see him all the same Douves is not far away

How far

Thirty miles Chantre has a car and he makes full use of it I can tell you

Then why do his hospital training at Douves if he'd see just as much of your employers

I said for professional reasons I didn't say they'd see quite as much of each other

Do you think your employers have a bad influence

I wouldn't say that specially, young folk are influenced by what they choose but it wouldn't be a bad thing for him not to enjoy himself quite so much

Is his health delicate

No

Well then

I've said it before I'll say it again for professional reasons he'd learn a lot more at Douves

What do you mean by influenced by what they choose

Just what I meant and no more

You said Chantre usually took your employers off on their travels, what travels

They've been twice to Italy once to Greece once to Sardinia, no I mean twice to Greece once to Sardinia one other time to Denmark and very often to Amsterdam for the week-end

How do they go to Amsterdam

They go to Douves by car and then by air now the flights are more frequent there are more and more tourists, they've added a new floor to the airoport for the new restaurant the old one was lousy my gentlemen used to say the food wasn't fit for pigs
Did they often eat there
No but there were occasions when they hadn't got time to make other arrangements they get in rather a state and like to be at the airport in plenty of time, the second time they went off to Italy they nearly missed the plane no that was Greece
Who used to keep the old restaurant
Beretti not to be confused with Barbatti who as I said runs the Trois-Abeilles, I went with them once to the aerodrome I had some job to do at Douves and they paid for my luncheon, I didn't find it so bad except for the corked wine Beretti came to apologise naturally not much of a manner but I don't find Fion any better, it's he who keeps the new restaurant before that he ran the Bécasse Rue Verru

Were your employers invited to Rivière's place in Amsterdam
Yes
Did the two ladies de Bois-Suspect and de Hem know Rivière
They'd seen him here though he didn't often come in June but I think the Duchess was in touch with him in Paris about his collection of forgeries
About these forgeries did Rivière know Térence Monnier
Yes
Did he work for him
I've no idea he has his own experts in Amsterdam I told you
Did the two ladies de Bois-Suspect and de Hem know Chantre
Of course one day even Madame Sham had a bit of a fling with him as they say, he didn't say nay they never told a soul and for a joke my gentlemen went to Rottard-Chizy to take them by surprise someone had told them they must be there, they arrived at the hotel said they were the police and they were shown up to

their bedroom, Madam Sham's hair was all ruffled and so was Chantre's they had a good laugh and they phoned the two young ladies Lacruseille and Saint-Foin who were there and finished the night with them, Marthe heard all about it when they came back

Why didn't you mention these two ladies straightaway de Bois-Suspect and de Hem among your employers' intimate friends

First I never said they were intimate friends and then I can't say it all in one go there are still heaps of other people they knew

What do you mean by intimate friends

People they often saw not only in June

What route do your employers take from their home to the airport

Leaving through the grounds at the rear they take the by-road for Crachon which climbs up to the Plateau and joins the main road from Sirancy, there's a dangerous cross-roads with a halt sign then follow the main road into town and it's straight on after that

What is the landscape like the topography

What was that

What kind of country do they pass through

Well along the by-road fields and trees at first mostly oaks and the woods of Sirancy that you see on the left, then the Plateau with chestnut trees and fields on the left the forest of Grance and the land that belongs to the Bonne-Mesures, on the right fields that fall away down to the river below and the same straight on all the way into town the road drops down again crosses the river by the Pont Bonaparte and on the other side the embankment, they come straight into the Quai des Moulins on the right there's the Rue des Oiseaux which with Henri-Vachon marks the end of the embankment, they cross over and take the Rue de Broy which makes a bee-line for the hospital that's the easiest way, mind you could take the Rue Octave-Serpent which goes more towards the station and then the Rue du Goret-Sifflard I mean the Rue des Bains, and the Rue des Halles which comes into the Avenue Dominique-Lapoire but those are narrow streets as I said with lots of cross-roads and two traffic lights, one at Les Marquises one at the Rue Charles it takes longer better to follow the Rue de Broy, they go past the girls' school at the corner of the Rue des Oiseaux opposite Les Marquises then the boys' school at the corner of the Rue des Genêts and straight on again to the Rue Prolot which forks into Dominique-Lapoire, they turn left into that till they reach the Avenue de Douves on the right, then take Douves cross Les Africains pass the casino and the station and straight on again till you're out of town with little houses and gardens on the outskirts, then fields and woods again for thirty miles to the airport it's two miles this side of the town, the entrance is straight off the main road on the right

You say there are chestnut trees on the Plateau

Big ones dotted about, once upon a time there were woods a few clumps left but it's chiefly fields

The woods of Sirancy are they chestnut trees

They're mixed because the ground falls away towards Sirancy chestnuts prefer higher ground

And the forest of Grance

There it's almost all oaks the finest forest in the district more than half of it's on the Bonne-Mesure estate, the old folks were still telling stories in my day about that forest and the men who'd been hanged eating acorns that made them grow tusks like the boars, and the Great Jackdaw that used to attack the women at nightfall

The river lies below you say

Well of course it skirts the Plateau and flows on down to find the lowest point as I've explained, it makes a great loop that ends up at Crachon and on the other side of the Manu it's quite flat for miles

Are there woods in this loop

The woods of Le Furet I told you which belong to my gentlemen, the people of Crachon have permission to collect the dead wood but often they cut it down and that causes endless trouble with the farmer who's the only one with the right to cut it

How does the bridge look the Pont Bonaparte

Like a bridge

Describe it

The main road dips down again and then straight into town on the right bank a little district that's called La Butte because it's on the side of the hill, there's the Rue de la Butte, that crosses the bridge it's a bridge how can I say with two arches it's called Bonaparte because of Napoleon, it's not the only trace of the emperor in this part of the world for example the Trois-Abeilles that comes

This road is called Rue de la Butte just as far as the bridge

It's not a long road for example there's hardly more than five or six shops apart from the Co-op

Is there an embankment on the right bank

The Quai des Bouchers with plane trees like the rest but narrower it's a favourite spot for the kids, with the remains of underground passages that have been walled up one that goes under the river it seems to link up with the monastery, when you think of the work in those times just imagine

What monastery

Saint Violon the monks used to be called the Violinists there aren't any now they used to specialise in making chestnut liqueur from the chestnut trees on the Plateau

Chestnut liqueur you say

It's written in the guide book anyway it's not made now

Are there still any fortifications round the town

They've been demolished all that's left on the Quai des Tanneurs is half a tower called Don Quixote's tower at the corner of the

Rue Matias, there's a little shop of children's books and records on the ground floor living quarters on the first, and on the Quai des Moulins a bit of the walls incorporated into the block of houses between the Rue des Rats and the Rue des Albigeois, towards Les Oublies too on the new site for the excavations there's quite a long stretch of wall you can see the Roman foundations underneath, they've laid them bare there was once a moat all along this side as far as the castle all that's left now is the name Fossés-Mahu a tiny street that leads into Les Oublies

Where is the casino

I told you Avenue des Africains it's on the corner of the Avenue de Douves there's the gaming-room the bar a restaurant not much good and a hall with a stage, during the season companies come in from Douves or somewhere I used to enjoy them once upon a time I saw the Guardian Angel with Pauline Colonna, she was superb that woman it was she played the guardian angel fighting for her home against the vamps

Is Mademoiselle Lorpailleur anything else but a novelist and journalist

She's a schoolmistress in town it's not her novels that keep her alive, my gentlemen the time when they used to talk about her said you could feel the schoolmarm in everything she wrote that's what I think about her articles in the papers, my gentlemen only read the Paris papers now the Sous-Préfet is always telling them off

What do you know about Doctor Mottard

He's the superintendent of the hospital a big tall man with a moustache not from our parts

Do your employers know him

Bound to everyone knows everyone else

Used he to visit them

No only once out of politeness Madam Sham asked if he could come and take tea she used to see him every day at the Baigneurs, they found him uninteresting as they say perhaps they'll change their minds

What do you mean

I mean that's all they know of him they don't go to the baths for their rheumatism as neither of them has got it and they've their own doctor at Douves, but if ever they did need treatment you never can tell they might see a bit more in him he's a good doctor

And Ducuze

He's old he doesn't go out much

Who is your employers' doctor

Doctor Georget very nice he often used to come to the house and not stuck-up in the middle of a meal he'd take the trouble to come and congratulate Marthe, one evening he helped us with the washing-up we were meant to be going to the circus I remember the only thing that annoyed me he used to get on well with the flunkey I'd rather he hadn't, yes Doctor Georget looked after Marthe when she broke her leg he happened to be there, she was taken straight to hospital and as Bompain wasn't there every day there was only an intern Georget did the operation himself, and he often came from Douves to see her she might have limped for the rest of her days if it hadn't been done properly, six months' rest he said we had someone to fill in I told you Marcelle Vieuxpont a woman who wasn't very clean I used to think she smelt but my gentlemen said she was a good cook

What did Georget look after your employers for

Because he's a friend

For what reason, for what illness

For flu sore throat laryngitis

Wasn't it easier for them to go to a local doctor

I told you he was a friend they used to phone him when something was wrong and he'd come

Do you mean that they were ill at the same time

I didn't say that I said Georget would come when they were ill either one or the other
Were they often ill
No more no less than anyone else
Do you know if he treated them for anything apart from flu or sore throats
Good Heavens I don't remember all their ailments it was for chills most of the time
Was it you who cleaned their rooms when one of them was ill
Me or the flunkey
You never noticed anything unusual about their medicaments
What do you mean
Syringes, phials
Yes at times for a bad sore throat or let me see bronchial pneumonia one of my gentlemen had the doctor would give injections
Were these syringes and phials used only in case of illness
Yes why
You don't think your employers or one of them made more frequent use of them
No why
Where were the syringes kept
In the medicine chest
Where was that
Each of my gentlemen had one in his bathroom
In normal circumstances were these syringes always in their right place, you never saw them left lying about
Never besides surely the doctor wouldn't have gone there to make an injection
What do you mean
You don't go to the W.C. to inject a patient
Have you ever noticed that your employers were in a more

nervous state than usual at certain times, did they not occasionally leave the table or the drawing-room to go to the bathroom

I said they were in a state yes at the airoport for example but as for going to the bathroom I should have thought anyone had the right to satisfy a personal need when he wanted to

Doctor Georget used he to come on his own

Sometimes on his own sometimes with Monsieur Raoul or other people to parties

Who is Monsieur Raoul

A friend of his

What does he do

He works in the hospital at Douves in the laboratory I think

Is he a nervy type

Quiet rather

Did he talk to your employers about their ailments, have you ever caught them whispering together

You forget I'm deaf

Describe this Raoul

He's tall about twenty-five fairly slim straight black hair he's often in blue jeans

Does he know your employers' friends

Yes he knows Monsieur de Longuepie and Monsieur de Ballaison and the others quite well

What others

All the others I can't give you the whole list again

Does he know the Duchess and the Princess

Yes they often used to go out together

How do you know about that

How do I know well I used to see them go off of course

Go off where

Leave the house

So they didn't stay in with your employers when they were all together

I wouldn't say that I mean often when these ladies were there they'd go off after their aperitifs so they could dine out
Especially with Raoul
Not specially
Why mention Raoul rather than anyone else
Because you asked me if he knew them I said yes and they used to like to go and dine out in the summer
Where did they take their aperitifs
I told you on the terrace
And in the winter
In the drawing-room but the ladies were never there in the winter
Who did your employers see in the winter
You're really after that list
Didn't some of their friends only turn up in the winter
I don't remember
Did this Raoul come from the district
No his parents settled here about fifteen years ago they're English by birth and came from Alexandria, their son talks English to the Princess it seems that's the thing to do in any case better than German
Doesn't the Princess speak French
Yes but for a change perhaps she gets tired hunting for her words and perhaps too it's to make people forget her nationality
Is she German or Austrian
German I think
Did she speak German with the man called Franz
No English I think
Did Raoul know Franz
Yes but they didn't get on nor did Gérard who can't stand the sight of him it seems he's like an iceberg the English are cold fish
Were Raoul's parents invited by your employers

No besides my gentlemen weren't too keen on their friends' families they said it was like a hornet's nest you'd have them all flying at each other's throats, better let sleeping dogs lie and have some peace and quiet, I think they're right

Did your employers speak English to the Princess

I think so occasionally and to the others too, while we're on that Marthe says one day there was a great argument about languages they were bickering all afternoon Morgione was reciting things in Italian Donéant in French Hotcock in English, Donéant went out slamming doors it nearly turned into a nasty rumpus if it hadn't been for Mademoiselle Lacruseille who's a bit more reasonable they'd have gone off without any dinner, still it was Morgione with his big mouth who finished the argument he said Dante was the greatest poet and Italian singers and actors and all the rest and they let him have his say

Did your employers know Doctor Tronc

Everyone knew him everyone loved him, he used to come to the house every week at midday on Thursdays there always had to be a water-ice for dessert he adored them old men are fond of their food, he was a hard drinker too alcohol is mother's milk for old men as he said good company a good talker, Marthe always used to have a chat with him after luncheon she went upstairs from the kitchen and they'd go into the garden together it was a tradition my gentlemen gave permission, she used to put down in her notebook a lot of the things he said I must try and remember let me see yes for example if you'll pardon the liberty he was pretty racy, your table's forlorn without a good horn meaning that for a woman to be a good cook she mustn't be alone in bed, Marthe used to protest she'd been a widow for seventeen years she said she didn't need that to be the best cook in the district on the contrary it takes your mind off everything else, and then what was it yes if at luncheon you're bored offer dinner to milord meaning that you invite the bore at midday and the friend in the evening, he didn't mean it seriously because it was he who didn't want to come in the evening any more staying up late used to tire him, and then there was a brat round the hoop means a hair in the soup I suppose that meant a woman can't see to her cooking and her child at the same time all this you know comes back to me thanks to the notebook, yes everyone really missed the Doctor they laid him to rest in the cemetery at Sirancy where he originally came from, the Abbé Quinche made such a long oration Marthe told me she could just imagine poor old Tronc saying to himself in his hole in the ground if you don't shut your trap I'll jump inside it, another of his expressions all the memories he left behind were jolly

Were there other English-speaking people among your employers' friends

Yes Lord Chastenoy and Lady Chastenoy his name is Mark with a k hers is Rosamond not Rosemonde I've seen Rosamond in her books Rosamond S. Chastenoy, they come for the season too but in September and stay at the Hôtel des Bains which is not so modern as I said, one year they stayed with my gentlemen they weren't meant to be coming that year but they changed their minds at the last moment and the room they usually have at the Hôtel des Bains wasn't available for them as they didn't want any other my gentlemen told them to come to the house for a couple of weeks until it was free for them they turned up with a load of luggage we put them in two of the bedrooms on the second floor, Lord Chastenoy wanted to be woken every morning at seven o'clock I had to take him his tea and two stinking biscuits he'd brought the tin down to the pantry himself, at ten to eight he'd go out in the garden with his walking stick and his red silk scarf he'd go for a walk in the kitchen garden, in September there was a lot of dew and the ground was soft he'd be back regularly at half past nine all muddy for his Brekkers with Lady Chastenoy who'd be up by then, the whole fortnight she was telling him you are impossible which means *vous êtes impossible*, it seems they always say *vous* to each other in English to the dogs too there's no difference it doesn't seem very polite to me it's Marthe who used to hear her say that in her squeaky voice, because of the mud he used to go and change his trousers and his shoes I wondered if he didn't do it just to annoy Lady Chastenoy she wasn't a bad sort but a rather difficult woman, she used to make him change three times a day so that's once in the morning then at midday and again in the evening if it wasn't sports clothes in the afternoon as well to go and watch my gentlemen playing tennis, but when it came to tips we couldn't complain we were hard at it pressing suits or her dresses every day the housemaid never had a minute, we had only one hitch and that was the laundry Leduc scorched one of milady's nightgowns while it was being pressed it appears it was her grandmother's lace irreplaceable or her great-grandmother's, my gentlemen offered her a new one that they took her into town to buy the very same day, she never wanted them to go in the shop for a nightgown she said that was shocking, mind she didn't say no when they suggested going into town she must have been very particular about having the right number of nightgowns that was her all over the little we knew of her anyway, she's a super-fusspot her Brekkers for example the first day the eggs weren't cooked the way she wanted and she wouldn't eat them she never said a word it's Marthe who asked her, she came down to the kitchen to show her the result was just the same

Did Lady Chastenoy write

Who to

Didn't you mention her books

The books she used to read I've seen them in her I've seen them

Where

In her bedroom yes I had no business to be there it was only the chambermaid was meant to

Didn't you say the chambermaid only looked after the linen

Yes but for a lady especially English my gentlemen had made a point of only letting the chambermaid do the tidying up, the flunkey or me we did Lord Chastenoy's room
 Did he have any books
 I only saw one about dogs
 Why did he choose the kitchen garden for his walk
 Some pet idea of his I suppose
 Where is the kitchen garden
 Next to the farm and the gardener's I told you
 Do you think Lord Chastenoy was interested in the vegetables
 He must have been but for a whole fortnight to spend more than an hour a day inspecting the tomatoes and the beans seems a bit strange
 Are there no other vegetables
 At that time of year there's not much except tomatoes and beans the cabbages are starting and there's always the lettuce but for interesting vegetables it's better in the spring
 What do you mean by interesting vegetables
 Asparagus for example or artichokes
 Do you think they'd be sufficiently interesting to justify more than an hour's walk
 I wouldn't say that on the contrary I found it very odd he chose the kitchen garden
 Don't you think he must have discovered some special attraction there
 I can't see what
 The farmer or the farmer's wife the gardener and his wife or the gardener's daughter
 If that was it I'd have heard from Pompom, no as I said he may have done it to annoy Lady Chastenoy
 Are there no other places in the park where you could get muddy
 I should say

Well
Well well I don't know
You say your employers used to play tennis
Yes
Where is the tennis-court
Behind the house by that I mean let's say the north-east, on the other side of the main drive
In the grounds
Yes
Why haven't you mentioned it
I forgot
Didn't Lord Chastenoy play tennis
He watched them playing he was rheumaticky and that prevented him besides at his age
What age was he
In the seventies Lady Chastenoy the same but she was very erect you've no idea
So it interested her too to watch them playing
So it would seem it appears to be a tradition in their country as for croquet I used to play that as a child it's easy but tennis is strenuous
Did the Chastenoys go and take the waters when they were staying with your employers
Naturally that's what they came for
When did they go, at what time
If I remember right they used to go off at ten o'clock with the flunkey who drove them in the big car they'd be in town by half-past ten, they'd stay at the baths till half-past twelve and the flunkey would go and fetch them we'd have luncheon later than usual
Did your employers have several cars
The big Ford they never wanted to change that they said it was good enough it's still going now and the little one a Fiat they've changed that several times

Where is the garage
In the basement next to the kitchen there's a concrete ramp
Where did the chambermaid press the clothes
In the linen room
Where is the linen room
In the basement too a small room that leads into the pantry
Why did you mention neither the garage nor the linen room in the plan of the house
You never asked me
Can you go from the garage to the linen room or the kitchen
No why
How are these basement rooms laid out
The garage to the left of the main entrance on the right the steps that go down to the kitchen, after the kitchen the pantry and the linen room which leads into the boiler room which leads into a large room that's used for lumber where we pile up the logs for the big fireplace and where the chambermaid hangs up the smalls, the big wash goes to Leduc as I said
Is there no door in the garage that communicates with any of these rooms
The small door at the back leads into the wine cellar
Is this door from the garage the only way into the wine cellar
If you really want to know it communicates with the boiler room as well I never gave it a thought it's much easier to go through the garage to get to the wine cellar, anyway we didn't see to the wine my gentlemen always did that
How do you get from the kitchen to the dining-room
By the staircase that goes up from the entrance hall the door's on one side, in the corner of the dining-room there's a serving hatch it all had to be carefully arranged with Marthe my gentlemen wouldn't have anyone talking through the serving hatch and that complicated things, often we were obliged to go all the way down instead of asking from upstairs, it's true about the

serving hatch instead of simplifying things it was just the opposite except it was handy to be able to come and go by the staircase without carrying anything

Didn't you say the flunkey had upset a dish of *quenelles*

It doesn't stop accidents happening when you're waiting at table besides that wasn't in the small dining-room but in the large one that was rarely used, on important occasions maybe once or twice a year, there's also a serving hatch there too that goes down to the other kitchen and the staircase goes straight into the dining-room

You say another kitchen

Yes in the south wing in the basement but I say it was rarely used Marthe was furious when she had to do the cooking in that one, obviously it's not so well fitted up she had to go and fetch whatever was missing it meant a lot of complications, she'd rather they'd kept to the usual system but my gentlemen objected not wanting us to pass right through the main drawing-room with the dishes, it didn't matter if Marthe was furious

Why didn't you mention this second kitchen

I forgot it was rarely used for me the kitchen means the other one

Are there other rooms in the basement

Next to the second kitchen another pantry and one other room and a small W.C. as on our side

What is this other room

A junk room where we stored old books my gentlemen used to read a lot and I don't know where they found the time, all the ones they weren't keeping went there till the hospital sent for them those at least that would interest the patients, the secretary had recently altered this room for himself they'd laid a kind of black and white lino on the floor against the damp and a radiator, there was also some business about the pipes to know whether it was better to link them up with those in the dining-room above or go straight into the boiler room

What did the secretary use this room for
 For work he used to say he couldn't settle down properly in his bedroom and he was always being disturbed in the office but I tell you it's quite recent
 Did he entertain in this room
 How could he in the basement it wasn't arranged for that, just for him a table and armchair and shelves for the books
 What kind of work did he do there
 Just work I don't know what his own work I suppose
 Would you have a rough idea from the papers or books he kept there
 We couldn't go in he used to keep the key, on the last occasion we brought some books down we had to ask him for it
 Didn't your employers have a second key
 I don't know
 When did he go and work there
 In the evenings I think
 Did he keep it clean himself like his own bedroom
 I think so or wait last time we took some books down he asked me to use the vacuum cleaner but it wasn't very dirty, yes he used to do it himself unless the flunkey did it for him
 The time you did it yourself you didn't notice what kind of books or papers were lying on the table
 They didn't interest me or yes just a minute under the bed there was a scrap of paper with writing on I couldn't read a word it was as if it was written the wrong way round
 The wrong way round
 Yes as if it was the wrong way round the letters formed the wrong way round how can I say, for example an a instead of having its belly like this it had it like that the tail on this side unless they weren't a's or letters at all, just I don't know something for fun but they looked like letters the wrong way round yes

And you left this paper under the bed
I put it in the wastepaper basket
The secretary didn't speak to you about it later
No
You say there was a bed in this room
Yes as well as the table and the armchair a divan in the right-hand corner going in
Did the secretary sleep there
No he had his bedroom on the second floor I told you
Who was this divan for
Not for anyone special it was for resting I suppose
You never saw the secretary come out of this room in the mornings
Never
How was it lit
At night by a table lamp, in the daytime through a cellar-light like everywhere else in the basement except in the kitchen where there are windows which look out on a kind of well if you see what I mean in concrete cut out of the terrace, the bottom half of the windows that is standing about three feet away it lets in a lot of light it's surprising
Is the other kitchen lit in the same way
The same
Did the secretary go to this room during the day
I never saw him go in
Did it communicate with the ground floor
By the kitchen staircase
Was there a telephone
A telephone in a cellar that would be the day
How did the secretary reach this room
Through the large dining-room and the kitchen
Could he not get there through the garage
I can't see why he'd go right through the basement

How did you carry the books down to this room

I repeat through the large dining-room you go down to the kitchen beneath cross through the pantry and you're there

In what part of the dining-room does this staircase emerge

It seems to me you'd find a plan quite useful, it comes out in the centre of the wall on the terrace side between two windows opposite the great round staircase that goes up to the first floor

So there are two staircases in the large dining-room

Yes

And normally it wasn't used at all

It was used as a drawing-room too it's not separated from the large drawing-room it all makes one huge room L-shaped if you like, the big table takes up perhaps a third of it yes a third there are ten chairs along each long side two at each end so you see we could entertain twenty-four people even more but my gentlemen didn't like grand dinner-parties, as many parties as you like up to fifty people but dinners no they used to entertain their friends six at the most the small dining-room was quite large enough you can entertain ten people there

You say there was an entrance hall

A small hall yes it's normally the service entrance between the garage and the kitchen but you can say it served for everyone, it's very smart it doesn't look as if it's for servants especially as the tradesmen used to go straight to the kitchen, the entrance from the main courtyard leads straight into the large drawing-room it was very rarely used not practical, besides the cloakroom and the washroom lead off the small hall and even for big parties they'd come in that way

Which are the rooms that lead off this hall

I told you the washroom which had a cloakroom large enough for most occasions on the left as you come in, facing you the door that cuts the hall in two, on the right the dining-room door

And the other half of the hall

On the left the door to the office, opposite an entrance into the large drawing-room with no door, on the right the opening into the dining-room also with no door

What did you use as a cloakroom for big parties

The office we pushed the furniture back and brought the coat-racks up from the cellar

How was the small dining-room furnished

Old style

Describe it

There's the table at the back with six chairs round and four other chairs two between the two back windows on the right as you come from the kitchen, two others between the back window and the French window on the left which leads into the courtyard, in the two corners at the back two corner-pieces with like bulging cheeks and wavy legs it's shaped like a kind of bow shall we say the two sides of each piece of furniture I mean a bow like the one Cubid has in the garden if you see what I mean, on the right still coming from the kitchen between the first and second windows a large serving-table it's a console in pink marble all gilt underneath with elaborate cross-pieces and a group of carved dogs lying down or sitting on the top, opposite so on the left a big sideboard packed with silver that's carved too all over there's a shell up above and rosettes with flowers round and on the sides flowers and squares and below an ornate pointed apron with at the centre another shell I think, no they're flowers and garlands the hinges of the doors above and below run all the way up both ends finishing in ornaments like fir-cones or flower-buds, so there's a cupboard in the top of the sideboard and a cupboard below the silver's on top the table-linen and the napkins below, between the two cupboards there's a shelf I'm explaining badly the cupboard above is set back further than the cupboard below which makes a shelf yes a shelf and just under it three drawers for the silver cutlery, there was never anything but silver on the table it was a lot of work for

Go on with your description of the furniture

So that was the sideboard and before that still on the left between the first window and the corner of the drawing-room another console table a smaller one with an enormous Chinese vase on it from before the flood as they say very expensive, what else the curtains on each side of the eight windows in green silk and large pictures very dark on the walls, over the serving-table there's a broad panomara of a battle you can see mounted men in wigs and armour in the background forests and little towns one all in smoke and lots of soldiers all over the place, the first horseman in the front on the right is Louis XIV he's not looking what he's doing he's looking at us the other horsemen too as if it was a photo when they've been told to watch the birdie, a horseman on the left is busy running another through with his sword who's falling backwards that one's not looking at us, further on between the second and the third windows a Dutch picture like the one on the main staircase but no flowers a jumble of fruit apples pears grapes plums even a pineapple Heaven knows why they don't all tumble down, in a metal bowl engraved with little dancing figures against a background all black in an enormous gilded frame Spanish it appears with three or four rows of leaves and garlands and rosettes, then on the right-hand corner-piece a stone statue on a black plinth that's Saint Nicholas, on the other two smaller statues coloured on blue plinths that's a king and a queen in period costume, then between the window and the French window another battle just as large but the figures are very small, you can see two armies colliding with pikes and lances everywhere there's a hill in the background with little men racing about deserters probably and on the right a windmill with an ass and chickens and children watching the battle, so then there's the sideboard and then well that's all, on the floor there's a

large patterned carpet some reddish colour birds and fishes and little dogs running all round the border some with only three legs
  And the large dining-room
Also old style
Describe it
Coming from the drawing-room on the right you have the main staircase in the corner and opposite in the left-hand corner the restored chimney-piece as I said with its mantel in large blocks of stone going up to the ceiling, there's red brick in the fireplace and two big andirons that come from the Château de Sirancy almost eighteen inches high representing lions eating a man I mean to say the lion's body is very long where you lay the logs, next to it just facing you there's a window then the first French window then another window then the small staircase from the kitchen and you've reached the middle of the dining-room, then a window again then the second French window and the last window on the south side, along the front side two windows like in the small dining-room and over the courtyard the same two windows and a French window, the table too is at the back when you come from the drawing-room it faces you longways on it's a table with fat bobbly legs and a cross-piece joining them underneath, the top is of grey marble with two large angels in the centre carved out of stone one half-lying the other sitting and stroking the first one, the chairs have high carved backs and are covered in real tapestry not much to look at green and grey flowers all twenty-four of them round the table, between the first window and the French window there's an armchair with elbow-rests and wavy legs a *bergère* as it's called covered in silk with green and blue lines and above it the portrait of an old man he's bare-chested he's a saint with a beard praying his eyes to Heaven, between the French window and the next window there's a commode which looks like a cauldron all pot-bellied in wood dark with brass fittings and three drawers, the pointed apron at

the bottom like flowing locks of hair on top there are two candelabra all curly too for five candles it's funny how that style nothing is straight, and above it a picture in a large gilded frame representing a fine lady down to the waist she's wearing a tall white wig with ribbons and a piece of lace she's turning to face us with a slight smile holding in her hand a fan painted with marguerites you can see quite clearly, on either side of the commode there's an armchair covered in tapestry sprays of flowers in various shades of blue, then the small staircase with a little wall round then still against the wall under the serving-hatch a serving-table far too small the few times I used it I never found it practical, when the former mayor of Sirancy failed to get re-elected soon after I went into service there my gentlemen gave a large dinner-party he was one of their friends and I put a second serving-table against the little wall, above the staircase there's a black plaque in cast-iron with the family crest like the one at the back of the fireplace, then between the next window and the second French window a large picture showing an historical banquet there are people half naked if you pardon the liberty men and women at least twelve larking about with satyrs and pot-bellied Bacchuses, there's lots of fruit and wine-jars on the table and in one corner some woman who's drunk kissing a goat, it's not as dark as the other pictures there's some colour in it especially red and blue very well drawn you can count all their toes even in the background a little satyr under a tree playing a flute, between the French window and the last window a commode the same kind as the other but not so complicated only the top is marquetry seven or eight woods of different colours to make a bouquet, it's very delicate the wood splits with changes in the temperature or for example a drop of water falls on it and that's that if you don't wipe it off at once the wood swells, my gentlemen take great care of their old treasures the cabinet-maker always has something to patch up and stick together, standing on it the same candelabra as on the other one with a round piece of felt underneath you can't put anything down on that commode and I know what I'm talking about right at the start I once put some flowers there what a song and dance, in this commode like the other one the table linen's kept there are three drawers and above it the portrait of a man in a white wig with a little tail and a ribbon a young girlish face he's in a poppy-red braided jacket a very frilly ruffle and he's holding a rose the Malmaison type those flat roses with a lot of petals you only find them in the old gardens now, there are three bushes in the rosary more like specimens nowadays the more a rose has fewer petals the better it is, it's back to the briar rose really this fashion business you can't explain it mind with regard to

The furniture

In the corner a large armchair just for show it's very uncomfortable with a straight back and no springs, it's an old cane chair covered in green material with tiny yellow lines like the one in the other corner my gentlemen wanted to get rid of it, when there aren't enough armchairs in the drawing-room they still don't use them then they'd rather take a plain chair, above it a big mirror hanging in the corner that's Spanish too the glass is all frosty these old mirrors you can't see yourself properly they make everything look so gloomy, there's a second one almost the same in the other corner except the glass got broken while it was being moved my gentlemen searched everywhere even at Vichy for an old piece of glass I mean an old frosty mirror, in the end they found one in Douves slightly smaller they had to insert a strip of gilded wood in the large one to hold the glass firm I ask you what a lot of fuss to make about a minor detail, in the middle of the wall on the garden side between the two windows there's a sideboard with four doors all moulded in star shapes it seems that's how they all used to be once upon a time glass was put in later, it's in pine wood my gentlemen found it in the Midi where they liked making furniture in pine it's not as valuable as really

fine wood but when you see the work, there are pigeons on the cornice and a mass of flowers all round no shelf between the two parts it must have been a bedroom piece because of the pigeons a wardrobe transformed into a sideboard, there are two big keys with a pigeon on the ring part we sometimes put the silver gilt there about six dozen soup plates about six dozen dinner plates about six doz
    Go on
    Well then the other corner as I said, then between the window and the French window on the courtyard a console table all in white and grey marble, the two legs very thick and bulbous with the big bulge facing you sculpted in the shape of big rhubarb leaves it's Italian untransportable with a vase on top standing on a pedestal in marble too three feet high, it's fretted all round like say little violins without the neck and the bottom with the same rhubarb leaves only smaller, then between the French window and the second window a very long picture it's a fête or rather a procession in the style of the banquet opposite some woman sitting on a chariot with nothing on but a crown of leaves round her head she's laughing and pinching one of her nipples with one hand, and with the other she's holding up a goblet that's spilling over you can see the wine running down over her stool decorated with grapes and vine leaves, there are men and women in different poses sucking grapes or feeding each other with them and round the chariot children dancing and looking at the women one of them has his hand on a woman's bottom, really I ask you the people who did those paintings what were they thinking about nowadays at least look for example in the cinemas the under-sixteens are not allowed in for the risky films after all we're not indecent like that, the chariot's drawn by two oxen garlanded with grapes the colours are about the same as the banquet except there are more clouds in the sky, then between the window and the staircase a table with bobbly legs and two drawers for the rest of the silver and on top of it a large silver bowl terribly heavy all

engraved inside, you can see soldiers in short skirts and helmets gladiators probably, there's a bull right in the middle disembowelling a dead man on the ground and a rearing horse and a small stand with people watching the gladiolery it's a very Roman-looking work you might say all round there are oak leaves on either side of the table an armchair covered in covered in I don't remember now, in green or grey yes in grey velvet grey it's coming back to me even that they're not exactly the same, one has a round back the other with a hump in the middle or rather two little humps they were both painted white my gentlemen had them scraped about five or six years ago now and that's all, sorry the carpet it's a Savonnière carpet it seems they show it to all their guests a big pattern of leaves and flowers with two rows of beans or rather beanstalks which weave in and out round the edge and in the centre under the table a kind of pink and green cauliflower the other patterns start from, on the ceiling the old beams the house wasn't built yesterday one very large one running across from the main staircase to just above the small one and the others longways up to the chimney-piece, as for the lights there's a spotlight in the marble vase another camouflaged by one of the beams which shines on the banquet another that lights the small staircase, and for big occasions they'd use the four candelabra which made twenty candles plus two candelabra with six candles each from the drawing-room which made twenty plus twelve thirty-two

Were there no curtains in this room

Yes long ones at each window and at the French windows with green and yellow stripes a very thick silk lined in pale green, to do the vacuum cleaning what a chore I had to add the extension piece and stand on the small steps and every month unhook them to clean them and take them down, we used to do that the same time as the carpets

Weren't there any cupboards in either of the dining-rooms

In the large one no just the best service in the sideboard but in the small one you're right there is a cupboard or shall I say half a cupboard over the serving-table hardly noticeable in the wall, it didn't do to leave finger-marks on the paintwork my gentlemen would always notice almost the very moment they're such fusspots a flat white paint like all the walls in the house, we kept a reserve stock of this paint in the lumber room for touching-up I used to do that myself, over the serving-hatch too there was a half-cupboard

How was the small dining-room lit

Like the large one a spotlight camouflaged by a beam which shone on Louis XIV another on the other battle and on the table we used to put two small electric lamps with pale yellow lampshades real parchment they were old candlesticks we'd put them out when we laid the table, the plug was under the table next to the bell you only had to press your foot to ring very practical in spite of the times it went wrong when someone's foot got caught in the lead under the table

You say the andirons in the main chimney-piece originally came from the Château de Sirancy

Yes one of the things my gentlemen purchased from Longuepie he's broke I told you he just sells off things from his place in order to repair a gutter or something like that, all the odd jobs he gets the Spaniards to do in the castle it's almost more pitiful than if he let the whole lot go to rack and ruin but folk like that tradition for them it means something they'd rather bleed themselves white and starve themselves to death, each time Longuepie could drag the conversation out till luncheon or dinner was so much money saved, you'll tell me they were friends right a friend's a friend but he was lucky my gentlemen weren't parsimonious and always ready for a visit they so hated being alone, but as I told you say what you like Longuepie was a scrounger mind there was no malice in it that's as clear as the nose on your face and it's better than his wife the way she went on, always seeming to oblige you when she was after *you* for something

Whereabouts is the castle

A little way outside the village, the place itself is called Longuepie not even a hamlet just a few houses left once upon a time it was more important, at any rate it's part of the Commune we call it the Château de Sirancy, two out of the five towers have collapsed and there's only one part of the main building left they've gradually got more and more cramped inside their farmers live there too, in what was once the guard-room in the rear wing it was very high they've made an extra floor for a hay loft, beside it there was a chapel that's used for stables there are still some things that came from there at Souaffe's the antique dealer the fragment of some pillar and odd bits of the choir-screen, Dame Longuepie pretends it wasn't from the chapel she's so pious it's an obsession Souaffe has to tell his customers it comes from the castle without any details, anyway it doesn't sell but we know the place inside-out just think as a lad I was always over at the Raisinets' place the old couple who were the farmers before I'd roam about everywhere, that was still in the days of the old couple Longuepie's parents' day *they* didn't put on airs they were poor and they admitted it, the old lady had a box of biscuits in the kitchen all soft they were which she gave to us children they had a musty taste we used to take one just to please her, you know what people are like only think of that Binet woman I told you Dame Longuepie was a Binet her mother lives with them she has treatment every year but you bet your life it's Madame Hartberg who pays, that Binet woman not even a *de* to her name she *had* to make changes so she could look down her nose and now when people talk of the Longuepies they no longer remember the old pair who were just the reverse, you see it only needs one woman to upset everything

Didn't these Binets have money

Pff oh they may have had some hard cash Longuepie wouldn't have ventured otherwise, but you know what it's like even then I mean before the wedding the Binets thought they were the cat's whiskers only visiting the gentry and of course they had to go to the school at Douves, they may not have been badly off but the children had to share out what each of them got between four I don't really know but Longuepie may have been hoping for more in any case what he received soon went on repairs, and all the land at Le Rouget sold off bit by bit and the land at Les Vernes to my gentlemen as I said he doesn't get what he could out of it, mind on top of the repairs he's got his household to keep going and their idiot daughter which all adds up

Didn't the parents sell anything during their lifetime

They'd rather have been hacked to pieces I tell you their lands go back almost to the Middle Ages, it appears that during the Revolution they passed on to the state like a kind of Trust but under the Empire or soon after they took possession of a large slice of them again it all brings back memories for them, they preferred to struggle to make ends meet it's not that their son is a brilliant businessman but *he does sell* he'll soon have nothing left but his eyes to weep with, if only that would do him any good but on top of the repairs and the rest old Dame Longuepie with her airs and graces oh no *she* mustn't lose face oh no *she* can't dress any old how and I ask you she even has to entertain in evening dress, not often I admit but still

Why do you think the peasants are always doing him down as you say

Well you see that's education believe me, the Longuepies the old couple penniless as they were they had class you don't find that any more now they liked people all the old folks remember, it was what you might call the family *esprit de corps* and they handed it on to their son who doesn't know how to look after himself Maître de Ballaison can warn him to be careful till he's blue in the face you'd think he did it on purpose letting himself be fleeced in one way it's almost better though, living on other people I don't like that but when you think of the Hartbergs for example the only class they can find comes from their purse

Whereabouts is the land at Le Rouget

On the foothills of the Rouget mountain chain, the high ones like the Trognon or the Pointe or the Visard aren't more than three thousand feet but they extend a long way to the west you can almost say as far as Rottard, everything that slopes down to our side of the river forests and pasture-land was part of the estate

And the land at Les Vernes

In the same area further to the south it's cut off from the rest by the Chie a small tributary of the Manu which has its source the other side of the Chanchèze

You say that as a child you were familiar with the castle

I said the farmers but we used to poke our noses everywhere to have a good look round

Can you give a general description of the buildings

That's easy the castle's on the last slopes of the Plateau on rising ground that dominates the river, when I say it's falling to rack and ruin I'm talking of the two parts that are no longer lived in and the outbuildings but what's left of it is still impressive, there's a large square tower with a tiled roof in two colours making a pattern Burgundy style and a gilded weathercock, the small building they live in has a view over the river and another tower a round one rather set back with a pointed roof we called it the Nid-de-Pie because of Longuepie and the wing for the farmers behind with another square tower at the corner, what's in ruins is all the second building facing the river between the Nid-de-Pie and a tower that collapsed and another building behind between the farmers' and the fifth tower, from below you don't realise half of it is uninhabitable they keep up the main front and that section of the roof, but from the courtyard I mean from inside you can see there's nothing left but the façade they've built a wall which cuts the courtyard in two to conceal it, from the village side after the farmers' all the ruined part is hidden by the trees which curve round in front and also hide the tower that collapsed, the outbuildings were lower down they're completely disappearing beneath the brambles, in the parents' time the façade hadn't been restored and the Nid-de-Pie had lost its roof and so had the small building or almost, they'd retreated into the tower with the weathercock only spending out enough to turn the rear wing into a farm

Why do you say the roofing of the tower was Burgundy style

Because I've seen them there the one at Sirancy is yellow and green each colour stepping up to the ridge and the roofing of the small building's the same with two golden balls on top, the roof of the Nid-de-Pie is plain brown it doesn't cost so much, the large tower behind is half in two colours half brown

Didn't you say that your employers had bought the land at Les Vernes and then sold it again at once

Yes

Who to

Strangers I hardly remember

Didn't you say they've visited your employers

Yes but who they were I can't remember I believe they were the type from the south but it would be easy to find out unless they've sold it again already

And they didn't remain in contact with your employers

Not as far as I know

Is the land at Les Vernes built on

No

How do you reach the Château de Sirancy

Along the by-road that comes from the village it goes round the hill and comes out in front of the castle on the river side but by the short cut you come smack into the back of it

Whereabouts is Le Chanchèze

The valley leaves the Le Rouget chain below the Pointe it runs southwards, it's all dried up stunted vegetation it was said to be full of rats

Where is the factory bought by Rufus

In the part where they've brought the water

Where does the tributary have its source

On the west slopes on the other side I told you it makes a little valley not very long that comes out into the Manu

What is this valley called

The valley of the Chie it's a very old name, the Curé maintains it comes from the Latin like *châtaigne* which used to be *castagne* without the ch so now it's Chie it used to be something like *quies* which means quiet or another word which means restless, Marthe made a note of that too

You say that Madame de Longuepie entertained

I didn't say she often did because of their being hard-up but it was evening dress

Used your employers to go to these parties

There were two or three times when they had to go but they came back early there was nothing to drink I must say between the two of them they can knock it back, when Longuepie came to the house after the last one he apologised and said it was his wife who fusses about formality

How far is the castle from the village

A couple of miles' walk

What sort of thing did Madame de Longuepie ask you to do

Oh I don't know I had to do with her chiefly about the fête I told you, things like staying on after half-past six or going into town for her really as if she meant you to feel you were lucky to do it

Did she ask favours of your employers

That would have been the day I told you they didn't get

on mind if she had they'd have been too polite to refuse
 When did they start work to turn that wing of the castle into a farm
 The parents had started it before I mean Raisinet was living there already but without amenities, he had to store his hay in a broken-down lean-to hence the extra floor for the hay loft and the major part of the work was done by the son but the chapel's been used as a stable since before the parents' time, the things you can find at Souaffe's have been there a long while
 Who is this Souaffe
 An antique dealer at Agapa
 Are there several there
 Five or six Souaffe in the Rue du Magnificat Blinville in the Rue Sainte Louvois in the Avenue des Africains Miette in the Rue du Cimetière
 Are your employers in contact with them
 Definitely all the time they're busy buying something
 From one of them in particular
 Miette yes they often buy from him last time it was some Chinese porcelain we never knew what to do with it finished up in one of the spare rooms
 Who is this Miette
 The antique dealer in the Rue du Cimetière
 What do you know about him used he to visit your employers
 He used to yes he's a tiny little man lives up to his name, very clean about his person always light grey suits even in the winter that he has made at Nantet's and a flower in his button-hole, he wears rings you can't help noticing a great diamond on the little finger on his left hand and a kind of greyish-white transparent stone on the right hand, he's not a hair left on his head he's neurotic about it, if he's so worried about his hair he's only got to wear a wig like Térence Monnier mind you can tell

Used he to come alone

That depends sometimes alone sometimes with friends not always the same, he's well-known in town a changeable disposition always in trouble with his friends

What kind of friends

Friends of his own kind

What do you mean by that

Antique dealers for example

Was he married

He wasn't up to three years ago it was a surprise, a plain woman I only saw her once in the shop for my gentlemen a note to hand over to her husband as much as she could do to thank me

Do you know her maiden name

No she's from Douves but as I always say marriages like that are always for worse and never for better

What do you mean by marriages like that

I mean between folk who aren't young any more used to their own freedom, he must be regretting it already it didn't solve his problems on the contrary and he doesn't bring her to the house

Will you explain once and for all what sort of problems you mean

Is there only one sort of problems there are thousands when you don't get on with people

How do you explain that none of your employers' married friends seemed anxious to bring their wives with them

I never said that I said several of them there are some who used to bring them

Mention some of Miette's friends

There was a big fair-haired removal man made you wonder what he could see in him I've forgotten his name now, there was a Monsieur Génois a big man too a wine merchant his warehouses are behind the station Rue du Salut, there was Frédy there was I don't know who anyway he used to know all my gentlemen's

friends Gérard Hottelier Chantre Luisot Donéant Cruchet the whole gang
 He wasn't friendly with Longuepie or Ballaison or Rivière
With them too
Was he alone at the shop before his marriage
No he was with Monsieur Léglise
This Monsieur Léglise did he visit your employers
 He came once or twice with Miette at the start then he stopped coming I don't think my gentlemen liked him unless it was Miette and his problems, *I* thought quite well of him he often bought me a drink at the little bistro near his shop now he works Avenue des Africains at Louvois' place
 You haven't seen him since
It's a part of town I rarely go to
Have you seen him again
Once or twice by accident
Where
In the street
Did he speak to you about his new employer
 Oh me you know nowadays what people say to me I was going to say it goes in one ear and out the other, and in the street what's more it's hopeless
 Do you know where the marquetry commode in the large dining-room came from
No I've always seen it there
Didn't you say that one of the mirrors in the dining-room had had its glass broken during the journey
Yes
What journey
When they were bringing it
When was that
 Five or six years ago now, there used to be a big picture there the portrait of a man full-length under glass my gentlemen

didn't like it any more it was sent to the attic when they found the other mirror
    Where did they find it
    At Blinville's
    What do you know about Blinville
    He's a bastard
    Explain
    Well my sister had an old Bible from her husband's family they were Huguenots by tradition which was handed down from father to son, when Edouard died she wanted to sell it you know what it is we're Catholic by tradition her husband's religion she never approved of, she didn't ask my advice and she offered this Bible to Blinville who told her it had no value, he gave her ten thousand francs for it in memory of her husband he said and I learned later from Léglise that he'd sold it again for a million to an Englishman at the Hôtel des Bains, I went to see him about it he told me at once that Léglise had made a mistake he was confusing it with another Bible, he pretended to search through his accounts to prove it to me and showed me a bill for twelve thousand for a Bible saying it was my sister's two thousand francs profit that's fair enough you know, but Léglise is sure it's not true just think of it a million my sister
    Who was this Englishman
    A Monsieur Barrymore he went back to his own country what can one do
    Whereabouts is the Grand Hôtel
    Place des Maures 21
    And the Hôtel des Bains
    On the corner of Dominique-Lapoire and the Avenue de Douves
    How many hotels are there at Agapa
    How many can there be about twenty maybe yes in the directory round about twenty counting all the small ones like the Deux-Gros

What is this Hôtel des Deux-Gros

A shady hotel I told you in the cul-de-sac of the Deux-Gros

Which are the other large hotels

After Les Bains and the Grand Hôtel let's say the Perroquet Noir Rue Prolot, the Hôtel de Broy Rue de Broy, the Hôtel des Etrangers Place de L'Hôtel-de-Ville, the Hôtel de la Gare opposite the station, the Hôtel des Africains Avenue des Africains, the Hôtel Brague Rue des Genêts all that lot supposedly first-class but there's no comparison with Les Bains or the Grand Hôtel, then in the class below hotels like the Grand Cerf or the Grenouillet or Les Arts Rue Magnasse or Fabien Rue Bassinoire and all the smaller hotels including the shady ones, I'm forgetting the Esquire which they've modernised it seems it's quite good but I wouldn't be too sure, Corinot the owner went to prison about fifteen years ago something political he'd been mixed up in the bread rolls business that's no recommendation, people forget but I wouldn't recommend him

What is this bread rolls business

A communist newspaper in Douves that got up a campaign to reduce the price of bread it was just a publicity stunt but it gave rise to demonstrations against the bakers' union, Corinot was on the action committee they discovered the money for the campaign had been taken from the bakers' union funds by one of his comrades called Faivre a misappropriation, the Prefecture made an order authorising an increase in the price of fancy bread rolls seeing they couldn't do anything about the price of bread that's all they got out of it, Corinot did a spell in jug with Faivre and several others like Leduc and his brother-in-law

Which Leduc

My gentlemen's laundryman he only had a week inside he wasn't on the committee

Where is Leduc's laundry

At Sirancy Rue du Savon near the main square

Do you know if he works for the hotels at Agapa
Definitely not there's no shortage of laundries in town
Did the Englishman Barrymore know your employers
No
Did he come regularly to Agapa
I don't know
Would you know whether he knew Lord and Lady Chastenoy
It would be easy enough to ask at the Hôtel des Bains but I don't see the point
Do you remember the name of the chambermaid who looked after Lady Chastenoy while she was staying with your employers
It must have been wait a minute it must have been Angèle or Camille, no Angèle yes Angèle Letournat a girl from Crachon who's got married since
Did she know Gabrielle the gardener's daughter
Yes I think they used to go out together
Did you never catch them out Angèle and Lord Chastenoy in some kind of complicity
Complicity what about
Some sort of understanding or familiarity
Well that would really take the biscuit
Answer
I never noticed anything
Do you remember what books you saw in Lady Chastenoy's rooms the day you committed your indiscretion
How could I they were all in English
Didn't you say the hospital sent to your employers to take away the books of interest to their patients
Yes
What do you mean by of interest to their patients
How do I know, books I mean for people not in good health
What did you do with the books that weren't taken by the hospital

They stayed in the cellar
Have you a rough idea what kind of books they were
They were books just like the others
Why did you say the flunkey may have done the cleaning in the room that was altered for the secretary
Just an idea
Give details
It was simply that as he didn't ask me he may have asked the flunkey
Did the secretary know Miette
Yes as he used to come to the house
What else do you know about Miette
What else do you mean
His private life
That's his own affair
Does he live in the town
Yes over his shop he had a little spiral staircase an iron one put in to communicate with the first floor when he got it, he waited something like fifteen years before he could there was an old woman there who didn't want to move out, Mademoiselle Lacruseille had tried to do something about it once she went to see this old woman to suggest a smaller apartment but she wanted to stick to her own
So Miette was in contact with Mademoiselle Lacruseille
They're cousins
Why did Mademoiselle Lacruseille intervene
Intervene in what
Why was she the one to make this proposition to the old woman
To do her cousin a favour, Mademoiselle Lacruseille likes a good chat they thought the old woman would come round more easily to talking to her especially as Miette's character was well-known he must have quarrelled with everyone in the house, makes

you wonder even if the old woman didn't stay on just on purpose to annoy him

Where did he live before

Rue des Chevaux-de-Luge

Alone

I've no idea

Did he already have this flat at the time when Léglise was working with him

No it was later

Do you know the flat

Yes my gentlemen asked me to go and give him a hand with the clearing-up after the painters had finished repainting everything

What does it consist of

By the small staircase you come up into a large room that overlooks the river and extends at the back up one step into another room it makes the ceiling so low you can touch it, and leading out of this room a bathroom on the left which he's had put in the old woman didn't have one, on the right the bedroom I suppose the furniture still hadn't arrived, the kitchen is right at the back a little corridor that leads off the low-ceilinged room and on the right in the corridor a glass door that leads onto a kind of little balcony-verandah they want to turn into a garden if I'm not mistaken, it's over the courtyard

Are the ceilings in the bathroom and the bedroom as low as in the central room

No you go down another step

What does the kitchen look out on

The courtyard

Describe this courtyard

I didn't pay much attention except that opposite there's the same sort of balcony with plants it's that which gave them the idea and in the middle of the courtyard an old well without water, the lodge for the concierge is painted red and on the right

I think a sign for the garage Peugeot which is on the Rue des Bains almost opposite the Oiseaux-Baigneurs

Do you know what firm Miette had applied to for the repainting

Robert Menteau his van was in front of the door with a young chap taking away the paint cans and brushes, I even remember commenting to Monsieur Miette they could have been more careful the parquet floor was all splashed with paint along the walls and the windows too

Was Miette's wife there

No

Is Robert Menteau a friend of Miette's

He's one of my gentlemen's friends anyway

Has he worked for them

He's the one they always ask when there's work to be done

Was Miette alone that day

There was Frédy

Who is this Frédy

A friend of his I told you

Describe him

Young about twenty-five to thirty fairly tall swarthy a bit of a wag, he's always up to some trick he works now with Souaffe

Where did he work before

At Miette's before Léglise

Is he still friendly with Miette

Yes that's what I say

Why when you mentioned Miette's friends did you say there was this one and that one, why there *was*

Because he didn't bring them all at the same time

Who was the big fair removal-man type

I can't remember his name I told you

Is he still one of his friends

I've no idea

Has he worked with him
No
Was he an antique dealer
I've no idea
Then why say that Miette's friends are generally antique dealers
I didn't say that I said some were
Which are they
Souaffe Blinville Louvois
Then why not mention them by name among his friends
You'll make a monkey out of me
Did Miette get married before he had his flat over the shop
Yes just before
So he lived in the Rue des Chevaux-de-Luge with his wife
I should imagine so yes
Then why say you didn't know whether he lived there alone

Because I thought it was before you were asking me, anyway he can't have lived there long with his wife they went off for a month's honeymoon, the Cimetière flat was practically ready as I said when they got back they were just in time to move

Where is the Rue des Chevaux-de-Luge

It leads into the Place de l'Hôpital second on the right as you come from the Rue de Broy, Miette's flat was number 46 on the same landing as Jonas stays and corsets who had that spot of bother with him

What spot of bother

It goes back a long way they were friends once Miette had some property at Lémiran where he got to know Pompom, it was he who found him a place with my gentlemen, Pompom used to work for him there he decided to come here when Miette sold up, but it's not the only reason he wasn't happy at Lémiran any more the old landowners were selling everything off one after the other because of the cement factory it changed the whole district, so yes Miette had this property he had his eye on a piece of land not far off which he knew the cement development company was going to buy I'm talking now of before the factory was built, he had his contacts he was dead set on it so as to sell it again double or treble the price and all at once he found out that Jonas had bought the land for himself he raised it with him of course, Jonas sold it again four times as much their quarrel goes back to that as I always say a smoking gun means the fun's begun the factory got built Miette kept his property another five years and sold it to a company that built a ten-storey block of leasehold flats on it it wasn't a bad deal but he couldn't swallow that land business, Jonas immediately after bought a house for himself on the Hottencourt road

Who is this Jonas

The stays and corset shop on the corner of the Rue des Chevaux-de-Luge and the Place de l'Hôpital, no-one ever knew where he came from exactly it seems he'd travelled a lot before he settled down cruises chiefly he's got contacts in the merchant navy and the transatlantic companies, his corset business is going well he's completely renovated the shop there are mirrors everywhere it makes a real salon for the ladies, he has a lady manager now one of the old gentry who was down on her luck just the person it appears it was Mademoiselle Saint-Foin who suggested her to him

Does Jonas know your employers

Yes but even after all this time it didn't do for Miette to be there

And this lady who used to belong to the gentry

Frou-Frou as they call her recently she came too, not so long ago, she's a special friend of the young ladies Saint-Foin and Lacruseille she goes to Rottard with them where they join up with a whole collection of other ladies, come to think of it people are like flies round a dung-heap

What do you mean by that

When there's one there are twenty
Why that image in connection with these ladies
It just came to me like that I was thinking the more they are the more they like it
Is Miette familiar with real estate transactions
What do you mean
Is it his habit to buy and sell property and houses
He may well have been interested, with Maître de Ballaison I think they used to talk about it in the past with Rivière too but let's say he'd do it rather as an amacher what he likes most is to look at old houses and discuss things with people, it's quite a time now since he sold Lémiran he's still not made up his mind to buy anything else, Marthe once told me he had designs on an old farm near Fantoine a kind of fortress which must have seen some exciting times the cellars are Merlovingian it's historical, the owner lives in Constantinaples every other year he comes for his treatment he's probably asking a lot for it, Miette has had the time to visit the whole district but he might come back to this idea it's my belief to live in it you'd practically have to knock it all down, the walls are six feet thick how can you make windows in that and the cellar's full of saltpetre unless Miette is richer than people think, he might wait for the right moment get the old barn off the Turk at a reasonable price and have it restored so it looks like a museum and build a place himself next door, there are eight or nine acres of land
What makes you imagine he's richer than people think
It wouldn't surprise me a bit he's just the type of little man knows how to handle his affairs all right we've always known him well enough off his shop must be just a screen a way of avoiding income tax, his property at Lémiran was worth a pretty penny what's he done with it all not all down the drain I'm sure and his mother was no pauper and now his marriage, that woman must have a packet

What do you mean by he had his contacts when he had his eyes on the ground bought by Jonas
I mean he'd been informed that the company was going to buy
Informed by whom
Someone who was in the know
Do you know who
No
You say he liked discussing things with Maître de Baillaison
At one time yes Miette and Ballaison used to have great discussions I can see them now walking round the garden, Ballaison always very sedate and polite in black and the other one small excitable never still waving his arms about, they'd start off round the ornamental lake before their aperitifs and sometimes they'd go down as far as the river we wouldn't get them back till we'd rung the bell a second time, I remember one day we didn't wait for them they arrived in time for the roast Ballaison was full of apologies and Miette as excitable as ever he didn't care as he went past the serving-table he knocked off the best decanter and crash my gentlemen laughed the wrong side of their face, next day he got Léglise to bring over two similar ones by way of apology my gentlemen were furious to know theirs wasn't the only one, they took it up with Souaffe who had sold it to them under guarantee but that decanter didn't exist any more and Souaffe found some differences with the ones Miette sent not cut in the same way and the stoppers weren't in period, Miette found out he came back a few days later with a reinforced decanter Louis-Philippe and with a big magnifying glass he proved that the stoppers were the same to the nearest cut, he brought some photos and some papers too that the decanters and the stoppers were genuine they came from Paris a friend of his come to think of it who knows Rivière too, Benjamin Latour
    Perhaps Ballaison and Miette were discussing something other than blocks of flats in the garden

That's possible but it would surprise me Ballaison and real estate that's his speciality that and inheritance, and I tell you Miette was going all over the district in search of a house by the way that reminds me he had offered to buy Malatraîne from Ballaison, Ballaison wouldn't have minded he has his house at Sirancy but his wife nearly hit the ceiling we found out from Pernette, she screamed like a fishwife that she'd rather burn her house down than see it become a den of vice

What did she mean by that in your opinion

How should I know a woman in a rage will say anything, she can't stand Miette he's a friend of my gentlemen's and she's had a row with them I told you unless Pernette made it up she hates her mistress

Who is this Pernette

Pernette Varussin the Ballaisons' maid

If she hates her mistress why does she stay on

She's no chicken you know what it's like she's got attached to the building rather than the people though Ballaison she's very devoted to him

Whereabouts is Malatraîne

Along the river on the Rouget side a little by-road that turns off to the left on the Hottencourt road, the manor doesn't overlook the river it's in the middle of the woods it used to be a hunting lodge marked in the guide book, grandfather Ballaison bought it for next to nothing it's very damp they go in the summer Madam insists says it's good for her daughters' health the three ugly ducklings, she does it out of sheer pig-headedness there's not even running water they wash in basins Pernette is fed to the teeth emptying the ladies' pails, you can understand that Madam's wild more than wild one day it will kill her to have missed the chance of getting Bonne-Mesure which has every comfort it's a different proposition

These woods round the manor are they the woods of Sirancy

No they're the woods of Malatraîne much further to the west after the bend in the Manu, all this part is marshy the manor is very isolated they have to go as far as Le Bérouse for their provisions a little hamlet with just a grocer's shop and a bistro, it's Gustave who makes the journey on his bicycle at his age the young ladies are bone idle and proud you could never ask that of them, their father's got his rattle-trap but when he's staying there he doesn't like moving around and La Ballaison doesn't drive it's not done

Didn't you say your brother Gustave was in Australia

Well you see this is another Gustave, Gustave Etrillot another one of Pompom's army pals

You say Ballaison has a house at Sirancy

His house yes they're only at Malatraîne in the summer, two months it used to be now only one, no-one likes it there

Ballaison didn't visit your employers when he was staying there

On the contrary he used to come more often than usual

Didn't you say he doesn't like moving about once he's there

Not to get provisions

Describe his house at Sirancy

It's the finest one in the village everyone will tell you the same three storeys plus the garret which is enormous, on the ground floor he has his study his office the clerk's and the typist's office a large waiting-room and an old kitchen where they keep all the files, on the first and second floors the living quarters, on the third floor Pernette's and Gustave's bedrooms and a tenant who rents two rooms at the front Professor Sagrin he gives lessons at the boys' school in town, every day he does his eight miles on a moped leaving at half-past seven he takes his machine out of the garage where Ballaison keeps his car, he's a real fusspot he lives all alone and has geraniums at the windows that he waters at a quarter-past seven and in the evening coming back from school he does his shopping, he calls first at the butcher's then at Vidolle's for his milk and his vegetables and a bottle of Loewenbräu beer and at six o'clock on Tuesdays and Fridays, seven o'clock on the other days you can see his windows being opened wide winter and summer alike he airs the place for five minutes he's got delicate health his face all pimples, my gentlemen used to call it *la peau de Sagrin*

Describe the front of the house in detail

It's taller than it's wide from the street fully timbered like the old houses in town with beams showing under the eaves, three latticed windows on each floor three dormers in the roof, on the ground floor they've made two bay windows to give more light to the office, the entrance stairs lead straight off the pavement three curved steps the door is carved in little panels with figures in the middle laughing or putting out their tongues, there are two doorbells one for the study one for the living quarters the garage is on the right an old barn transformed jutting onto one side of the house, at the back there's a garden shut off on the left by a small building they rent to Mademoiselle Miaille and her mother, at the back by a large house which belongs to them too rented to Chastel they've kept for themselves the right to use the garden, Mademoiselle Miaille has her front door in the Rue Neuve behind and Chastel in the Rue du Poisson-Pêcheur the three buildings all made one residence once upon a time and it's always belonged to the family, I think they want the small house back Mademoiselle Miaille is making it difficult for them saying her mother can't move at her age, on the left there's the little Place des Garances the façade is longer on that side four windows

Has Sagrin been a tenant for long

Something like six or seven years they're quite pleased with him Pernette says he's very clean she tidies up for him once a week, near the washbasin he's arranged one corner as his kitchen what's left of the two rooms is full of books it seems he works every evening till one o'clock in the morning, he's entitled to two baths a week he's very correct with his landlords who invite him from time to time to lunch on Sundays, he never stays long the girls don't like him they say he lays in wait for them on the stairs and doesn't pay enough rent, they probably wish he was running after them he's not bad to look at and the eldest one's just the age Pernette told Marthe if I've got it right that the girl went up one evening to knock on his door but he didn't answer, and she didn't dare try again as Pernette's room is too close

I suppose you don't know if Pernette and he

Definitely not Pernette would be only too pleased she's fifty-five and he's thirty-six she's bound to have told Marthe

He has no attachment in the village or in the town

They used to say he went with the Totton girl for a time but it didn't seem to come to anything he must lead some sort of life in town something at least but he's never invited anyone home, he knows the Lorpailleur woman and the things she writes in the paper he writes sometimes too I saw once he was on about one of her books but his speciality is grammar mistakes, last time it was on *attendez sur*, it's so stupid I've forgotten now

Does he know your employers

Ballaison brought him once for them to show him the park my gentlemen went round the gardens with him he stayed to dinner if I remember right

Is he asked to Malatraîne

It sometimes happened he'd go for a day or two before he went off on his holidays but not any more La Ballaison believes it's not proper for her girls

Who is this Totton girl

The daughter of Totton furniture mover it would have made a good match for him they've got money but as I say they're not seen together now at any rate not in the village, she's moved into town Mademoiselle Lacruseille knows her I think she invited her not long ago to go with her to Holland for her television

Is the Totton girl in that too
Not so far as I know
And you don't know if Sagrin still sees her in town
I've no idea
What do you mean by lead some sort of life in town
When you live in a village I should have thought it was obvious no
Does Sagrin know your employers' friends
He knows Chantre and Donéant yes Pernette says there are telephone calls to give him a message sometimes on Saturdays or Sundays
What kind of message
That they'll meet in the evening at Le Cygne for example or they'll come and fetch him to go into town
Does he often go out with them
According to Pernette no he works hard I told you
Have you any other sources of information about him
Marthe heard Donéant say Sagrin was getting depressed he doesn't see enough people, they try to take him out of himself but he's always got an excuse with his work he'll have wasted his youth in books and writing
Do you know where they see each other when they meet in town
He doesn't like the Colibri it seems but Chantre says it would do him good to shake up his ideas, they're meant to have gone there once and Sagrin said or did something terrible, Chantre brought him home in his car and that's why my gentlemen's friends have lost interest in him he's a misanthrogynist
How do you know Mademoiselle Lacruseille knows the Totton girl
I've seen them together in town and she told Marthe
Do you know if she invites her to Rottard-Chizy
No

Whereabouts is Lémiran

Quite a way to the south something like sixty miles it was residential, there were even people from Douves who had property there now the factory's changed all that

Does Pompom originally come from Lémiran

No he's Alsatian I told you he was about thirty when he went to settle there, married Jeannette who's a Mochaz and he used to look after a number of villas till the day when

Who is Benjamin Latour

An antique dealer from Paris a friend of Miette's and Rivière's I told you

Used he to visit your employers

That's how I got to know him the day of the decanters Miette took out his papers and there was Benjamin Latour printed on them I saw it, it was early in the morning my gentlemen were still taking their breakfast Miette arrived quite without warning, he asked me for the decanters and made his demonstration right in the middle of breakfast my gentlemen seemed embarrassed having believed Souaffe's stories, they all ended up with a good laugh that's their way out of all their difficulties I've often noticed you'd think that sort had nothing in their heads, so perhaps the friends they upset have nothing there either though I think it's more likely they try to keep in with my gentlemen because when he arrived Miette's face looked quite different, the idea anyone should think his antiques weren't genuine made him quite ill nervy people are like that

Where is Le Bérouse

Five miles from Malatraîne on the Vériville road the bus stops there but I tell you there are perhaps a hundred inhabitants, some petrol pumps have popped up along the road two years ago the brother of

Has Gustave Etrillot been in service to the Ballaison family a long time

Twenty years once he used to be with Mademoiselle Ariane, he left her after some argument between her and his wife Sophie Voiret who'd stolen some money according to Mademoiselle Ariane she wasn't an easy woman when she'd got an idea in her head, Sophie always denied it she died some time after, Gustave never went back to Bonne-Mesure makes you wonder if La Ballaison didn't slip up taking the Etrillots on just then Mademoiselle Ariane took it badly it was like publicly making her out to be crazy and unjust, I don't say she wasn't towards the end of her life

Did you know Mademoiselle Ariane

As children yes we used to go there my sister and I more often even than to Longuepie there were the old Etrillots the farmers, Gustave was already a man he's the same call-up year as Pompom I told you we used to play with his sister Etiennette who was ten years younger than him and their cousin Dédé he died of paupery at eighteen he was never very strong, the Etrillots had taken him in when his parents died in the railway accident on the line from Douves I'm talking now of more than forty years ago, it was still the Trundler as we called it a little train with open trucks still it managed to kill five people trapped underneath when it couldn't make the bend, yes Dédé and Nénette what became of her for a long time Gustave believed she was in a convent in Belgium she must be dead now too

Say what you know about Ariane de Bonne-Mesure

She was a fat spinster with white hair sitting on the terrace under her parasol with Mademoiselle Fernande her companion she used to do embroidery, she used to call us scamps and forbade us to walk on the grass we used to go as far as the linen room which is on the other side to see Mademoiselle Passaquin and Marguerite who did the ironing, old Passaquin had a graveyard cough all pale and crouched over her sewing machine we used to block the pedal from underneath with bits of wood so she had to bend down and she'd cough and cough

Mademoiselle de Bonne-Mesure

She was a bit daft but a good woman at heart she had her niece and nephew who used to come and see her every year, the niece is Mademoiselle Francine who's still at the Château I told you the nephew was Louis the lieutenant who used to come in the hunting season with a group of friends and take the house over for a week there are thirty rooms, it was he who paid for the rearing of the pheasants two thousand of them the hatching was done by the hens we'd take over to the forest in crates and then let out, there were two gamekeepers who used to sleep in tents to keep an eye on everything and the year after they'd go shooting there Mademoiselle Ariane called it their slaughter-house and refused to contribute a penny, the gamekeepers too were paid by Monsieur Louis I remember one-eyed Gaston

Mademoiselle de Bonne-Mesure

Oh yes well as I was saying she had her nephew and niece and Mademoiselle Fernande who died a year after her and all the old women she employed more out of charity it seems to me now she can't have needed so many people, a woman for the linen and the ironing and the washerwoman who had a goitre that size she used to tell us the Good Lord had punished her for sucking her thumb as a child and made her neck swell, who else her two maids Charlotte and Valérie who knocked up at least a hundred and fifty years between them and the valet and the farmers and all, she also used to entertain Monseigneur from Douves Emilien de Bonne-Mesure a relative who was before Bougecroupe, he was mad about cheese soufflés Adeline the cook when he used to come would make a soufflé for six we always used to hope there'd be some left

Mademoiselle de Bonne-Mesure went mad you say

She was deranged towards the end she used to dress any old how even wouldn't dress at all, one day Mademoiselle Fernande found her in the forest without a stitch on engaged in eating an apple, her heirs used to come and make a fuss of her, when she died they tried to contest the will but there was no way out it was dated six years back she was healthy in mind all right quite a sly one even as she'd managed to disinherit La Ballaison

You said she disinherited her brother or her sister

I think so yes La Ballaison is the daughter of her brother or her sister, of her brother I think yes so she must

Didn't you also say Mademoiselle Francine was her niece

Her niece yes wait a minute, in fact no she must be her great-niece her great-niece that's it with not so strong a claim, it's all so complicated especially as there was a half-brother from her father's second marriage, perhaps La Ballaison

What do you know about this Mademoiselle Francine

I don't know anything I told you she never goes out and I haven't been back to Bonne-Mesure for ages my memories date from Mademoiselle Ariane's time, when I went there six or seven years ago with Clément I only saw that they'd cut down the great plane tree on the terrace

Didn't you say you'd seen Mademoiselle Francine at her window

Yes I said that I haven't seen her since

Does she live alone at the Château

She has her companion a relation of Monsieur Chantre's I told you but the name

Have you never been tempted to find out more about her and this Château where you've memories of your childhood

No all I know is that it's not as it used to be, Bonne-Mesure is not talked about as it was in the days of Mademoiselle Ariane there's no more hunting no more nothing, no you just stick to your memories

Are you sure you know nothing else about Mademoiselle Francine

Yes

Wouldn't her companion perhaps be more of a nurse
Yes I think she is a nurse
And Monsieur Chantre as a doctor and a relative of this nurse never spoke of her to your employers
It's possible but it's no concern of mine Marthe knows more than I do so do my gentlemen why not question my gentlemen, no I don't know anything else let sleeping dogs lie and leave the rest alone
Do you feel nervous when you're being questioned about Bonne-Mesure
Memories memories I told you why don't you leave me in peace
In Mademoiselle Ariane's time was there anything else at the Château that made an impression on you
Everything made an impression on me, the great terrace the towers the roofs the plane tree and the parasol and all those pheasants running wild in the woods, the forest we used to know by heart as far as the sheep farm
Is that the forest of Grance
It starts there round the house it's not so thick there we called it the wood, the forest further on we used to walk miles and the mushrooms at the end of the summer white caps fairy stools grey ladies
What is the sheep farm
An old stable where we used to shelter on rainy days there was more water inside than out, the storms used to frighten us they still used to tell tales about the forest as I said
Ghost stories
Yes like the Lady Stone in the clearing with the willow herb it would bring the dead back to life, and the owl who'd drive anyone who saw him crazy but stories like that you can say what you like there's a basis of truth to them, the Curé used to say they were old wives' tales still his maid died after a walk in the forest I mean the Curé in my day the Abbé Dufaux

Do you still believe this forest is evil

What once was ever will be as they say the best proof of it is still Mademoiselle Francine

The proximity of the forest you mean is

You never can tell when I talked to my gentlemen about Grance they thought I was simple-minded still I've got my proof all right

What else

Yes

For example

Nothing

Explain

You'll never believe me it's better to keep one's memories to oneself

Are these the reasons why you never went back to Bonne-Mesure

Those reasons and others, when you're young you're like the Curé Dufaux later you get to thinking it out but all this you know it's every man to his

Who was this Demoiselle Fernande

Mademoiselle Ariane's housekeeper an old spinster very erect with that hat of hers she said she couldn't stand the sun she was from Vériville where she had a brother the stationmaster, she used to speak English to Mademoiselle Francine she accompanied Mademoiselle Ariane to Mass every Sunday we used to go on foot there, she had black net gloves and her bag stuffed with newspaper clippings she used to say people were ignorant, when Mass was over she had her clippings read out to the ladies and she used to buy an almond cake at Nanar's

Who is Nanar

He died a long time ago he was the baker in the square a big man who used to walk his mother round in an invalid chair she was ninety-five when she died their name is Narre, his daughter Sophie is still the local gazette it's a disease with her telling tales anyway she invents half of them, Marthe knows her well too she used to do some ironing in Mahu's time now she lives on her income

And this Mahu

A crackpot always prowling around he used to tell Sophie what he heard about people, she said he was off his rocker but she let him have his say and her stories came partly from him, the name Mahu is a local one originally they came from Fantoine I told you there's a Rue des Fossés-Mahu at Agapa

Whereabouts is Fantoine

About six miles from Sirancy in the direction of Vériville there's still a Mahu there who must be the crackpot's nephew he married the Clope girl they run the café, it's the brother-in-law Chinze who put up the money they hadn't a bean neither of them my gentlemen always used to say that Fantoine was the home of all the local good-for-nothings, I must say the population in my day was a pretty job lot, on account of it was so isolated I suppose in the old days people usen't to move around so much it's a poor bit of country this side the land's no good there must have been a lot of inter-marriage

And this Chinze

A cousin of the cobbler's the father of Marie Chinze no-one knows what she died of everyone wondered at the time, Levert was more or less mixed up in it or his son we never knew Levert's wife took drugs he finished up in a ditch, Marie's brother that's Minet

And the Clope girl

The daughter of a boozer who used to doss down in the station he had to be chucked out

Did your employers know the Levert woman

I think so yes they had mutual friends she died before I entered my gentlemen's service

You say she used to take drugs

That's what people said Sophie Narre would tell you more than I can

Do you know if she used to visit your employers

I don't know what I do know is that in her last years she never left the house, father Levert took to the bottle after she died that was his excuse at the start and Philippe often came to see my gentlemen then he left the district and nothing's been heard of him since, Marthe thinks he's in America for her America's a dumping ground for drunks

Who is this Philippe

The Levert's son his mother's death sent him off the rails it appears that was the excuse *he* used for drinking too pity he was such a nice boy, they used to have the Villa Les Roches where he entertained a great deal then his father forbade it and Philippe stopped coming except to my gentlemen's or to the Colibri, he was a friend of Gérard's and Luisot's

Did Levert visit your employers

In any case not after his wife's death before I don't know but I'd be surprised he was quite a character always alone

Who were these mutual friends of your employers' and Madame Levert's

Doctor Tronc I think and Chantre's mother

And Marthe never told you she'd seen Madame Levert at your employers' in the company of Doctor Tronc or this Chantre woman

I tell you she'd stopped going out

And this Chantre woman

What about the Chantre woman

Did she visit your employers

She came once she's a very sick person she'll end up like Madame Levert

What do you mean by that

She'll die of course

Do you think she takes drugs
Not unless it's infectious I've no idea
Why do you mention Madame Levert in connection with the death of Madame Chantre
Because she's ill and doesn't go out now either
Did Chantre speak of his mother to your employers
I should think they had other subjects of conversation
Such as
I mean he only thought about having fun
Why didn't you refer to Madame Chantre among your employers' friends
Because she didn't visit
Did Doctor Tronc speak of her
I've no idea
Didn't he speak to Marthe about her when they had their chats in the garden
He must have told her he looked after Madame Chantre
Why
Her illness
Why did people say Madame Levert took drugs
You know what people say she had a maid who used to talk, the medicine chest full of goodness-knows-what Madame Levert all upset if she ran out of one of her medicaments always trailing round the house in her dressing-gown, people jump to conclusions straight away when someone lives different from everyone else
Do you believe Levert took drugs too
I shouldn't think he needed to he was always dead drunk every man to his taste, their son's been criticised right enough but how else could he turn out with parents
Used Levert to go to the Colibri
He used to go to the village chiefly but he's been seen everywhere, yes at the Colibri it seems one evening Boubou had got him all to herself they were both in a fine state, as usual Levert

was asking everyone about his son Boubou told him he was at her place they went off together and Philippe who was in the corner half-seas over is meant to have drunk the old boy's health

Who is Boubou

A negress I told you

Who was this maid of Madame Levert's

Lina Schmidt a German girl it's old fat Hem who had her brought here she's with the Foissets now

Does Madame Chantre have a maid

I don't know

Who are these Foissets

Friends of the Hartbergs my gentlemen couldn't stand them either I must say I sympathise, Heaven save us from the new rich she's a Dondard people of no importance her father used to work at the printing shop in the Rue du Rabot type-setter as they call it, her mother spent her life in hospital tubercular from head to foot lived on charity their daughter met Foisset when he was still a salesman for vacuum cleaners he was an orphan no father, old mother Foisset kept a stall in the market you see the type it's a mystery how he got on so well he's manager of the Kitou factories refrigerators two or three thousand employees, they've a villa at Hottencourt one of those buildings all cubes one on top of the other, it appears they never spend under a hundred thousand francs when they go out with the Hartbergs the proprietor of the Mouton Gras knows them well, when they arrive in their Rolls-Royce he puts on his formal face and when they've gone he has a good laugh the way the ladies have got themselves up the Foisset woman in particular with her emeralds and her diamonds she looks like the Queen of Sheba as they say, fifty million if it's not enough to make you sick they've been known to whip off to London for dinner and be back on the one-fifteen plane, he owns the cinema at Hottencourt too and the California at Sirancy and the Bijou at Agapa opposite the station, he's meant to be keeping a tart at Douves according to Lina he must be spending three million a month on her she manages the Petit-Théâtre used to be an orange-seller straight out of the casbah that lot what's she called now chichi houri she'd like to be introduced into society it's as much as she can do to speak French, he slips her his lolly to keep the theatre going what an idea Lina saw her this this the name's on the tip of my tongue with him one evening in town apparently she had one of those minx coats on that Madame Rufus had brought back for Goldshitt if you remember Lina recognised it, the Rufus's know her employers when Madame Rufus came back

You say the Princesse de Hem had sent for this Lina
Yes
Do you know if she remained in contact with her
The Princess and Lina how on earth could she interest her
Did the Princess know Madame Levert
I don't know
Do you know if she knows Madame Chantre
I think so yes Marthe said she used to go and see her at Douves
Did the Princess never ask Chantre about his mother when they met at your employers'
I don't know
Would Marthe know
Possibly
Do you know if this Lina would be interested in finding a place with Madame Chantre

I don't see the connection anyway she never told us she's more likely to be interested in giving up work altogether, she used to have savings her brother frittered them all away poor Lina had lent him it must be four or five years ago now a handsome sum Hans wanted to start up a stationer's business it lasted six months, when you're as daft as that you don't get other people to fork out for you mind Lina doesn't hold it against him by no means she just says Mein Gott and that's that

And you say Philippe Levert was a friend of Gérard's

Yes they often had a gay time together my gentlemen were quite fond of him too he went off with them to Greece no to Italy with Chantre, Philippe came back with a collection of little statues that were quite valueless according to Miette, he managed to palm them off on the Englishwomen through Gérard who made them believe they'd been found among the ruins and he got a good lump sum for them, I remember Philippe and him treating my gentlemen to champagne two crates that arrived from Reims, my gentlemen still hang on to one of those statues as a souvenir they always play the same trick on the new guests, it's some little woman in her nightshirt as they used to dress at the time she's been put on a marble plinth the kind of joke they like to go in for

What else do you know about Philippe Levert

He was very fond of little dogs for example the last one was a belington bedington something like that, a frizzy little beast all grey and quivering he always took it with him like the basset he had before, Sham he was called it was the Duchess who gave him her nickname

Didn't you say your employers had a dog too

Yes Albert they took him with them on their trips I don't mean their long journeys but wherever they went in the district, a Great Dane who was always slobbering towards the end all he could eat was fillet steak or failing that game always stretched out in the drawing-room on his rug, I used to get ticked off if it smelt it had to be cleaned every Saturday Albert hated that he used to sneeze three or four times whenever I put his rug back clean

Who is Bougecroupe

The Bishop of Douves and Agapa he took over from Monseigneur a long time ago that's what we called him from the start not anywhere near the same class as Monseigneur he's common-or-garden not the same style, a red-faced man who tried to lay it on thick it was difficult taking over from Monseigneur everyone realised that straightaway he never managed to make much impression, he lives in the bishop's palace at Douves and comes to Sainte-Fiduce on holy days you have to look in the guide-book for them he stays at the parsonage next to the cathedral, the Curé Archdeacon or Canon I've forgotten which he's called Trochard receives him like an ambassador a carpet they put down on the pavement and Bougecroupe gets out of his car crossing himself again and again he's grown very fat with the years, Trochard's always got to ensure when he goes from the parsonage to the cathedral that he's not obliged to turn and face the statue of Karl Marx, one day there was quite a to-do crowds of people in the square for some commemoration or other the children from the orphanage had arrived late and been unable to take up their position on the right side, Bougecroupe went straight past without blessing them the Petit Photographe at once published a picture of it and you can see quite well, the editor who's anti-clerical that's Poussinet wrote up an article where he found it distressing I remember that the ecclesiastical powers-that-be should consider formalities more important than charity, the parish magazine replied in similar vein that it was distressing to think such thoughts could arise in the mind of brothers in God, everyone knows that in the short journey from the parsonage to the cathedral Monseigneur is simply concentrating on the holy sacrifice he is about to celebrate if we grasped the full significance of his lofty mission etc etc

Trochard the Curé is he all alone to look after the parish

No there are two Abbés I believe in any case one called Pienne who fails the children for their catechism that seems to have caused some trouble too, Poussinet again according to him this man Pienne used to go and wait at the gates of the kindergarten school with a group of Wolf Cubs to attract the other children coming out he claimed he just happened to be there by chance playing with his Wolf Cubs, Poussinet said Catholic scouts spend too much time proselytising instead of developing their muscles what we need is boys that are tough and go-getting the men of tomorrow, he took the opportunity to mention the Gymnastics Society where they've started a new section for the toddlers but this man Pienne Léglise had said about him before that if there was an improper way to show his zeal he'd choose it, for his young nephew his brother's child that is is always hanging round the Abbé's skirts wanting to take Communion all the time it's bad for a boy his sister-in-law has quite a battle, they've only one fear that he turns parson several times they've tried to send him to his grandmother Volland's on Sundays but the kid gets up an hour earlier to go to Mass, it would be easy to stop him but for Grandma Léglise who backs him up she goes off the deep end about it keeps it up all day long they've even thought about moving away from the parish

Are there several parishes at Agapa

There's also the Church of Saint-Véron near the Town Hall that's Curé Rondin more like the poor parish all that area, for a time they had a worker priest who was employed by Boche he got a factory girl into trouble it was an experiment a priest from Paris, the Sous-Préfet had to intervene to hush things up the Abbé came out of it with a clean sheet the girl managed to get married a month later thanks to Simonot, they say the Pope forked out for the dowry

Say what you know about Poussinet

He's editor as I said of the Petit Photographe a left-wing newspaper he's got backing, Simonot has a lot of trouble with him over the casino you see every year when the theatre company from Douves comes back for the season he pulls them to pieces, it's bad publicity for the town the visitors will lose interest in the theatre Poussinet would like to see a little less Boulevard as he calls it and more Heaven-knows-what, the Lorpailleur woman is there behind it all too one year they tried to invite a company from Paris it didn't work as they've not enough money and it's the same for the concerts the Lyric Society's quite enough here every single time Poussinet finds some way to have a dig at Raymond Pie the conductor who comes specially from Sirancy for the rehearsals and all, a good dozen of them chiefly violins the clarinet is Soupot's boy he won a competition at Douves I mean to say, when there's a chorus they ask for the cathedral choir Poussinet sees red at once and the orchestra gets it in the neck though once my gentlemen went to a concert at the casino and they said it was very how was it they said very

Who's the manager of the casino

Monsieur Ange Bottu the brother of the Mayor of Sirancy my gentlemen get on very well with him Monsieur Ange has asked quite a few favours of them, Marthe says if the casino still keeps going the entertainments I mean it's thanks to them they don't like Poussinet it wouldn't surprise me if they managed to get him kicked out and that business of bringing in other groups they don't agree, everyone in the district has a right to some say in the season it's the same with the orchestra they're honoured members of the club as they provide the money by the way people used to say

Isn't the casino a paying concern

Not really no more and more people are going to the one at Sirancy the stakes are higher and for entertainment they have a streep-teeze better than in town it seems, I don't think Simonot is against developing Sirancy they haven't any baths, two towns where you can amuse yourself that's good for visitors it makes a bit of life, this is just a detail but even for petrol now there are ten places in the seven odd miles between Agapa and Sirancy and for honeymoons say what you like about it people feel much freer at Sirancy for example at the Hôtel du Château

Is that the hotel where Gérard's fiancée

That's it yes there's the Hôtel Fortuna as well next to the casino and the Chasseur which gets fuller all the time, Barbatti's brother that is he doesn't ask for passports it seems it's a real you-know-what-I-mean, he's sticking his neck out

What sort of contact do your employers have with the Abbé Trochard

They have no contact with him their parish is Sirancy

And with the Bishop

None by that I mean at the start Bougecroupe tried to keep Monseigneur's connections going I wasn't with my gentlemen then, I believe Bougecroupe paid them a visit as a gesture to his predecessor, didn't do any good my gentlemen's connections with Monseigneur were through the family like Mademoiselle Ariane's I don't actually know whether he used to visit my gentlemen, they'd made a few gifts to the cathedral the ostensory I think and one of those what-do-you-call-its a chasuble or a cassock, Bougecroupe must have known it came from my gentlemen and a cow's always good for milking they had no reason to butter him up they're not practising I told you, their relationship with the Abbé Quinche that's friendship I don't suppose Quinche missed a chance to mention them to Bougecroupe who put his foot in it but I tell you that's all ages ago

Do you know if Bougecroupe maintained relations with Francine de Bonne-Mesure

Mademoiselle Francine kept up her aunt's tradition at first she used to invite the Bishop to the Château but gradually she stopped inviting anyone

Do you know if any other people in the district still entertain the Bishop

Dame Longuepie yes I think Bougecroupe lunches at the castle once a year, La Ballaison can hardly help doing the same as well Pernette told us he used to go to Malatraîne it was quite a business Monsieur had to see about the provisions for the occasion the young ladies coped with the kitchen and Gustave waited at table which used to make us laugh he's never been trained, Pernette had come along with Riquet she said to him you can be Gustave and I'll be Madam, and Riquet passed the dishes the wrong way round he did it on purpose Marthe and I

Who is Riquet

Pernette's nephew he's a hairdresser in town it's he who cuts my gentlemen's hair Pernette told him how Gustave

This Riquet used to come and see you then

Sometimes yes my gentlemen used to invite him he used to come to the kitchen first at the start shall we say before he'd got all his clients, Riquet-la-Houppe they call him he's the best hairdresser in town all my gentlemen's friends go to him he's really made his mark you should just see, there's a salon for the gentlemen and a salon for the ladies three girl hairdressers a manicurist two lads and himself which makes, no, I mean three lads for the gentlemen two lads for the ladies and three girl hairdressers and a manicurist with him that makes ten, the salon for the ladies you'd say it was a proper clinic all that apparatus and everyone in white and behind I'm forgetting a salon for the beauticians as they call them, kinds of nurses to fix your face make-up and all which is ten plus two twelve, twelve people

You say he used to visit your employers

Their hairdresser after all it's only natural especially him now he's a gentleman you'd never recognise him, without my gentlemen I think he'd still be sweating it out at the station barber's

Did they help him financially

According to Marthe who got it from Pernette yes they're meant to have advanced him a sum of money he didn't have all that staff at first but that's what launched him as they say

Had they known him a long time

Yes they knew him when he was still a young barber's assistant at Julien's

Who is Julien
The station barber
Used Riquet to visit your employers before he opened his new business
I don't know, when I first went to my gentlemen's he'd just got established the salon was half the size for gentlemen only he had just two assistants who have left now anyway, not the reliable type by what my gentlemen said
And did he often visit your employers after that
Often yes he was introduced to my gentlemen's friends at parties he cuts all their hair now, he even suggested to me I went along there once but with all that mob fluttering around it didn't suit me, mind he did me a favour it seems he only performs himself on the big-wigs my gentlemen and the ladies fight for him, Mademoiselle Lacruseille told Marthe you can't find his equal at Douves the Duchess used to go every third day, in the season naturally he has to take on extra staff a lad and two girl hairdressers who work at the back with the beauticians, the other hairdressers hate him he's drained off all their clients that's competition for you say what you like every job it's the same
What's the name of this Riquet
His name is Henri, Henri Varussin but it's the salon that's called Henri they call him Riquet or Riquet-la-Houppe
Do you know if apart from your employers he was specially friendly with any of their men or lady-friends
Monsieur Hotcock and he were great friends and young Duval, Martin Coulon I mean to say when he was still here before going into films they went to America with Hotcock one summer when he was going home, Duval stayed on there he was in his element Riquet came back half crazy about it talked of nothing else, according to Pernette he thought everything here was lousy for his salon he's meant to have asked Hotcock about a specialist from over there to fit it up he didn't like Ducreux

In spite of the fact your employers advanced him the money

I'm talking of when he made the second lot of alterations he was more friendly with Hotcock then they used to go on holiday together

Weren't your employers sorry

Sorry about what

Sorry to see Varussin more involved with Hotcock

They're not like that on the contrary they used to like people to meet at their place they always had friends there, Hotcock and Riquet for example often stayed on to sleep at the house we used to give them the blue room which Riquet liked best there was a large picture he was keen on having for himself, my gentlemen ended up by giving it to him shortly before I left it's horses in the act of

You say Hotcock and Varussin were given the same room

Yes why

Weren't there enough rooms

There was no point them using half a dozen the rest besides were sometimes occupied by other friends

How many beds were there in this blue room

Two beds like in the others three even in one of them, my gentlemen's friends weren't fussy anyway it was all hail-fellow-well-met

What other friends most often stayed the night

I told you Chantre and Gérard and Hottelier and also Miette and Mesdemoiselles Lacruseille and Saint-Foin and the Duchess and the others it varied

Were Mesdemoiselles Lacruseille and Saint-Foin given the same bedroom

They're together in their own place they're used to it

And Gérard for example what bedroom was he given

It varied either one of the bedrooms on the first floor or perhaps on the second

Did he also share his bedroom with someone else
It all depended on the rooms available I tell you they always worked it out somehow
How many beds are there in your employers' bedrooms
Two in each
Were certain guests invited to share their bedrooms
I tell you they always worked it out to fit in with the rest, whenever there were a lot of people staying they'd make use of the second bed
Who for particularly
I've no idea
Didn't you serve them breakfast
Everyone took it in the dining-room
Were there sometimes other ladies apart from those you mention
Yes but with so much coming and going how do you expect me to remember
What other ladies for example
I don't know the Princess Mademoiselle Lili Frou-Frou and the rest
Who is this Lili
An actress friend of Morgione's
Used she to stay the night with Morgione
That wasn't my pigeon
Say what you know about Mademoiselle Lili
Nothing more than I say she's an actress friend of Morgione's, she often came to parties she knew Mesdemoiselles Lacruseille and Saint-Foin quite well I think she was in television too, Marthe used to say all these little actors save their bacon with television it's like radio for helping them out in my day that sort would have kipped down under the arches or joined a circus, I don't mean Mademoiselle Lili was stuck-up no but it's the principle of the thing

Did she know Riquet and Hotcock
Of course she knew them
Why haven't you mentioned either Riquet or Mademoiselle Lili before
I tell you I can't think of everything at once
Do you know if Mademoiselle Lili was a client of Riquet's
One of his best clients she stays here right through the year, Mademoiselle Lacruseille told Marthe Lili had gone through all the colours of the rainbow before turning blonde we've always known her blonde, she was very soft-mannered but I think when it comes to swigging it down as they say she'd do her fair share
Didn't you say you never waited in the evenings
At parties I said
But didn't you say your employers could have entertained the Pope and you wouldn't have known
Yes I said that especially in recent years when my work's over I'm not asked to do anything else
During these recent years did Mademoiselle Lili stop coming to parties
No
How do you know
Because she stayed on after dinner of course
Couldn't she have left after you'd gone up to your room
She could if she'd wanted to
How do you know she stayed on
Because I sometimes happened to see her next day
When did you finish your work in the evening
After the washing up
Did you wait at dinner
To start with yes later it was usually the flunkey or the extras for the big dinners but I often used to lend a hand
Didn't you say the extras came for the parties

Yes but once or twice they came earlier, I told you the big dinners were very rare
If they were so rare why mention them
I don't understand the question
Why speak of these extras coming for these rare big dinner parties
Because I couldn't stand them and whether the dinners were rare or not the people weren't rare enough
You couldn't stand any of them
It's not perhaps that I couldn't stand them but you know what it's like when you're doing a job you don't want half-trained half-wits getting in your way
But didn't you say it was mostly the flunkey who had to do with them
That didn't stop them hanging round the kitchen
And what did you think of them all individually
I've no opinions at all about people who mean nothing to me
So you considered them rather undesirable company
I've told you all about that except for Cyrille Mauvoisin he's the serious type
How do you explain that your employers could keep company with them
I didn't say that
You said that Frédy knew all your gentlemen's friends Gérard Hottelier Chantre Luisot Donéant Cruchet the whole band
Well if I did say it that's too bad
Why did you dislike almost all your employers' friends
I never said that I said some of them were worse than others and Luisot and Cruchet were not among the best
Once again how do you explain that your employers did not share your opinion
I wasn't in their shoes
Say what you know about this Frou-Frou

She's a Polish lady I think I don't know her name, she was a Countess apparently more or less a refugee she got married here to a business agent who left her very unhappy and unprovided for, Mademoiselle Saint-Foin found her one day in the street she'd just committed suicide she'd tried with aspirins and slept for three days she still looked then as if she was asleep, the sun was very hot and she appears to have been wearing a filthy old macintosh Mademoiselle Saint-Foin took her up to her flat and Frou-Frou explained it all to her, she stayed with the young ladies for a while before they introduced her to Jonas and he engaged her at once saying he needed a well brought-up person like her the young ladies brought her to the house where she went down very well, Riquet for example would have liked to have her in charge of the girl hairdressers but she preferred the corsets he changed the colour of her hair too the first time we saw her she was a redhead then a patna blonde as they say, before she committed suicide it seems she'd tried to read the lines in her hand when Marthe heard that at once she wanted Frou-Frou to read hers, Marthe noted it all down in her book she guessed Marthe had had her misfortune she predicted her husband was dead and she'd lost her money Marthe was quite shattered and even her house I think she told her about that too, Marthe asked her about her book on the convicts she said it was a very good book and ah now I remember she also predicted she had two children, Marthe said yes they're a long way away the two of them but Frou-Frou said you'll receive a letter and three weeks later the letter came from Jeannot who's in Belgium say what you like there *is* such a thing as second sight

Did this Frou-Frou stay on with Mesdemoiselles Lacruseille and Saint-Foin

No she has a flat near the station

What do you know about her husband the business agent

Nothing I don't even know his name she's divorced

Does she live alone

I don't know probably, she's no time at all for men she says it's them responsible for suicides fifty per cent of the time Mademoiselle Lacruseille told Marthe and she wrote it down in her book, when I saw that I said you could say as much about women

Didn't you say that Marthe had had two or three situations before going to your employers

Yes the first time at Douves just after her misfortune she was with Evincet the banker, difficult people Madame Evincet spent her days in bed with her masseuse and she was on a diet which Marthe said was impossible always cooking something special for her, he's just the opposite a real gourmet it was from them Marthe got the *tournedos Pavlova* my gentlemen were very fond of them with *foie gras*, the recipe is for swan's liver they used to talk about it with the Evincets when they were still coming to the house right at the start before they had quarrelled, it's a recipe passed on to Madame Evincet by her grandmother who had married a Russian her first marriage anyway Marthe was happy enough with them in spite of the diet but their daughter when she came back from America hadn't a good word to say for cooking in butter or sauces or anything, Marthe didn't enjoy her work any more she got a situation with a friend of theirs Monsieur Drille a dotty old man from Agapa who my gentlemen knew too he used to collect flies he'd even go to the South Sea Islands for them, Marthe had to learn a lot of recipes from places like that she did some for us sometimes especially rice dishes, Drille got it badly for her she couldn't move without finding him at her elbow him with his boxes of flies a wonder he didn't sleep with them, it used to make Marthe sick waiting at table with all those flies pinned to scraps of cotton-wool or corks masses of them besides apparently they smell Drille didn't suit her she only stayed two years, then she went to Miette's sister's place Madame Monachou her husband's related to the wine merchant she's so mean she wouldn't let the tiniest piece of cheese-rind out of her sight and she never paid Marthe the wages she'd promised she said the stuff she'd wasted was worth far more than the money owing to her even Miette couldn't help, she left at the end of her month so it was through Miette she came to my gentlemen like Pompom my gentlemen used to call him their employment exchange

Who are the Evincets

He's a banker as I said the Evincet and Romano Bank they've had a branch at Agapa for several years he's very rich but a sick man every year he goes to Rottard or Vichy it seems he never comes to the end of his treatment without an attack of liver, he can't stop eating and drinking while his wife's always getting herself massaged Marthe said it was a real homsession she had three masseuses one who came all the way from Agapa and a special bathroom for showers and all, she only went out in the evening and when she came back her laxative always had to be left ready with boiling water and never infused in advance, when it was too late Marthe used to put it in a thermos flask before she went to bed there were times when her mistress would wake her up to show her the water wasn't hot enough, what with that and the diet it was a bit much for Marthe but they paid her well and her bedroom looked out on the street a lovely room she's always been sorry she had to leave that, when their daughter came back from New York Marthe had to serve everything raw and sterilised or boiled in water and make mince every day, the daughter used to come and teach her how to cook potatoes or boil an egg Marthe couldn't stand it any more she told herself she'd have lost the knack by the time she had to look for a new place and off she went, Evincet was furious he found another cook in the end but according to my gentlemen

Why did your employers quarrel with them

I don't know over some money business

And Drille you say your employers knew him

Yes there was a time when he came to the house but we haven't seen him since he got another cook Violette Chenu he married her she's a cousin of the manager of the Hôtel Fortuna at Sirancy, she was the one who took him there first and since he came to know the hotel the old boy can't tear himself away at weekends, Gérard and Riquet have often seen him with women now they say when he married his cook he married his pot but he's trying his luck elsewhere

Who is the manager of the Hôtel Fortuna

Antoine Chenu I knew his father well a bit potty about religion he used to run the Choral Society at Sirancy before Raymond Pie every year he went to Lourdes as a stretcher-bearer, I must say the hotel's very well kept with a terrace raised above the pavement and geraniums all through the season, they've a Turkish bath in the hotel too for gentlemen that's for losing weight they say you can lose up to four pounds a time it's always full in the season they queue up for it it seems Chenu's thinking of enlarging the premises

Did Gérard and Riquet frequent this Turkish bath

Yes they often used to go to keep slim as they said

Do you know if they used to meet Drille there

I don't know they used to see him with women on the terrace one day even he's meant to have asked them not to tell his wife if they saw her he pretended he came to Sirancy for his flies, there's a naturist shop with a lot of insects and creatures in the window Martinet and Fêtard the bird-sellers they've got two shops next door to each other

You say Barbatti's brother also had one of these hotels

The Chasseur yes before he took it over it was a small hotel for commercial travellers old Ma Lemove a great fat woman ensconced at the reception desk drinking all day long, she only had two chambermaids and the hall porter Gnafron he used to tout for custom in front of the station with his umbrella, *Sasseur*

Sasseur he used to shout Italian he was, as children we'd often run off with a suitcase

What about Barbatti

He took the hotel over from Lemove's heirs they'd just kept it going as a small hotel without renovations he renovated the whole place the hotel trade he's got that in his blood like his brother, he set up a restaurant in the basement in an old wine cellar it's called La Sainte-Table with religious statues and candles like a refectory in a monastery, the waiters are dressed as monks and there are two monks who sing bawdy songs during dinner you get the words on a slip of paper separate from the menu on the table, the wine's drawn from a big cask at the back Totor took me all round once to entertain people what you have to get up to, it's three thousand francs the menu my gentlemen often used to go the Duchess too got on well with Barbatti he's a good-looking man like his brother, Sicilians very dark and talkative and when it comes to business I tell you it's in the family

Did this Barbatti visit your employers

No he's not the type for my gentlemen neither is his brother Guido who runs the Trois-Abeilles but they used to like going to their places

What do you know about the Duchess and Barbatti

People said they didn't twiddle their thumbs together Gérard was in the know always hanging round there for his tourists, but if I had to count all the fellows she played around with we'd be here for the night, just to give you an idea one year Marthe worked out that in one single month she'd had six locals and five tourists

Who is Totor

He'd had his go too he was one of the waiters Victor Prunet one of the oldest at the Chasseur he must be head waiter by now

How did Marthe come to hear of the Duchess's goings-on

Through Gérard and Pernette everything gets known in a small place

What do you mean when you say the Barbatti brothers are not the type for your employers

I mean they wouldn't have invited them

Didn't they entertain people who weren't their social equals

People who were young and gay oh yes of course but the two Barbattis what must they be somewhere between forty and fifty and Italians you know what they're like on the whole not specially distinguished

Didn't you say that Cruchet Luisot and Gérard for example had no education

Yes but to start with Cruchet and Luisot didn't come as guests and then Gérard is young and he was friendly with everyone with the Barbattis it's not the same they've their own little world, which is not the same as my gentlemen's

Well then how do you explain about the Duchess

Oh when it comes to feelings

Did she never try to bring Barbatti along to your employers'

After all she knew what she was doing

Do you think she'd have brought him if Barbatti had been young

No

So there was something else apart from age and education

You can't answer questions like this just like that it's more a matter of knowing people you can tell at once if it will work or not and I tell you for the Barbattis it's no

Would you mind recalling the whereabouts of the ruins at Sirancy

You mean the theatre it's on the right of the village as you come from Agapa by road as I explained just over a mile on foot, the little road the coaches take is quite a joke a lot of tourists ask to get off in the village so they can go on foot, you walk along by a stream through clumps of oak trees and come out at the theatre it's been cleaned up in recent years, there used to be some huts stuck on top now they've taken them all away you've a car park for twenty cars and the coach and on the right a new little ticket office with a window that's the way you go in, all round the theatre there's barbed wire it's old man Rognot who gives out the tickets he's got two rooms at the back for himself and his wife, the theatre's about a hundred yards away you don't have to follow the guide, what's left is the surrounding wall with something like ten or fifteen steps in tiers quite steep it's stone from Chanchèze and a piece of the wall at the back it's explained in the special guide-book three hundred francs at the ticket office, it used to be much higher with niches for statues very well restored by Georges Trapaz the painter, the stage is raised up a bit they did start re-doing the floor in stone but one year when a theatrical company was coming to act there they put down a concrete floor provisionally and it's remained, beneath the seats there's a vaulted corridor the walls are all messed up by the tourists who write their names in spite of the warning notice Rognot isn't strict enough people do their little jobs in the odd corners instead of going to the W.C's at the entrance, behind the theatre there are still the foundations of a small room and a mosaic very knocked about that's been restored by Trapaz too it's a wild boar and two little round trees they tell you it must have been the actors' green-room, they've installed a refreshment bar at the side under a pergola with tables old mother Rognot serves the drinks with a young girl at the height of the season generally from the village, one day Ducreux wrote in the papers that this refreshment bar was a monstrosity I don't agree they've grown a Virginia creeper all round it, it's very nice to spend a few minutes there with some oak trees for shade it's a very sheltered corner they explain too that the Romans knew how to choose the right site, beside the window there's a place where Rognot sells postcards of the theatre and photos, one taken from above with the trees at the back in colour the other black and white taken from below you can pick out the steps another is the mosaic in black and white and another Trapaz' restored version in colour black yellow and white, there are maps of the district as well showing the roads and little letter-cards with photos of the area, he sells souvenir ash-trays too in terra cotta of the theatre and pots from the potter in the Rue du Son I told you about him he takes every chance he can get to show off his pots, and dolls too in regional costume for your car it's a wide black skirt with red and blue bands at the bottom a blouse in white lace and an embroidered black scarf and a little black head-dress stuck on their head, Trapaz puts his pictures up for sale there too several of the theatre in different colours it's the work of a real artist and the countryside round Sirancy seen from the Plateau or from the river, one very beautiful at sunset you can see all the reflections in the water that one he sold to Gérard's Englishwoman, those that go down best he always does them again he says he doesn't like modern painters they're all Picassos, it's what you feel about it that counts or as you might say what you'd most like to have in your own home

You said there were still some ruins in the village too

A well and an underground passage the coach stops there ten minutes not Roman, the same period as the fortifications at Agapa probably

There's no official guide for these visits

No Rognot and the driver ought to be enough in theory but they've got into the habit of bringing a fellow from Douves with the tourists or picking him up on the way at Agapa where the coach stops at Les Oublies and at the museum too, that's what Gérard used to do

You say Gérard knows this Georges Trapaz

Yes they were school-fellows but Georges doesn't like Gérard's friends now they don't see each other much except at odd times to do one another a favour like selling Georges's pictures, Gérard won't take a percentage

Is Georges Trapaz from Sirancy

Yes they're an old family from these parts his father and his grandfather were local councillors and now it's his brother Joseph a big agriculturalist, he wouldn't at all mind being Mayor in place of Bottu but the opposition says Trapaz doesn't make enough impression to represent all our interests, it's not that he's badly placed I mean where money's concerned but he hasn't done enough studying as he took over the running of the farm very young and Sirancy with its holiday-makers and seasonal visitors who come for the waters is changing its character more and more it's almost a branch of the town, we need someone who could make a speech on occasion and who knows how to stand up to the Sous-Préfet about loans for improving local amenities, and the ruins that's important too to know the dates and all a useful stand-by mind you Bottu wasn't very popular but still he was a school-teacher before he retired and his wife had a villa anyway he made more impression at the time than some old pig-breeder, they didn't want Longuepie that was natural Longuepie's father was Mayor once then the Left took control they had a Communist Mayor before Bottu now it's the Right again, if they can't have Longuepie who shouted from the rooftops he was no longer interested in politics they don't want Trapaz either I always say about the opposition this business of prestige in my view it shouldn't come into it putting up a show for strangers not when your own district is at stake, an old family like the Trapaz knows the needs of folk who work on the land how to discuss crops and prices you can trust them for that with your eyes shut and you can say what you like about tourism it's all well and good but suppose something awful happens I don't know what, fashions might change and nobody take any more interest in the ruins in the waters of Agapa the main resources of the district are in the soil and always will be and Bottu proves it the experiment's not a success he's losing ground I told you

Georges Trapaz

He's Joseph's elder brother he did his studies at Douves but he's a sort of tramp when all's said and done, he's never wanted to do anything else but his painting they're hard to sell and when it comes to marriage after all there are plenty of rich farmers' daughters who'd be pleased enough to have him after all he is a Trapaz, but there's always been some snag I don't know how he gets away with it only recently with the Lemanchon girl Marthe told me they'd been engaged since last year's fête she knows through Pernette and blowed if he didn't break it off four months ago no-one knows why, or rather we guess it's because the Lemanchon girl was too serious he's meant to have told Riquet once he was a pal of his too that women are like pipes if they're too mellow you're an unlucky fellow, artists are like that but it's no good complaining he has to do his own shopping always moaning when you meet him, mind you as a person he's better than his old friends who are making their way in the world he's got character and it ought to take him somewhere

Did he keep company with your employers

Not at all

Do you know if he has anything to do with the holiday-makers as you call them and the people who stay at the Fortuna and the Chasseur

I've no idea but even if he did you could hardly hold it against him he's still young and the winter's pretty dull, in any case they wouldn't be the same ones as those Gérard knows or Hottelier or Riquet though perhaps they could, Chenu has bought some of his pictures there are some in the entrance hall

Do you know if he visits the Turkish bath

No

Does Chenu know your employers

Very well yes he's been to the house
So he's more their type as you say than Barbatti
That's right yes
Carry on
Carry on what
Did he often visit your employers
Often that's hardly the word but sometimes yes with a number of his patrons, that one he was a creeping Jesus all right you'd only to watch him in front of the pictures and the furniture it was a sight for sore eyes, I remember the big sofa in the drawing-room he'd go round it in circles and make an awful fuss before he'd sit on it all put on he can't know that much about it a hotel-keeper that's all
Is he married
No
Do you know anything about him personally
I know he gave me a nice fat tip the day when
His life, his companions
His patrons of course and his staff all the usual problems of a hotel-keeper
Carry on about his visits to your employers
Yes a creeping Jesus there's no other word for him that sort of thing you can't pull the wool over my eyes, all smiles he was and over the furniture as I said he was always raising his arms to Heaven every time the same is that any way to go on, I mean over that pedestal table where I used to put the coffee one day I could see my gentlemen were on the point of offering it to him
Describe the furniture in the drawing-room
That'll keep us busy for a while
Fire away
When you come in from the main courtyard you've got the other door facing you at the back it makes it look more spacious though God knows the drawing-room doesn't need it it runs the whole length of the house on the courtyard side like my gentle-

men's two large bedrooms on the first floor or the four bedrooms on the second, there are six windows looking out on the courtyard plus the French window and on the opposite side the same plus the two windows beside the chimney which makes sixteen in all, you can imagine without heating what it would be like especially for my gentlemen such chilly mortals it always had to be twenty-one degrees I told you it used up an enormous quantity of oil, it's they who once decided to have the dividing walls knocked down so if we start going round from the left, between the door and the first window there's a high-backed armchair the same type as the chairs in the large dining-room covered in light grey silk with little white birds at the top separated by a pale pink line it was the most delicate we put it there so it'd be used as little as possible, over that there's the portrait of a man with a goatee beard and a thin curling moustache in a lace collar it's meant to be a King of England who's said to have stayed with the Bonne-Mesures I ask you three hundred years ago now, they say he presented Antonin de Bonne-Mesure with a silver-gilt dinner service that Mademoiselle Ariane was still meant to have in her possession but it disappeared, between the first and the second windows a scalloped gilt table and round it three armchairs with wavy legs covered in salmon-pink silk with green and black sprays of flowers, on the table a big lamp in black metal Chinese or rather a vase made into a lamp with an open-work pattern of birds and fishes between the claws of a dragon whose head is under the lampshade if I had to describe *that* in detail, the shade is yellow silk with a crinkly edge my gentlemen wanted to have it changed it seems it's not in fashion any more, and over that an old map of the district in the style of the one in Plumet's bookshop it's the area round Malatraîne where the marshes are there are lots of little clumps of reeds, you can see the manor almost as it is to-day except it's only one chimney and no stone staircase at the front and Le Bérouse looks more important with a church, the Abbé Quinche said it was a quirk of the carto carto of the man who made the map Le Bérouse has never had a church it's behind glass in a gilded frame, between the second and third windows a large show-case where they put the rarest pieces from their collections which are in the billiard-room I told you, there are some Chinese objects on the top shelf pale green dishes and statuettes in pink or white stone very complicated each with several figures, lower down some items from Mexico they're in terra cotta most of them little squatting men pulling faces and the small head of a woman alive on one side dead on the other terrifying carved in black stone and some necklaces, lower down again some large negro statues in wood they'd better have left in the billiard-room you should just see some of the details, below that some old books and some pages from an andivonal that's its name in parchment the first letter illuminated and all the notes for a choir, the show-case is an old converted wardrobe one of those Norman monstrosities it takes a whole day to clean and what's more a cornice at the top that's not properly fixed, almost every time on that ladder to dust it bang a clumsy movement and down it nearly came, then between the third window and the corner a commode the same sort as the others only not so dark with fittings shaped like horses with a fish's tail we always caught ourselves on the keys, there's a Chinese vase on top in grey porcelain quite plain which you'd expect to find in the show-case it seems it's worth as much as the whole of the small dining-room put together I've forgotten what century, and up above it a huge picture they're gods mythological sitting on clouds a big fat woman holding out her arms to a soldier below who's got his foot hooked in the branch of some tree he's tripped up looking at her, beside her there's a man with one hand on her shoulder and the other holding the reins of a four-horse chariot flying off round to the left towards a patch of sky with just enough room for some little angels with plump behinds who make a chain to link up with another woman on the cloud, her head's covered in flowers and she's gingerly holding a mandoline you'd think she was going to drop it on the soldier underneath it was painted by a butcher yes Boucher famous in his time it appears, then there's the passage from the drawing-room to the small dining-room it's a continuation of the entrance-hall that's been cut off in the middle on the left the main opening into the dining-room on the right the door of the study at the back the door to the hall, on either side of the study a portrait the one on the left a lady in blue in a bonnet a grandmother with a thin rather sunken mouth and eyes like pinpricks, she has a patterned cashmere shawl over her shoulders and one hand holding it with a ring on the first finger and round her neck a wimple as they called it in fine tulle on account of her wrinkles, on the right a man in a cravat rolled round several times and tied in a knot white which gives him a very fat neck he's in a dark brown frock-coat with a collar and has short untidy hair a big nose and raised eyebrows they're mementos of the family, then going on round the drawing-room a huge kidney-shaped sofa covered in grey velvet and armchairs to match on either side that reach out in a circle round a low lacquered table with gilt mouldings on its tiny feet and round the inset table-top, it's got gold flowers painted on it too it's very delicate upset a cup of coffee on that and it needs wiping up at once I used to serve it on the pedestal table near the window so as not to have any trouble, over the sofa there's a picture that runs right along the wall it's religious The Circumcision on the first of January a crowd of characters from the Bible in a church with fat pillars standing round Jesus in his mother's arms she's holding him out to the priest who's bending over him with his knife, the characters all round don't know what to do they know they're being looked at that's what I don't like in these paintings on the right there's a group of men in robes who pretend they're talking to each other a serving-girl is offering them fruit, another group's sitting down looking at a book another walking towards the back and talking and the same sort of thing to the left of the priest his assistants, one holding a dish another a cloth the third one's turning to the fourth one to whisper in his ear and a group of people some in hats and some without who are moving in the same direction as those the other side towards the back where the pillars get smaller and smaller and there are niches for saints right up to the ceiling, which makes at least fifty people in all not counting the very small ones at the back who aren't bothered about the Mass, they must be the vergers busy polishing the brass or getting things ready a little scene all in greys, the Holy Virgin is in blue as usual and the priest has an enormous hat and a gold robe the others are in various colours getting greyer as they recede into the background, there are lamps hanging down from the ceiling on long cords you can see the little red flame my gentlemen had it off an Italian dealer who got it from a disinfected church in the south of Italy there was probably an epidermic and the moveables had to be sold, apparently it was in a very bad state Térence Monnier's studio took six months to restore it the frame is gilt all open-work vine leaves at least a foot wide, then in the corner before the first window at the back my pedestal table and a very low sofa with big poufs all round in leather and fur it makes a cosy little alcove the radiogram is tucked away by the settee it's big but a low one, above the sofa there's some shelving for the records my gentlemen used to make up concerts for themselves but it had to be jazz for their friends it was Hottelier who saw to buying the new ones my gentlemen weren't interested, next to that a standard lamp in shaped wood with a salmon-pink shade, a white bearskin rug on the floor that's the place where they listen to music when it's too hot near the fireplace where there's a second loudspeaker, you sit on the floor or on the sofa the lighting's restful so long as you switch off the spotlight on the big picture which shines right in your eyes it's fixed in a recess that runs instead of a moulding all round the drawing-room ceiling where the beams don't show, this corner then was a bit of a mess and my gentlemen were sick of it but it was just what their friends liked best you felt you could relax there, up above the sofa on the window side there's a small picture musical a lot of ladies in powdered wigs sitting in a circle round a little violinist and a double bass with a miniature white piano played by a little girl it's eighteenth century, then the first window then between that and the second another large portrait a red cardinal sitting on the edge of his chair very stiff with both hands on the elbow rests ready to spring out at you, he's a yellow complexion and thin with the kind of spectacles they used to make then a Spaniard he's above a folding card-table with a chequered marquetry top, green baize inside for bridge and four armchairs round with knobbly legs covered in green and purple tapestry in a badly drawn floral pattern, when the table was folded there was a Holy Virgin on it in badly pitted wood painted pink and blue what was left of it the face was still well preserved with great round black-rimmed eyes it came from Miette's, he'd found it near some cathedral Chartres or Amiens at a small antique dealer's who didn't know about prices it was a good bargain, that sort of thing's very popular these days you'd think the more it's been knocked about the better it is they call it rustic, between the second and third windows an enormous commode more brass than wood the legs curved like the others but they finish up at the bottom as animals' paws and at the top as women's heads with an elaborate hairstyle, the big bulging part that's their breasts not a bad idea and the top's in reddish-brown marble, there are only two drawers where my gentlemen kept their holiday snaps and empty albums for later and the glue they'd spend at least a fortnight after the holidays sticking the snapshots in, on the commode there's an old clock with a brass angel on top holding an hour-glass and another below unrolling a ribbon which runs all round the clock making bows, it was the worst of all to polish that and the commode the slightest trace of white in the hollows and my gentlemen would throw a fit, above it there's a mirror with all angels' faces round in gilded wood one of the faces at the bottom was missing for a long time before Miette or Louvois I think it was Louvois found one slightly smaller that he hacked off an odd piece from a wooden bedstead, between the third window and the French window a big black chest carved in relief just the front of it, on one side Adam and Eve driven out of Paradise with their hands to their faces weeping and making for the corner with the Good Lord turning towards them just his head in an artichoke that's like a tree, his beard goes sailing off round the other side where they're just eating the apple they look stiff and awkward and the serpent's gliding between their legs with another tree to balance the first, the whole thing surrounded with several fat mouldings and little squares in relief like false teeth, on the chest a stone statue it's a saint with a long face holding his belly that's rustic too, with St. Mary Magdalene above kneeling life-size leaning right forward towards a death's head her hair all over her face and her dress torn off her shoulders the rocks of her cave on the right, on the left the forest and a mountain you'd think was cardboard the colours are gloomy and the frame is black, after the French window another chest that's the pagan side as my gentlemen used to say carved with little men and women in their bareskins chasing each other round in opposite directions till they come to the lock, and on top the trunk of a man his privates are missing it's Greek they appeared to be proud of that but Greek or not a man's always the same on a marble plinth with a bar that sticks into him from behind to hold him up, up above the portrait of Venus the Goddess of Love all naked life-size she's walking along holding her child by the hand a German painting, she's expecting another baby that's easy to see she's got a red and white hat with a feather she's holding her head at an angle to look at an orange tree on the right covered in oranges, on the left there's a small tree with blue flowers which the child wants to pull her over to see but she prefers the oranges, in the background horsemen on a road that climbs up to the drawbridge of a fortress with a gibbet and a man hanging funny sort of advertisement for slap and tickle you can say what you like the Germans are not like us, the frame is black to match the Magdalene then between the first and second windows a commode like the other one except it's got three drawers where they used to keep papers under lock and key, and on top two candelabra each for six candles which are like the ones in the large dining-room but gilt and with angels round the base, above that there's a mirror almost plain just a bouquet on top and pointed like a crown below the flowers, between the second and third windows a large old-style desk smothered in brass it's been placed the other way round sticking out towards the centre of the room if you get the idea, endways on let's say and a very heavy gilt armchair with big knobs and cross-pieces underneath covered in red tapestry with fringes all round, that's where my gentlemen did their accounts and their writing there are two drawers in the desk and a leather top like the secretary's with a big inkwell shaped like a wedding cake gilt and three holes for the hen's-quill pens just for show they had their fountain pens, and two ashtrays like flattened frogs which always had to be the same distance from the inkwell and a candlestick at either end, to work in the evening they'd use the lamp which is on the table in the middle I'll deal with that later, they never left anything lying about on that desk the drawers were locked too, above the desk the full-length portrait of a lady it's some queen squat-looking in that dress with a pointed bodice coming down below her waist and a wide skirt grey and pink in thick folds, and over her shoulder a black cloak lined with ermine which falls back one side over the corner of a table, three or four pearl necklaces and pearls all over her dress a huge lace collar standing up and a little crown perched on her frizzy grey hair long ear-drops and a sad face with a hook nose and a double chin, following us with her eyes though she can't turn her head her left arm's hanging down with a handkerchief in her hand her right arm's resting on the back of a chair, behind her there's a red curtain that's pulled back held in position by gilded lion's-head clasps, between the third and the fourth windows by rights you should be in the large dining-room but the drawing-room goes on up to the chimney-piece there's another large Norman wardrobe made into a show-case for the books they make most use of to save going up to the library, dictionaries books on painting novels and on the middle shelf three framed engravings, one's got lizards all over the page and salamanders with all the little marks and scales on the skin touched in, their tails all curling where there's room, the other one is serpents arranged in the same way and in the centre a letter from the King Louis XIV to the Prince de Condé which was given to my gentlemen by Ariane de Bonne-Mesure, between the fourth and fifth windows a gilt settee with tassels and fringes covered with tapestry in a large red and blue pattern and two armchairs the same, over it a broad landscape it's a city on a hill with fortifications and belfrys and two roads going up through the cornfields, you can see the peasants harvesting the women with their skirts tucked up and the men in shirt sleeves like nowadays there are some horses and dogs and a child in one corner peeing on a cabbage and right at the bottom some rooks foraging, it's the brightest landscape in the house because of all that corn the frame is gilded wood with two rows of leaves the one for the queen has three, then between the last window and the chimney-piece the armchairs start all round it in a circle in grey or pink velvet the wood painted white all old-style there are six of them, the chimney is in large blocks of stone from Le Trognon I told you and red brick inside with a plaque at the back like the one in the dining-room only bigger, the hearth is very high I could just stand upright and the stone mantel ends in a point there's a little ledge where Chantre always wanted to put some flat candlesticks but not my gentlemen, there's just a stag's head carved in stone in the middle I always wondered how on earth they could have made the horns without splitting the stone, the andirons I've told you already, so then there's the large dining-room, the only thing I left out was the wall on the courtyard side to the right of the entrance if we start with the round staircase in the corner between the curving balustrade and the first window there's room for an armchair with an oval back and straight legs which doesn't go with the rest, covered in white silk with green bouquets my gentlemen kept it in memory of a friend of theirs a lady who died and left it to them, with a jewel box above it kept in a little niche in front of a big two-handled marble vase where I used to put flowers though there wasn't enough light in that corner, between the first and second windows one of those large pendulum clocks as tall as a wardrobe it's always been kept going you only had to wind up the weights every evening they weigh at least five pounds apiece, it used to strike the hours and the half-hours I can hear it now you might almost say its voice and every now and again a weight would suddenly drop and start off the striking mechanism it was a wheel that slipped out of place you could easily put the catch back, there's a little cornice at the top of the clock representing a whole lot of farmyard animals with the cock in the middle the comb's been broken, on each side of the clock there are two little console tables gilt with only one leg each of them has a candelabra with six candles, between the second and the third windows a black commode plainer than the others with coloured flowers painted on the drawers and on top, another one it's impossible to put anything down on there's just one statue with felt underneath a group of satyrs in bronze lifting up a lady she's got her arms in the air and she's holding a garland, above that there's a glass-framed map like the other side it's the Château de Sirancy as it used to be with its five towers and all its weathercocks you can see the farm buildings on the right down below and the hamlet which has gone now the trees in the courtyard have just been planted, Monsieur de Longuepie has got the same one at his place without the trees there's writing in the top corner on the left Longuepye with a y, on each side of the commode but pulled forward a bit there are two small lacquered armchairs black with sprays of flowers painted on the back the same idea as the commode and with cane seats, between the third window and the French window the same high-backed armchair as on the other side covered in a silk that's not so delicate, pale green and black stripes with white dots and above it the portrait of a young girl in a large hat covered with a piece of veil her dress leaves her shoulders bare and she's a black ribbon round her neck with a medallion, she's pointing to a little grey cat she's holding the cat's face looks terrible you'd think it was a monkey and that's the end of the tour round the drawing-room, in the middle on the right there's a large round table on one pot-shaped leg with three flat star-shaped feet underneath to keep it firm, the top is all encrusted with pieces of mother-of-pearl which are like a series of crowns round the centre, on top that's where we put the lamp I told you about a crystal candelabra with a white lace shade, round the table the same little black armchairs that go with the commode the backs are all in one piece with elbow-rests filled in at the side, on the cane seats there's a pink or black cushion and on the small dining-room side a long marble table on one leg that broadens out at each end carved in the shape of animals, one on the left one on the right they're goats with birds' legs their wings and their horns meet in the middle, on the table there's a bowl of fruit in marble the fruit too I mean Italian and nothing round that table, on the ceiling three chandeliers with drops of Venetian glass huge ones for real candles we never used to light too much work, the lighting for the drawing-room was spotlights for the pictures the crystal lamp the Chinese lamp and the salmon-pink lamp and the candles on the candlelabra for parties which doesn't make much really for so much space but my gentlemen hated too much light, there's only the carpets left now fifteen in all four enormous ones and eleven smaller ones scattered about even on top of the big ones, and salmon-pink curtains at all the windows and that's it

Where was the imitation statuette that Philippe brought back

On the shelving for the records you see there are some things I can't help forgetting the vases the ashtrays the

You say you used to hear the clock striking

In the early days yes I've never been able to get it out of my head

What kind of snapshots did your employers take during the holidays

Snaps as souvenirs of themselves and their friends on the beach for example or eating out at a restaurant they're really photographers' photos, there was one funny one where you see Chantre with a dunce's cap hitting a lady on the head with a spoon, everyone's laughing the waiter's got his eyes shut because of the light and lots of other photos of the sea and the mountains in Greece with temples and in Italy old streets and fountains one of Philippe clinging on to the statue of some old boy, anything they wanted to take as souvenirs, I often looked at those albums all except one which had a fastening you could lock in brass that's the one made their friends laugh most I never saw that

Who was the lady in the one of the restaurant

I don't know she had a very low-cut dress and a necklace that sparkled and a flower sticking out

What kind of photos do you suppose were kept in the locked album

Amusing photos I should think

Wasn't the restaurant photo amusing

Yes why

Then why wasn't it in the locked album

Because it was in the other one
  Do you think it wasn't amusing enough for the locked album
  I've no idea I tell you I never saw it
  It never crossed your mind that these photos were of a special kind
  They must have been specially funny I suppose
  Don't pretend you don't understand
  I don't understand
  Pornographic for example
  I don't know what that means
  Licentious
  I don't know
  If they didn't hide amusing photographs like the restaurant one why do you think they hid the others
  I've no idea
  Did Marthe or the flunkey know what that album contained
  Marthe didn't anyway, the flunkey perhaps
  You were never tempted to ask him
  I'm not curious
  Then why did you look at the other albums
  For fun
  When did the silver-gilt dinner-set disappear from Mademoiselle de Bonne-Mesure's place
  It was never found after she died
  How do you know
  Through Pernette who told Marthe her mistress is still meant to have seen it when she paid her last visits
  And your employers weren't concerned about it
  It was before I went there
  How do you know this dinner-set originally came from England
  Because my gentlemen told me when I told them Pernette had told us a dinner-set had disappeared
  What was the letter from Louis XIV to the Prince de Condé about

It was too difficult to read very cramped handwriting with lots of loops everywhere except for Condé at the top, and in the middle I think crown and France twice and Holland and the signature Louis in letters four times as big as the others

How do you know it had to do with Louis XIV and Condé

It's written on a small card underneath

Why do you think your employers hated light

I never said that I said too much light in the evenings especially electricity we couldn't be lighting candles the whole time

Why not

Because for them on their own or one or two friends they didn't think it worth it, they were close-fisted about little things like that they weren't frightened of spending large sums only small ones

Were there any more strange engravings in the house like the ones with the salamanders and the serpents

Yes a lot of them in the bedrooms and in the library, insects plants and monsters one especially with several figures a child with a calf's head and frog's feet and next to him a headless woman with her eyes and her mouth in her stomach and arms covered in feathers, and above her I think it's no below her it's a man with elephant's ears and a small head where his privates should be and feet that turn in with spurs on and higher up another child with four arms and an ostrich's head, I wonder if all that really existed

I suppose it could have been before Jesus Christ they say the Egyptians had queens who were half jackals it's Marthe who knows about that

Is this Antoine Chenu the same as the Monsieur Antoine you mentioned at the beginning

No the other one used to come with Carré he's not from these parts he travels, a very well turned out gentlemen with his small very tight-fitting shirt collars I think he's a dress-designer

And this Monsieur Carré

He's the President of the Archaeological Society I told you an expert when it comes to ruins, now he's at Sirancy all the year round if they don't want Trapaz for Mayor he'd fit the bill very well and where agriculture's concerned what with his farm and all he'd know how to keep his end up, he's a man you have confidence in even Abbé Quinche respects him although he's non-practising too he knows how to explain about names

Used he to be a resident of Agapa

He's always been a resident of Sirancy at La Fenière but he used to spend the winters in his house in the Rue Dombre next to the Maison-Bertrand, now he rents it to the Voirizels since the death of his wife three years ago

What is La Fenière

A large estate the lower side of the Plateau beyond Longuepie there must be about twelve acres, the farm is one of the largest in the area Passavoine the farmer goes in for breeding he's got about a hundred cows and chickens more than a thousand as well as pigs, Monsieur Carré's house is smaller than my gentlemen's since he became a widower he's been letting the first floor to Monsieur Hallinger the dress-designer who has business dealings with Monsieur Antoine, he lives in Paris for his collections he only comes in the summer it's a money-making profession, Marthe used to see his name in the women's magazines once when she was at Douves she saw a dress made by Hallinger Paris in the window of Leroy's she went in to find out the price it cost something like two hundred thousand francs

Who was Madame Carré

A Darmally it's she who had the money, Carré was a teacher at Douves but you don't make much at that she was very nice, a fat lady everyone was fond of her she died of cancer

Used she to visit your employers

Yes but you might say how shall I put it that she wasn't quite at home there though everyone thought a lot of her, naturally she didn't drink then how shall I put it she didn't enjoy herself perhaps in the same way they did if you see what I mean, besides when she came it used to be for luncheon, what a kind face she had Marthe used to say her husband had made her unhappy but it didn't show

Did she know Mesdemoiselles Lacruseille and Saint-Foin

Yes the young ladies had a high opinion of her but she wasn't the kind of lady you'd have seen at the Colibri or at Rottard I used to take my hat off to her as they say, when I thought about La Ballaison or Dame Longuepie for example who everyone detested they'd watch over their husbands like Cerverus and the way they used to talk, whereas she poor woman for two years she went around with that muck in her throat she'd had an operation for it Doctor Bompain, her husband and my gentlemen were the only ones who knew it seems there was no hope and so did she I think we all know how it ends that sort of thing

During her lifetime did Carré ever visit your employers without her

Yes for parties

Why does Marthe think she was unhappy

It may be her husband didn't spend enough time with her or perhaps because she had no children, she helped out a lot at the day nursery

You say this Hallinger had business dealings with Antoine

Yes Monsieur Antoine was constantly travelling about to Paris London New York for his dress-designing, he used to be invited to La Fenière even in Madame Carré's time it must be through him that Carré got to know Hallinger

Why do you say even in Madame Carré's time

Because it was before she died

Do you think she felt any aversion for Antoine

Certainly not she liked everyone

Then why even
I say even while she was still here afterwards they saw a lot more of each other
So she was more or less opposed to their being together
That's not what I said really sometimes your questions
Was Hallinger married
I don't think so no
Why don't you think so
Because Marthe said dress-designers never marry
Have you any idea why
It must be because they've got too much work with all their collections, Marthe said she'd actually read about Hallinger that he used to work night and day and when he takes some time off he's probably not short of women he's got six mannequins it seems, of course I know if they're like this that what was she called I told you about her Donéant's sister their figure's as flat as a pancake forgive me if I think that's funny

Since Hallinger rented the first floor at La Fenière does Antoine stay with him or with Carré
Those questions again how do I know it's the same house
Who is this Passavoine
The brother of the baker in the Rue Allouet, he's made a nice packet at La Fenière though I must say he works like a nigger but Madame Carré advanced him a tidy sum for his equipment and his cattle, Sophie Narre said it was two or three million that was a small fortune at the time he's meant to have paid it all back, his wife is an Audrelat from Le Rouget a little dark thing who keeps everyone on the hop they've got three sons who work with their father the youngest must be about fifteen

There's a day nursery at Sirancy you say
Yes in the Chemin des Cerisiers it's a little outside the village Madame Carré put a lot of money into it they must have something like fifty children now, the head Mademoiselle Poulinot is a

friend of Mademoiselle Lacruseille's she's a very live wire as they say, she went scooting about like a fireman the night of the fire that was four years ago now Pernette happened to be on the spot coming back by the night coach ten minutes past twelve, they stopped at Les Cerisiers when they saw the fire it was the washhouse that almost touches the children's building everyone lent a hand Mademoiselle Poulinot got burns on her arms it could have been a disaster another minute just imagine all those little ones roasted, Riquet said they were like sucking-pig the same flavour anyone would think he'd tasted some

Which coach was that you mentioned

The night coach I told you which gets in from Agapa ten past twelve it stays at the depot all night and leaves again next morning at twenty past six for Agapa and Douves

Did you yourself usually go to Sirancy by coach

Yes there's a stop about five hundred yards from my gentlemen's place but I'd quite often find myself doing the three odd miles on foot

Whereabouts is the Chemin des Cerisiers in relation to the centre

As you come from the town it's just before you enter Sirancy on your right before you pass the Cours Clemenceau

Give a general idea of the plan of Sirancy

It's called the village but it's really a small town I told you it's surrounded by a kind of boulevard or avenue which at first is called the Cours Clemenceau, as you follow it along to the right the Cours Ratebose then the Cours Carrin-Tonneau then the Cours Gabriel-Tomès, if you're coming from Agapa you take the Rue Chavirat and go straight on it's one of the four principal streets you pass the Rue Poussegrain on your left, then on your right the Rue Evangéline-Vouache on your left the Rue Sirotte, then you cross the Rue Merveille and you still go straight on you've the Hôtel Fortuna on the right and on the left the

Casino opposite, then the Rue de Pince-Bouc then on your right the Hôtel du Château and opposite on the left the Chasseur and you come out in the main square on the right you've the Town Hall, then the Rue du Savon which is one of the four and continues on the opposite side as the Rue du Velours-de-Paille which runs right through the town then still in the square to give you a rough idea you have the Rue Marcel-Atitré which is a continuation of Chavirat then on the left the boys' school and the church of Saint-Chu then of course Velours-de-Paille then the girls' school, if you carry on along Marcel-Atitré you leave behind on your right and your left the Rue des Grands-Traversots which marks the start of the Rue du Dimanche and still carrying straight on you arrive at the other end in the Cours Ratebose

At Sirancy is there a favourite place you patronise as there is at Agapa

My favourite place I suppose it was Le Cygne in the square next to the Town Hall or Julot's Place de la Goutte-Blanche, my favourite walk was always round that little square near the Cours Clemenceau which is right on the edge of the countryside, from Julot's place I used to take either the Rue Crosse-Besogne which crosses Clemenceau and on the other side joins the Chemin des Cerisiers which is on the road for Le Camp, or I'd take the road for Le Zodiaque you cross over Clemenceau and take the right fork the Chemin des Guêpes or even Claude-Boutade a bit further on where the gardens are better kept in the spring, with those little dwarfs if you see what I mean for gardens you stand them under a tree or in the middle of the lawn for example it looks more cosy, then on the left the Chemin Doux which runs into the Chemin des Guêpes you follow that up on the left where at Fricot's there's a lovely little pond in front of the lodge with a miniature mill and three of these dwarfs bearing sacks, Fricot's a retired railway man if he's out of doors we have a talk he's worried about his daughter Hélène who's a bit flighty, she works in some offices in town she's already had three or four affairs with the clerks and trouble over miscarriages her mother's quite shaken when she talks about her says there must have been a cuckoo in the nest, then the Chemin de la Tramontane on the right which joins the road for Le Camp right opposite the Chemin Philibert-Lepoivre which goes zig-zagging through the fields, it's all bee-hives round there the honey from Sirancy is well-known even at Douves

Whereabouts is Ballaison's house

Rue Marcel-Atitré almost on the corner of the Grands-Traversots there's just the Place des Garances between

Who is this woman tenant Miaille

The mistress at the girls' school, someone in the fifties not easy to get on with I told you she's making trouble for Ballaison about leaving her mother's meant to be too old but the old girl trots about as well as you or me, the father's dead run over by a tourist twelve years ago for several years Madame Miaille was secretary at the hospital in Agapa reception desk, she used to terrify the patients with her questionnaires she's meant to have added some of her own just to embarrass you, when my sister had her pendicitis she damn nearly gave her the idea it was cancer and that just an hour before the operation, she kept us hanging about searching through her pigeon-holes for the right form to fill in and all it's a shame when people are in pain my sister never forgave her, the daughter's no more soft-hearted than her mother the children loathe her

And the tenant of the other house

Chastel yes we call him Barbouse he's been studying up the streets of Sirancy and Agapa for twenty years for a dictionary it seems the Curé knows something about it, the Miaille woman was barmy about him once always watching for him at her window, she even started going out after him chasing into town when her classes were over to the Library looking up books and old newspapers, she used to meet Chastel there and they'd have tea at Gorin's we were sure they were going to settle down together and then nothing, he's still by himself but the Curé's not so sure of him Chastel looks more and more bonkers with his black cape and his pince-nez constantly falling off his nose, he's meant to have started learning Turkish says you can't explain everything with Latin, he's been going out at five to four always to the same place Pernette says for quite a while now, from the Rue du Poisson-Pêcheur he turns off right into the Rue de Givry then the Rue du Savon as far as the square, he crosses that and at four o'clock he's where the schools come out on the corner of the Rue du Velours-de-Paille he gives the children sweets and kisses them and pets them especially the little girls, already some people call him Jesus

Has he been a tenant for a long time

It must be about thirty years yes Madame Chastel died about ten years after they moved in, and as he got married at thirty after all his troubles yes he must have been forty when the Miaille woman was after him he's in the sixties now

What troubles

He wanted to become a priest he'd almost finished his studies as an inseminarist and I don't know what happened, one day he came home to his mother's and he got married five years later with a Goupil from Hottencourt older than him, they had a son never got on he's somewhere near Paris a removal man with some firm that covers the suburbs

What does Chastel do

Now I tell you nothing but his dictionary he's retired he taught history at the boys' *lycée* in town, I think it was he who brought Sagrin to Ballaison's

Do Sagrin and Chastel go about together

Pernette says from time to time Sagrin goes to the other man's place for his dictionary

Does Sagrin also teach history

No Latin I think and French

Didn't you say it's a large house that Chastel lives in

Yes I see what you mean why doesn't he share with Sagrin, because he doesn't want anyone else at home he's got money from his dead wife he pays regularly, anyway it's not *his* house Ballaison's after it's the small one where the Miailles are that he'd like to get back again it joins onto his he'd only have to knock down the walls where the doors were blocked up, as I explained once it was all one building

Who was this Goupil woman from Hottencourt

A relation of the retail stationer's Chastel got to know her at the fête she was nearly forty, he married her straightaway and rented from Ballaison leaving his mother in the small house in the Rue Chauffe-Manche which he'd gone back to as I said, Madame Chastel never got on with her mother-in-law a nice woman though we knew her quite well we used to live in the Rue Joly fifty yards away

Was Madame Chastel also a religious crank

Pretty well yes but you can't say it did her much good she didn't like people, she spent her time making trouble for the tradesmen and always ailing having children so late in life had tired her, she was on a diet of boiled rice until she died the child was brought up by his father who let him have all his own way, it didn't do him much good either

You say it's only been a short while since Chastel's been waiting for the children to come out of school

Pernette says it got into him about six months ago, before she always used to see him going off in the direction of La Goutte-Blanche he used to go walking in my little lanes, Fricot knows him well

Used you to meet him

No the afternoons that wasn't my time of day

And you say the little girls attract him specially
So it seems though he gives them all sweets but when it comes to kissing it's more likely the girls
And no mother has complained
I don't think so no at least no I don't think so
Say what you do know
Well according to Pernette Petite-Fiente's mother is meant to have made some remark about her daughter coming home late from school one day, the child never said where she'd been Barbouse didn't bring her home with him anyway but according to what another girl's meant to have said the mother has her suspicions but as she's well-known for making a drama out of everything and as Petite-Fiente's a horrid little beast no-one said any more about it
Who is Petite-Fiente
Sorbet's little girl Noémie everyone calls her Petite-Fiente she gets on well with the boys when it comes to playing dirty tricks on people, you'll tell me it's only kids' stuff but the Miaille woman's at her wit's end
What's this other little girl meant to have said about Chastel
That he'd kissed her probably or I don't know you know how children are
Was the incident ever repeated
Not so far as I know besides if it had been Chastel would have got into trouble, no it's just that he's starved of affection you can understand at sixty all by himself with his dictionary and that son a removal man he never sees
Is Pernette likely to have questioned Sagrin about Chastel
She asked him how he got on living alone, Sagrin said it was filthy both floors in a terrible mess with all Madame Chastel's things still there he works down below in a room next to the kitchen where he has his bed a long time ago Pernette offered to

go and do his housework but he doesn't want her, as for Ballaison he doesn't care so long as Barbouse pays up but it seems the roof's in a bad way, that'll give him a chance to drop in and have a look
    And does Sagrin know anything about the little girls
    No all that's just gossip I told you if he really did that it would soon be known he's not the one who'd tell Sagrin about it anyhow just think
    Is Pernette sure that Sagrin goes to his place about the dictionary
    That's what he told her yes, now the Curé's losing interest he needs someone now and then to explain things
    Is it Sagrin who says that Chastel is learning Turkish
    Yes but as a joke I suppose, Turkish Turkish for *our* street names I mean to say
    Has Sagrin ever been seen as well when they come out of school
    No he's in town at that time
    What do they say about him in Agapa
    What do you mean what do they say about him
    That he might be interested for example in little girls
    I told you he was at the *lycée* for boys
    In boys then
    What on earth are you getting at now, the slightest thing you're told you dig up something dirty
    Why is the Curé losing interest in Chastel's work
    It's not the work he's losing interest in he asks Sagrin how it's going but Barbouse, have to admit he's getting strange the way he looks he stares at you sometimes without recognising you, the Curé says it's Barbouse who doesn't want his help any more but it's my idea he's the one who's dropped *him* he doesn't like to be contradicted when he's explaining his Latin Barbouse probably did bound to have done that and I expect he told Sagrin that the Curé was Latin mad and thought everything came from Latin
    Don't you think it might have something to do with Chastel's new habits

I tell you no it hasn't Chastel's got no new habits he's chosen a new place for his walks and that's all there is to it
  The Curé is in touch with Sagrin then
  They meet occasionally Sagrin goes to the parsonage to talk about Latin he takes the chance of asking Quinche what Barbouse wants to know but this is all quite recent I tell you, Sagrin never went to the parsonage before and anyway Quinche and Barbouse are sure to make it up it's stronger than they are a common interest unless Quinche gets the push before that
  What is it that makes you suppose Sagrin and the Curé discuss questions of etymology
  I didn't say that I said Latin
  What makes you suppose that
  It's Sagrin who told Pernette
  Why might the Curé be getting the push as you call it
  Because people are fed up with him if it does happen he'll go to his sister's at Fantoine
  At what time of day did you go for your walks round Fricot's place
  Wednesday mornings and Sundays or even in the afternoons but always before four o'clock I never met Barbouse
  Do you often see Pernette
  Fairly yes
  And you can understand *her*
  Not well but she's a very high-pitched voice and when she shouts sometimes it's all right
  Better than Marthe
  I don't know
  Didn't you say now Marthe wrote down what she had to tell you
  I said at Gorin's she doesn't like shouting when it's full of people but even in her kitchen she has to write things down for me when I can't manage, there are some off-days as she says

When people shout very loud like this do you understand
What
When people shout very loud do you understand
I can't hear write it down
Does Pernette write things down for you
Yes it depends on the day
Why haven't you mentioned this question of days before
Because I never thought about it besides off or on it's no joke really
Why didn't you say you were seeing Marthe again in her kitchen
Because you never asked me anyway we meet more often in town
Are there other people you could understand without having them write things down
It depends on the day and above all on the voices yours is no good, they have to shout anyway and that upsets me you don't know what it's like
Can't you do a little lip-reading
A word here and there but only people I'm used to
Do you understand this
Say it again
Do you understand this
I don't understand write it down
Repeat the name of the maid to Curé Quinche
Phyllis Legouard, Quinche calls her Marie and the children Scalawag
Is Pernette in touch with her
No more than anyone else it's chiefly Marthe who used to invite her I told you, she's seventy-six but sound enough in the head she knows what's going on in the parish about the Curé getting the push she always says they won't dare, Marthe wrote some of her ideas down one day something about them all being

crazy about their Republic Church isn't a republic it's the kingdom of the Good Lord he's the one who decides, she was a militant royalist when she was young I remember seeing her at a meeting in the square after Mass there was a speech made that was still in the Abbé Dufaux's time before she went to the parsonage, she was carrying a white flag those banners people have at Corpus Christi and she shouted Long Live Louis XVI Long Live Saint Louis, some of the men made a counter-demonstration I remember asking my poor mother what was going on nothing she told me just politics

What are your new lodgings like

In the Rue Tétin not far from our old house in the Rue Joly just before the Rue Allouet on the left as you come from Chavirat along the Rue Poussegrain opposite the Rue des Tailleurs, I found it through my sister she's kept up all her contacts at Sirancy friends of my first brother-in-law the Arminces, they let me the bedroom on the second floor which used to be their son's it's not large but there's running water and for an extra cupboard I make use of the one in the corridor after all we all have a few little things of our own, the trouble is the smells there's a cheap café in the courtyard and well I mean to say when you've been used to decent cooking all your life

How do you spend your days

I get up at six impossible to sleep a minute longer and I heat up my coffee, I've got a spirit stove I don't trust all their newfangled butagas and I wash and tidy up what else can I say, at eight o'clock I go down the Rue des Tailleurs and the Rue du Cordon into Velours-de-Paille on my way to the Cygne, in the square going past the church I buy my newspaper and at a quarter past eight I'm at Monnard's they open at eight I order a glass of white sitting at the second table on the left as you go in, Cyrille is always nice to me so is Monnard mind and Henriette his wife she's at the cash desk but I know Cyrille better, Eugène or Blimbraz are often in their corner we sometimes have a game of dominoes together but usually I read my newspaper and I think, my meditation as Marthe calls it I think a lot you see my meditation at my table the paper usually slips out of my hands, it'll soon be a year since I left my gentlemen after seeing such a lot and knowing people suddenly no-one nothing to make me run about do this do that nothing to force me now I realise how shall I say, you go on out of habit at first it took getting used to that was ages ago making the effort I mean but not knowing quite how, other people other people it's easy to talk but them who told them the reason why it makes me think now it's all over you go on and it leads nowhere, my glass in front of me the coat rack the window with the square and its fountain Henriette at the cash desk the men at the counter and the customers for tobacco, Monnard in the morning giving out change the civil servants at a quarter to nine arriving at the Town Hall we knew them all and it happens more often if you've nothing to reply you don't bother it's of no importance any more they're just people, they could be different people in a different town me a different person at a different table wouldn't I still think the same I don't know if I'd been in three or four wars or revolutions or chopped off heads I could still have got away with it and found a cushy job, sitting at that table somewhere else would I still think the same these people they're all alike dead or alive the same old story long or short sweet or sour with the same faces anxious about burying their mother or catching a train or paying a bill, the same smile for a woman when they're twenty the same fatigue every day a struggle every day a struggle no better no worse than the next man for nothing only to stay alive I don't know what it means any more I don't get it, just to see the same eyes the same ears suits shoes bicycles dogs all alike all alike at my time of life now with my glass the paper the coat rack in front of me or at my gentlemen's beating the carpets out on the grass polishing a tea-pot the secretary taking the car out Marthe peeling potatoes my newspaper what was I saying, there comes a day when none of it matters to you any more what's the point of it all that trouble and strife suddenly it's all wiped off the blackboard something written on it I couldn't read I can't be bothered any more suddenly I don't know a thing any more I feel underneath my desk my little ten o'clock snack in a minute the birds don't you hear the birds I mean sometimes the birds like bells they stay with you keep you company, at my desk in the old days thinking one day it would come back the blackboard without the voices no-one around not Thursdays or Sundays not the table or the kitchen or her either all alone in front of me the blackboard disappears the last word left to read what's it all about there was too much to do, the marquetry commode the fish service in my hands that's something you don't wonder whether it'll do it's got to be done, shopping in the village the baker my sister to see in my head something that doesn't expect an answer my life right enough so what then I could do the same things again scrub out my room but I don't have to now all that belongs somewhere else somewhere else other people's places who tell you to do the silver brush my suit there's nothing of me left now my paper slips from my fingers, if Cyrille put out the light or pulled the curtains I wouldn't realise, it's not me at the Cygne any more than when I'm heating my coffee or serving aperitifs in the drawing-room I've slipped through my own fingers like that glass on the table how shall I say yes slipped away, what brought me alive was not being my own master and that's it I'd like to see my sister a bit more often like her to say come round Sunday or come round Thursday to stiffen something inside, get a firm grip on my newspaper that's the worst of it you're lost to the world

   Sorry to interrupt your meditation you must answer
   Answer what
   Do you still go for walks round Fricot's place
   Do I still go for walks

Pull yourself together, we're on to your life now at Sirancy, answer, do you still go for walks

Yes I go back round my little lanes occasionally when I've read the paper or else in the afternoon after lunch

Where do you have lunch

At the Armince's they give me my board

Who are these Arminces

Friends of my first brother-in-law I told you my sister's in town married again, Paul Armince and Clothilde he's an insurance agent never been able to make a career for himself, she's a cashier at the Magasins-Prix we were fairly close in my brother-in-law's time less so after but my sister's kept in touch, the little I give them for my keep they don't turn their noses up at that but I find them changed I wouldn't say on the make but almost being short of cash isn't good for people, they've dug quite deep into their savings for Clothilde's illness and I don't think their son's very shy by what they say about borrowing from them

What did the Armince boy do

I've no idea he went off two or three years ago my sister said let's hope he gets a proper start at last, it was for some timber business with a pal they were meant to start a saw-mill in some valley Le Rouget way we heard it didn't work out but he never came back, it seems he's gone as a page-boy in a hotel at Vichy I forget who's meant to have seen him there, he'll end up in Paris too

Where do you buy your newspaper and which paper

Next to the church old Ma Attention's kiosk I take the Petit-Photographe or the Agapa Echo sometimes the Fantoniard

Whereabouts is the Rue Allouet

It's the turning after the Rue Tétin as you go towards the Cours Tomès it continues as the Boule-Menue

What do you know about Passavoine the baker

The brother of Carré's farmer he took over his father's business who was our baker before him, the Ballaisons get their bread from him although it's quite a way but he bakes the best bread and he delivers which isn't very common these days, to think in the old days you could have had just one trouser button delivered

Who are these Voirizels who Carré lets to

They own the Magasins-Prix with branches all round the district, it's good business for them not so much for the customer when you look at the quality although in one way I'd almost change my opinion now, when you're alone rather than chasing everywhere you've got everything to hand, at my gentlemen's we'd never have mentioned the name neither Marthe nor me she's still against it mind but as I say when you've got to do it all yourself it's tempting, if Marthe could hear me

Do these Voirizels have any family

They've two children a girl and a boy about fifteen the kind of teenagers who go in for negro music, the girl's dressed so you feel uncomfortable for her trousers so tight she can hardly sit down, I saw her recently on the terrace of the Fortuna in a shirt more like a brassière one doesn't want to be prudish but you must admit

In what part of Agapa is the Rue Dombre

Near Les Moulins first on the right off the Rue des Rats as you come from Les Marquises, it leads into the Rue Gou

Who are the Darmallys

People from Vériville Madame Carré's father owned the watch factory he's meant to be Swiss originally, the mother's still alive she's gone eighty Monsieur Carré goes to see her every month, she came to my gentlemen's with him once she's as deaf as I am, to see her start smiling before you speak to her and then go on a moment too long you'd almost feel sorry for her if you didn't know what an old witch she was, the day nursery for example Madame Carré her daughter often tried to get her interested she's got all she wants living alone, even without making a donation there was a time when she could have done some knitting for the children Madame Carré would have provided the wool, she preferred to do nothing at all rather than knit for a bad lot like that the nursery school obviously it's mostly children without fathers it would have been a comfort to her if they'd died of cold, it's hard to imagine an old woman as wicked as that it's Monsieur Carré's maid who used to tell Marthe everything, Julia she's been in love with Carré for twenty years she used to play every dirty trick imaginable on her poor mistress like upsetting sauces all over her or forgetting to order or spreading tales all round about Carré not sleeping with her almost ever since their honeymoon it was a rotten marriage and all, Marthe told her she was wrong to be like that they even quarrelled for a while because Julia had taken one of Madame Carré's brooches which she thought she'd dropped in the coach, there's no knowing really she didn't suspect it was Julia but good as she was she didn't want to accuse her, Marthe managed to get Julia to put the brooch back somewhere in the bedroom two or three weeks later, Julia didn't want to quarrel with Marthe after all she hadn't got many people to chat to, you can't say she was really no good as she used to tell it all to Marthe but curious yes curious, come to think of it it's difficult to say any one thing about anyone I mean that they're this or that because when you think about it they're not quite like that either in things that are not important at first sight but are really important deep down it's like

How did Julia know that Carré failed to observe his matrimonial obligations

I'd have been surprised if you hadn't picked on that, yes she knew because they didn't have the same bedroom and she had hers on the same floor at any rate at La Fenière it was a maid's privilege in return for long service she used to say, she'd leave her door ajar to know who was coming and going as she's a light sleeper almost not sleeping at all, every evening she used to wait for Carré and Madame to retire to their separate rooms he'd say to her goodnight my dear and kiss her hand, Julia didn't miss a thing like a bitch in heat there's no other word for it her Jean-Jacques Marthe had an earful, now Madame Carré's not there any more and the first floor of La Fenière has been let Julia's had to move up to a maid's bedroom it's enough to make her ill though her mind's at rest too as he's got no woman with him

Do you know who are the members of the Archaeological Society

Yes there's Carré then the president and the committee Monsieur Turina Chastel Sagrin Plumet who else, Doctor Mottard who took the place of Doctor Tronc and the Sous-Préfet as honorary member with the Abbé Quinche and all the people who pay their subscriptions are members like Marthe

Who is Turina

The one in charge of the excavations he's not there all the time unfortunately he lives in Douves, he's an expert perhaps but his team no thanks very much they may be specialists but the damage they do I told you, mind you if Turina received more money from the Commune he could afford different workmen you can't tell me specialists would bring a whole wall tumbling down as they did at Les Oublies, that's what Poussinet said in the Petit-Photographe under the photo

Do the members of the society have meetings

Once a month there's a lecture

So the Curé has an opportunity to meet Chastel

Yes probably they talk mostly about the ruins at the committee meeting according to Pite, the new site at Les Oublies Turina keeps them up to date then he gives a lecture that's on Sunday afternoon, about Agapa in Roman times for example or the invasions at the last one for instance he said no-one knows where the name Agapa comes from, there's meant to have been a Pope called Agapet and the Agapètes who were a type of early Christians but Agapa existed before that perhaps it changed its name at that time, the inhabitants are still called Agapètes anyway Marthe noted it down she was there I saw her afterwards, there were about fifteen people she saw La Ballaison who pretended not to see her she was explaining the tapestry in the hall to a lady, the lecture was in the committee room it was cold Marthe was frozen stiff when she came to meet me at Gorin's but as education it's a good thing I'd like to be able to go, the members have an annual banquet at Racosset's at about the same time as the fête Sagrin says the food's good but I'd be more inclined to agree with Monsieur de Ballaison who said the standard wasn't any better than at the Bécasse and the chef doesn't inspire me with confidence, chap called Sudervie a Gascon who puts more garlic in a sauce than Marthe in a whole year's cooking, not very subtle their cooking all the members can go to the banquet if they pay a thousand francs but there are never more than about ten people including the committee it's embarrassing having to talk when you don't know anything, Marthe's never been to it

Are these public lectures

What do you mean

Are they reserved for members only

No everyone can go if they pay a hundred francs it's announced in the papers and there's a poster on the door of the Maison-Bertrand

Who is this Pite

The caretaker of the house the concierge he has his rooms at the entrance in the courtyard Pompom got to know him through Lémiran, it's he who sends the notices out to the members his daughter's a typist, they used to send out cards they had printed at Loriot's but it cost too much

Where does the Pite girl work as a typist

At Renoir's export firm she's a friend of the Totton girl or used to be anyhow

Say who the Totton girl is again
The one Sagrin used to go with she's a friend of Mademoiselle Lacruseille's now
Whereabouts is Renoir's export firm
In town they've an office Rue de Biron and a warehouse at the station
Who is this Racosset
The owner of the restaurant in the Rue Filière not far from the Mouton Gras, he wanted the same sort of place and had red wall-seats and palms put in but that doesn't make for good food, Philippard he at least never went in for alterations and he's as good as the Mouton Gras I told you, I'd like to have ordered Marthe's niece's wedding breakfast from him but they wanted a place in Sirancy where the bride lived
Who is this niece of Marthe's
Mireille her brother Alfred's daughter he lives at Hottencourt now Marthe doesn't often see him and Solange isn't our sort, about the wedding breakfast they'd asked Marthe to ask me at first I suggested Philippard but they wanted it done at Sirancy, so first I thought about the Fortuna the restaurant isn't bad but Chenu wanted too much he was always adding on fresh items, in the end it came to three thousand francs a head and Alfred didn't want more than two thousand Chenu's last offer was to make it two thousand five hundred it was still too much, so I went to see Dontoire Rue Gaston-Routine it was one of the best restaurants in my day it's gone right down but I thought perhaps for a special occasion Félix would make an effort, it was a good choice he was satisfied with two thousand a head all in, so I made up the menu with him oysters we ordered through Philippard it was easier that way he's got special contacts and he didn't tack anything on, then a *vol-au-vent* then a *filet-en-croûte* which always used to be Félix's speciality, then a *gratin de coeurs d'artichauts* based on one of Marthe's recipes Félix didn't mind her explaining

it to him, then salad cheese ices and fruit for two thousand francs couldn't do better these days

Who was this Mireille marrying

Pierre-André Dumans a cousin of Dumans the transport man a steady lad who used to be secretary at the Town Hall, now he's with Pégin the undertaker's in the Rue Croquette where he earns a lot more, Mireille was very taken with him she'd got to know him through the papers just think of it as she'd gone thirty her parents were getting worried, they'd put an advertisement in one of the Douves papers and Dumans answered just by chance it mightn't have been anything genuine at all, when he realised it was Mireille who lived three streets away from his place he nearly went round the bend he'd never have had an inkling because of the way her parents put it on can't think why by the way Alfred is a civil servant with the Customs and Solange is a Bianle from Crachon, still he wrote off and Mireille when she discovered it was him she was bowled right over she told us after that for ten years she'd had her eye on Pierre-André and he'd never looked at her they made a go of it from the start, the parents tried to make trouble Pierre-André is an orphan with no money behind him and they'd been banking on God-knows-who for Mireille, anyway they agreed only too pleased but of course it's Alfred who had to pay for the wedding breakfast and the ceremony at the church

Apart from the family who was at the banquet from the village

Apart from the family let me see apart from the family, no I'll have to start with the family so there must have been Solange and Alfred, the bridal pair that makes four, Dumans transport and his wife six, Antonie Bianle and Amédée Chatton eight, Marthe and me ten Bottu and his wife twelve Thiéroux the builder and his wife fourteen, the Curé fifteen and number sixteen Léonie Dothoit who's related to Pierre-André a cousin of his poor mother's, we thought about her at the last moment I'd asked Alfred to make a round figure it was easier for the table and odd numbers mean bad luck, I almost regretted it afterwards it was so difficult to arrange the seating at table but it was too late she'd been invited, so who was there not from the family there were the Bottus the Thiérouxs Amédée and me and the Curé which makes seven, I can see it all now as if it was yesterday you've no idea the work it makes I'd started like my gentlemen do for their big occasions making a plan with the oval table from the first floor reception room putting Mireille in the middle on one of the long sides and Pierre-André opposite, on the right of Mireille her father of course and on the left the Curé, on the right of Pierre-André Madame Dumans his cousin and nearest relative on the left Madame Bottu the Mayoress, it's Solange who insisted on inviting them though they're not specially close but she could tell everyone they were there and for her son-in-law's sake so he'd know he wasn't just marrying anyone, Alfred didn't see things in the same light he said as Pierre-André was secretary at the Town Hall it was normal to invite Bottu and anyway it might be useful for him in the future you never know but at rock bottom it flattered his vanity too, it was difficult talking things over with them Marthe came with me three evenings running to their place and wrote everything down later I made up my plan with her, so where was I yes on the left of Pierre-André Madame Bottu, on the left of Madame Bottu Amédée he's a childhood friend of Pierre-André's he was best man, on his left Antonie Bianle Solange's sister on the left of Antonie in the middle of the short side let's say the end of the table Thiéroux they're very friendly with the Alfreds they couldn't do anything else they gave a table runner three thousand francs from Tripeau's, opposite him at the other end his wife and on her left that's where I had an empty place, I realised after it couldn't be a man or a woman because the Mayor was on the left on Madame Duman's right so I should have got rid of Léonie Dothoit as she was bound to come on Madame Thiéroux's left and two ladies together that's not done, and if it was a man he'd have been next to Bottu there was no way out, like me being next to Thiéroux it all came from the fact that you had to start with the married couple who should be opposite one another each with their proper neighbours, you can't help bringing two ladies and two men together at either end with sixteen people, so on the right of Madame Thiéroux it was Dumans and on his right Solange that's it for one side, on the other Alfred on his right Marthe her sister and me on Marthe's right I couldn't put myself anywhere else they'd invited me to thank me for looking after everything, there was only one other place I could have put myself that was next to Madame Thiéroux in the place of Léonie and Léonie next to Marthe as they're friends but I was next to Bottu, he loves talking and there was only Madame Dumans on his left who never could say boo to a goose Marthe will tell you she's well-known for it though she's not stupid it seems but it comes to the same, I couldn't be in Amédée's place either he had to take Antonie's arm to escort her to the church, they had to be kept together nor next to Solange of course she'd never have agreed to a servant, no Marthe that was the only place for me we gave it plenty of thought but I tell you until we'd sorted it out, mind you with the Curé for example I said at once it would have to be on the left of the bride as her father's on the right you can't put him anywhere else, the only thing apart from Léonie was Bottu who wasn't next to the bride I think in a case like that it's better for the Curé to come first especially as Quinche is old and I couldn't put a man next to the bridegroom, but in the end we found our plan worked out quite well Marthe and me Alfred too it was a start, then we had to think about decorating the room Madame Félix suggested a garland all round in laurel leaves we tried it out for a short stretch but it looked gloomy, I suggested the garlands from the fête that we keep in cardboard boxes in the loft at the Town Hall Bottu gave permission, we did it with

Pierre-André quite simply one pink and one white attached to the pictures on the walls it's paper cut in a pattern that pulls out like an accordion if you see what I mean and we thought on the table two bunches of peonies and irises, I was chary of lilies because of the smell just two in each bunch, for the wines with the oysters and the *vol-au-vent* the local white wine you can't really do better than that, for the roast Félix had in his cellar about fifteen bottles of St. Emilion that needed opening he gave me some to try I think another year it would have been too late, and for the dessert some Mousseux ordered by Julot from Lantoy's they let me have it at a special price I had to make do with what I had, for Marthe's *gratin* we went round to Félix's three days in advance he'd got to try it out and he made it as well as Marthe, and the day came round even sooner than we thought when you're constantly busy with the same thing time goes quickly, in a way for Marthe and me it was our day I'll always remember her coming out of her room in her blue dress and lace collar with a black straw hat and a little veil and a bunch of cherries on the side, she'd asked me if it wouldn't be too much but for a wedding it was just right, I wore a suit one of my gentlemen's black jackets still quite good it was only the trousers had to be lengthened I didn't want to put on the dress coat I've got for big occasions so as not to stand out too much and a carnation in my buttonhole, we caught the coach and at nine o'clock we were at Alfred's there was no-one else there yet they made us sit down in Alfred's bedroom, Solange and the bride were in a fine state in the next bedroom they couldn't find the pins for the bride's head-dress Mireille had bought them a week before at Tripeau's pearl-headed ones, we had to move everything out of the way of Mireille's mirror-wardrobe when she remembered she'd put them inside Alfred was getting impatient, they sent us down to the drawing-room next to the kitchen where it wasn't so untidy to wait for the others, Pierre-André turned up at half past he wasn't allowed up straightaway he went up to kiss his wife-to-be just before the others arrived about quarter to and we formed up into a procession on the pavement, Madame Dumans couldn't find her handbag I told Marthe it would be like the pins, we didn't know who should be Léonie's escort I'd only thought about my table and Alfred hadn't given it a moment's thought there's always something at the last moment but of course neither the Bottus nor the Curé were in the procession so that made three people less, Léonie was the odd one out as she was at table we put her behind Amédée and Antonie, so at the front there was the bridegroom and Madame Dumans she's twenty years older than he is and could take the place of his mother as we'd arranged she had a grey dress on and a black hat with a white plume that Marthe thought looked distinguished, then Amédée and Antonie in a brown dress with a yellow scarf and handbag to match, so then came Léonie all alone we couldn't do anything else then Marthe and me then the Thiérouxs who started bickering because Thiéroux wanted to take his wife's arm and his hand was sticky with perspiration I said she'd better take *his* arm, then Solange in a pink dress now was that very suitable for the bride's mother Alfred hadn't wanted to upset her although he didn't like it, she had a hat covered in little flowers like lilac pink and white the children who were watching us started laughing she was escorted by Dumans transport, and who brought up the rear the bride very sweet with her little veil and a short dress she could easily dye Marthe told me with her father as escort his chin was all trembling, he was about to lose his carnation as he'd broken the stalk and Solange had to fix it with a pin at the back, we started off for the Town Hall where the ceremony was due at a quarter past ten we only had to take the Rue du Pince-Bouc as far as Chavirat and then cross over at the Hôtel du Château to arrive at the Town Hall on the right, it all went off well as far as Le Cygne where Cyrille was chucking Blimbraz out on the pavement he was drunk already, he's always had it in for Dumans ever since some transport bill twenty years ago that Dumans had got him to settle by issuing an official order to pay some business about freestone from Chanchèze when Blimbraz was still in contracting, when he saw the wedding he wanted to hit Madame Dumans Cyrille pulled him off at once by the sleeve but Blimbraz fell over, Cyrille and I picked him up his head was bleeding luckily Cruze the chemist isn't far Cyrille ran off at once to fetch him I told the others to go on without me and when Cruze saw it was nothing serious I caught them up just before they went in to the registrar's, there I must say it's always rather moving one's memories you know Marthe could see I wasn't quite myself I don't suppose she was either and we squeezed up to each other a bit everyone took their seats round the table and Bottu in his municipal sash shook us all by the hand and started reading the declaration under a bust of the Republic, luckily the speech didn't last long I couldn't face the bridal pair or Marthe or Alfred no-one looks quite himself on these occasions they get you all worked up, then he made them sign the book and we stayed there a while the church service was at eleven o'clock, Solange took the chance of talking to Bottu and his wife she was in black with a kind of smock embroidered grey that Marthe found distinguished too that's what she always finds when she likes something, then we went out again the Bottus in front of Léonie we crossed the square to the church where Quinche was waiting for us on the steps, he was wearing his surplice and two choirboys with him two little lads I didn't know made me think of Pipi and Tourniquet long ago who used to play marbles while they officiated at Mass, there were other children on the steps waiting for the sweets Alfred had asked me to deal with that so I'd left the bag under the counter at Le Cygne Cyrille was meant to bring it along as I came out, the Curé shook everyone by the hand you have to make a grab at it he can hardly see a thing now and he went on in front of us into the church with the choirboys while Raymond Pie played the harmonium, Marthe told me it was quite soft we were sitting near the choir where Scalawag had put bunches of lilies I could smell them even from where I was I got hot round the collar thinking of the lilies on the table perhaps I ought to remove them before the wedding breakfast, then Quinche said the blessing and made his speech I saw Solange wiping her eyes and Léonie too which surprised me she always looks so self-possessed but with things like that you can never tell, beside me Bottu twiddled his thumbs to show he didn't believe in it all but no-one noticed him, I could see the stained-glass window at the east end that represents Saint Chu the Holy Virgin had a hole right through her middle kids who must have been throwing stones and I don't know why I suddenly thought I've not forgotten you see, I thought that broken window was a bit like the beginning of the end, all these ceremonies these Masses at church in my day they were people's life now we don't believe so much in it all what's to become of everyone I wondered, suddenly I saw the window with no glass nothing and the bridal pair in front of a gaping void as you might say, when all that was something solid it was like a sort of guarantee the ideas that come into your head, at one moment Bottu sneezed he asked his wife for a handkerchief she took one of those little ladies' hankies out for him he blew his nose and got it all over his fingers, he wiped them under the back of the pew in front when you can't hear you keep your eyes open, with the service over we went out Cyrille was there with his sweets Pierre-André and the bride threw them to the children it always ends up in a fight, Petite-Fiente was there she attacked anyone who had more than she had Pierre-André had to separate them, it was a nice sunny day and Amédée wanted to take some photos but he couldn't decide on the right place it took such a time especially with the sun in your eyes every couple one after the other, Marthe and me he gave us ours

Marthe kept it in her drawer it'd be quite good if Marthe wasn't screwing up her mouth a bit turning her head to one side you can't see it's her she must have been thinking about something else, there were people at the church door to congratulate the happy pair friends of his and hers and the family's a lot of old folk too that's what they like I won't say their names always the same ones, Amédée went on taking photos once stepping backwards he nearly fell off the pavement, we were with Pernette and Cyrille he was trying to tell me why the bag of sweets was torn, Marthe told me afterwards one of the children had spotted the hiding-place under the counter Cyrille had had to run out in the square after him the bag had burst open on the ground but there can only have been a few missing, he went on explaining to Marthe while I was watching everyone talking on occasions like that people form into groups that wouldn't normally go together, I said to myself that's all you need a boy and a girl who fancy each other people forget their barriers and their troubles and come and wish them happiness as if that little word alone which doesn't really mean much because you say it to others made you forget your own woes, that's what I was thinking and Marthe who doesn't miss much gave me a dig with her elbow she could see I was going off in my own thoughts, I said I felt lonely at my gentlemen's it's only now I realise how much Marthe meant to me we both had our misfortunes that's enough for people to understand each other, I remember my mother one day had made it up with an old friend she'd quarrelled with just by thinking twenty years after how unhappy she'd been with her husband that's it you see

The wedding

Right the others went off home and we made our way to Félix's place without joining the procession, I was starting to think about my lilies again the smell but when we arrived at Félix's place there was such a nice smell of cooking that even in

the reception room you could only smell the lilies if you bent right over them anyway they took the flowers away half way through the meal you couldn't see your opposite number, Félix to start with offered us aperitifs downstairs it was a good thing to do it got known and brought him some customers, he served us martinis and pastis it gets people going straightaway and after that kind of ceremony you get a dry throat, people who say it's wrong even to drink an occasional glass they can't often feel much excitement you need something to put you right and what's more it helps to keep the conversation going anyway everyone felt much better, Solange got quite friendly she fingered Marthe's hat her bunch of cherries and Léonie was having a chat with Bottu I was relieved as they were going to sit next to each other, the bride went round everyone in turn her glass in her hand without the martini she'd never have done that you see she's a shy one, in twenty years I've never seen Félix anything like it he almost had tears in his eyes to see so many people at his place, then we went up and they all admired our decorations especially the flowers and the table so nicely laid Madame Félix had produced a dinner service *she* hadn't used for twenty years, again you could almost say it's twenty years since anyone felt so good, but I couldn't hear what people were talking about Marthe wrote a lot down in her notebook about the wedding it was her day too, anything I can say apart from what I saw it's thanks to that
   Go on
   We all sat down at our places I'd put the names on little cards in front of each plate the Thiéroux's went right round the table twice they'd mistaken Monsieur for Madame, when everyone had been seated Félix served the white wine he just had room to pass behind the chairs, Popo and Josette were waiting with their dishes of oysters near the door that was the only snag it was a bottle-neck passing through then we went on serving the wines ourselves me on my side and Dumans on his it simplified things,

the oysters then four dishes two dozen on each I'd worked out half a dozen per person from Bélon
  Who are Popo and Josette
  Pauline Planche an old woman who still gets hired for special occasions and Josette Valentin Félix's waitress he'd just taken her on
  Go on
  So yes a half dozen Bélon oysters I couldn't rise to more, several people like Madame Thiéroux and Antonie and Bottu didn't even eat all six they gave their share away, Bottu said he preferred snails the Curé's meant to have told him he couldn't renounce his birthright meaning that Bottu's a country bumpkin, everyone laughed but Bottu didn't get angry he's meant to have answered that priests never mind reminding us that we're made of clay not when it suits their book on the other hand the bridegroom asked everyone if he hadn't got too much he'd have wolfed the lot, someone made the joke about knowing that oysters are good for bridegrooms naturally that sort of joke at weddings it's what shall I say it's natural, so after the oysters the girls brought on the *vol-au-vent* it made an impression all right with two celluloid doves on top Mireille had to put one in her hair and Pierre-André in his jacket pocket, then Félix served it out and the girls passed it round at once at the first mouthful I found it was a bit filling as they say the sauce too thick and the pastry too soft but Félix got nothing but congratulations, Madame Dumans mistook the meat balls for bulls' testicles Amédée told her no that gave rise to some fresh jokes, at one time I thought we were going to run out of white wine but Félix had ordered some more from Monachou, it was just we had to wait to bring some bottles up he didn't expect they'd get through it so quickly, I could see Madame Bottu all flushed as if she was being inflated someone drew attention and they all turned to look, Bottu explained that wine had this effect on her but it didn't stop her drinking we were well away as they say, when the *filet en croûte*

arrived I'd no more appetite left neither had Marthe, when the bridegroom saw the dish all garnished with lemons shaped like flowers by Madame Félix he got up and called for her Madame Félix came up from her kitchen dripping perspiration and he kissed her and drank her health then he kissed Félix and told him to go and kiss the bride and he did, Mireille kissed him on both cheeks and then *she* got up to go and kiss Madame Félix who burst into tears it made for a lot of coming and going round behind the chairs then Alfred said to sit down again and tackle the fillet, Madame Félix went back downstairs waving goodbye as if she was off on a journey it was the excitement and the white wine she'd already drunk in her kitchen, Félix cut his fillet up like a lover cutting up I mean a lover in love with his fillet and the girls passed the dish round, it was a success very tender still pink inside Marthe let me know like this with her hands she's one you can really trust, when it came to the St. Emilion which Bottu tasted first I was a bit frightened so was Félix he might find it was beginning to go off as I said but after the aperitifs and all the white wine we'd drunk already no-one noticed, Félix gave me a wink everything was all right everyone took a second helping even an old chap like the Curé it's amazing I told myself what he can put away, talk about eat like an octogenarian it's perfectly true but then all at once Madame Bottu began to go pale and flopped out in her plate, Pierre-André and Amédée got up at once to help her Bottu explained it was nothing she often did it just passes out for a minute for want of air, in fact everyone was too hot we opened the window while Pierre-André and Bottu were laying Madame Bottu out on the floor, the little bride looked quite put out but Madame Bottu opened her eyes again straight-away and a moment later she was able to sit back at the table it was just that she had to stop drinking, so then there was Marthe's cheese dish and there I really think it was too much for everyone even Quinche lifted his arms in protest but he ate some all the

same so did I so as not to disappoint Marthe, more than half got left but somebody must have enjoyed it later, I was finding the St. Emilion more and more drinkable I told myself to watch out you've got to keep an eye on everything if something goes wrong you're responsible, I must admit Marthe started putting her hand on my glass as well, then the salad lamb's-lettuce and beetroot then the cheeses four kinds Bleu d'Auvergne Saint-Nectaire Camembert from Doince's that I'd chosen myself and some creamy cottage cheese for the ladies, Thiéroux next to me took a large piece of each what a constitution I had come to a stop so had Marthe, Alfred took some blue the bride some white and she helped the Curé who couldn't see which cheeses they were I can't remember what he took after that Solange didn't
 Cut it short
 After the cheese the ice-cream from Gorin's Marthe had wanted pistachio the one she prefers but it mightn't have pleased everyone, so we'd decided on vanilla and pistachio Félix got a round of applause when he brought it in on the shooting-club's big platter which is usually downstairs on a shelf with the other prizes it was the only one that was right for size, Gorin had dressed it like a kind of tower of Babel two moulds one on top of the other one large and one small which made four tiers vanilla at the bottom pistachio vanilla and pistachio on top with some birds made of sugar and squirts of whipped cream everyone took copious helpings it helps to get the rest down, I told Alfred we'd serve the *mousseux* after that, the first round was the signal for the speeches I started pouring and he stood up his chin was trembling even more than at the Town Hall Mireille all flushed didn't dare look at him he started speaking and straightaway he was crying Mireille Solange Léonie as well all the ladies and Pierre-André were red about the eyes, Alfred went on Marthe wrote down roughly what he said a great wedding day everyone gathered together round a new warming-pan the parents have done their

duty up to the young 'uns to do theirs, then he talked about future happiness and sacrifices it was quite long I could see some of the guests stealing a spoonful of ice-cream it was melting on the plates, in the end he raised his glass and we had the toast it was the Curé's turn next Mireille asked him to do it sitting down and he made a short speech saying he was happy to be at this wedding perhaps his last, he had taken to Mireille as a devout young girl in the choir and he told Pierre-André a woman is a treasure or rather a vase that contains a treasure if the husband doesn't make an effort like Jesus Christ the treasure gradually disappears and the Church falls on evil days he was warning them about it, we had another toast then Bottu his was the best speech he said the family is the cell that forms the egg of the fatherland and nothing holds together without it, every marriage is a fresh cell and a fresh egg which provides the basic structural elements of a community Pierre-André knew something about that being secretary in the Town Hall, the important thing in life is respect for the rights of each citizen who is the foundation-stone of the future, to end up he read a poem by his aunt Louise D'Isimance a local girl who died thirty years ago she'd changed her name to be a poetess in Paris, Marthe asked him to write it down it goes like this a happy pair on the road of life plight their troth through joy and strife love grants escape from death's attack to pilgrims of the beaten track, he explained that the beaten track that means everyone since time began who does his duty at the polls and is the father of a family, we had another toast and as Alfred stood up and leant over the table to shake him by the hand he dipped his jacket in the ice-cream he had to take it off and Popo had to wipe it down she was drinking the toast with Josette and the bridal pair and the Félix's, Madame Félix had come upstairs again for the speeches she was still the one who shed the most tears she was kissing Léonie and Madame Thiéroux and even Bottu it was just then that Amédée cheered us all up again by singing that march about the soldier setting off with a flower on his rifle you know it's patriotic, his fiancée's weeping at the window and he says take heart take heart take heart war will yield to love our souls are more united than earth to the tree above, it's a song that ends badly because he doesn't come back but Marthe told me he didn't sing the last stanza, there was a lot of clapping it seems he's got a nice treble voice, then Thiéroux sang a song too he obviously had a struggle to get to his feet he sang down in the forest something stirs he upset both the glasses trying to drink a toast, Antonie was annoyed her scarf caught some Félix took it downstairs to the kitchen to pour hot water through we still had the fruit to eat and the nuts for the philippine game with the double almonds I had a go with Marthe and she won it the following week, everyone was beginning to want to move they were standing up or throwing almond shells at each other, Félix brought the coffee and the liqueurs and Mireille cut off a small piece for everyone from the bottom of her veil to keep up the custom, she went to the window where the young people were calling her from below they were waiting for the wedding breakfast to end to start the dance in the ballroom, it was five o'clock everyone went off to the Town Hall it was Bottu who provided the refreshments the young people danced you might say the whole village was there, Marthe and I found a quiet corner with the Alfreds near the stage, it's a hall that's used for the shows the scouts put on for the jumble sale we were only just warm enough sitting quiet the hall's not heated and spring was late that year, Mireille was very nice to Marthe always coming to ask her if she was all right she wanted her to dance with Pierre-André, Marthe gave me her bag to look after and she realised she'd left her hat at Félix's I hadn't noticed either, Pierre-André ran off to fetch it he brought it back all knocked about the kids had invaded Félix's place to eat up the left-overs and they'd had a fine time with her hat the bunch of cherries was missing and the wings pulled about Marthe was most upset, Solange at once offered to buy her another I must be fair to her, still Marthe did have a dance with Pierre-André I watched all those people spinning round there was a record-player behind us like the one at my gentlemen's and young Robert saw to the records it seems you can hear very well thanks to the loudspeaker at the other end of the hall, the record-player doesn't belong to the parish but the electrical arrangements were made by the scouts I was feeling tired I must have dropped off for a moment when I

Who is young Robert

The grandson of Scalawag's brother, François Legouard he was well-known in my day as a local official he was against everyone at the same time the priest the gentry the tradesmen the civil servants, it was he who suggested demolishing the church to have a sports ground in its place it was at the time when sport was starting he'd got interested straightaway, he was mad about football and aviation the way he talked about Blériot you'd think he was a saint, he founded a Society for Friends of the Propeller and made my father join my father was never interested in anything outside his slippers but François was so wildly enthusiastic in the end my father read what they published about the first trial flights it was Douves to Sirancy at the start

Who is Philippard

The owner of the Truite au Bleu Rue Prolot where my gentlemen often used to go for the Vosne-Romanée I told you, he's the brother of the builder who'd worked for my gentlemen before I arrived then he started drinking and hasn't done much serious work since, his daughter Madeleine took her own life no-one ever knew what had happened Philippard never got over it and the bottle did the rest, his friends Mortin and Verveine who works with Cruze have been trying for a long time to help him back on his feet and find work for him but what can you do he was never on the site and people got fed up you can feel sorry for a while but if the other chap won't pull up his own socks, it's a sad business old Ma Philippard goes out charring at her age and with the way they used to live, round our way any woman down on her luck falls back on that

And Cruze

The chemist in the Square next to the Post Office he's an old man now it's Verveine who does everything his old apprentice, he must have interested him in the business but Cruze is still there his only pleasure is being in the shop and buttonholing the customers

What memories did the ceremony at the Town Hall bring back to you

Old memories

Personal

Memories are always personal

Were you ever married

Even other people's weddings all those people you've known

Answer

I'd rather not talk about them you keep your memories to yourself

Answer, were you ever married

Yes

When

Twenty years ago

What happened to your wife

She's dead

When

Ten years after our marriage

How old were you when you married

Thirty

What did your wife die of

A nasty chill

In what circumstances

In the forest

Was she delicate
No
What happened
We found out too late there was something wrong with her lungs at least that's what the doctor said
Who was she
Marie Nolé
Why didn't you say before that you were married
It's an old story now I thought there was no need
What memories do you have of your married life
Two people sharing life together
Give details
Ups and downs
Did your wife have a difficult disposition
Everyone has his own disposition
Were you already in service at that time
Yes
Who with
The Emmerands
Who are the Emmerands
My old employers
Pull yourself together, you're meant to be giving a detailed answer
Perhaps I didn't want you to question me about that everyone has a right to some privacy
You must answer, who are these Emmerands
They're dead
Who were they
Property owners
Where
At Le Bouset
Whereabouts is Le Bouset
Between Sirancy and Agapa

Explain about the Emmerands

They were elderly friends of my gentlemen and I didn't like them we stayed on because we were comfortably housed but they brought us bad luck

How long did you stay there

Ten years

Why did they bring you bad luck

They used to converse with the dead

Spiritualists

They both had their noses in their books and their experiments they used to entertain friends at night they used to see dead people and talk to them especially her, she told Marie she could see our child

You had a child

Our little Claude he died when he was eight, for two years after that Marie didn't want to leave because Madame Emmerand used to tell her what he was doing the other side and that he was happy I never wanted to get mixed up in it

Why do you say it brought you bad luck

Because there are some things one's not meant to do I should have left as soon as I found out, I tell you we were comfortably housed and Marie had our little one straightaway she didn't want to leave she said we'd never find another position like that our employers could do whatever they liked with their dead it was no concern of ours, but gradually she became intrigued she often used to talk to Madame Emmerand in the end she used to ask her regularly for news of her dear ones first her father and her mother, Madame Emmerand told her what they wanted her to do it was almost always a walk in the forest which was a favourite place for the dead, Marie was meant to be getting more and more responsive and be able to hear them herself that wretched woman wanted her to get like her, Marie didn't tell me at once or I didn't want to believe she did it to get like Madame Emmerand

I thought she can have news of her dear ones if she wants to so long as it doesn't go any further but I should have left I knew it wasn't right

In what way do you think this brought you bad luck

I think that's what caused the death of our little one I think Madame Emmerand wanted another death to have someone else to talk to especially a child she knew, it was easier for her to guess what he was doing the other side and in her conversations with the others she must have asked them to let him join them so she could hang on to Marie afterwards and make her more like her, I should have been wise to all this I was sure it would come to no good but Marie always used to say think about our little one he's well-off here, and when he died then she couldn't leave any more it's a terrible business when you get caught up in it Marie wasn't the same any more every day every day she'd stay for hours at night with Madame Emmerand to talk to the little one, I'm positive she caused her death as well as the child's I couldn't get over it I told her Marie had never been ill before, the doctor said she was a real chest case when he came shortly before she died we thought it was a nasty chill quite straightforward he said it was too late there was no hope but he was a friend of the Emmerands he'd never have wanted to say anything else

What did your little boy die of

Meningitis in three days it was over

Who was this doctor

Doctor Vernet from Douves

When did the Emmerands die

Her six years ago and him three

What did they die of

I've no idea

Used they to visit your employers

Sometimes because they'd known one another quite a while but my gentlemen didn't believe in their experiments they always told me grief had turned my mind to say Madame Emmerand was responsible, that she was a very respectable woman in touch with some Spiritual College in America where she was born but I feel sure she was wicked, she had dealings with the devil the devil yes he turns up wherever such things are done at night he comes to tell me it's a good thing Marie and our child are dead, I can see Madame Emmerand holding his hand and she's laughing with her black teeth more and more often now more and more often they come I can't sleep in the dark any more at midnight they switch off the light and tell me their horrible tales I can't sleep any more they're going to kill me they're going

Calm yourself, did Marthe know about your sleepless nights

Yes she told me it was all in my head that it wasn't true and I should think about something else to get to sleep count sheep but all my sheep had the face of the devil, I used to tell her if everything you've got in your head's not true how can you go on living it's bound to exist somewhere the good things and the bad, Marie and the little one aren't here any more they're in my head but that doesn't mean it's not true, if you had to be wondering that all the time well I ask you it would be too easy to say the good things are true but not the others and I wouldn't really call that easy, our little one and Marie you could say it's not true because it upsets me so you see I didn't agree with Marthe the devil exists all right, I can't help wondering how they manage people who don't think about him I must say when I was at my gentlemen's I thought a lot less about him I slept better then though I'd only just lost my wife, it's now it takes hold of me more and more after ten years

How do you see the devil

It's better not to talk about that

Answer

He doesn't always have the same face he doesn't always come the same way generally I'm aware of him before I go to bed things don't look the same you'd think they'd been moved around or suddenly no more water in the tap or my bedroom door that won't shut properly, I don't mean to be going to bed but it's him who pushes me down I try to stay on my feet it's impossible, once I'm lying down I leave the light on I know he's waiting and suddenly the light goes out I can't see him straightaway he's a hat down over his eyes when he takes it off he looks like Marie with a hooked nose or Madame Emmerand who bursts out laughing or else they're holding hands they've got almost the same face, I say my prayers and they say that's right say your prayers and out of their sack they pull the head of my little child his mouth all twisted up no I don't want they'll be coming no I don't want

Don't get so excited, is it always your wife and child they talk to you about

Always

Never about your life at your gentlemen's

No unless they take the face of someone I've only seen once at their place and suddenly I remember

Why do you say the light goes out

Because it's true

Don't you think you really put it out yourself when you're half asleep

When I was young that happened but not any more it's him

Is Doctor Vernet still alive

Yes

Is it he who diagnosed your child's illness

Yes he took him to hospital straightaway but it was too late

You've never thought of seeing the doctor again, asking him for more details

I'd rather die though he'll die before I do

What do you know about that

I know

How
I can't say
Answer
Because he's been stuck with pins
What do you mean
If you don't understand what's the good
Answer
His photograph I stuck it with pins
And that will make him die
Yes
Did you do this with the photographs of Monsieur and Madame Emmerand
Yes
And you don't feel responsible for their death
It wasn't me it was God
How was it God
He told me
He inspired you to do it like that
Yes
Have you killed anyone else in this way
It's not me they're being punished for bloodshed
Have you done it to anyone else
No
So death in such a case is not immediate
You have to stick them in for a long time
Does the devil help you
You don't believe in him you'd better watch out
Watch out for what
For him
Why
He's beside you
Here
The lamp moved he's going to touch you watch out

Can you see him

Calm down, answer
He touched you
Where
He's gone
What was he like
Your face
Will he come back
I don't know
When did you see him for the first time

Answer, when did you see him for the first time
After Marie died but I'd felt him before as soon as we went to the Emmerands' they'd chosen the right spot
What do you mean
Le Bouset is near Grance
Used they often to walk in the forest
Every day they'd bring stones and branches back
Used you to go there too
Not since Marie started listening to them
Have you gone back there since
No only to Bonne-Mesure that time I told you
Where exactly is Le Bouset
Coming along the road from Sirancy there's a turning the same side as Bonne-Mesure a big bend, Le Bouset's not far from there on the left a little hamlet squashed between the quarry at Vaguemort and the forest
What is this quarry at Vaguemort
An old quarry with a farm disinfected no-one will live there any more that's where he comes you can see fires burning there at night, in the morning people say there's no trace of what caused the fire and the noises, Madame Emmerand was always

going there to pick her mint so she said she did show it to us but she gathered other plants as well that she never did show us Marie knew that, one day a pine tree close beside her was struck by lightning you can still see it and she came home full of revelations Marie stayed with her till two o'clock in the morning and for a whole week she wouldn't eat she talked of the dead day and night, Doctor Vernet came to treat her with injections and a diet looking back on it now how could we have stayed there so long I knew it would bring us bad luck but Marie was stubborn women are like that and always for the wrong reasons, before the little lad died she used to say if I looked round for something else I'd be to blame if we ran into difficulties, if you really want to know she used to go to Vaguemort too and stay there sometimes all afternoon, if you hold out your little finger to things like that they've soon got you by the arm that's where the trouble starts

What did your work consist of at the Emmerands'

Housework

And your wife could have whole afternoons off

Once that wretched woman got her claws into her she didn't give a damn whether the clothes were clean or the washing up done or anything

What kind of people did the Emmerands entertain

The kind that go in for table-turning and rappings on the wall they write down their revelations, I never wanted to get mixed up in it but naturally Marie told me about it especially after the little one died he didn't tap so loud he'd go on saying he wanted he'd go on saying he wanted

What did he go on saying

We were both meant to go to Vaguemort and lie down there on the ground so he could feed himself

Feed himself you say

He was hungry he had to feed himself it's when we're asleep he's able to eat

Didn't Madame Emmerand say he was happy

She used to say so at first to get Marie involved later she knew he wasn't happy he had to feed himself those were her revelations they feed on us death must be a slow process, we wouldn't mind doing it I wouldn't anyway if it weren't for the devil I'd do it all the same yes for Marie and the child but you've got to pass through him and that you see that's not right that's not truth it's a sin, he wants us to be living corpses we know all about that we don't need priests they want us to pay them to pay them to tell us about the love of God they ought to be burnt burnt the lot of them burnt such people everyone burnt

Calm down, don't let your imagination run away with you

There's no difference it's all there in your head your whole life through no difference

Do you drink a lot

It's in your head your whole life through the same

Answer, do you drink

What do you expect me to do all day long I told you with Pompom a glass here a glass there

And without Pompom

There's always someone at Julot's or at Le Cygne they haven't cast me off, even Julot when I'm all alone has a drink with me but don't try and make out I'm a drunkard the drinks you have don't change your head for you, if it starts going round at the time all the better it's a relief and if the devil calls up the dead to torment us in a sort of way he's right it's our fault, all those snares of his we fall into serves us right for doing the wrong thing if I'd left the Emmerands we wouldn't be in the state we are now what's got to be done is burn Vaguemort that's the source of the infection burn Vaguemort and people like the Emmerands and the doctor burn them straightaway don't put it off but he'll die I tell you, you have to pay for it causing the death of other people those that die every day a normal death that's life you can't stop people dying and living on in our heads, it's all these goings-on you pay for he'll leave me be one of these days and Marie and my little boy will really be at peace we must burn Vaguemort *I* must burn Vaguemort, Marthe says I'm just getting ideas I listen to her because at bottom I'm still afraid it may all come back on me I've been a funk all my life

Don't get excited, burning Vaguemort won't put anything straight, Marthe's right, talk about your little boy

You want me to talk about him

Yes, how you used to live at the Emmerands' with him and your wife

When he was born we called him Claude as Marie wanted it was her brother's name a lad I used to know he was always spoiling for a fight and had never done a hand's turn but a kind heart Marthe used to say he died in 'fourteen, the baby weighed eight pounds a beautiful baby we'd made the cradle out of a laundry basket Marie had sewn a blue frill all round it as she was sure it would be a boy and for the palliasse there was no shortage of bran, Madame Emmerand provided us with the baby linen and when the moment came she sent for Vernet Marie gave birth in our bedroom, for a first one it seems it went off all right four hours from ten o'clock in the evening till two in the morning, as for me I was waiting in the garden and in the kitchen when Vernet came to tell me it was a boy I was very thrilled but a girl would have had the same effect, Monsieur Emmerand stood us champagne I tell you they did everything right up to the end to make us trust them we were their friends they used to say they almost adapted the child straightaway and quite spoiled him from the start, three days old he had an attack of jaundice then all the children's complaints I mean when he was three or four, chickenpox measles scarlatina whooping-cough the lot but he was well looked after coddled by everyone that's why Marie stopped wanting to leave, when he was five he nearly got impaled on a fence climbed up he had to go and retrieve his balloon he always kept the scar Madame Emmerand wanted us to send him to school the sooner you start the better it is, he was a credit to us straightaway always a good boy always came first it didn't seem normal to me I used to tell Marie I'd never got on at school, she said he must take after *her* father and coming from a well-fed home that counted, Madame Emmerand never even had to help him with his homework he did it all by himself aged seven he'd learnt how to read it used to worry me to see him like that he didn't spend enough time playing, Vernet ought to have done something he could see the little chap you had to tear him away from his books to get him to eat but they were always giving him books he had at least twenty, I used to tell him to go in the garden I'd go out walks with him as often as I could but my time wasn't always my own and there, three days were enough to take him away from us

You say Madame Emmerand was American

Emmerand had met her over there they got married and came to settle down here ten years later it was she who bought Le Bouset they had everything altered, we had a real apartment all to ourselves a spare room and a lavatory and then a bedroom for the child, she had her ideas about Marie from the very beginning and I tell you even if Marie hadn't done a thing even if she'd told her nothing she was all sweetness and light her method worked she got hold of my poor wife but she didn't lead her to Paradise

Was Monsieur Emmerand also in the habit of conversing with the dead

Yes all the time they were in league together but she was the one who led Marie into it a woman it was easier

What became of the property at Le Bouset after their death

I told you three years he outlived her, when he died the property passed to a nephew he carried out fresh alterations he didn't want to be reminded of them the house has changed completely it appears

You say there was a farm

Yes and some farmers they'd really chosen the right folk to be left in peace it was no good talking to people like that neither Marie nor I liked their company

Is it through the Emmerands that you got to know your gentlemen

Yes when I didn't want to stay on they told me to come to them

Before you went to the Emmerands had you already had a post

With Monsieur d'Eterville it was at his place I learnt my job I got married the year I left him and went to the Emmerands Marie was pregnant by then

Why did you leave Monsieur d'Eterville

Because I didn't like it there and I wanted to get married and it was impossible to stay at his place

Used he also to converse with the dead

I only found out when I went to the Emmerands that's why he used to go there

Say something about Monsieur d'Eterville

He was a difficult man to get on with he couldn't stand the slightest sound even a light switch would wake him in the morning, I used to have to start my work with a petrol lamp that I trailed round from room to room I used to do all the work except the cooking and often when I was waiting at table he'd suddenly wave me away he'd want to be alone, afterwards I realised it was his revelations

Used he to entertain

Usually on Sunday evenings and Wednesdays but he didn't get up to these tricks with the others in his own home

Who did he entertain

The Emmerands and the Flammards and sometimes my gentlemen that's where I first saw them, and old ladies like

Madame Tocsin and the Marquise de Nutre one of my gentlemen's relatives she's dead now
   Who was this Marquise
   One of my gentlemen's relatives I just said
   Where did she live
   At Nutre of course
   Where's that
   Further on than Le Bouset along the little lane you can get there on the main road too it's after Agapa in the direction of Douves, Madame de Nutre used to arrive about seven in her brougham she never wanted to buy a car, in winter those machines it's asking to catch your death though that's what she died of anyway a chill, I can still see her stepping out of her boneshaker Brindon the coachman would go and open the door for her she'd be buried beneath her rugs he'd give her his arm or Monsieur would and as soon as she reached the drawing-room she'd sit down in the yellow armchair and say Fernand I'm played out, that meant she wanted her port straightaway but it didn't do for it to be ready served which is what I did once she said to me do you take me for a tippler, everything had to be done properly but I must confess she was no laughing matter she was more likely to make our blood run cold she was really high-class only removed her gloves to go into dinner and put them on again immediately after, she used to call her bag her ridicule that's the old name for it she talked of nothing but her estate and the trouble she had with her farmers, she loathed Mademoiselle Ariane said she was raving mad but they were family squabbles all these people loathe one another
   What's this story about her brougham
   It's not a story it's the truth in the provinces people were full of crazes about that time, a little horse-drawn vehicle my gentlemen sent to the museum when the Marquise died it was historical royalty had ridden in it, there was a coat of arms on the doors the coronet of Nutre they've repainted them at the museum

Who was Brindon

A good sort he used to come and eat in the kitchen with us and have a chat he'd travelled round a bit with his last employer he told us about the countries he'd seen, we used to put the horse in the stable with his peck of oats which Brindon brought, Clotho that was the horse's name a dappled grey I always called him Coco an old nag who passed on just after the Marquise

Madame de Nutre used she to go to the Emmerands'

No you couldn't shift her except for Monsieur d'Eterville and for the Ballaisons

She knew the Ballaisons

She was related

Did she entertain at Nutre

Yes it was really quite a to-do she used to send off paste-boards as they call them a month in advance but according to Monsieur d'Eterville and my gentlemen too it was a big bore for everyone nothing but old folk

Did you see her again at your employers'

Twice yes, the second time just before she died three days I think

Do you think she knew what d'Eterville went to the Emmerands' for

It was only at their place I found out, she's meant to have told him she'd never see him again if he carried on

Did d'Eterville go to Vaguemort

Yes I only found that out later too

Whereabouts is the farm in relation to the quarry

You want me to talk about *that* again

Answer

You know as well as I do

What makes you think that

He wouldn't have come just now if you hadn't known

Once again your imagination's leading you astray, answer

You haven't answered either
We don't know anything
Watch out
Answer
 He'll be back again he doesn't frighten me he won't get Marie he won't get the child I'll burn Vaguemort and myself with it if necessary
 Take it easy, whereabouts is the farm
 Make the sign of the Cross
 Does that put your mind at rest
 Yes
 Why don't you do it to drive him away in the night
 It doesn't work every time
 Answer, whereabouts is the farm
 Next to the quarry
 Give details
 There's no point if it's him you want me to talk about
 It's not about him it's the farm, answer
 They're all in the same sort of place you know as well as I do, with grass growing all round and an abandoned quarry holes inscriptions you can see them from here you can catch the smell
 Are there several of them in the district
 All on the borderline so we slip over the other side
 Why on the borderline
 In your head the borderline in your head what you know and what you don't know that's where it is
 Does Vaguemort exist outside your head
 In yours too
 Answer
 I don't want to
 Answer
 Vaguemort is at Vaguemort I told you near Le Bouset on the right of the little lane it's got to be burnt

Do you think Grance has got to be burnt too
Why not the whole district while you're about it
Who worked in the kitchen at d'Eterville's
Maurice Duparc he's still there
Have you seen him again since you gave up your post
Yes
Did you speak to him about the Emmerands' goings-on
As soon as I suspected I told him but he didn't believe me anyway he didn't care
Did you remain in contact with him
I went back to see him in the Emmerands' day afterwards we met at Julot's or at Le Cygne
Do you still see him
Hardly ever he doesn't go out much now
At the Emmerands' was there any other staff apart from yourself and your wife
No
Were your gentlemen's friends aware of what used to go on at the Emmerands'
Yes but for all of them it was a load of tripe once even the Duchess wanted to start turning my pedestal table they laughed themselves silly, my gentlemen never invited the Emmerands unless they were alone or with d'Eterville but not very often it was out of politeness they'd known one another a very long time I told you, I think Monsieur Emmerand had been in the same form as one of them
Where did Monsieur d'Eterville live
18 Cours Carin-Tonneau
What did he do
What do you mean what did he do
What were his occupations
He was in his study all day except when he went out for a walk he never stopped writing and he read a lot sometimes

he'd say to me I haven't done enough and he'd work all night
What did he write
I don't know
You never asked him
I said I'm not curious
You never had to put his papers in order, tidy up his desk
Yes but he locked his writings up
The cook didn't know either
No but I'm willing to bet it was his revelations he must have had quite a number just imagine to write like that, when I take two hours to write three lines Marthe was always pulling my leg
Who were the Emmerands' farmers
Clots I tell you you couldn't say a word to them they got everything all wrong, Marie used to try at first but every time you chatted to her the woman always used to say p'raps it is p'raps it isn't and he was the same when they'd finished their work they'd both sit there on the bench their mouths open wide not doing a thing
Were they good at their work
There wasn't anything complicated there was the garden to keep up not many crops and no livestock except in the farmyard, they kept geese
Did Monsieur Emmerand do any gardening
He was mad about concrete he used to put it everywhere little walls round the vegetable patches, concrete rafts under the lean-to's and round the water pump and even a whole path as far as the gates, he didn't know how to go about it he was always having to start again it would keep him busy till five o'clock then he'd read in his room
And Madame Emmerand
She didn't do anything but read and go for walks she had a little dog she was training like a circus dog he knew how to open the doors and dance and what's more he'd eat all the sugar in the

cupboards, how many times did I have to put it in a different place Jimmy would find it even on top of a wardrobe he'd climb anything like a cat, our little Claude had a lot of fun with him they were inseparable, the dog used to go with him to school and went to fetch him at exactly the right time when I think about all that it's like twisting a knife in the wound the easy life we led had lulled me right off to sleep, asleep I was yes and I couldn't wake myself up it would seem that any happiness you find ought to be thrown right off before it smothers you you can't make a move any more you look at your wife and your child and you're powerless to do anything

Did your boy go to school alone

No there were two or three from Le Bouset who made the journey together as far as Sirancy, one was Popaul who was bigger it set our minds at rest nothing ever happened to them

How far were you from Sirancy

Two kilometres on foot we were just outside the hamlet about half a mile, the first year he went he was six Marie went with him at first then she let him go off with the others there wasn't any danger

Who were these friends of the Emmerands who used to come in the evenings

Ordinary people like the Lemoves relations of the former manageress of Le Chasseur and the Flammards and Madame Tocsin they used to meet at d'Eterville's too

Why do you think the seances only took place at the Emmerands'

I don't know according to Marthe some places are more propitious than others and Le Bouset being isolated nobody or shall we say not so many people could be suspicious whereas at Sirancy it would have got around at once

Did Monsieur d'Eterville live alone

He had his sister Rue de Jivry who used to come and see him

almost every day, a poor old spinster so deformed you'd wonder how she could get about it took her a quarter of an hour to come round

Was she entertained by the Emmerands

No she only saw her brother she was another who used to read a lot too I think, she used to read what he wrote I've often seen her with his manuscripts on the sofa and when she stayed to dinner they must have talked about it but never a word in front of me

You still had your hearing at that time

Yes

So you think she was perfectly well aware of her brother's goings-on

I'm sure she was yes but she didn't give the same impression as the others there was something rather disgusting about them rather I can't find the word yes disgusting when they were together even on their own, something that set them apart which didn't inspire confidence but not her as if she was outside it all and looked on him as a child she must have been good which is unusual with people deformed like that, she died in hospital the same year as our boy

Explain where the Rue de Jivry is again

At the end of the Rue du Poisson-Pêcheur it runs between the Rue du Savon and the Grands-Traversots

Where did your impressions of d'Eterville's sister come from

Where did they come from

Yes are you sure you never heard her talk about these things

Positive I can't see why I wouldn't say so if I had

Apart from his sister and his friends d'Eterville didn't see anyone

No

Who were the Flammards

He was a business agent he had his office Rue Chavirat not far from the Fortuna it's not a very respectable profession, I know one or two who are gnashing their teeth to think they went to him you only find out later that their little tips aren't straight and the commission he used to tack on I ask you, as for her he quite simply picked her off the street but she knew how to set about pleasing people, d'Eterville thought she had all the virtues even the Marquise fell under her spell and that's what I call the limit she got all she wanted by flattery but she was never invited to Nutre I mean to say

Do you think d'Eterville was running after her

Hard on her heels yes

Explain

It seems clear enough to me even Flammard was in the know but he didn't want to lose his contacts, to be entertained by d'Eterville that was something where business was concerned it must have lasted a good year she used to come in the afternoon and they'd do it with the port on the divan in the drawing-room, what did they take me for a half-wit he told me she was interested in his writing but those stains on the divan beg pardon they might just as well have gone upstairs

Did they go on seeing each other after that year

Yes he always hoped it would start up again some day or other, she'd found a Mexican who was meant to be going back home and in the end he settled down here mind you a woman like her wouldn't be fussy about keeping the two of them going but I suppose d'Eterville couldn't give her enough, and physically as they say he wasn't very appetising anyway Maurice used to call him the ram he smelt so strong

Did he have any other affairs

Before the Flammard woman he'd been six years with Raymonde Guersec an assistant in the toy shop in the Rue Atitré she finished up getting married, and before that I don't know I wasn't there

And after
He didn't take up with anyone again once a week he used to go to the Balançoire
Is that a bawdy house
It was
Do you know why d'Eterville and Madame Flammard didn't go up to the bedroom
I've often wondered, perhaps because it started in the winter there was an open fire to remind them or him at least, but according to Maurice there are some people it excites them to do it not in the proper place and perhaps she didn't want to go up either and for him to get undressed
You know that he didn't undress
I saw them from the garden once they hadn't pulled the curtain as I was passing I saw them mind you it may have been the only time he didn't undress I was intrigued I stayed there, at moments like that people aren't so aware of things
What did you see
What I told you
Give details
It's not the sort of thing you can talk about
Give details you must
Oh well he was sitting on the divan and she was doing it to him just like that
That's all you saw
I don't see the need to
Do you think we're interrogating you for fun, tell us everything you saw
She knelt down in front of him and that's the way she finished him off
And did he go up to his room with Raymonde Guersec
Yes
How many times did she come in a week

Monday and Thursday and sometimes Saturday

Did you catch them at it too

No, only when you listened at the door you could hear the two of them, Maurice it used to get him quite excited and he used to yes every time he used to listen

And he used to what

He was excited

What did he do

What a man may do when he's excited and alone

And you joined in this exhibition

I had no need for that I had my girl-friend

You had a girl-friend

After all I was twenty

Who was she

Ninette Lapache

Why didn't you marry her

The questions you ask because I didn't want to

Did she marry

Yes Ernest Plantin the grocer in the Rue du Cordon, sometimes, when I see her again I say to myself Heavens age doesn't do much for your looks

Why did d'Eterville have an unpleasant smell, didn't he wash himself

Oh yes two baths a week not always so many he had eczema but above all he had one of those skins that have a strong smell it happens sometimes, I had it once with my feet though I used to wash them every Saturday but I couldn't get rid of the smell I used to dab them with pure alcohol it's good for perspiration mind you d'Eterville wasn't aware of his smell it was us and the Flammard woman of course

Why did you say d'Eterville didn't keep company with anyone except his sister and his friends

Because sentimental questions are personal

You were a lot more reticent about such questions with regard to your employers, why

Because by going on so you pushed me into it but anyway with my gentlemen it's not the same

Why

Because

Answer

Because it's not the same people don't understand anything yet you're meant to tell the truth and it's not easy so it's better to say nothing

Why not

Because things of that sort I realise they're this way or that way even if it's difficult to talk about them they're true and only concern the people who do them, and you've got them mixed up with morality that's what's really dirty and I don't want to discuss it with you because I don't know you

Does it matter to you so much all of a sudden the good opinion we might have of your employers

It's not that it's because of the truth I've just told you it's too difficult, if I've seemed prudish or let's say if I *am* I can't do anything about it now we've got all these barriers in our head and your questions don't help me to get rid of them, it all needs a lot of thought and you won't get me on that subject again

In other words the details you're giving about d'Eterville you refuse to give about your employers

I repeat you pushed me into it and I repeat if people can't understand one another it's because of folk like you who don't want to understand and who get their morality all mixed up in things where it's no business to be

If you're so sure that's not what morality is why do you refuse to talk about your employers without fear or favour

I *am* without fear or favour they can do whatever they like and so can you and everyone else, what I *don't* want is to talk any old how about things that don't concern me and besides if you really want to know I never caught my gentlemen out at anything, I wasn't twenty any more and none of that was of much interest to me

You admit having been fairly curious when you were young

If you can call that curiosity it's more like your blood pumping you up

So it's not just chance that led you to catch d'Eterville and his mistress

If you start talking about chance there's no end to it it's impossible to know what pushes you this way or that way especially when you're young one day you stumble on something and that's that, I haven't any book-learning but when it comes to chance or love or the way you behave with people at a certain time in your life ideas just come to you you don't need to go out and look for them, they come and install themselves without warning they're yours and when you come to think of it they've got nothing to do with what so-called respectable people would like you to believe, that's what I mean by my meditation everything slowly loses its importance I mean it doesn't torment you any more it's life that's important, the older you get the more you grow aware of things that can't be explained and you can take my word I'm not talking for the sake of talking if you gave any serious thought to things you wouldn't be pestering me for details like flies round a carcass

Your change of attitude is surprising, how do you explain it

What change

These humanitarian feelings all of a sudden

I don't know whether I'm humanitarian but I do know I haven't changed

You seemed ready enough to criticise up till now

I criticise what I have to criticise and I'll go on doing so that's my right

Who was Madame Tocsin

The widow of a General she's still alive she's past ninety, she's bed-ridden she can't move and she does her job there if you'll pardon the expression every time her maid tells her you could have rung for me before but when the old woman rings it's too late, her maid is Mademoiselle Germaine she knows Marthe quite well she used to come and tell her sometimes that she was fed up wiping her clean she doesn't feel like doing the cooking afterwards, it's sad and funny both at the same time like the story of the gentleman in the inn comes a moment when he wants to go to the toilet the innkeeper explains to him where it is in the courtyard and a minute later the gentleman comes back saying it's impossible to take his trousers down in there there are too many flies, and the innkeeper says wait half an hour it's too early at midday they're all in the kitchen

So Madame Tocsin was in her sixties in d'Eterville's time

That's right yes ninety take away ten eighty take away ten seventy take away ten sixty that's it, she was a friend of the Marquise one of the gentry when she was a girl she had estates in Brittany where she used to go in the summer, in the winter she lived in the Rue Evangéline-Vouache one day I had to accompany her home it was worse than a museum there was such a clutter there was hardly room to move she pointed out they were souvenirs of her late husband, the kind of thing that comes from Algeria or Tunisia handbags pieces of material daggers cushions drums coffee-pots even a horse's saddle, all higgledy-piggledy she wouldn't touch a thing they hadn't been disturbed since the General's time and they must be there still unless Mademoiselle Germaine has had a clear-out now her mistress is bed-ridden

Did you by any chance ever go to the Marquise de Nutre's place

Yes once she asked me to go as an extra for a party

Describe her house

It's not a house it's a château though it hasn't any towers still it's called the Château de Nutre, it's not as old as Bonne-Mesure or Sirancy the original one was destroyed at the Revolution and this one reconstructed later after the style I think of the one built for Antoinette Trianon, there's only one storey above the ground floor entirely made up of reception rooms it's almost as big as my gentlemen's and all panelled light grey if I remember, there were several chimney-pieces and some fine furniture like the little armchair by the staircase at my gentlemen's and all light and airy yes that's what I remember about it, pale blue carpets and curtains and chandeliers with the candles lit there wasn't a single electric lamp I don't think there was even electricity at all, in the kitchen we had to work with a petrol lamp that's right it all went with the style of the Marquise, that evening she was even more made-up than usual her cheeks obviously rouged which looked funny on her old face it seems it was the fashion once upon a time, the party was after dinner they'd drunk some champagne first and some old maid no longer very young started to sing what was her name she had a low-cut dress over her scraggy shoulders and an old-fashioned hair-do a black ribbon round her head to fasten the bun, what was her name Croissant Croissy it'll come back she sang accompanied on the piano not a real piano a tiny little clackachord as it's called it sounds like a musical box and everyone listened as if they were in church, now I'm talking about it you see it's funny how things come back words release your memories Monsieur d'Eterville was next to La Ballaison she was young at that time, he had his eyes glued to her bosom and I think he was playing footy with her in the front row they were sitting I thought to myself what a nerve, after all Ballaison was at the back with my gentlemen or perhaps they weren't there, yes they were and the General's wife and some others I don't remember any more God how far away it all is now but that singer Coissat that's it, Mademoiselle Coissat that's the name Coissat I can see her now holding a handkerchief between her hands that's the way people sing in society and her voice has stayed in my mind like my bells and my chimes

Do you remember who she was this Demoiselle Coissat

She must have been a relative just a minute of the General's wife I think I'm not quite sure but she used to sing all over the place that I do remember, at the Ballaisons' I saw her too they had a real piano

Had Pernette started working for the Ballaisons then

By Jove I believe she had yes she was there by then poor girl she'd just gone there probably she must have been twenty

Who accompanied Mademoiselle Coissat at the clavichord

Clavichord there you are what am I talking about with my clackachord clavichord, who accompanied her well as for that La Ballaison perhaps but no because she was sitting in front who was it *I* don't know perhaps the Marquise, yes it was the Marquise she had a white shawl over her shoulders a white shawl with black birds on it who'd have thought I'd remember that, a white shawl that's it with

Did the recital come at the end of the evening

No there was supper as there always was at Madame de Nutre's, I was very young then it was the first time I'd served a supper it's not made up like a dinner it's all nothing but delicacies, liver pâté and stuff like that and caviar I remember it was a great luxury all the rage at the time she always had it at her place d'Eterville used to say, she sent for it from Douves from Demaison's that's where I always used to order it for my gentlemen, caviar what do *you* think of it *I* don't like it it's like cod liver oil anyway that supper I served for the first time, d'Eterville dropped me a hint now and then for the things I was forgetting and wait just a minute there was a moment when the Marquise dropped something her pince-nez or her lorgnette, was she the one who had a lorgnette or the Dowager d'Aircule no the Marquise had a lorgnette I rushed forward to pick it up under the table, d'Eterville told me afterwards that everything had to be done more sedately the Marquise said thank you my man but looked the other way, she never looked at the people she was talking to except her intimate friends I mean she didn't look at the servants or people she didn't know or who didn't belong to her world, that often struck me it seems to me it's the least you can do to be polite when you're meant to be well brought-up but it doesn't appear so

Who was the Dowager d'Aircule

Another old lady she came back to me just like that when I was talking she lived in the Rue Tétin on the corner of the Boulevard an old house like the Ballaisons', she was worth a fortune and lived like a pauper by what people said, her heirs had the house done up from top to bottom all the time I seem to be saying the same thing about old people dying and houses being done up

Do you remember who else there was at this party

Old memories like that does it matter

Try to remember

It's difficult when you try, it comes back better when you're talking

Go on about the supper

That's just it I don't remember any more

Come on now there was the Marquise the Ballaisons the Dowager your employers the General's wife Mademoiselle Coissat, who else

Longuepie how stupid of me Longuepie of course he still wasn't married then and the lady he used to go out with at the time Madame Madame what was her name a widow very young with black hair

So there weren't only old people there

Yes most of them were old that's why I forgot, I've seen the others a lot more often or I still see them now

Were there a great many guests

About fifty people when she entertained it was by the bus load

Try to remember their names

I should have to think back over those who used to come to my gentlemen's that would be easier wait, there was an old man I saw at their place at the start but that was a good bit later twenty years almost during the Marquise's time he can't have been so old, it's no good I'll never remember

Who was this old man

My gentlemen used to call him Architruc he was sort of loony there's no other word he called himself the king of somewhere or other or he'd been king once, Marthe thought he was mad and his servant too who went with him on his travels so-called but without a penny to his name where could he travel to, he used to call him his minister of state to my mind he must have been one of those old Russians you remember they were all princes of something, my gentlemen let him think they believed it yes I remember him and his minister they must have kicked the bucket not long after, my gentlemen never heard any more of them

What age might they have been

They're ageless people like that

And you think the master was an intimate friend of the Marquise

I've got an idea yes unless I'm mixing him up with someone else who d'Eterville used to call the Wandering Jew, he had a mania for travelling too but he *had* taken a few trips I did see him at the Emmerands' but it's all vague what can you expect I had no reason to take much interest, all that's from another life as my mother used to say it doesn't take long to bury us

So there were other people went to the Emmerands' apart from those you mentioned

Yes but not for their seances they used to see other people separately, people passing through strangers but I've no wish to talk about them again

What happened to the Château de Nutre after the Marquise died

It was left to her daughter Madame Grossbirke the wife of a

German who came to take the waters, she'd gone back with him and only returned to the district when her mother died
  What do you know about these Grossbirkes
  They weren't in my gentlemen's circle but I used to know their servant fellow called Johann he used to come and see Marthe he even made propositions to her imagine that
  What was so surprising about that
  Surprising nothing but I mean to say
  You mean to say what
  She had a narrow squeak
  What happened
  Here we go again there's no end to it
  Answer
  He was a killer
  A killer you say
  He's what I call a killer a type who's chopped up three people
  Who, in what circumstances
  It started four years ago while the Grossbirkes were in Germany, a girl from Les Vernes Marceline Fouaron went missing from the village and they didn't start a search for her instead the police were satisfied with the explanations given by the parents of her fiancé Gilbert Stoffel, they said Marceline had followed him to Austria where they'd come from they'd been settled in the district for about ten years and Gilbert had never got used to it he used to go about with Marceline everyone knew that's why the police were satisfied with the explanation, of course old Mother Fouaron said that wasn't good enough for *her* she wanted to know where her daughter was but in the end the Stoffels calmed her down too by saying they'd had letters from Gilbert they were both in good health and married, old Mother Fouaron wasn't particularly surprised her daughter had told her nothing they hadn't been on good terms since Marceline started going out with Gilbert and to cut a long story short it wasn't talked of

again until the following year when a girl went missing from Le Rouget I mean the village of Le Rouget, there wasn't even an enquiry her parents had received a letter from a fellow called Karas who they used to take as a lodger during the holidays with his sister Nadine, it said in the letter he'd asked Paulette to join him in his own country he was in love with her and he'd married her she was even expecting a child, which the Truets had already found out a month before their daughter disappeared but without suspecting it was Karas for the very good reason that while he was there on holiday with them Paulette had gone harvesting near Vériville, the Truets thought she'd got herself in trouble while she was there and didn't want to say and yet it was still possible it might have been Karas the father because Paulette had seen him two days before she went harvesting, and when I say it was at that time the first business was talked about again I mean just by Marthe and me and Pernette and a few others like Pompom people didn't really put two and two together, even old Mother Fouaron felt almost relieved when she found out her daughter wasn't the only one to have left the district in a hurry but we said to ourselves it wasn't normal nothing like that had happened before, I admit there are sometimes epidermics that suddenly affect young people all at once they all want to do the same thing that's what Pompom thought but still I was suspicious because of the time of year it was the same, so it was in November while the Grossbirkes were in Germany but we only found that out later I mean we only made the connection later we had no reason to suspect Johann, until two years ago when the same thing happened at Sirancy this time Doucette's daughter who didn't come home from work one evening, her father's the worrying type he was very fond of his daughter being a widower and he went to the police about two o'clock in the morning after almost combing the village, he woke up Lorduz who says but I saw Aimée about eleven o'clock at Nutre she didn't see me she was making for the Château I thought to myself she's going to see Johann as his employers are away for some job she's meant to do for them, I should explain she was a seamstress-dressmaker by profession she'd done some work for Madame Grossbirke before curtains foot-rugs that sort of thing, anyway Doucette asks him to go with him to the Château they take the motor-bike they arrive at Nutre they ring the bell and after a while Johann comes to let them in he tells them he hasn't seen Aimée and suggests going to the village with them to have a look round, off they go and find nothing so that

Cut it short

So that next day the police take up the search and a week later they dug up their far-from-inviting treasure-trove it was Aimée with her throat cut in the cellar and already buried next to the two others

And all this was Johann's good work

The last time yes he was on his own but for Marceline he was with Stoffel and for Paulette with Karas

Did Stoffel and Karas really play a part in it, it wasn't blackmail

No they were both involved

So Stoffel was still there for the murder of Paulette

No I mean each of them was involved in his own affair, Stoffel with Marceline and Karas with Paulette

Explain the case of Marceline, who was she

The Vernes girl I told you she worked at Buchet the grocer's she was left with only her mother and she started to go out with Stoffel she must have been twenty-seven or twenty-eight it lasted two years maybe, Johann knew all about the local love-affairs he told us quite a bit we thought he was joking it was later we found out he was a maniac homsessed as they say, so he made up to Stoffel and it appears he told him it was more exciting to do it with a girl that was dead or dying Stoffel must have been round the bend to believe him and get caught up in it, they planned it for November when the Grossbirkes were in Germany they always used to go off at the start of October till March and one evening Stoffel took Marceline to Nutre she never suspected a thing as you can imagine, all this we learned from the papers last year at the trial and they cut her throat and they did it one after the other on top of her while she was bleeding to death, then they buried her and Stoffel sloped off to Austria but his parents found out why it was, Johann paid them a nice fat sum so they'd say they were getting letters he'd saved up some money several millions imagine that a servant, he'd been running some racket in his own country

Did it come out at the trial he'd already gone in for these macabre experiments in his homeland

No, only that he'd been trafficking in a number of things to get money, he was forty-eight when he went into service with the Grossbirkes it was then these ideas came to him and he couldn't get them out of his head

Did the Stoffels really get letters from their son

Yes it was Johann who had told him to write they had the first at the end of November and the second at Christmas

And Madame Fouaron was satisfied with this explanation

I told you she was

Did the Stoffels know Marceline was buried in the cellars at the Château

No, only that Gilbert had killed her

Tell about the Truet business

Same thing, Johann knew Paulette was going out with a lad from Hottencourt Jules Martino he'd caught them together one day in the woods but he didn't approach Martino as he had Stoffel, he got Karas involved who'd been coming on holiday for two years with his sister to the Truets', they were a couple of young foreigners of good family they used to spend a fortnight at Le Rouget on their way back from the seaside, they'd discovered the Truets took lodgers the first year they came you'll ask me why they chose such a God-forsaken spot lost in the mountains I've no idea, and why they went back the following year

They didn't stay in town or at Sirancy before going up to Le Rouget

The first time yes for a week in the Hôtel du Chasseur but not the second time, mind you they'd a very nice car and they could come into town when they felt like it

When did Johann make contact with Karas

At the beginning of his stay at Le Rouget end of October

How is it that Karas and his sister took their holidays in the mountains at that time of year

That's exactly what we wondered it's horribly cold and no snow even, it seems it's the time they liked best it was a change, even the sea they liked better in the autumn

Did Karas's sister know about the crime her brother committed

She found out just before they left they took the plane the next day

Was Johann really alone when he had his final fling

I told you yes

When did the trial take place

Last year at the same season

At the law courts in town

Yes

What was Johann's attitude during the hearing

He didn't say a word the two days I was there it was his counsel who spoke, he said Johann wasn't responsible there were some doctors experts to read their reports that he wasn't normal I saw it in the paper later but he was sentenced to death all the same so was Stoffel the police had had him brought back as soon as they discovered Aimée, his counsel said he was a hypnotic case there was an expert to say Johann was hypnotic too but it didn't do any good

And Karas

He did himself to death when he found out they were looking for him but his sister was there she was acquitted and Stoffel's parents sentenced to prison, Marthe used to say the whole pack of them there was nothing to choose between them and d'Eterville was no different either

Why d'Eterville, was he charged too

No but the Emmerands' goings-on came up for an airing as well *he* had to answer, as they'd departed this world

Why the Emmerands, used they to know Johann

Yes

How

It's all old history

Answer

Because Johann was with them before he went to the Grossbirkes

Why didn't you say so

It didn't occur to me

Was he aware of his employers' practices

Yes

Say what you know

Yes he was aware all right yes he knew everything he was a filthy German when Marie used to talk to him I could have hit her

How do you mean when Marie used to talk to him

When she used to talk to him outside our duties

So he was with the Emmerands at the same time as you

Yes

Why did you say you were alone you and your wife working for them

Because I didn't want to talk about him just then

Why did you see him again afterwards if you detested him

I said he used to come and see Marthe he used to try and get her too

Had he tried with your wife
Yes and a lot of good it did him
Did it by any chance come out at the trial that the Emmerands' practices had something to do with his taste for necrophilia
What's that
His liking for dead women
That's what his counsel put forward saying it had upset the balance of his mind but he wasn't successful they're two different things it appears but Marthe's right all these psychos are tarred with the same brush
Were the Grossbirkes at the trial
Yes to give evidence as to his character they said Johann had always given them satisfaction
Who were the experts
Two doctors specialists from Douves I've forgotten their names, one fat one with glasses and a small one who gesticulated Suroni yes or Surino something like that
Any other doctors
The ones who made out the report how they found Aimée and the remains of the two others it was in the paper too enough to make you sick
Whereabouts is the village of Le Rouget
In the valley of Ensemeur which links up with Le Chanchèze at the other end it's fifteen hundred feet up
Who were the Karases
Young foreigners I told you
From what country, what age
He was twenty-seven she twenty-five they were Judoslavs
Did anyone discover the reason why they used to take their holidays together
Why just to be together I suppose
Nothing else
I don't know what you're getting at

Some reason which might have led them to be more than brother and sister for example

That they went to bed together, I've no idea about that

Nothing of the sort came up at the trial

No Nadine said she was on holiday with her brother and he'd told her about the crime before they left she didn't dare say anything, she wept a great deal her photo was in the Echo the jurymen felt sorry for her and the Truets said she was very correct paying regularly, or rather it was Nadine's counsel who asked them the question

Was it established whether the child Paulette was expecting was Martino's or Karas's

It was Martino he said he was sure he was the father, Paulette had never slept with Karas and that's what Nadine said too she knew all about her brother's love-affairs and she didn't hide it

Who did Paulette go harvesting for at Vériville

Emmanuel Moigneau he gave evidence that Paulette was very reliable and a good worker

Who was this father Doucette

The mechanic in the Rue Crosse-Besogne he's had nothing but bad luck in his life his first wife died a year after their wedding and the second who brought him Aimée was run over by the coach slap in front of the post office five years ago

Was Aimée Doucette going out with anyone

Now we know Johann was homsessed we've no more reason to believe what he said

What did he say

That she used to sleep with everyone even with Grossbirke, he said she used to go to the Fortuna and the Chasseur on Saturdays and Sundays for a drink before dinner he's meant to have seen her with God knows how many men, I'm sure it wasn't true in any case I never saw her with anyone and always simply dressed not at all the same type as the others there's no mistaking them

What others

The girls who go with the visitors they have a new one every season my mother would have called them *cocottes* that's the word, come to that I'd rather have a girl like Viviane you know where you are you see with her she doesn't put on airs when she's with someone she gets on with the job flat out as they say, not like those little tarts girls you knew when they were born they'd have you on for all they're worth, at least Viviane doesn't stick with anyone ships that pass in the night isn't that more

Was it known why Aimée came to be at Nutre at eleven o'clock in the evening

Yes it was Lorduz who got it right she had to take some measurements for the curtains in an upstairs bedroom we found that out from Odile, she'd had a meal with her in town after work and she'd borrowed her bicycle to go to Nutre and back, she'd intended to catch the last bus for Sirancy Odile said she wanted these measurements, as she meant to work the next day which was Saturday she just had time to go to Nutre and back before the last bus a conscientious girl like that is she the type that drinks before dinner, her father was too late when he saw the note she'd left for him in the kitchen saying I'm having a meal with Odile don't worry the counsel read it, Marthe said it made quite an impression hearing the voice as you might say of the dead girl afterwards

Who is this Odile

A friend of Aimée's who works at Jasmin's too

And Jasmin

The bedding shop Rue des Chevaux-de-Luge

Didn't you say the first crime took place four years ago

Yes

And that Emmerand died three years ago

Yes

So Johann still hadn't gone to the Grossbirkes

He left Emmerand when his wife died six years ago

Did Emmerand carry on with his practices after his wife died

I should think it's likely yes

It didn't come out at the trial that he might have taken part in the first crime

No except that the lawyer said the Emmerands had twisted Johann's mind but when it comes to understanding all the ins and outs I tell you these psychos

Didn't you say Johann had been running some racket in his own country to have made such a pile before he went into service

Yes I said that

How long did he stay in service with the Emmerands

He arrived five years after us

So as you were there ten years he was there with you five years

Yes

Plus five years as Madame Emmerand died six years ago and you left your gentlemen going on a year

How do you mean

Five years with you and five years without you that makes ten

That makes ten yes

As the first crime took place four years ago and Johann left the Emmerands six years ago he'd been with the Grossbirkes two years when he murdered Marceline

Two years I think yes

What do you mean you think

All these calculations, for me you know

And yet it's clear that ten years plus two years makes twelve years of service for Johann

Twelve years yes that's right

So, twelve years before going into service he had piled up several millions you said

Several millions yes

What reason did his counsel give for this to say the least peculiar behaviour
I don't remember
Could it not be considered that the fact of going into other people's service with savings to the tune of several millions already suggested something abnormal in his conduct
I understand you mean he was already round the bend before that it's quite possible that is yes
Did nothing come out at the trial to suggest he might have earned these millions not before but afterwards partly at least, in other words that he went on trafficking while he was in service
I don't remember them mentioning it
Did the Emmerands never have discussions about money while you were with them
Yes he had some trouble he was always going away on business
Where did he go
To Germany I think
Didn't Monsieur Flammard discuss money matters with your employers outside their spiritualist meetings
Yes, I never understood a word
Could you remember any particular names that came up in their conversations
Even if I did hear better then than now I didn't listen at doors
When they discussed money matters it wasn't in front of you
No
How do you know then
Marie used to tell me
She used to be present at these conversations
I've no idea I tell you she was more intelligent than me she used to grasp things
Answer the question, was she present at these conversations
She never told me
But you knew she was present at their spiritualist meetings

Yes

Couldn't financial matters have come up during these seances

I've no idea

The business Flammard carried on wasn't quite above board you said

Yes I did say that

How did you know

Because that's what people said and we talked about it with Maurice at d'Eterville's

Do you think if Maurice wasn't interested in questions of spiritualism he could on occasion have served as confidant to d'Eterville in matters concerning finance

He talked to him that's all I know

Do you think d'Eterville apart from his indulgence in spiritualism could be mixed up in Flammard's shady business transactions

How should I know

Didn't you say that Flammard's complaisance concerning his wife's liaison with d'Eterville had a financial motive

I said d'Eterville was the right person to know in other people's eyes when it came to business

What did d'Eterville talk about with his guests if he wasn't engaged in spiritualism

This and that the sort of things one talks about

Did Maurice know

He made out he knew everything but there was another one he was psych I mean he was letting it go to his head he thought he was so important and all because Monsieur occasionally asked him to accompany him to the Emmerands'

Did he accompany him there

Sometimes yes

Did you see him again at the Emmerands' later

Yes sometimes

Who were these Lemoves who were entertained by the Emmerands

He was a business agent also related to the former manageress of the Chasseur I told you

Talk about the Lemoves

What can you say about them just people like their friends people like anyone else all this to me now you know

Answer

He still has his office in town Avenue des Africains not far from the Casino, it seems he's turned over a new leaf if you know what that means but people only want to believe what they're told so long as it suits them, he keeps up his contacts perhaps because of her I've never known what to think Marthe used to say she had strings to pull in the police force a sergeant or even better she wasn't much to look at either, they've got two sons who must be between twenty-five and thirty twins, both of them settled at Douves one's a vet for animals the second's in chemistry I think they're always being mistaken one for the other even my gentlemen used to mix them up sometimes when they came but I haven't seen them for ages since then, all the time you're asking me questions it seems to me I'm back in the café on my chair as if I was talking about something else something else somewhere else I'm not here any more, we could invent other people no matter who yes make them say anything we liked it would be just like what happened between the real ones all of them in our heads they're dead, your questions give me the impression we're forcing them to speak but mistakes are not important they'd talk just the same whether it's true or false and we'll still be in the same boat when other people ask questions about us, someone will answer them this or that it won't make any difference our life will have been our own and no-one can do anything about it other people I mean, and whether you answer them yes or no the result will be the same they'll mix you up with me I'll be the one who asks the

questions and you'll do the answering true or false what does it matter
 You mean you're not making any effort to be objective
 What's that
 Any effort to tell the truth
 Yes I am on the contrary I am making an effort I'm even trying too hard and the truth lies to one side, in what I don't know any more or what I don't know yet or what you forget to ask me and there we are going off into things that we're sure are true because of our efforts I'm finding it less tiring all the time but the truth has been left a long way behind it was just where we didn't expect it, perhaps because it was too simple and we've been racking our brains to say something different because of our efforts and we get left with a fine mess that has nothing to do with the truth and perhaps that's what our life is, like a sort of boxroom we lumber up with things we don't want any more we say they're our memories it's helped me to get where I am and twenty years later we turn them out again and we've no longer any idea what they mean, papers photos notes notes all those notes
 According to what you heard from your wife, what kind of business used Lemove to discuss with your employers
 I don't know I've forgotten I wasn't there neither was she
 Answer
 I can't remember now
 Try and remember
 Remember remember how can you remember you've done two or three things what you've seen won't amount to much more you keep barely the half of it in your head, those things in the past how can you remember you tell stories but someone in your head has changed them over the years they're not the same any more or they wouldn't still be there, when they happened you didn't try to remember them you had other things on your mind and when they come back to you ten twenty years later

they've been altered no-one would recognise them again you don't know who it is who's making them look like this, no they're not memories any more they're something you may have wanted misfortune you even want that without knowing and you run up against something here or there that could make it happen and it's later very much later that you notice it did happen it's there you have to call it a memory but it's not, if I think of Marie and our child in my head it's a misfortune but when I was with them I wasn't unhappy I thought to myself the little lad will grow up I had plans we'd have had our own house we wouldn't have gone on staying with other people, I've thought about all this I can't tell my memories any more they're not mine any more Marie and the child were happy so was I but I don't remember that any longer, I couldn't even tell you what time our boy used to get up I was up already I couldn't even tell you what he used to do except for his books, I couldn't even tell you what his voice was like I don't remember his voice any more or his face except for the photo I've forgotten the face of our child that's the misfortune you see he's not a part of life afterwards he's in our head which is poisoned with all that stuff people want us to call memories, what we ought to call memories is what we've got in front of us now yes what we've got in front of us, afterwards it's all over

Pull yourself together, say what you know about Madame Lemove

What are you trying to get at

Answer

I said what are you trying to get at how will you be better off for knowing what I can tell about Madame Lemove

Answer

No I won't answer I don't want to Madame Lemove is nothing there's nothing to say about her and you won't be any the wiser for making me talk about her, it's my turn to ask you what are you trying to find out what are you trying to get out of me, I only know bits and pieces I don't know the truth never shall and we'll die not knowing and all the people like you who are mad to find out other people's secrets they'll die first they'll wear themselves out, they don't know how to ask questions though they know how to plant the answers and that's not the way to ask

Well what's your secret then tell it

If I did have one that's not the way I'd tell it but I haven't don't worry I'm like one of those people who take their little troubles always the same ones off to the café to drink to make a secret for themselves, they haven't got one any more than you have they'd like to make one out of their petty little problems so they can really *be* something and they go on drinking till they've been found lying in a ditch a note in their pocket with goodbye written on, all of them all of them that's what they die of but is that a secret the same one everyone has no it's life my life and you know it because I've told you yet you go on carving me up

Who did you lose

Who did I lose why go on trying to fool me, who did I lose I told you and all the others how could I know their troubles their lives everything that goes on round us that we detest how could I know it was helping me as you might say to pass the time why no I thought I'll be rid of all that one of these days I'll be left in peace, well you see the only thing that stayed with me was that after all and now I don't pass the time any more and there's nothing to stop me jumping off the bridge, all the bad reasons you had to keep going were really the right ones and the ones you thought would drive them away were the wrong ones, so after that don't ask me again why

Answer, what do you know about Madame Lemove

And always Marthe and me we used to say later on, later on, but we must be mad what is it that blinkers us till the day our eyes are closed for good, even Marthe and her house she'll never succeed in getting it back again she'll have nothing but worry till the bitter end and the day she's able to move her things back in before she's had time to put one foot on the stairs she'll have dropped dead on the pavement

Answer, what do you know about Madame Lemove

It's like my gentlemen with all their la-di-da makes you wonder what they're after in life you'd think they're all right with their money and their friends but it's just the opposite, they couldn't be alone for one minute without getting the blues and they used to make plans really hare-brained schemes, plans for selling the house and buying another one somewhere else in order to start again start what again

For the last time what do you know about Madame Lemove

No that's not what the truth is it's not just waiting believe me the truth is having something in front of you you can't see because you've got something else to do, and loving your own folk that's what it is it's *not*-thinking about it and going to empty the chamber-pots and polishing the drawing-room and doing the garden and going back to your room in the evening whacked without even thinking of having your wife because by the time you think about it it's too late, all there's left to do is to make up memories that won't be the same ten years later, you've spanned a great chunk of your life it's ten years later already and you're wondering if it was a happy one and answering no and tormenting yourself already ten years later with what we've got left of these memories which aren't even ours any more, no the truth I think the truth is doing what you have to do without taking anything in and without asking for anything, as soon as you start asking you're ready for the cemetery and anyone not forgetting me who talks to you about happiness had better keep quiet so as not to kick the bucket for talking cuts life short as well we go on from one stage to the next and we can't tell which is the best, but to work without saying a word keeps you going quite steady and no-one will worry you much when you reach the end

You are required to say what you know about Madame Lemove

I told you she was the wife of a business agent

What was her name before she married

Lucie Golard

Who was she, who were these Golards

They're still in the world of the living don't worry she's two brothers and two sisters she must be about fifty, she married Lemove twenty-five years ago they've got three children, the Golards the old couple are dead that's where you get with all your questions, I'll answer you'll have more than you bargained for the old Golard couple had a delicatessen Rue Jules-Zéphirat they used to sell pig sausage sauerkraut mince balls

Don't take that tone of voice, answer as you did before

Meat balls black pudding bacon prepared dishes you only had to warm up, they were well known in the district in my day for Madame Golard's get-up she used to dress like a duchess all from Leroy's they nearly went bankrupt because of that they bought one of the first motor-cars they expanded the delicatessen to take in three shops and were talking of starting a trade union to cover the whole district all this for Madame Golard *he* had no ambition, they produced five children two boys and three girls Daniel Alexandre Lucie Dorothée and Patricia Golard, Daniel took over the delicatessen he whittled it down to just one shop as it used to be he married Gabrielle Monachou-Loblong he's got two children and one idiot a mongrel very good-natured it seems they're more lovable than the others but I still can't imagine you'd wish it on anyone, for a long time he was in a special school for mongrel idiots at Douves to try

Cut it short

Alexandre took the Dussoigne delicatessen off him that's in town Rue des Clous on the corner by the crossing of Les Oublies, he's a man about fifty-five with a black moustache two tiny

blue eyes or grey-blue shall we say a nose like a potato a chin
Once again don't take that tone of voice

A chin like a German's he married Sicilia Monachou-Loblong so he's the brother-in-law of his own brother Daniel, he's got four children Maxime Chantal Valérie and Ghislaine Golard normal all four of them and on the blond side if you can call that blond a sort of light tan a bit greyish, every morning his wife goes off with her maid to the market in the Place Karl-Marx except on Sundays when there isn't one and on Mondays she goes to the little market in the area of La Butte Rue Amorinz, since she gave up the cash-desk in the delicatessen they've got someone called Claudine Abatis who's connected to the former farmers from Nutre what can they be now those two in their seventies, they're both in the old people's home in Agapa which is in the Avenue de l'Hôtel de Ville at the far end the entrance is in the Rue Donneau number 24 or 26, well this Claudine

You're running more risks than you realise going on in that tone

You want details

About Madame Lemove

She's no more interesting than Claudine

Go on about Madame Lemove, her affair with the police officer

It's Marthe who used to say that I don't know his name a chap from the police station in the Rue des Tatoués in town, Lorduz is more or less under him I think

Whereabouts is the police station at Sirancy

It's the gendarmerie in the square next to the post office

Describe the square at Sirancy

I've done it already

Every building in detail

When you come along Chavirat first you have on your right the café Le Cygne with the other shop that makes the corner the former shoemaker's Chinze, it's a small shoeshop now set up by Topiron a branch of his firm in Agapa he's made a shop window in plastic and painted all the outside light grey, the house has two upper floors and a slate roof very steep it's old an irregular shape and follows the line of the street and the square if you see what I mean set further back let's say on the square side with green shutters, and Le Cygne has been repainted red they've left the old sign in wrought iron just painted it black it's a swan in a circle hanging from a bracket, Monnard's never made any alterations to his café I told you he lives over it three windows on the square, Madame Monnard always has flower-pots on her window sills and over them Cyrille lets a bedroom to Raviuz, the entrance to the upper floors is next to the café on the square a little passage rather dark the Monnards never use it as they have a staircase in the café that goes straight up to their rooms, next to this house there's another butting on to it higher and narrower with three upper floors the ground floor is raised up by two steps above the pavement it belongs to Philippard he doesn't live there he has tenants, it's well looked-after painted white with dark brown shutters and a tile roof not so steep as Le Cygne they repaired it about three years ago, on the first floor live the Gassets on the second Lucien Morenne and on the third the Jouvins Louis the brother of Emile, they've got four children they'd like Philippard to turn the attic into bedrooms for them which they'd let I don't know what Philippard will decide, then there's a space of between twenty and thirty yards before the Town Hall with an iron gate at the back separating the square from the garden of the Hôtel du Château which has a lot of little chestnut trees and tables underneath during the season, from the upper floors of Philippard's house they have a fine view over this garden but it's noisy in the evenings and all flood-lit like they do nowadays a green light beneath the trees, for me who knew this part in the old days it's unrecognisable it used to be a small yard where the blacksmith stored his material under a shed, all that's gone they've knocked down the walls and now the garden joins on to the one at the back of the Town Hall and stretches as far as the Rue du Pince-Bouc, well after Philippard there's the Town Hall it juts out quite a bit into the square it's historical since the seventeenth century it used to be the town house of Valère de Bonne-Mesure there's a plaque sixteen hundred and thirty-five to seventeen hundred and two over the door, the Mayor has a right to the flats on the second floor there are eight rooms and on the first floor the offices of the District Surveyor and on the ground floor offices too and the room you get married in Social Welfare's just on the right as you go in, the house-front on the square has four windows either side of the door and nine on the two floors above, as for the height of the ground floor it's almost raised up a storey by a flight of five steps and a balustrade in wrought iron curving round at either end like the main staircase at my gentlemen's, on the first floor over the door there's a balcony supported by two men with beards down to their thighs carved out of stone which has an iron guard-rail with little gilded suns, all the windows have the same iron-work as a safety-rail and over each one a carved head at the top in a triangle, on the ground floor men on the first floor women on the second angels and right over the whole front a big triangle they call that a peddermint with a bull's eye in the middle like the ones in the roof except that they're in dormers, the roof is slate not steep but when you're inside the loft seems very high you could make rooms in there anyway they're the archives as Pierre-André used to say, all the old records and papers that are not used any more they're insured for two million makes you wonder why when you think of it all those dead people most of them were country bumpkins they're hardly of any interest now, so on the other side there's the garden with a lawn and rose trees and a little fountain beneath an arbour seventeenth century which represents Diana patron saint of hunters she's got a crescent on her head as she was patron saint of the moon too, old Ma Bottu must think she's God-knows-who when she's knitting in her garden, she's grown honeysuckle along the back of the house which won't do it any good but they haven't got much longer at the Town Hall we can still do something about it, Pierre-André had his bedroom overlooking the garden on the first floor next to his office he used to say when he saw Madame Bottu on the terrace

Go on

There's the same number of windows if I remember over the garden as over the square, and in the roof one of the bull's eyes is a pigeon house you can see the pigeons going in and coming out and flying all round they make an awful mess on the steps but they're decorative as they say, there's a print at Plumets of the Town Hall just as it is now except for the steps a bit wider it seems where there are figures getting out of a four-horse carriage and a lady on the balcony, it must be a party at that Valère's as it's dated sixteen hundred and eighty-four Plumet says he won't sell it for less than a hundred thousand francs as it was done by a well-known painter, you can't see the houses at the side the trees in the garden block the view on the left but it appears the garden never went any further on that side there used to be a tilery demolished now, Plumet says it was the fashion in those days for painters not to be realistic in order to flatter people then they'd be more willing to buy their portraits or their house, well after the Town Hall there's the Impasse du Coulis which leads to Mademoiselle Eydouard's lodge an old woman who's still working she paints lampshades and plates for Ortez in the Rue du Velours-de-Paille, her father left her this lodge but she lives in poverty refusing to sell her little garden to the Town Hall which would make her some money, and on the left there's a garage and the entrance to the kitchen of the Pitut house the wine merchant's which is the corner house, and another entrance on the square as well it's a tiny little house an old timbered one with a pointed roof and an elaborate period gutter and a procession of little men carved under the eaves, the front door is no wider than that on the right of it you can still see where there used to be a small shop which has been walled up, Pitut has made a way through inside into the house next door which belongs to him as well, in the small one there's only a kitchen downstairs and a bedroom on the first floor and three minute windows, the other one's new painted pale yellow and two upper floors, four windows on each storey at the front and a tiled mansard roof with a large bay window he had put in recently for his son who wants to be an architect he's just started his studies at Douves he needs light for his work, his name is Raoul he says his father has ruined the little house by sticking the other one up against it he ought to have done his rebuilding further off but to young folk anything the old 'uns do is always wrong come to think of it, they can make as much fuss as they like their turn will come one day sometimes I wonder what our child would have blamed me for later on everything I expect, next butting on to the Pitut house there's a big modern one on the corner of the Rue du Savon, six floors plus the ground floor with the California cinema and the Co-op food shop on the square and on the Rue du Savon a watchmaker's and the tourist agency, the entrance is from the square with glass doors and a large hall in artificial marble there's not a single piece of local stone it's all in concrete and imitation people who live there complain about the noise it rebounds like a barrel, the flats were let before it was built but some people have left already though it's very comfortable inside small flats with fridge and rubbish shoot and under-floor heating, how many windows are there on the front wait a minute eight I think yes eight French windows, plus the small window on the right, and twelve over the Rue du Savon with a large balcony that runs all the way round on every floor and bits of the façade painted blue or yellow to look gay and a flat roof with television aerials, it's the most modern building in Sirancy there was a lot of bother when it was being put up but Bottu held out he wanted it to be done during his term of office, from those flats even on the third floor you've a view over the whole country on the Rouget side as far as Saint-Porvan on the left and beyond Le Bérouse on the right, and from the fifth floor you can see as far as Grance on the other side and from the sixth you can even catch Nutre in the distance, so if some people criticise they can't say there isn't a view from the upper floors and that's progress for you though I couldn't care less, when I'm at home I don't often look outside but for the children for example on the balconies they get the sun and people

What is Saint-Porvan

It used to be an abbey on the lower slopes of Le Rouget it's historical, the little cloister's still left and a part of the church there's a special coach service to visit it, the normal tour of the ruins doesn't go there it's too far and the tourists are mostly interested in Roman stuff those who do go don't regret it and the situation's very beautiful too in the evening at sunset far away you can see the plateau and the plain in the direction of Lémiran the monks had chosen their position all right even now it's not built up round about, the abbey isn't far from the little valley of Entre which joins up with Chanchèze nothing grows there but wild sloes and bread and cheese

What exactly is left of the abbey

I told you the little cloister a vaulted roof and columns round a little garden with a fountain and bits of wall joining it to the church only the choir's left now, a very high vault and three pillars three storeys high it was all patched together in the old days with staples and cement but it's not been looked after the grass is growing everywhere and soon what was left of the sacristy will be completely covered in brambles, in one way it's a pity but in another for those who like it it's a change from advertisements refreshment room and all that lark

Go on about the square at Sirancy

Where had I got to oh yes the corner of the Rue du Savon the Co-op, it's Juan Simon who's the manager suits him all right except he's always got to look for ideas to show off his merchandise customers expect more from a new shop, it was started up two years ago but last year he's already made a few alterations in the display shelves for example on the right as you come in

And the California cinema

On the right of the entrance to the flats there's a small booking hall open to the square painted orange with the ticket-office and in two show-cases the photographs of the film that's on they change it Wednesdays and Saturdays, the seats are in the basement young people say it's no good because the screen's too high and the encaustics too low I don't really know me and the cinema

Go on

So then there's the Rue du Savon and on the other side you come to the Restaurant Pommeau let's say what used to be the Restaurant Pommeau, it's a Vieuxpont the brother of that Marcelle who used to come to my gentlemen's who took it over three or four years ago, it's going down no-one goes there now except the tourists who get stung, Vieuxpont tried to be clever he didn't think much of Pommeau's customers he put the prices up straightaway without changing the quality of the food just threw in serviettes and ashtrays and a different staff, instead of Lulu and Maggy there's a barmy waiter and a manageress with the full tra-la-la asking you how you found it whether it was good and all, the people who used to go to Pommeau's were workmen and small tradespeople if they went it's because they found it was good and not dear they don't like to be fussed over they want to be left to eat in peace and they almost all dropped it at once, Vieuxpont doesn't think he's beaten he's made some alterations and he's on the look-out for tourists during the season but in the winter he hardly gets anyone people are quite pleased they say that'll teach him, it's true it takes time to attract fresh customers

Go on

The house is painted mauve, downstairs there's the large dining-room on the first floor the small one which can't be needed at all now on the second floor is the flat on the third floor lives Grenier the watchmaker opposite, in front on the pavement there's a little terrace that Vieuxpont has laid out with tubs of laurels and a plywood cook offering the menu it's Trapaz who did that, so that house is on the corner and next door there's the Abarons' a large old house which still had all its beams showing in my day, it was rough-rendered all over in yellow by Augustin when he inherited it from his father and the little balconies removed, down below there's Gaston Letourneur's bicycle shop he's a mechanic and Songier the grocer who's got a hard job to hold out against the Co-op, they're trying to keep their prices down but it's not possible though they do have some customers who think the Co-op's too common, the house has three upper floors very large ones the Abarons have the first and the second, the third is shared between Raymond Pie and Latirail the teacher from the boys' school he writes in the newspaper like the Lorpailleur woman and ever since I've known him he's been saying he's working on a novel true or not to make himself interesting, I've never lived in a big city but how pretentious people can be in a small one, his wife works in town they must be making quite a packet between the two of them they've got three windows at the front and three behind Raymond has the three others at the front and two at the side, next squashed between Abaron and the post office is the Gendarmerie a small two-storey house Lorduz complains it's too small and not normal he should be on his own now Sirancy's got so many strangers during the season, and it's true he only has one room upstairs for himself and his wife they've split it into two to make a kitchen which used to be in a cupboard where they've put a shower, Madame Lorduz says that's all right for the troops but a woman's got to have a bathtub she never talks of anything else, so next the post office done up all modern painted blue and inside a telephone box and three windows at the counter I don't even know the employees, in the old one there used to be Sinture just him and his wife who used to relieve him the number of faux-pas they made the two of them, Sinture especially a man homsessed you might say he'd started steaming the letters open to read them but they got to the bottom of it just when he was about to retire and he got thrown into clink

Go on

Above the door there's the Miserables' flat the ironmongers from the Rue Sirotte he and his wife and their son who's just got married, he lives at his parents' with his wife a Dodieu from Le Bérouse while he's waiting to find something else Pernette says the young wife's been through it already with her mother-in-law, over them there's Mademoiselle Filin she's had a hard life too none of her folk left now, her two sisters were killed in a plane crash on their way to the Canaries it must be seven years ago, while their parents were alive they'd already lost all their money if you talked about the Filins in my day it was really something a big demolition firm the only one in the district now it's Adolphe Possier from Douves

Go on

The house has only got two floors now it used to be a villa, one side it's got a turret with a roof in ceramic tiles and over the entrance steps to the flats that is to say on the left of the post office a canopy in coloured glass with two little blue lions on either side of the stairs, I remember as a child those lions we used to

Go on

Next door the Villa Hong Kong also with a turret ceramic tiles round the windows it's the same style as the post office but the steps are enclosed behind glass, there's a bit of garden in front with a rustic fountain in rockery stone and dwarf palm trees yuccas which stand up well to the winter, the garden goes on at the back where I remember having seen the Chinese pergola being built by the former owner with two little roofs one on top of the other in ceramic tiles and a balustrade of iron dragons all round, it stands on a base of yellow tiles and in the middle I mean to say what must it be ten feet across there's a round bench lacquered red, on that side in the old days you could see Ballaison's house on the left on past the Rue de Jivry opposite, now the new houses cut off the view and the garden seems very shut in the Villa's been up for sale for two years, I think at the moment there's an American Society after it who'd like to do I don't know what with it something to do with chemical products, next door there's a new five-storey house with the Bank of the Crédit Agricole on the ground and first floors and flats let out to the staff, the front is white with dark brown shutters it's not so modern in style as the one in the Rue du Savon but it appears it's less noisy inside, the director Monsieur Larvillier lives on the fourth floor he's got a terrace on the roof, next comes the Impasse des Frotte-Bougres which leads to the garage for the Bank on the site of a small lodge that doesn't exist any more and on the left an old house the same period as the Town Hall but smaller and badly looked after, down below there's Vérassou's warehouse and on the upper floors a small hosiery firm as they still say, it's machine knitwear they call Sirancy-Sport it seems it's very badly paid the wages haven't shifted for five or six years

Go on

Next adjoining the warehouse there's the corner house very well built for its time but tastes have changed, balconies with columns on every floor by that I mean the columns are the whole height of each floor if you see what I mean, they join onto the balconies above with stucco decorations and windows shaped like the stained-glass ones in church, there are six storeys it was only rich people lived there the ceilings of the flats are all decorated too, they had one of the first lots of central heating there in Sirancy it was a Society from Douves who built it a Mutual Trust Company I think or Mutual Help

Go on

Now they've turned it into flatlets studios as they call them, one room and bathroom or three rooms at the most which are rented monthly furnished by holiday-makers or permanent lettings to young couples, that's just where the Miserable boy thought he'd find something but it's still too dear for him obviously they've got to

Go on go on

There's a round entrance on the corner like the Hôtel du Château's and a kind of dome on the roof which corresponds to another one in the Rue Marcel-Atitré, there are at least eight windows at the front over the square there are offices and facing the street first a draper's that has changed its name at least a dozen times in all, now it's called Textilor before that it was Le Petit-Louvre before that it was Marius Nibière before that

The square

On the opposite side on the corner the boys' school which has its playground in the Rue Atitré it's a ramshackle little building not very large with a school bell on the roof, Latirail pulls it when he arrives and when he leaves, there's another master for the tiny tots a trainee teacher who lodges in the school generally from Douves it's cheaper for the Commune than paying two school-teachers but they're going to have to change their system with the population increasing so fast you could hardly call them a luxury, from the square you can see the school kids bent over their desks and Latirail holding his cane, even now it affects me somehow our boy was in the first form with the little ones when he came out of school there used to be a woman selling cakes at the gate who'd sell off the stale ones from Duvoisin's Rue du

Dimanche at half price I used to buy some off her for the boy

Didn't your child come back from school with his little friends

Yes but sometimes I'd happen to be there and we'd go back together, I even remember one day Big Fat Bertha as we called her had upset her barrow just as the kids were coming out they made a rush and then scampered off with the cakes the schoolmaster ran after them, he set them some lines to write I must not steal cakes and the parents had to pay Big Fat Bertha back, it caused quite a commotion everywhere naturally with kids they each said of course *they* hadn't taken anything and the parents

Go on

Next door butting onto the school there's the Café des Marronniers, they've kept the name although there aren't any horse chestnuts left in the square any more they were cut down just after 'fourteen as they'd got some disease and some catalpas put there instead, that was the tree in fashion at the time planted all round the centre of the square

The café

It's a good twenty years since I went there not since Blache took over from Edouard Fafarou, Blache played me a dirty trick not the sort of thing you forget his café's not popular with everyone, he gets by all right in the season with the room he's set up next door where he serves tea to the English it's written up five o'clock at all hours, Marthe's been there it appears the tea's no good, there are three upper floors he's had it done up in the old style with mock timbers painted on and the room for the English is all imitation beams apparently a chimney-piece and copper saucepans on the walls, there are some of Trapaz' pictures he sells to the tourists and a chandelier made from an old spinning-wheel all got up with little lampshades red and white check this room communicates

The outside

Three floors above, Blache lives on the first his married

daughter on the second and the third is rented by Théophile Gourdin the business agent a shyster who's only there once a week when he's doing his rounds, there's been a string of young things through that flat he picks them up in town proper little love nest by what people say with a bed covered with those doll-shaped cushions he buys at the local fairgrounds a whole collection he's a weirdie that one
   Go on
   Over the door to the tea room there's a sign Old England and the windows are all little leadlights, when you open the door there's a bell that apparently plays the opening bars of the Engleesh National Anthem Blache knows his onions, next door there's the butcher's Molletiére's painted red Ferdinand was an old school-fellow I go and say hello now and then, his wife died last year so he's thinking of marrying again one of the Charbois girls she's twenty-five which makes more than twenty-five years difference between them but try and make him see, he's like a college boy with a photo of his girl-friend in his wallet she's this that and the other enough to make you think the older you are the stupider you get, does he think he's got looks with all those warts he's got cash and there you are, the house belongs to him almost as big as Abaron's with a very high pointed roof and a weather-cock that comes from the Château, he bought it for five thousand francs Longuepie wanted ten it came from one of the towers that collapsed and was kept in the family, there are only three storeys but you could almost make another two in the loft, five windows on the front the entrance door has a knocker like a frog and on the left there's Wendt's dairy which has a struggle against the Co-op too, old man Wendt's stubborn his wife's been wanting to find something somewhere else for ages, they've got two little girls they had when they'd been married ten years very sweet except that one wears astigmatised glasses they both go to school, Madame Wendt was a Loiseau from Hottencourt I used

to know her uncle he was between my generation and my father's he must be round about sixty-five he used to run the Nursery Gardeners' Union as he himself had

The square

Then there's the old Hôtel du Relais a narrow timbered house it was bought up a good fifteen or sixteen years ago by Monsieur Hartberg, it's been restored exactly as it used to be even before it was a hotel, the philosopher Descartes spent a month there one July sixteen hundred and ten he was fourteen there's a plaque inside which explains the Method of Queen Christina and all you can visit without paying my gentlemen used to say that with people like Hartberg it was anything for publicity no wonder when everyone can read on the plaque this property is owned by Monsieur Hartberg of Hottencourt, he'll hand it over to the Commune probably it'll be the museum the keeper is Denis Mouton Hartberg pays his wages, he's got two little rooms at the back where the garden is with flower-beds full of wallflowers, the garden joins on the one at the vicarage which is the next house along set back a little grey with four green shutters, the Curé lives on the ground floor and Scalawag on the first that house hasn't changed any more than the Church has that's still the same, the big clock's always out of order but there's one at the school, it's a bit grim to talk about a church as if everything you've seen going on there gave you the impression life would be better if there were no ceremonies at all, the more you make of the main events in life the faster you bring it to a close what do we need all that for always stressing the end it'll come right enough all by itself and this soul they're always telling us about after all that's different it's rather like

Go on

Next to the Church there's the newspaper kiosk I told you the paperseller is old Ma Attention she's been there for years she doesn't change, her husband's been paralysed for ten years he used to be a shoemaker I don't know what she must earn with her papers they've got two rooms in the lodge in the Route du Camp, in the days when he used to work I'd give him my shoes for re-soling he had a shop Rue Bapluie almost on the corner of the Grands-Traversots, he'd travelled a lot when he was young he went to Constantinaples working on a ship then he was hall porter in a hotel there, he more or less got married and came back for the war the first one I mean leaving his wife and child behind he's never seen them again you remember the fuss there was then over papers and passports, he took up his travels again after the war as far as Denmark where he learnt the shoemaker's trade with some type who nearly strangled him over a woman, then he came back here and married Denise Vantard his present wife that is she was a dressmaker in those days she wouldn't hear of him being a shoemaker and he got a job with Romain Prout the shoeshop Rue Chavirat where he stayed four or five years I guess before going back to shoemaking, his wife had given up fashion to become manageress of the little perfumery Place des Garances and when her husband fell ill she left to take on the kiosk a year or two later

Go on

After that well there's the Rue du Velours-de-Paille and on the corner opposite the florist Aubier, it's a new shop that won't last long he only does business in the season he was too ambitious, but you can't say he lacked advice he knows Léglise quite well his old neighbour in town where flowers sell much better than here, the house has two floors of flats Aubier moved in on the first and on the second it's Gimol the hairdresser who has his little shop next door I always remember him being there he does the men and his wife the women not dear and very good, according to Marthe it's well up to Riquet's where she had to stop going because of the price she tried the new one too next to the Hôtel du Chasseur and was furious to have paid so much for her hair and so badly done,

Louis and Louisette they are it's rather the same type as Riquet's but not so luxurious with several assistants and blue leather in the gentlemen's salon, pink in the ladies' the custom's chiefly in the season

The square

Over the third storey of Aubier's house as it has a flat roof there's a kind of small loggia set back a bit we used to call a studio, it was made in my day for someone called Laviaud a painter who used to have studios built for him on all the roofs a rum character odd man out, he used to work a week here a week there in the village or in town he had studios there too there's still one at 12 Rue des Rats and another Rue des Chanoines on the corner of the Rue Pisson the rest have been demolished, well at Sirancy there's still this one of Aubier's and another Cours Gabriel-Tomès until last year another Rue de la Croûte-Bigle on the way to the station, it was one of our outings to go and see Laviaud's new studios this one has a pigeon house as well all decorated with fretwood that Sartout the joiner had made to Laviaud's designs with his apprentice I remember, a little ridge along the top and holes shaped like kidneys it was all fitted to the framework of the pigeon house and painted blue, the Town Hall pigeons used to come and brood there Laviaud used to watch them from his hide-out he made a lot of pictures of pigeons you can still see them in lots of people's homes, the studio's been empty for a long time it *could* still be let though it would need some heating it was

Go on

Next to that there's the Hôtel de la Balance for business men, four storeys the front's repainted light green right at the top almost under the eaves they wanted to keep one of Laviaud's paintings that runs all the way across, it shows a tall woman in the middle holding a pair of scales and on each side peasants on their carts or in front of their stalls in the market with the Church in the background and the Castle and full of pigeons, everyone remembers him working on that scaffolding and his paint pots but the colours haven't lasted well and Nénès instead of asking Trapaz to see to it asked the fellow who repainted the house front, he said he was an artist and he's touched up all the colours it's much brighter but you can't distinguish the faces any more and the woman with the scales looks like a big brown patch of plaster, and one of the horses on the right looks more like a mule all that to save a few sous Georges wouldn't have asked much to do it, there's a slate porch over the entrance on the left as you go in a small sitting-room with a potted palm it was a cutting or rather the first one was a cutting that Pompom took from Miette's hothouse at Lémiran

Go on

There's a piano too where the commercial travellers strum away to pass the time in the evenings, once upon a time Madame Nénès used to make a good job of the March of the Dragoons

The house front

Four windows on each floor, there are sixteen rooms in all during the season with the holiday-makers as well it's always full, from the rooms at the back you can see the little square in the Rue du Cordon on the right and on the left the garden of the Hôtel du Chasseur, it seems some of these commercial traveller gentlemen spend their nights with their field-glasses trained on the bedrooms at the Chasseur every man to his taste, one of the two chambermaids is Maimaine she's available by what they say to the ones with no field-glasses, Madame Nénès says there's always trouble because of her but Nénès says no she's a girl that gets through the work of three always up at five she does the laundry as well and waits at table with the other girl, they've a restaurant on the ground floor it's cheap and clean Madame Nénès' speciality is

Go on

Alongside there's the Impasse du Caneçon which leads to the

back of Dourzat's vinegar factory a small firm that's been there for fifty years but they won't keep going much longer their gherkins

Go on go on

On the left at the end of the cul-de-sac there's a way into the garden of the Chasseur with a kind of pergola they've made into a sort of aquarium for the customers in the spring it's shady the sun beats down just there, a pity the playground for the girls' school adjoins the garden the guests complain of the noise but there's nothing can be done, they've put up a screen of thuyas six feet high to hide the wall

The square

So next there's the girls' school similar to the boys' with another schoolmistress as well as Mademoiselle Miaille she's a Mademoiselle Rapi and lives in the school her window's on the corner of the Rue Chavirat, when classes are over you can see her forever peeping out behind her curtain the children call her Cow's-eye she's almost retiring age and I expect they'll take a trainee teacher, there's a classroom on the ground floor with a large window frosted glass half way up and another the Chavirat side and a second classroom on the second floor as there is for the boys, there was a fuss in the Echo and the Fantoniard over the gymnasium downstairs which has no modern equipment unlike the boys', people couldn't understand why the girls should do gymnastics too, Poussinet wrote an article on moral health about hygiene having something to do with the muscular control they need in childbirth and all that, there's a small bell-tower but no bell the roofing was repaired two years ago now dearer than was expected which again made people say with the gymnasium there'd be no end to it, girls just ought to learn sewing as they did in our day we don't want women acrobats in the Moscow style, Poussinet got very worked up against the people who used to say that he called them reactionaries blockheads clodhoppers capitalists

The square

Well that's all except for the war memorial in the middle it's a statue by Chapouillot from Agapa of a footslogger with fixed bayonet dying in the arms of the Republic, his wife's kneeling down in tears clinging on to his cape, in one hand the Republic's holding a crown she's about to place on the soldier's head, I remember the day of the unveiling before he made his speech the Mayor had to pull aside the curtain that hid the memorial, he pulled it back a bit but the curtain got caught between the bayonet and the Republic's elbow some little lad had to go and unhook it, it's meant to be one of the best things Chapouillot's done he was specially noted for his tombstones every cemetery in the district's got some, he died a very wealthy man somewhere about six seven years ago he'd retired to Douves he was the biggest shareholder in the Atlantis cabaret it seems, so round the memorial there are these catalpas I told you about six and a patch of grass with a long narrow flower-bed where every year now they make a pattern with different plants, another excuse for people to say the Corporation's throwing money down the drain, but these little details amuse the holiday-makers and it makes publicity to attract those who come for their health

Who's this Topiron in the shoe-shop

The man who has his shop in town Rue Charles almost opposite the market, in the old days he used to be Rue de l'Enfant-Dieu now business isn't up to much round there he moved away in time, the shops in the market area and near Dominique-Lapoire the way the prices have gone up since three or four years ago

And Raviuz

He's a retired gas man it's his wife used to run the flat, Cyrille says the smell of cooking and old socks is so strong he's always having to keep his window open, old Mother Raviuz shuts it again for him every day saying the smell comes from the café below which is impossible considering the little yard is on the other side but people stand on their dignity when it comes to a thing like smells they never want to admit

And the Gassets

They're both office workers, he's at the bank and she's with Dualia the insurance company they're very common-or-garden you can't say a word to them without they get it all wrong, always having a go at the neighbours Cyrille will tell you but when it comes to asking a favour there are no half measures a litre of beer from the bistro to save themselves the trouble, Cyrille's been instructed to stop taking things up to them

And Lucien Morenne

He works at the printer's in the Rue des Bossus next to the football ground, all that area's being demolished they're going to put up some working-class flats, it's after the Grands-Traversots let's say between the Rue Bapluie and the Rue du Dimanche there are two or three small streets like the Rue Soifetier the Rue des Chaises and the Rue Christian-Miel where there's not a single house still standing, Lucien's a pal of Cyrille's he makes his best-wishes cards at Christmas for him for nothing, Cyrille sends them to people he knows it's an English custom my gentlemen used to do it too but just their visiting card it's more distinguished

Did this Morenne visit your employers

No he's a shy one not my gentlemen's type Cyrille brought him once Lucien didn't like it

Who are the Jouvins

Louis Jouvin Emile's brother and his wife who was a Romayer their four children are a burden, Pernette is godmother to little Alain she spoils him as much as she can but you can't make too much of one because of the others and when she knits it makes four pullovers or four pairs of socks, Marthe tried her hand at it once Madame Jouvin didn't know how to thank her enough she came to help Marthe out one day after a big party, she's one of those pale things you wonder how they hang on to life but who'll bury us all in the end, when she's working she doesn't say a word very close you'd think she was about to render accounts for her children's lives I've noticed before, women like that provide a settled home life but if they're always living on their nerves

Who is Emile Jouvin

The charcoal merchant in the Rue Croûte-Bigle it doesn't look like much but it's far more profitable than people think, he has some retail drink trade and the fuel business wood and coal plus the hiring-out of carts, he gets on very well with his brother as he's no children his firm will probably pass to Louis' eldest boy Jacques who's thirteen he's already taking him round there on Saturdays to get him used to the customers.

What does Louis Jouvin do

He's a cashier with Roux and Company in the Rue Zéphirat

Who runs the Hôtel du Château

The widow Pruneau she worked hard at the hotel in her husband's time he died ten years ago, no-one would have suspected she was so attached to him she didn't want to see anyone for four years, she put a manager in charge while she took refuge with her family and then she came back to run the hotel, there's a photo of Etienne in all the main rooms and in her bedroom a portrait she got Georges to do from the photo, she's kept all her husband's linen and even now people say she wears his shirts as nightshirts

Who was the manager for those four years

Olivier Quignon he stayed on as under-manager

Do you know where the name Croûte-Bigle comes from

Chastel used to say it was a deformation of the old name for the street Rue de l'Ecrou-d'Olbig who was a barbarian chieftain he's meant to have been imprisoned by someone just there, we know more or less where it was somewhere near number 12 opposite the fire station but there's nothing left of the old foundations, the area round the station was pulled down to make way for the railway line it's like the Impasse des Frottebougres the Curé used to say it came from the Latin *fortiche* and a name that means fortified village, probably the square was where Sirancy started the cradle of the town as they say unless it was on higher ground and you could look down on the fortified village from there the Curé thinks it more likely to have been near the Rue Chauffe-Manche

And the Rue Chauffe-Manche

Still according to the Curé it should be something like *covinus* or *cavinus* which is one of those chariots with scythes fixed to the wheels used by the invaders and the other word *manicule* which in fact means handle, but Chastel is sure it isn't he told Marthe it was much more recent at that spot there used to be a kind of canteen for the soldiers of the Comte de Sirancy but at one time the Castle was completely razed to the ground by the lords of Longuepie so then it would mean to warm up the food *chauffe-mange* which developed into Chauffe-Manche, I think Sagrin agrees with Barbouse

Did you find out through your employers who Valère de Bonne-Mesure was

I think he was the younger brother of the one who owned the Château at that time, he's meant to have gone to Court in Paris where he had some official position I don't remember what and he had his private house built here where he spent the summer, I believe the Cardinal in the large drawing-room at my gentlemen's must have more or less come from there or perhaps it was the Saint in the dining-room

Who is Mademoiselle Eydouard

She's no chicken she must be almost eighty, she knew Bottu's aunt that Louise d'Isimance she even went to Paris with where she stayed for a time I believe, my mother used to talk of her in a guarded way she was meant to have been very pretty and attracted some actor but things like that don't last long and she came back without having managed

Who is this Ortez Rue du Velours-de-Paille

The one who buys the lampshades and the plates from Mademoiselle Eydouard, a small shop sort of junk shop where you can find odd things to match up a plate for example or cutlery, I remember once at my gentlemen's having had a long search for some silver cutlery that must have been chucked into the dustbin unless it took the fancy of one of the extras, well I found one exactly the same at Ortez' I only had to have the monogram put on

Who is this Pitut the wine merchant

He has his warehouse near the station on the other side of the Cours Clemenceau it's his father who started the business, La Vinasse as we called him he was too fond of his own wares he died of psychosis of the liver

Was it his son Raoul who used to come to your employers' with Doctor Georget

No Georget's friend is older about twenty-five I told you, Raoul Pitut is seventeen

What is this travel agency Rue du Savon

The same as the one at Agapa a small branch, there's only one assistant Mademoiselle Thonac she deals with the booking of seats in the coach for the tourists and the hotel rooms she telephones the town, she has practically nothing to do in the winter for the agency so she types out the papers of a lawyer from Agapa who lives here Rue Mereveille, Maître Lierre quite a card by what people say

What happened to the previous restaurant owner Pommeau

Not much I must say he went off to Douves thinking he could start a good business there but he must have done badly or he'd have been back to see us, he got taken in by some type who promised him the moon with dancing and a cabaret several even that they were meant to start up together, I think at the moment Pommeau is looking after the cloakroom he put up a small fortune to be able to run it but this other cove let him down that's what we think

Did the waitresses Lulu and Maggy find another job in the district

Yes Lulu went to the Mouton Gras so I mean to say she's quite somebody and Maggy to the airoport to Fion's

Who is this man Vieuxpont who took Pommeau's place

He's none too smart that's all you can say you don't start up a restaurant do you without knowing your job, he had a grocer's shop in town Rue Prolot which was doing well the last few years since they built all those offices Avenue Dominique-Lapoire it went to his head and he bought a car on top of having the van and Pommeau didn't exactly give him the restaurant away

And Grenier

The watchmaker he's Cruchet's uncle they don't get on since Jean-Pierre blew his mother's money at the Casino I told you, Jean-Pierre borrowed from Grenier and he can't pay him back it's always the same, old man Grenier can't understand how people can enjoy themselves while they still owe money he belongs to the old school Jean-Pierre's just the opposite he used to tell Marthe the poorer you are the less you should go without

Didn't you say Jean-Pierre Cruchet worked at Nantet's the tailor's

Yes I did

Where is Nantet's place

In town Avenue Paul-Colonel

Who are the Abarons

Big landowners with property all over the place round Sirancy, the grandparents were still peasants they had the farm off the Route Du Camp between the main road and the lane called Philibert-Lepoivre, it's Augustin's father who bought the house in the square he put another farmer into the farm Augustin goes on looking after his affairs with his brother-in-law Fouaron Marceline's cousin, they're always thrashing out some deal or other buying or selling land they're good customers for Ballaison

And Gaston Letourneur and Songier the grocer

Gaston used to be a racing cyclist he opened his shop ten years ago when he had to give up sport because of his heart, his pal Pierre Leduc is in it with him the laundryman's brother he used to be a racing cyclist too, he does the repairs when he's not at Le Cygne he's a confirmed bachelor as they say always having his little joke, he gets on well with his neighbour Songier who'd always be in the bistro if it weren't for his wife she keeps a firm grip on him obviously she has to if they want to hold out against the Co-op

Do you remember who was the owner of the Villa Hong Kong

Yes Monsieur Herbas-Degoin he used to scare the pants off us children always in a black suit he used to take a real Pekinese dog out for walks he said he brought him back from there, he'd been in China for years and he used to give lectures at the Town Hall we went there once me and my mother that's a good way back, he told us all about his travels with a map on the wall and said some Chinese words that made us laugh he talked about the people and the rickshaws and all, old Ma Pintonnat our washer-woman had seen his flat it was full of dragons and buddhas in every corner and a bedroom entirely lined in embroidered silk with incense-burners, he must have left quite a few things when he died to Mademoiselle Ariane he was very friendly with her and it may be even some of the statues in my gentlemen's showcase come from there, Herbas-Degoin is buried in the cemetery at Agapa he'd ordered his tomb while he was alive it's a square column with a miniature pagoda and all written in Chinese according to his last wishes

And Larvillier

The director of the Crédit though he's a banker he's not so very rich it all belongs to the company, he's been there for eight or nine years before that it was what was his name now what *was* it

Has this Larvillier any family

He's his wife and three children the two boys are at boarding school in Douves and the daughter's still with them Mademoiselle Elizabeth she's about sixteen very reserved, she never goes out without her parents sometimes they go to the California or else into town no need to be sorry for them mind they go to the Mouton Gras

Did they associate with your employers

No they're not the type, my gentlemen had their bank in town but almost all the people from Sirancy kept an account with the Crédit Louisette for example and Passavoine and Cyrille

What about Vérassou's warehouse

The warehouses for the cardboard factory in the Cours Ratebose by that I mean the factory used to be Rue du Balais, a tiny little factory they moved to the Cours Ratebose and the warehouse in the square they only use now to put the soiled goods, they've got other storerooms in the new place but Vérassou kept on the old one so as to make a better deal he's waiting to sell to the highest bidder, the whole building belongs to him the hosiery may have to clear out almost sure to there have already been articles in the paper by Monsieur Carré and by the members of the Archaeological Society about the scandal as they call it of such an historical house coming down to this, Poussinet answered it's the people that count industry and freedom for the workers but still he has to admit the warehouse should be fully used, and the wages at the hosiery he mentions them too the gossips say that's because he's got a girl-friend who knits there

Who runs this hosiery

Doctor Mottard's brother

Does the Duvoisin bakery still exist in the Rue du Dimanche

Still there yes

Didn't you say there was a bakery called Narre's in the square
In the old days yes
Whereabouts exactly
Where the new apartment block is Rue du Savon, it was an old timbered house with a bit of a garden which used to belong to the General's wife brought her quite a bit in at the time I don't think nowadays you'd be allowed to demolish houses like that
You mean the wife of General Tocsin
Yes
Who was Big Fat Bertha
An Alsatian her name was Bertha so obviously she was called Big Fat Bertha she's dead by the way she took to drink
Who are Blache and Fafarou
I told you
What sort of dirty trick did Blache play on you
It's an old story
Answer
I'd rather not
Answer
It's to do with Marie
What happened
He said something to the Emmerands
Explain
He said she was flighty and I was only just married so I gave him what for
What exactly did he say
That she was sleeping with Johann
Didn't you say Johann only went to the Emmerands' five years after you
Yes I did but that didn't stop Blache saying he was hanging round Marie and just went to the Emmerands' in order to be with her
And there wasn't a word of truth in it of course

Not a word
Where is the normal residence of Gourdin the shady business agent
Douves
Who gave you details about his flat
Marthe she found out from Sophie Narre
Is Sophie Narre Gourdin's mistress
Is that meant to be funny she's an old spinster I told you, she knows about things because she worms out people's secrets or else she invents them
Who is Molletière
Ferdinand a school-mate I told you
And the Charbois girl
One of the daughters of Marc Charbois the antique dealer's brother they're related to Dontoire
Who is Dontoire again
The owner of the restaurant where we had Mireille's wedding
Are there antique dealers at Sirancy too
I should say with the tourists it's a paying concern
Where is Charbois' antique shop
Rue du Pince-Bouc not far from the Casino
Who are the other antique dealers at Sirancy
Mademoiselle Louvois Léglise's boss's sister, my gentlemen used to say she knew nothing about it without her brother she couldn't get by anything she has that's any good it's Louvois who buys it for her there's something at my gentlemen's that comes from her what is it I remember when they bought it
Was she in your employers' circle
No she's a shy disposition but Mademoiselle Lacruseille used to say she was very interesting
She was one of her friends
I don't know
What other antique dealers

Bouboule as he's called in the Rue Tétin it's more like a second-hand shop he was there even in my mother's time, you had to pay to look at him in the street and what's more he'd take it, also there's Victor Nippet in the Rue Chavirat he knows my gentlemen quite well

Why haven't you mentioned him before

You asked me about the antique dealers from Agapa

Tell about Nippet

My gentlemen used to call him Nirot I never knew why, he didn't like Miette but Marthe thought he was more distinguished he's a bit sickly he has to follow some treatment for areophagia a sort of bronchitis I think

Used he to come to your employers'

Not so often as Miette, that's it now Rivière used to work with him too

Is he married

Not so far as I know

Has he anyone with him in his shop

His mother an elderly woman that every year you think she won't last out and she does, she broke her ankle last year when there was that snowfall in January and she walks with a stick now, I see her going by in the square at nine o'clock every morning she's the one who opens the shop, Nippet doesn't arrive before eleven

Does Scalawag have her kitchen on the first floor of the vicarage

You're forgetting Denis Mouton

What do you mean

If you think I haven't noticed you're going round the square again you're wrong

Do you think it's a trap

You never can tell

Say what you know about Denis Mouton

He was Johann's best friend
His accomplice
Perhaps
Why didn't you say so
It's not true
He wasn't his friend
No
Say exactly what you do know
Nothing special, he's an old man who lives alone and he's got a niece to come and do the housework once a week
And he didn't know Johann
Everyone knew him
Not specially
No I tell you
Go on
Nothing else he's from Nutre he never goes out of the house, Monsieur Hartberg
From Nutre you say
He was born there seventy years ago but he's spent his whole life at Hottencourt in service with the Hartbergs now he's retired as you might say
Why are you lying
It's the truth I tell you, I just wanted to see what would happen and you believed me as if other people's affairs were of no account compared to Johann's because he was a murderer, I suppose that's because people latch on straightaway to anything out of the ordinary they think it's much more important than the average man who carries on without killing anyone they forget
Say something about the vicarage
The kitchen's downstairs it leads into the garden
Is Ma Attention a nickname
No it's the name of René her husband
Is this René from the district

Yes

Are there any other Attentions

There are at Rottard-Chizy the commune they first came from René has a brother and two or three cousins who've stayed on there his brother's pensioned off

And Romain Prout

He's Rue Chavirat too immediately on the left coming from the Cours Clemenceau before the Rue Poussegrain, he's not from the district and his wife even less so she's Spanish, even now Pernette says you can't understand a word she says their sons have gone back to their mother's country they're both married

Are there any other shops except for the perfumery in the little Place des Garances

Well now you've hit it Ballaison's doing his utmost so there should be no tradesfolk at all he says it's historical too, he's already got the Mayor and the Sous-Préfet to intervene over the dairy which had to pack up they're waiting for the lease of the perfumer to run out so they can stop the owner renewing it he'll have to be compensated, the Archaeological Society got mixed up in it too but in fact people say it upsets Ballaison personally because his windows look out on the square but it must be admitted it's better without tradespeople, the three other houses are as old as the solicitor's there are little plane trees all round it's intimate they're talking of getting the coach to stop there too

Whereabouts are the old well and the underground passage

Rue Fougère near Goutte-Blanche

What route does the coach take to go to the Roman theatre

Coming from Agapa it goes up Chavirat as far as the square where it picks up the tourists in front of the agency, then the Rue du Savon and the second on the right is the Rue Fougère it stops for ten minutes at the well I told you, then it crosses Goutte-Blanche follows the Rue du Zodiaque and joins up with Clemenceau it goes along that as far as the Chemin de l'Aiguille on the right, comes out on the Route du Camp and a hundred and fifty yards on there's the little road for the theatre

What sort of detour would it have to make to stop in the Place des Garances

It would just have to pick up the tourists in front of the California for example so as not to have to turn off into the Rue du Savon and it would go straight into Marcel-Atitré, the Place des Garances leads off that

And then to get back into the Rue Fougère

No problem it would take the Grands-Traversots on the right then Jivry again on the right then Rue du Savon and Rue Fougère

How would you go for example from the Hôtel du Chasseur to the Rue Fougère

On foot of course

Which way

You take the Rue du Pince-Bouc which leads straight into it

How much time does that take

Five minutes

How do you account for the fact that the coach picks up the tourists at the agency instead of at the well which is so much nearer

It's a rule at the agency that the coach stops in front and the driver always has a message for Mademoiselle Thonac or vice versa

Are there any tourists who walk straight to the well from their hotel to wait for the coach there

There are always some

Aubier the florist is a friend of Léglise you say

I didn't say a friend I said an acquaintance

There was a flower shop near Léglise's shop

Miette's shop you mean Rue du Cimetiére yes just next door

Did he know Miette too

As neighbours

Did he know your employers
No
So he was Léglise's neighbour before Léglise worked for Louvois Avenue des Africains
It could hardly have been after
Will you stop being so aggressive
I don't understand what you want me to say, yes it was at the time when Léglise was at Miette's
Has Aubier any family
No he's a bachelor
Has he anyone with him in his shop
Mademoiselle Rancet
Who is she
I don't know her she's from Douves
Who is this Nénès
Ernest Laviron and his wife is a Terry from Le Rouget, they're hard workers but he never set the Thames on fire as they say considering the time they've been there they ought to be doing better business specially with Maimaine, she saves them some money that girl she's been there nearly fifteen years
Do you think that as well as certain customers she's been willing to oblige Nénès
Yes that's what people said Madame Nénès is meant to have held it against her that's why she says she causes a lot of trouble unless she says it just to save face she's only too happy to keep her, they only employ two women I tell you she's a good bargain
Who is the other woman
Anne Juvy a cousin of Marguerite Juvy's
Who is Marguerite Juvy again
The wife of Soulevert André Mademoiselle Lacruseille's concierge
Who were you thinking about when you said one of the extras

might have taken a fancy to the cutlery that disappeared from your employers'
  No-one in particular but if I must say most likely Poulet
  You said this Poulet had no regular occupation
  I don't know what he used to do but it can't have been much
  Does he still go as an extra to your employers'
  I don't know
  Where does he live
  He used to live Rue des Bossus last he was always moving, before that it was Rue Joly before that Rue du Cordon no Rue du Cordon after the Rue Joly before it was
  Couldn't you have found out through someone in the village Sophie Narre for example what he lived on
  Sophie Narre couldn't abide him she'd have said anything that came into her head
  What *did* she say
  You know what women are when they've got it in for someone
  What did she say
  That he was a street-walker if you pardon the expression
  Do you mean that after the fashion of Gérard he used to pick up strange women
  Well
  Answer
  Sophie said strange men
  And the police didn't intervene
  What police Lorduz is not the man to get involved in things like that after all he's an honest man
  Because Poulet only operated in Sirancy
  For the sort of clients he must have found in the season there are as many at Sirancy as in town no need to go chasing about but that wouldn't explain what he lived on out of season
  Are you sure he didn't go into town, to the Colibri for example

It wasn't my job to trail him and I tell you all this is just Sophie's yarns
   What did Marthe think about it
   She didn't like him either
   And your employers put up with a boy of that type being in their service
   Got to know first if it was true and whether they knew
   Do you honestly think they knew
   If someone suited them they weren't so particular I mean provided he did his work well that was enough for them
   Did he do it well
   Personally I didn't think so but the secretary said he did
   Did the secretary protect him
   Apparently yes
   Why do you think he protected him
   That was his affair
   Do you think it was because of his morals
   I've no idea
   And your employers
   Now you're back on that again
   Answer
   I've no idea
   Didn't you say the secretary got on well with the flunkey
   Yes I did
   Did the flunkey get on well with Poulet
   No better than with the others
   Didn't you say the secretary's day off was Tuesday
   Yes
   And the flunkey's day off
   Thursday
   Are you sure the secretary shut himself up in his room all day on Tuesdays
   Yes

You don't think he could have had company
Who
Poulet for example
Poulet wasn't part of the household he only came as an extra and even then only on days when there were lots of guests, usually we asked Cruchet and Luisot
What do you think the secretary used to do with his day off
I said I've no idea we always wondered Marthe and me though we also used to say that was his own affair
Can you be sure he saw no friends on those days
I told you he had no friends no-one visited him
Didn't you say the flunkey might have joined up with him after he left
How can anyone know
Why did you make this supposition
Because one was as unpleasant as the other and birds of a feather flock together
But you still go on maintaining that the secretary had no friends
Depends what you mean by that, if you call being friends always looking as if you're plotting in dark corners then let's say they were
And with Poulet
Same sort of thing yes
Didn't you say that when the secretary was talking to the flunkey he looked as though he took a certain pleasure in it
The pleasure of getting on at other people's expense
What do you think they were plotting
I've no idea
Where did the secretary go when he took the car
To run errands for my gentlemen
Did he go into town or to the village
Both
And you were unable to find out through the tradespeople

where he preferred to go when he went into Sirancy for example

He went to the places where he'd given small orders, for the important things it was the town

He didn't by any chance go to the Rue des Bossus

To the printer's, what would he have gone there for

To see Poulet

I should be very surprised it must have been a hovel he'd never have wanted to be seen going in there nor to the Rue Joly, besides if he wanted to see Poulet he could have met him somewhere else but I should be very surprised if he'd done that during the day he was always in too much of a hurry

And in the evening

He could see anyone he liked it was of no interest to me though that too that would surprise me, in the evening he worked for himself I told you he'd had his office fitted up in the cellar to be left in peace

What work did he do according to you

I've already told you I don't know

And you still don't know what there was written on the note found under the bed

No it was written the wrong way round

And that didn't intrigue you

Not at all except I told myself the letters were the wrong way round, unless it was just for fun like when he used to telephone always scribbling something on his pad it didn't mean anything at all

What kind of scribbling

Sort of squiggles

Not letters

Might have been yes

The wrong way round

I don't remember

When you were studying the note found under the bed you didn't see any connection between those letters made the wrong way round and the squiggles on his pad

Why no I didn't

And you're sure he didn't speak to you about that note again

Yes

When he went into Agapa where did he go

To the tradesfolk or my gentlemen's friends, Miette for example or the young ladies Lacruseille and Saint-Foin or else to the Hotel

What Hotel

The Grand Hôtel where the Duchess and La Hem used to stay or else he went somewhere else I don't know how should I I wasn't him

Why did you mention the printer's rather than Poulet's lodgings when we talked about the Rue des Bossus

Because I tell you Poulet was constantly moving he hadn't been in the Rue des Bossus long two months perhaps

Didn't you say that Lucien Morenne worked at the printer's

Yes

And that he was a friend of Cyrille's

Yes

What was the relationship between Poulet and Cyrille

How do you mean relationship

Did they get on well together

They hadn't quarrelled as far as I know

Didn't you make a difference however between Cyrille's type whose company you were quite willing to keep at Le Cygne and Poulet's

So what

In other words Cyrille might have shared with Poulet interests you disapproved of

I don't understand the question

Knowing Poulet's morals you weren't surprised he could get on with Cyrille

Your filthiness again I repeat it was Sophie said that about Poulet and I didn't have to believe her

Do you know if Cyrille knew Professor Sagrin

Yes he knew him

And Lucien Morenne

He knew him too yes

How do you know

Cyrille must have told me

Did he also tell you where he used to see Sagrin as Sagrin didn't receive visitors at home

He saw him he saw him *I* don't know at the café I suppose

Why this hesitation

Because hang it I've no idea I wasn't one of their gang

Their gang, explain yourself

Their group if you like

So they did form a group and saw each other regularly

In everything you say you're following some idea I don't understand

Answer

I know they knew each other full stop that's all

And the secretary was one of the group

I think so yes

You see he did have friends then and several even

If it pleases you to think so yes he had some but I still say he didn't receive any visitors

So you admit their meetings took place at Le Cygne since neither Sagrin nor the secretary entertained at home

I don't admit anything at all it could have been at Cyrille's why not

Then it couldn't have been any time but the evening if it was at Cyrille's

Yes the evening
So the secretary didn't spend all his evenings working
I never said that I said most of the time
Did Raoul Pitut know Cyrille
I think so yes
Did he know Doctor Georget
I I don't know
Don't get so worked up say yes or no
I think so yes
How do you know
It's Cyrille who must have told me
He's a young man of twenty-five with black hair you said
Yes or dark-brown perhaps you might even say light-brown
Why do you persist in concealing the truth
What truth
That he was Georget's friend and that he and the other Raoul are one and the same person
Because
Because what, why were you hiding this
Because I don't like to be made to say things that are none of my business that you take the wrong way with your mania for
Why did you pretend Raoul's parents were English people from Alexandria
Because
And that he didn't get on with Gérard
That *is* true
How can anyone believe you when you've tried to disguise the truth several times already
I'm not asking you to believe me my conscience is my own
How do you explain that the secretary had friends outside your employers only a few of whom used to visit them
I don't explain it
Say how it strikes you

If you want to know well here's what I really think, they used to get together because they'd found ways and means of fiddling their income tax forms and it was the secretary who had most of the tips and that's why they used to meet without my gentlemen who didn't want to be told anything about it

And you think Sagrim and Morenne who used not visit your employers' would have done it if they could have talked to them about it

I don't say that I mean the others met on their own because of that

And all year round they'd talk about their taxes

According to Pernette yes

How did she know

Through her nephew Riquet

He was one of the gang

Yes

And you what did you think about it

Me nothing

Cyrille didn't tell you anything

Perhaps you can see him shouting that out in the café

And Pitut was interested in these tax matters

He used to make out all his father's forms

And Poulet the wide boy

He knew almost as much about it as the secretary he used to

He used to what

He used to make out other people's forms

What people

Just people

Which ones

That's no concern of mine

Say what you know

According to Pernette it's meant to have been Topiron and the Gassets and Emile Jouvin and Passavoine and Duvoisin and the

three Hotels Château Chasseur and Fortuna and also Nénès and Ortez and Pitut of course and
  The whole of Sirancy
  I don't say the whole but a lot of it
  And Riquet used to talk about this fraudulent organisation to his aunt
  Well I mean it wasn't directly through Riquet she found out it was through one of his women assistants
  Which one
  This wife of Max the cashier needless to say *he's* in the know
  Doesn't Riquet work in town
  What difference does that make
  And Max's wife confides in Pernette
  She does her hair for her they go out together on a Sunday or a Monday
  All the tradespeople in Agapa are probably part of this mafia too
  I think there are quite a few
  And yet you were wondering what Poulet could live on out of season
  I still wonder
  Don't you know this little game of defrauding the Inland Revenue is very lucrative
  I didn't know
  Perhaps you know who's at the head of this jolly little organisation
  Maître de Ballaison
  Are you still trying to be clever
  I say what I know
  So Cyrille's gang very probably used to meet at Ballaison's
  I've no idea and if you don't believe me there's no point in our going on
  Why did you say the flunkey knew how to write what he shouldn't

    I don't understand the question
    When you complained the flunkey never spoke a word to you you said he could have written you a note from time to time as he knew quite well how to write what he shouldn't in a different context
    I suppose I was thinking about the letters he used to write or rather about the calculations he used to do for their false declarations
    He used to go in for that too
    I think so yes
    Tell the truth
    I believe the secretary gave him calculations to do
    And he did these calculations in front of you
    No
    Where
    In his room
    You used to go into his room
    Only once one day when he wasn't there
    And what are these letters he used to write
    Letters
    What sort of letters
    Filthy ones
    Who to
    That was his business
    Answer
    I don't want to
    Letters to women perhaps
    No yes
    Yes or no
    I won't say
    So although you said you weren't you *were* guilty of certain indiscretions
    It happened very occasionally

And the billiard room
What about the billiard room
You said it was immediately below your rooms didn't you
Why do you ask me that
Answer yes or no
Yes
And you never by any chance stumbled on anything special in there
No why
Be careful how you answer
Why do you ask me that
Answer
I saw the secretary once one night
Alone
With Monsieur Rivière
What were they doing
They were sitting at the little table they were reading some papers
What sort of papers
I don't know
Be careful
I swear I don't know
Where was this little table in relation to the billiard table
At the far end on the bathroom side
Describe the billiard room
It covers all the north wing except for the bathroom on the east front, the walls are papered red there's a
Didn't you say all the walls in the house were white
It's possible the billiard room must have slipped my mind
Go on
The billiard table is on the right there's a dustcover over it my gentlemen didn't play any more and their guests didn't enjoy it much on the whole, the room is almost as large as the dining-room I used to find it gloomy because of all that red but

there are lots of pictures and some fine furniture like the rest
How is it reached
By a small staircase that comes up from the library
You never mentioned this staircase before
I haven't talked about the billiard room yet and I tell you you might say no-one ever went there
You didn't keep it clean
Oh yes I did that
Go on with the description
You want me to say everything
Everything precisely
When you get to the top of the staircase immediately on the right
Whereabouts is this staircase
In the same corner as the one from the kitchen which comes up into the hall in fact really it's the same staircase
Except that it breaks off between the small dining-room and the library
That's right yes
Go on
So on the right between the landing and the first window on the north side
How many windows are there
If you keep on interrupting me I won't be able to tell you
Answer
There are five windows on the north side the kitchen side that is, two windows over the garden three windows over the courtyard that makes ten
Go on
So yes on the right to start with before the first window there's an old rocking-chair the rattan or cane type that my gentlemen thought was awful, it was Gérard who wanted us to leave it there till he could move it to a place of his own when he'd found

a home he was still living with his mother, and over it on the wall an old print in a heavy frame which shows billiard players of the period in their wigs and candles placed on the table which can't have been very practical, my gentlemen thought a lot of that print they were afraid it was getting more and more spotty I didn't find the spots were increasing but they said

Go on

Between the first window and the second there's a mechanical organ as large as a sideboard it's very old they found it in Germany or in Switzerland I think, you can see all the pipes with their little whistle and three cymbals on the top and in front it looks like a theatre, great painted heads all round and in the middle on the left there's a village wedding the bride and the bridegroom in front of the priest and the family sitting on little benches, when you turn the handle it starts playing if I put my ear close I could just hear a little but what I really liked was to watch it all moving when I used to do the cleaning I'd turn the handle, first of all you see the great heads start opening their mouths and winking their eyes, there's a big cuckoo up above that comes out of its cage and bows three times then the priest starts blessing the happy pair he can hardly move any more his arm's got stuck but his head still turns, the bridegroom holds out his hand to the bride and that's when the family moves one of the children goes the rounds jerking along and holding out his arm to pass the plate, it lasts for a moment like that and suddenly a bell rings and the cymbals start up and the door opens on the right and you can see the ball in progress, the bride exactly like the other one dancing with her husband and the family too but there's only one figure that still moves now that's the little man with the grey hat the others try but they can't get started, the great heads all round go on making eyes at you and the Good Lord comes out of his cage below the cuckoo and bows then the devil comes out and shows us his arse and an angel with a broom shuts the door on him then the cuckoo comes out again and bows and that's the end, the organ's gilded all over as well as being coloured there are snails and scallops and bells and balls like on a Christmas tree, you can certainly see they weren't afraid of work I often used to sit in front of it and I'd think

Go on

On either side of the organ there's a little wooden chair a straight one all painted with flowers and cows and birds that's Swiss too, one of them's got a broken leg I stuck together again but the radiator's too close it comes unstuck, then between the second and the third windows there's a big picture on the wall of peasants playing all kinds of games like blind man's buff, in the left-hand corner you can see a girl with a band round her eyes and the boys all round larking about one of them's lifting her skirt or else no that's in the middle, on the left there are some people playing croquet that's it on the left the croquet and one of the players is turning to the blind man's buff girl and lifting his mallet as though he's going to conk her one, another one's trying to get through the hoop you can see him leaning forward and taking aim and right on the extreme left that's it now it's coming back to me there's a player pushing the ball with his foot while the others have got their backs turned, on the right there's a girl on a swing hanging from the branch of a tree and a boy pushing her from behind and another one in front peeping up her skirts the ideas are always the same really country bumpkins or whoever it is, other peasants in the background chasing after each other or climbing up trees and two lovers in the grass the boy's got hold of the girl's leg while he's trying to kiss her with a mongrel pulling at his jacket from behind, the frame's painted red and black but it's in a bad condition there's a great split down one side, under the picture there's a rustic table with heavy legs painted green and white with three little drawers you can't open if you don't know the trick, there's a little catch underneath that you've got to pull to release the first drawer which when you open it releases the second and the second releases the third in the same way, on the table there were some genuine old examples of the cup-and-ball game they're balls on the end of a cord you have to fling in the air and catch in the hole in the handle I could never manage it what's more they're a ton weight, and on either side of the table some old high-chairs for children what I mean is they're raised up on some wooden contraption which folds down to make a little moveable pen where children used to be put in my day, Louvois used to say that in a few years' time they'd be as sought-after as lots of other old things people can't know what to do with their money buying stuff like that, the one on the left is painted red it's a little smaller than the other one plain wood and in front of the seat there's an abacus and under the seat you can hang the chamber-pot there's a little lid for that, between the third and the fourth windows there's a show-case stuffed full of china it's the worst thing to dust, even with a feather duster you can break off a finger or a flower I used to tell them I'd dusted it but I only did it every other time, they were almost all groups of people in period costume some of them of eight or ten people like the ones on the top shelf hunters on their horses with bugles and guns just imagine the guns you couldn't as much as touch them, I broke a few at the start and the tail off a dog there was a group of dogs too and the stag all alone jumping a hedge with its antlers when you had to stick them together I ask you, when you really come to think of it that sort of thing I wouldn't be half surprised if it was just to train the servants, they get packed away in glass cases no-one ever looks at, what proves it is that now people don't keep so many servants they've stopped making them, on top of the case there are two dark blue vases too high up for anyone to see them with gilded handles and each one a different scene painted on one of them shows young ladies playing at ball the other one boys fishing with a net but it's wasted up there, between the fourth

and the fifth windows another glass case with stuffed birds this one, all the birds of our nation on the top shelf there's a magpie a jay a woodcock a little owl a falcon, below that a wild duck a water-hen a seagull a baby swan a kingfisher, below that two swallows a robin some tits a nightjar a finch a wagtail, below that a nightingale a blackbird a lark some warblers a stonechat
  Cut it short
  They're so well preserved you'd think they were about to take wing, on branches or imitation grass or the swallows for example they're perched on their nest, all the back of the case is lined with a special paper country scenes sky and trees you'd think
  Cut it short
  On either side of the case there's a black chair with slender rails covered in tapestry and above that a little oval passe-partout picture with butterflies more or less exotic, a large Brazilian blue and an orange one all flecked with green you'd think
  Cut it short if you don't mind
  You don't like nature
  Go on
  Right then there's the corner and we're at the wall on the garden side, before the first window there's a large passe-partout with all the insects grasshoppers beetles the lot and below that a small console table painted red and blue rustic, I think it must have been a table which had its two back legs sawn off, on it there's a clock under a glass dome like you used to see in the past it's in the form of a man who's holding the dial in one arm, or rather he's setting it down on a kind of treetrunk and on the left a woman in an apron is cocking her head to listen I didn't dust that the dome is thermetical as they say, so then there's the first window over the garden from where you can just see the row of statues on the right after the ornamental lake you'd think they'd measured exactly from here to the centre of the window, after that there's only one picture so as not to get in the way of the billiard table it's

a soldier like the Pope's bodyguard with baggy trousers and a lance, after that before the corner another little sawn-off table painted red and white and gilt with an imitation bunch of flowers on top all in finigrane and coloured pearls under a dome and above that a passe-partout of insects to make a pair with the other one, after that between the corner and the first window over the courtyard there's the doings for walking sticks, then between the first window and the second two big horses off a merry-go-round one white the other black with eyes made of agate and fringed saddles in red leather, they're supported by a rod under their bellies that's planted in a great plinth on the floor my gentlemen had found them in Douves and Chantre was very keen they should keep them in the drawing-room a young man's idea all right why not pigs and goats like the ones at the fair, above them fixed to the wall on great big brackets there's a tiny old Guignol theatre with all the puppets, Guignol Gnafron the Gendarme the Devil in painted wood with great big eyes and other characters with smaller faces in papier mâché Claudine the Marquis the Country Policeman and the Dog, there's a little curtain that still comes down quite well and a scene at the back you can turn round, on one side it's a room and on the other a street with the prison I used to look at that for ages too they're memories that really stay with you, when Gnafron got the Gendarme drunk and Guignol who wanted to marry his daughter to the Country Policeman who wanted
   Cut it short
   It's painted light green and all gilded round the edge with Guignol written on top in red, then between the second and the third windows yet another glass case with a collection of ships all kinds, from Primitive Man to the Queen Mary and all the sailing ships it would have taken a week every time to keep them all clean, then between the third window and the door which leads into a bedroom there's a glass case that covers the whole wall like the big one at the far end next to the bathroom where there were

negro masks and stiff-looking statues of horsemen and goats' heads with horns I call them goats you can't really tell, these negro things how can anyone like them there are some that are quite frightening I wouldn't have been too keen to go in there on an evening with all those heads grimacing, on the upper shelf

You say there was a door leading into a bedroom

Yes

Go on

On the upper shelf

Cut it short

Go on cut it short I don't know what I'm meant to be doing

Go on without too much detail

What do you want me to say

The large show-case at the far end

It was the same more of those negro things and costumes in feathers or pearls and horrid things from Mexico like the little woman in the drawing-room, almost always death's heads or those little men with tiny legs and monkeys' faces some putting out their tongue three tongues even one of them, and axes catapults sorts of potato mashers all those savages' implements of war and cooking utensils and even something Christians shouldn't have in their homes, the mummy of a real dead woman on her knees all dry and crumpled up in a coffin you just don't show things like that, as if you once you were dead you were

Go on

In front of the large show-case there's a round table the same kind as the black mother-of-pearl one in the drawing-room and armchairs round it covered in red velvet and a lamp with globes hanging from the ceiling like the one over the billiard table, four white globes crosswise which once used to work with oil in addition to the lights in the show-cases and I think that's all

You say no-one ever went into this room, are you sure your employers didn't go to look at their collections

They may have gone but the guests never stayed there long
It's at this mother-of-pearl table that you caught the secretary and Rivière one evening
Yes
How did it come about
I'd been to check that the shutters were closed in my gentlemen's bedrooms they were away and I went up to the billiard room to check as well
They were away where
They'd gone to London just for two or three days
And Rivière was staying in the house
He'd arrived unexpectedly
Was he on a business trip or did he have a special purpose in coming
He's not likely to have told me but I think he must have been on a trip as he turned up unexpectedly
What time did he arrive
Round seven o'clock I think my gentlemen had taken the three o'clock plane the secretary had gone with them in the car, he'd been back about an hour I guess he'd already told Marthe he'd a lot of jobs to do in Douves
Where were you when Rivière arrived
In the kitchen
Give details about Rivière's arrival
What do you want me to give details about he arrived as usual and I let him into the drawing-room and telephoned the secretary he'd come
So the secretary wasn't at home
Yes he was, I mean the telephone in the house he used it all the time to give the staff orders so did my gentlemen and we did too to announce that someone had come, mind you it was usually the flunkey I couldn't hear anything
The flunkey wasn't there

No it was his day off
He didn't come back before dinner
Not that evening he took advantage of the fact his bosses were away
What did the secretary say when he heard Rivière had arrived
I tell you me and the telephone
What was his attitude when he saw him
I'd gone back to the kitchen and he ordered something extra from Marthe for Rivière
Did you serve an aperitif
Yes
Did Rivière seem at all disturbed
Not at all
And the secretary
No more did he
Did Marthe make any suppositions about this visit
She was always making suppositions
Which ones on this occasion
She said he'd come on purpose while my gentlemen were away but I had no reason to believe her
Why did she think that
You'll start getting ideas again if you listen to Marthe
Answer
She said it was connected with Johann, that Rivière must have come to see the Stoffels
It was after the trial
No before it was already being talked about Johann was in presentative detention
Why would Rivière have been interested in that affair
That's exactly what *I* said but she said everyone was responsible everyone should be judged guilty
What did she found her suspicions on

I tell you she was like that she could see connections everywhere, she used to say the tax gang was in league with Johann and Rivière too and the Princess everyone

Once again had she any precise fact to go on

She'd seen the Stoffel woman the day before in the village talking with Miette at Blache's and Poulet's meant to have joined them and she's meant to have heard them talking about Nutre and Karas, they didn't see her she was at the back behind the partition that cuts off the rear of the room

What exactly did she hear

That's all just names but with the ideas she has and the next evening when Miette arrived after Rivière she said what did I tell you

Miette was there too

He came about ten

Was he with the secretary and Rivière in the billiard room

No it was after he'd left by then

And Marthe didn't try to find out what they were saying to each other

Yes I think she listened for a bit she went up to the hall to put some things away in a cupboard

What did she hear

They were talking about the Grossbirkes and about Johann and everything and they looked at some plans

What plans

Some plans that Miette had

Probably the papers you saw Rivière and the secretary studying together

I've no idea

Did she hear anything that could have made her think they had any responsibility for the crime

I repeat she had her ideas and everything she heard confirmed them for her though you can be sure if it was the truth they'd have been talked about at the time but nothing of the sort, still that didn't help to make her change her mind

And you why did you think they'd met

Only because the secretary had phoned Miette to come and take advantage of Rivière's visit and talk business with him, perhaps a house that Miette was after I told you he was looking for one and he wanted Rivière's advice or something like that, and if they talked about Johann and the others it was because everyone was talking about it at the time

Why do you think they both retired to the billiard room later

Well really I've no idea they had the whole house

Are you quite sure that Miette left earlier

Yes about half past eleven twelve o'clock

You were still up

Yes

Wasn't it your habit to go to bed earlier

Yes but as the flunkey wasn't there in case they asked for something

And the chambermaid

She never sat up my gentlemen didn't want her to

There was no-one else in the house

Chantre and Gérard had been there for a few days

Why didn't you say so

I didn't think about it they were often there but they weren't likely to do the servants' duties

Why didn't you say they'd dined with the secretary and Rivière

Because they didn't dine with them

Where did they dine

In town I think they came back about eleven Marthe heard them

They didn't pass through the hall

No through the drawing-room

Did they stay up with the others
Yes
Where were Chantre and Gérard sleeping
Both of them that time on the first floor in the rooms in the south wing
Describe these rooms briefly
The one at the end has two windows overlooking the ornamental lake and one over the terrace, the other two windows over the terrace
Haven't they any windows over the courtyard
No there's a corridor that leads to both their rooms on that side
Does this corridor exist on the second floor
No
Describe these first-floor rooms
The one at the end is furnished in green with white stripes the bed and the armchairs and the curtains I mean it's the one Gérard likes best, the bed is Empire very heavy in light wood with swans head and foot in bronze which made the shape of the bed rather like a bathtub, it's not very long for a boy as tall as Gérard he probably had to sleep curled-up
Cut it short
There's a table in figured walnut with lions' feet and armchairs the same and a commode the same and a divan the same if you want me to hurry, and another tall commode in mahogany with a mirror and a whole assortment of ivory brushes monographed and modern sliding cupboards along the wall that separates it from the other bedroom, you can't see they're cupboards on each door they've stuck an old painting, two landscapes with ruins and two ladies in dresses like nightshirts with their waists up under their arms, the carpet is green with patterns in yellow it's a woven period one a large one circular with the signs of the zodiac and bees in the corners, the lamps are green too over the bed there's a landscape it's the island of St. Helena where the

Emperor died a prisoner, and a view of the sea at sunset a large sailing ship on the right and in front a fishing boat, over the lighter of the two commodes there's the portrait of a lady in a grey and black turban she looks right at you with her hand on a book next to an ink-well with a quill pen

Does this bedroom communicate with the other one

Yes there's a door between the cupboards

Pass on to the next room

It's red with cream lines the same bed with swans but with a canopy too and an eagle on the top, the furniture is almost the same except that there are two flower-stands on columns with lions' feet the carpet is red with a yellow pattern round the border, between the two windows over the commode there's a portrait of the Emperor on horseback and soldiers in the background it must be during some battle but which one, between the corner and the window

There's no bathroom

There's the large bathroom which also serves for these two rooms that's the inconvenience of the one at the end passing through the corridor but for Chantre and Gérard that didn't matter

What do you mean by that

Being buddies I don't suppose they minded

Where did Rivière sleep

It all depended not always in the same room

The evening we're talking of

Where did he sleep now wait in one of the bedrooms on the second floor yes the blue room next to the small bathroom, we call it the small bathroom because it's half the size of my gentlemen's but I don't mind telling you it would do me for lodgings, all delft tiles different designs and a sunken bath like a film star's the same and an absorbent carpet heated from below it's all thought out you should just see, exactly the temperature of the feet normal feet I mean when you

Is this the secretary's bathroom too
No he has the other half for himself in grey and yellow delftware just as beautiful except there's no absorbent carpet
Didn't you say before there were two beds in all the bedrooms
Yes I said that three even in one
Why don't you mention the two beds in the rooms on the first floor
The divan in the end room can be used as a bed and in the other there's a period camp-bed but you're in such a hurry
Do you know what time Rivière went to bed that evening
No
And the secretary
Nor him he went down to his office
What office
The one in the cellar
Rivière didn't go down with him
No
How do you know
Because I saw him
Where
I was in the dining-room closing the shutters
You were closing the shutters at that hour of the night
I'd forgotten that evening
After ten years in the house you were forgetting your duties
It so happens it was the flunkey's job
Did the secretary say anything to you
He nodded good-evening
Was it some time after you'd caught him in the billiard room
Half an hour maybe
Which way did you go up to your room
Up the stairs of course
The main staircase
The servants' staircase

Where's that

Right at the corner of the rear of the building let's say the north-east corner for you to get your bearings

It starts from the kitchen

You're all wrong it starts from the garage it's so narrow two people can't pass on it a real bottleneck, it comes out next to the toilets in the corridor that leads to our rooms

Where's the little refrigerator you mentioned on your floor

At the other end of the corridor

Which rooms do you pass through as you go up the servants' staircase

You don't pass through any it's built in the wall as you might say, all it does is take up the corner of the cloakroom and the bathrooms above

So the secretary's bedroom was over the bedrooms of Chantre and Gérard

The bedrooms of Chantre and Gérard how you go on, they weren't *theirs* they were spare rooms, the secretary was over the first one

Was there another next to his

Yes very impractical because there was no corridor, the secretary kept his things in there

Couldn't he have made his second office there instead of relegating himself to the basement

My gentlemen used to say it might always come in useful

From the garage when you went down the servants' staircase how did you reach the kitchen

Through the door of course

What door

Why the door the door of the wine-cellar

And you had to go round through the wine-cellar, the boiler-room, the airing-room and the pantry to reach the kitchen

You look as though you know the basement better than the rest of the house
Answer
Well all right then yes there was a door from the garage into the kitchen
Why didn't you want to say so when you were talking about the basement
I don't know
Answer
I don't know I tell you perhaps because
Because what
Because I was ashamed
Ashamed of what
That we always had to pass through that garage we servants as if they couldn't have made the kitchen where the garage is, but no they didn't care they thought it was more practical so we could jolly well pass through the garage to go to bed, and that brute of a staircase Marthe could hardly get up it as time wore on is that a way to treat your servants
How is this staircase lit
Two little openings one on the first floor one on the second
On the main front
No the garage side
Does the main staircase go up into the attic
Yes but it's in wood after the second floor and steeper
Still it's easier to negotiate than the servants' staircase
It's not difficult
From where it stops can you get to your bedrooms
Yes
How
There's a long corridor that runs along the back of the house
Where does this corridor end
At the flunkey's bedroom and mine

It's not joined to the corridor with the refrigerator
No it's on the other side
So your bedroom and the flunkey's have two doors, one into each corridor
That's right yes
Whereas Marthe's and the chambermaid's only had one leading into the corridor with the refrigerator
Yes that's right
Which was your room, the first one or the second
The second
So the flunkey's was next to the toilets
You've got it yes
And you never used the main staircase to go up to your rooms
It wasn't for us
Even when your employers were away
It did happen
The evening we're talking of are you sure you took the servants' staircase
Sure sure how do you expect me to be sure
Think
It's possible I didn't
So as you went up you could have passed the blue room
I may be mixing up one time with another
Tell the truth
Let's assume I did go that way
Did you notice a light in the bedroom
I don't remember I don't know
Think, any light under the door of the blue room the bedroom occupied by Rivière the evening we're talking about, you were alone in the house the flunkey hadn't come back you had just closed the shutters in the large dining-room, the secretary was in his office in the basement Marthe was in her bedroom she'd gone up this same main staircase before you did to save herself the stiff

climb up the other one, your employers' bedrooms were empty
Chantre and Gérard had retired into theirs Rivière was in the blue
room the blue room any light under the door of the blue room
answer
  Yes
  Did you try and find out what was going on inside
  I looked through the keyhole
  What did you see
  He was sitting at the table reading his papers
  You didn't knock on the door
  Me knock why knock
  Answer, you didn't knock
  Yes I did knock
  What did he answer
  You're forgetting my affliction
  Did you go in
  I waited for him to open
  What did you say to him
  I asked if he wanted me to wake him up in the morning
  What did he answer
  He indicated eight o'clock with his fingers
  What did you do after that
  I went up to bed
  Had Marthe already put her light out
  No
  Did you go into her room
  Yes
  What did you say to her
  That they'd all retired for the night one to his office the other
to his bedroom
  Why go and tell her that
  Because she asked me to before I went to bed
  Well what did she say

She shushed me with her finger she couldn't shout that I was to go to bed
She didn't write you a note
Nothing that matters
Answer
She wrote be careful of Rivière Miette knows something, her eternal suppositions I went to bed
What was she supposing
I've told you again and again I no longer know what I'm saying
Did the flunkey usually close the shutters all through the house
Yes
At what time
At six o'clock in winter and eight in the summer
At what time did Rivière get up the next day
At eight o'clock when I woke him
Was he meant to be leaving
Yes
At what time
Something like half-past nine
By car
Yes
Did the secretary go with him
No
Do you know where Rivière was going
No
Did Marthe happen to know
According to Pernette he stopped in the village
At whose place
At Blache's
To do what
I don't know
Don't be so tongue-tied, say what you know
What a lot of fuss about nothing all this is leading us nowhere

Answer

According to Pernette he went straight to the Salle des Anglais to talk things over with Blache and Poulet and also Nénès and Monsieur Larvillier, I'm sure she made a mistake what could Monsieur Larvillier be doing there especially with Poulet

She was watching them from the street

She pretended she'd mistaken the door for the bistro but she couldn't listen to what they were saying Madame Blache took her straight off to the kitchen

Did she see them come out again

Yes they went opposite to Gaston Letourneur's who was talking to the Miserable boy I think, Monsieur Larvillier is meant to have left them to go to his bank and they went into Gaston's where they didn't stay long, Blache went up to his flat and Rivière took Poulet in his car they went off towards the town at least along Chavirat that's all she saw it started to rain so she went home

Why did you pretend not to remember going up the main staircase on the evening in question

I wasn't pretending anything at all I remembered because you went on so

You were particularly intrigued admit by Rivière's arrival

No I tell you that was Marthe

Why did you look through the keyhole

You don't know what it is to be deaf and to like your job, other people would have listened at the door before knocking but what can I do you can't be always disturbing people and how can you suddenly turn up like a bad penny, no I tell you for me it's normal even my gentlemen never complained about it

You must have stumbled on quite a few things in this way

What do you mean

In your employers' bedrooms for example

If you want the confessions of a chambermaid I've already warned you that's not my style

What is there between your bedrooms and the spot where the main staircase comes into the roof
The corridor I told you
So along all the courtyard side there's considerable waste space, what was it used for
A sort of loft
Just one room
Three
What is there in these rooms
Everything they didn't use any more or else things they hadn't decided where to put, furniture they'd bought
And all this was bundled into the three rooms
Bundled up no they hated untidiness
How was it kept then
In the first room there was all the stuff that used to be in the small dining-room, in the two others their old bedroom furniture
What was this old bedroom furniture of theirs
In the first bedroom a large black bed all carved with columns and figures the same style as the chests in the drawing-room, the head of the bed much higher than the foot and right at the top a sort of little shallow cupboard with two panels you can open and inside there are three pictures, the one in the middle the manger and the animals and the left-hand panel a wise man in a fur hat and the right-hand panel a shepherd, there's room for at least three people in that bed covered in a thick red material with big green flowers, Miette was after buying it it was worth a million and high-backed chairs four I believe yes and two elaborate Spanish armchairs upholstered in gold I'm sure of that, a material with real gold thread and a pattern of flowers it came from one of their grandmothers a marquise or God-knows-what, and a wardrobe black like the bed where they temporarily stored a collection of things for the church candelabras statues holy water

basin even an ostensory with shelves of fine pearls, and another wardrobe quite different with its doors all painted clodhoppers on the spree in natural surroundings, things for the church in that one too mixed up with negro masks they didn't know where to put and rosaries not Catholic I don't know what religion, on the walls there were two mirrors

You say on the walls, so the room was properly arranged

Yes

Could it be used as it stood

Yes except that the wardrobes were full

Did you count it among the total number of rooms

No it's the loft you don't count the loft

And yet you counted the basement

No I included the kitchen then it was you who asked me for the rest

Was the furniture in these rooms protected by dust covers

No

So you had to keep them clean

We hadn't got time there was a woman who came once a week for the loft

Did these three rooms show the mansard roof

They had dormer windows but a proper ceiling

Go on with your description of the first bedroom

There was also a desk-table with wavy legs and four drawers full of old papers and pictures to be framed like botanical flowers and pages from a dictionary, and also an old toilet-table with a little mirror that swivels round on the other side there's a picture by the same butcher as the one in the drawing-room

What does it represent

Some woman on her bed doing something filthy with a little negro boy now you're satisfied

Go on

I think that's all no wait there's a large statue near the door it almost reaches the ceiling, it's a man twisting round and raising his arms he's going to die on a marble plinth with little columns and on the floor a large sort of fitted carpet but not tacked down there's a surround and it kicks up when

The second bedroom

All this for the loft we'll never come to the end

Describe it

There's another bed not so heavy as the first one in light wood like the Empire one but without the swans just with lions' feet, covered with a fur that was getting moth-eaten I pointed it out to my gentlemen several times it ought to have been better looked-after but they said it'll last till it's really seen its day, and the chairs and the armchairs in the same wood covered in blue, blue velvet, the armchairs have got elbow-rests which start at the top of the back if you see what I mean sloping down, they finish off in a pad at the bottom and the chairs have a removable seat by that I mean they're square and can be fitted into the chairs and you can take them out, there's a round table they wanted to move down to the drawing-room the leg is bronze the top of it is in some figured exotic wood fine workmanship, two oil lamps with cut-glass globes four medallions for each of the seasons, spring's a young man summer's a woman holding

Cut it short

There's a large wardrobe again full of collections and another next to it with not enough room full of linen still in good condition, sheets that Marthe would have liked to have pure white linen my gentlemen didn't want them any more they'd changed all their bedding to pink or blue or green, just like the handtowels

Cut it short

There's a complicated console table I'd be really surprised if that was a piece of French furniture, the front legs are women with wings smothered in clusters of angels and little birds and buds and the edge of the table-top is birds round a basket of cucumbers, and a third leg flat at the back not round but flush with the wall all decorated with angels too, the top is in blue stone like marble much more precious it appears and on it a Chinese woman in painted porcelain, her sunshade is pink stone she has a little dog in her arms and she used to be in the case in the drawing-room but Miette's meant to have said it wasn't pure period, what else is there yes two pictures over the bed the one on the right a man and a woman under a tree the woman has a bunch of flowers and the man is milking a goat with one hand, and the one on the left also a goat giving milk to a fat baby the parents are stroking a sort of parrot that's climbed on its back, I was forgetting the little wardrobe next to the bed not much higher than the black console table with four drawers encrusted with sea shells, the inside is lined in red velvet and on five shelves a collection of little bells all shapes and sizes from all the countries and I think that's all, the carpet and the curtains are blue

Is there a door between the two rooms

Yes

You say that in the third one that is to say the first one as you come up the staircase there was furniture from the dining-room

Yes apparently my gentlemen couldn't stomach it any more

Was this room properly arranged too

Yes

Did it communicate with the first bedroom

Yes

Describe it

I've had enough

Describe it

I've had enough of your little ways you're trying to get me to make mistakes about details you'd far better be asking me important things

Describe this dining-room

There's a table some chairs a sideboard

Would you mind giving details

They're rustic style foreign with all the legs at an angle pointing out like the legs of a stool, they come down from the seat or the table top and instead of going straight down they splay out on the ground I can't explain better, the table top is that thick it's heavier than a wardrobe with a tiny little drawer you can't open any more, the chairs are all wooden with a hole in the middle of the back, the sideboard is in two parts the top half is open like a dresser and in the bottom half there was a part of the old dinner service the rest was in a painted wardrobe like the one in the bedroom, there are also two wooden cradles which can be used as flower stands and three big chests full of table linen they didn't want any more red or blue check, or else embroidered table-cloths that Marthe found more beautiful than the ones we used and that's it

Nothing on the walls

Yes two large pictures in glass frames which are collections of postcards, almost all of mountain shepherds and cows and little houses with white windows the Black Forest as they call it with its dwarfs and soldiers with hair like women and I was forgetting a collection of clocks in another wardrobe, something like thirty or forty clocks Louvois was interested in them

How do you explain that the billiard room table was covered with a dust sheet when the furniture in the loft which no-one ever used wasn't

I've no idea perhaps they enjoyed going to look at their old rooms again occasionally

Are you sure nobody used them

Who do you think would have used them

Friends from time to time

Perhaps one was used once when there were a lot of people I can't even remember when now

What exactly was this bathroom next to the billiard room

The second bathroom for the bedrooms
How did you get there
Through the bedrooms or along the corridor
Didn't you say there were only two bedrooms on the floor below
Yes my gentlemen's two bedrooms
Was there a corridor at the back
No
You could go from one to the other then
Well yes I suppose so
They must have been huge if they corresponded to the large drawing-room on the ground floor
Huge yes
Describe them
Couldn't we give these two a miss I'm tired
When did your employers get back after the Rivière evening
I told you two or three days later
You don't remember now what day
No
Didn't you say the flunkey was off duty the day they went away
By Jove yes you're right so it was Thursday they must have come back on the Friday evening or the Saturday, wait no it was the Sunday the Sunday evening that's right Marthe had just come back from the village
Do you know what they said when they heard that Rivière had been
No
Did the secretary speak to the flunkey about it
I don't know
You were asking for important questions these are, try and remember
In any case the flunkey didn't chat to me, he might have said

something to Marthe I don't remember wait yes I do, no it's the secretary who asked her if she'd heard the flunkey come in during the Thursday night and she couldn't say, she told me about it she asked me if I'd seen any light I said I hadn't

It's important to find out your employers' reaction to Rivière's visit

Well I've no idea

What did they do the next day

Wait a minute they went into town in the afternoon with Marthe it was her day off

And Marthe didn't speak to them of Rivière's visit

She didn't tell me

Did she know where they were going

I think they said they were going to Doctor Bompain

Were they ill

No but he's there on Monday afternoons

Was Doctor Bompain a friend of Rivière's

I don't think so specially

Do you know what sort of interest your employers could have had going to see Bompain apart from their health

For their health they had Doctor Georget from Douves I told you Doctor Bompain was just a friend

Were they very friendly

Not particularly

Did Bompain often visit your employers

Not very much no

Why do you say he was a friend

Shall we say an acquaintance

Wasn't he the one who had operated on Madame Carré

Yes and my sister for her pendicitis

And you don't know why they went to see Bompain that particular day

Good God no I tell you

Bompain was a friend of Miette's

They saw each other I think over their mania for houses

Would you know whether Bompain was closely or vaguely involved in the tax business

I don't know

Would Pernette know

She never said anything

Say what you know about Doctor Bompain

He's a very good doctor a specialist for operations he studied in Paris before settling down with us his family comes from there, he came here when he was about thirty and married Mademoiselle Hénon the daughter of the last Superintendent of the Hospital who he'd met in Paris, when Hénon died they inherited the house in the Avenue de l'Hôtel-de-Ville and a handsome sum of money and they came to live in the district, he's got a very good practice people even come from Douves for their operations he makes a packet, some people say he's a bear that's not right how many times I've seen him in town having a drink with some shabby crowd, I think it's just he doesn't care a damn for the upper set he makes them pay and then good riddance, with Marthe for example he didn't want her to pay a bean it's my gentlemen who made him a present, he's a little man with a mane of white hair all round his head and rimless spectacles he's got blue eyes that take in everything at once and when he laughs he's got all gold teeth, his children used to call him Pain-sec because he used to make them eat stale bread in the old style, not that he's stingy it was like that at home we used to be made to

You say he drinks

No I said he didn't worry about having a drink at the bistro in the Rue de Broy with old patients of his he'd operated on *gratis pro Deo* sitting on the terrace with them large as life, Servien for example he operated on for prostate poor wretch he'd go through fire and water for Bompain

Who are these Hénons

Hénon the father was from Hottencourt, it must be forty years ago now he bought the large house on the corner of the Rue Saint-Véron from the Baroness Mons, when they extended the street as far as the Avenue the property was cut down to nearly half the size and the Baroness didn't want it any more, once upon a time there were large gardens in that area now it's all built up Madame Hénon the mother was related to the Foissets my mother used to say

You say Bompain has children

Grown-up children now the eldest must easily be thirty-five he's gone as a doctor too to Paris and the daughter married someone in industry from Rottard six years ago just after Bompain had had that trouble in the newspaper

What trouble

They blamed him for bringing pressure to bear on the new Superintendent about the way the operations were organised there were some funds for the Hospital gardens and Bompain's meant to have said his operations should take first place he needed modern equipment, the Superintendent should never have let Bompain have his way when you take on responsibilities especially in a good cause but Bompain didn't give à damn so long as he could look after his patients and the gardens have stayed as they were, it was all part of Poussinet's jiggery-pokery he never misses a chance to get folk talking about him and the influential ones who don't like Bompain were glad to see him in trouble

Has Doctor Bompain a practice outside the Hospital

Yes he has consulting hours at home for people who can pay

Where exactly is his house situated

I told you on the corner of the Rue Saint-Véron and the Avenue, the villa's too near the street since they cut off the garden and what's more all those new blocks have taken off some of its value, cubes for the workers and the spaghetti factory, when you come into town that way it's not very pretty the old people's home's been spoilt too it was a beautiful house in my time with a park that's been sold three-quarters of it

Did Bompain by any chance visit your employers after the Rivière evening

Yes a few days later he dropped by the kitchen to say good-day to Marthe

Just like a regular visitor

Yes that's true

And he wasn't one really

What

A regular visitor at your employers'

How many times do I have to tell you no

And Marthe wasn't surprised to see him turn up just at that very moment

I wouldn't say surprised she was very pleased to be able to talk to him about her health

She didn't make any suppositions concerning Rivière's visit

She said he was coming for the same old reason all right but I told her off you can imagine always the same ideas

Be more precise

About Johann and all the gang

Did Bompain know Johann

He treated him for a time for his intestines

And Poulet

I don't know

How long did Chantre and Gérard stay on after your employers returned

Something like a week

They weren't working either of them

Gérard worked when he felt like it I told you and Chantre must have been on holiday or he was taking one you know what students are

Did Marthe try to find out what they said to your employers during that period

She tried yes

What did she learn

They were planning an evening party in the park there were masses of things to order on top of the drinks and the eatables, fireworks new Chinese lanterns an orchestra the whole bag of tricks they didn't do things by halves and the list of people to be invited that was always a headache, not for my gentlemen they'd have invited absolutely anyone but for the young ones they were so jealous, always squabbling with this one or that one or someone who knew someone else and all that

Tell about this evening party

Good Lord where to begin, the Tuesday or the Wednesday I think my gentlemen took us into town, Chantre and Gérard were meant to see about the fireworks and the whole caboodle I was going to check the secretary's orders for the drinks and the rest, not check that's not the word confirm rather confirm, my gentlemen were always saying the telephone's all very well when you're in a hurry but it's better to see people especially tradespeople, seeing me after a telephone call they'd take things more seriously the delivery date and the quality, I took the chance of telling them whatever you do not this or that but exactly what I wanted, you have to din the same thing into them time and time again people are so careless

Go on

So yes they dropped me as usual at Les Oublies and I went to do my jobs then I

Who did you see and in what order

Well if I can remember let's see, I went straight to Riz-de-Veau as we call him that's Rivoz the delicatessen opposite the Mouton-Gras that's where we order the Black and White he gives my gentlemen special terms, for the Johnny Walker they used to get that from Douves one of their friends and wait now it's coming back Riz-de-Veau only had forty bottles left he was going to make up with White Label which my gentlemen hate, I said forty would be enough we still had about thirty of the Johnny, and then again for the *foie-gras* whatever you do not the Périgord which tastes of farmyard, the pretzels what else the olives the whole lot, then I had to go to Touchouze for the brains my gentlemen had planned on something hot after midnight forcemeat balls brains and mushrooms with rice, actually it was the girl who spoke to me that's right she knew nothing about the telephone call Touchouze was out, I don't like dealing with her as soon as you start insisting she gets on her high horse and looks offended she damn nearly tells you to go next door but they generally have the freshest brains, then for the forcemeat balls I went to the Rue du Cimetière to Loulou's Marthe couldn't do everything on her own and Pernette was away just at that time as she'd had to go to Lémiran to a relative, Loulou used to be cook at the Grand Hôtel Marthe's very fond of working with him I'm too busy on big occasions and no question of using the extras, when Loulou wasn't able to we'd ask the cleaning woman who's a fairly good cook but you know how they are people like Marthe they have their little ways and the cleaning woman used to answer back, Loulou was taking his siesta he's a character as my mother used to say he's saved a little and he still stands in or goes as an extra, he lives on the second floor over the Poinçot garage a flat that would just suit me the kitchen and a little

Cut it short

He doesn't like me much it gets on his nerves to shout and it doesn't always do any good, I had my gentlemen's note and he wrote all right for the eleventh that was the day before the party he'd sleep at the house, he was quite pleased all the same knowing my gentlemen pay well he offered me a wee drop and I went off to Octave-Serpent, I had to see Ogier the bicycle shop for a new saddle ours had packed up

You used to use a bicycle

It happened sometimes I'd go to the village but it was chiefly the flunkey who used it and the chambermaid, it was a woman's bike with a skirt protector over the back wheel

And you didn't try Letourneur's

Usually I did but as I was on the spot

Go on

Then I had to go along the Quai des Moulins, I dawdled a bit in my favourite corner and went past the Pou-qui-rote or was that another day, no that was the time the owner of the Colibri had almost run his car into the front of the little cobbler's shop only missed by a hair's breadth, people had gathered all round and the policeman was writing in his notebook on account of a fruit-seller whose barrow had been damaged, the fuss she made the fuss she made her cherries had been shot all over the place

Cut it short

I took the Rue Dombre to go to Gratien's Rue Surtout for the candles, every time I'm round there I get some from him my gentlemen hated running out of candles they're the best in the town pre-war quality, what they make nowadays in the big shops is no good at all and you can't always find white candles, then the Rue Croquette as far as the Avenue Paul-Colonel where I had to call at the ice-house my gentlemen had suddenly thought in the car that the secretary hadn't ordered enough ice you need an enormous quantity for a hundred people all night long in summer, there are never enough containers we did have some old tubs for the wine harvest at the farm

Go on

Then wait now perhaps I did take a swig at Fifine's Rue des Trouble-Fête yes perhaps I did, the poor woman had been very lonely since Florent died Marthe specially used to get anxious

saying she was looking more and more on the black side, she was just the age too and in cases like that there's nothing you can do either it passes or it doesn't, how many women we know who are in that state they drag on to the end complaining about nothing at all with their set ideas you think they're mad and they *are* in a way, I can see my poor mother
   Cut it short
   You're harrying me again
   Go on
Well a swig at Fifine's before going to Lesdière's Rue des Singes for the syphons my gentlemen had thought the secretary's order was too small for them as well, Lesdière received me with a bandage over half his face he was just back from the Hospital from what I could understand a syphon had burst he didn't explain how, I hadn't brought a note from my gentlemen so he began to get in a state he couldn't hear anything with his bandage the kids were running round our feet Madame Lesdière wasn't there in the end I wrote it down for him thirty extra bottles, then next door to Bruce's for the mushrooms then what, Rue Duport I think no Rue des Clous that's right to go back to Les Oublies, I had to call at Renard's Rue des Fossés-Mahu for the cakes some of them the rest my gentlemen were seeing to on their own Avenue des Africains, Renard specialises in *petits-fours* that we used to call Chinese because of their pointed shape I wanted to tell them to leave off the sugar violet if they could put a hazelnut on them all it's more distinguished, anyway I got called names by Gérard after the party he was furious but I know very well it wasn't for that those Chinese things you can imagine what did he care anyway, then it must have been easily six o'clock or did I do anything else
   Why was Gérard furious
   I'll talk about that later
   Answer

You told me to talk about the party I can't begin at the end, that's it I must have gone straight to the Grand Café Place des Oublies my gentlemen had given us a rendezvous at six o'clock at the counter, and I'm not the one who'd risk keeping them waiting, they arrived at six o'clock sharp Chantre and Gérard weren't there they bought me a drink meanwhile and the two others turned up at twenty-past six I didn't get the impression they apologised, we went home calling in at Noirette's for the champagne I think and that's all for that day, Chantre and Gérard had already got the lanterns and the rockets they'd ordered a special set-piece we were afraid wouldn't turn up at the last moment I remember, a week for an order from Paris was cutting it too fine

You say there were to be a hundred people

Yes plus all the village I mean those who wanted to come they were invited

Wasn't it the secretary's job to go and confirm his orders and check the goods

Yes normally it was him he did it the next few days but that day something prevented him can't remember what, my gentlemen asked me they had as much confidence in me as in him for things like that I'd even say more, when it comes to quality you can't put one over me

Go on about the preparations

For days after that the flunkey and I had a special thorough clean-up we weren't too keen on that the party was taking place in the garden it was completely pointless except if it rained so why do it but fussy as they were, it was the carpets that always gave us the worst trouble it was really hot what's more we sweated like pigs in that dust there's always some whatever you do, it's lucky they didn't make us clean the loft it took us a good two days still they found a way to make us turn out the cupboard in the dining-room and all the glasses to wipe, fetch the reserves up from the cellar all the plates and silver to polish you can't imagine the turn-up in a house, for days after that I had to help Pompom in the garden it was always impeccable but for this occasion it was the full works, just think the bronzes round the Amphibitis lake and make the fish shine like new and scrape some of the statues in the centre driveway which are getting black in places, old Mother MacMiche for example some woman holding a witch's mask in front of her eyes it seems she's acting comic, she's always in the shade and in such a damp corner she used to get patchy and the Apollo Velvetear too the bum he's got on him I tell you, everything to be scraped with sand three days we took over it Pompom had to freshen up the lawns too it wasn't really the season to mow them but once they get an idea, I must admit we had Pipi and Tourniquet to give us a hand for that kind of work they know the ropes, as for Marthe she had Jeannette and the farmer's wife for the heavy work then the chairs had to be put out in front of the large pond for the show, my gentlemen had gone to a firm from Douves to arrange the seating two of them came but I had to do everything after them all over again and their truck had gone over one of the lawns all that at the last moment, Chantre and Gérard only saw to their decorations they put lanterns everywhere even in the paths at the side going down to the river where my gentlemen had asked Perruchon for about ten boats it's Fifi and Cyrille who fitted them up with Poulet to look like gondolas, it was their job to see to the buffet to put the table up under a marquee they had a job it kept on collapsing the firm from Douves must have forgotten one of the assembly pieces, we put it right by sticking an iron bar underneath we were bound to take rain into consideration or all the food would have got soaked, the second buffet in a marquee too was in the main courtyard on the left Luisot came to see to the tables and Donéant as well they looked after the orchestra, Raymond Pie had asked if it was possible to rig up a platform because of the sound apparently we asked the scouts to put it up for us they're good sorts but muddlers I had all the trouble in the world to keep them quiet all that bunch want to do is chase about, and then what else the buffet near the kitchen for the village and the fourth one in the orangery, we had to push the plants back to the far end luckily most of them were outside at that time of year the orange trees and the palm trees but even then Pipi wrenched his back all right turning a crate round, thank goodness my gentlemen didn't want electric lighting as Gérard had suggested we'd have had to cope with electricians lurking in every corner there's nothing worse than that lot for arsing things up pardon the expression

How many statues are there along the main drive

Ten on each side, the first on the left is Jupiter I think he's bigger than the others sitting on an eagle and holding a stick his gown falls over his knees, opposite it's the patron saint of war I can't remember his name a helmet on his head and nothing else on he's lowering his shield and looks rather tired, then on the left it's a Diana like the one at the Town Hall except that she's stroking a doe she's in a short dress walking along, opposite it's Mynerve the patron saint of philosophers or something like that she's got a helmet on too and she's holding a screech-owl in her right hand that was an awful job to scrape, there was a sort of fungus not the same as MacMiche's which comes from the oaks and the plane trees she's got one lip broken anyway, then on the left a bearded man with his fig leaf and another one opposite almost the same except for his shoes laced up to the calves, then on the left a group of three women holding a distaff by that I mean one's holding the distaff another the spindle and the third one a pair of shears they had the same fungus as Mynerve, opposite there's an old man writhing about among a lot of serpents with his children, then on the left I don't remember, yes some other woman in a mask crying then old Mother MacMiche and the Cubid, opposite there's an actor and some others I don't know

333

their names one taking a thorn from his foot, another playing the flute his shirt rolled up under his armpits or no it's not that he's got his shirt over one shoulder there's another in a sort of camisole that turns up and a little hat, and to end with the Velvetear on the left and opposite Venus Aphrobitis it's funny when you think of the names they had

Go on about the preparations

The next day the eatables arrived

It all took more than a week then

I can't keep every day in my mind after all this time perhaps we had

Go on

The next day the eatables arrived Marthe noticed at once that the mushrooms weren't over-fresh, the secretary had to make a hurried dash into town to fetch some more my gentlemen have given up Bruce's since, it needs a bit of cheek after all with customers like them to treat them like that I'd been very particular too you see you can never repeat things too often, anyway Marthe started to cook her brains and the rice only needed warming up next day for so many people she couldn't manage any other way, Loulou had arrived at eight o'clock in the coach and he and Jeannette worked very hard, finally the cleaning woman had come too with me and the flunkey she helped pile up the china and the glasses on the tables, Luisot and Poulet helped us as well when we had to cart the things down to the river or the hot-house it's miles away, someone had to be there all the time till the following day to keep an eye on everything specially down by the river a fisherman or a passer-by it's quickly done, during the evening the lads took it in turn and Cyrille slept the night in the buffet marquee it was glorious weather, I remember having a row with that great lout Hottelier he stood there idling about watching us cart the china around he was probably afraid of rumpling his well-pressed trousers, Chantre told him off too and he vanished till the next day but it seems to me I'm forgetting something, yes we had a little accident when Fifi set fire to the packing material near the hot-houses and a petrol can near by burst into flames, half the glass panes in the hot-house blew out on that side my gentlemen were furious a bundle of nerves and no wonder there wasn't time to have them put back luckily the roof wasn't damaged we still had to move the drawing-room furniture in case it rained and make up notices please keep off the grass for the village people, Gérard even got up a little place before the big bend near the spinney of beech trees for their personal needs you know what people are like when you let them do as they please ah that's what I was forgetting the ice-cream, it arrived from Gorin's the following afternoon and the fruit at that time of year was morello cherries, the farmers had picked a good fifty kilos it was far too much Marthe had to start making jam straightaway after the party she hadn't meant to start for a week, did I mention the champagne I can't remember now and the ice in our tubs I forget the half of it

The day of the party

We'd done such a lot already we were a bit played out everyone got up early but there wasn't much left to do, I still had the coat-stands to put up in the small office but everyone came without a coat in that heat we were half-expecting a storm about midday but no it was fine settled weather the whole week, everyone took luncheon out of doors on the terrace my gentlemen to take the load off Marthe even went into town to get a cold meal, then the younger ones went right round the park to check that everything was in its right place I'd taken over the job of look-out by the river from Donéant, I was sitting on the steps thinking over everything we might have forgotten and I dozed off Cyrille came to shake me, we'd forgotten to change the candles in the house in case of rain he didn't know where I'd put them I'd had to find a different place for them because

When did the guests arrive
They arri they I
What's the matter
Nothing it's nothing
Pull yourself together, answer
I don't know it's nothing a little turn
When did they arrive
Having to say all that again you have to try and get back into it it's so far away now
Yet it wasn't long before you left, not much more than a year ago
Yes not long before so much effort for so little, I mean now now what's left how could we I mean how, that's life it's like dying another death to talk about that
Answer
That's what they say yes I won't get caught a second time but who is there to think about catching you, that's it that's what it was it makes you feel so fed up there was no way out I mean for us now it means being on the outside till the end
Answer
Have I really told you everything about the preparations
Talk about the party, what time did the first guests arrive
I still want to tell you about the previous day the things I've forgotten there were
For the last time, when did they arrive
At ten o'clock the Duchess and La Hem arrived with Rivière that I do remember as for the others well the whole lot arrived almost at the same time, Poulet was directing the cars we'd arranged for the parking in the large meadow on the left before the bend it's rather a long way from the house but we couldn't get cluttered up with cars in the garden, I was in the cloakroom by that I mean at the door of the small hall to watch them arriving they went straight to the main courtyard where my gentlemen

were waiting for them, it was still light the Duchess made a detour to come and leave her furs with me she always makes more fuss than everyone else the other ladies didn't have any or only a little one they kept just in case, I only had twenty coats and three umbrellas for a hundred people

Who were these hundred people

I can't say them all it's impossible only the regulars there was the Duchess La Hem Rivière Miette Longuepie with Madame for once, Ballaison all alone Georget Raoul Carré Rufus the Chastenoys the Ducreux Hotcock Riquet Mesdemoiselles Lacruseille and Saint-Foin Morgione as well as the young ones but when it comes to the rest

You never had a chance to look at the list

No

Try to forget as few as possible

There were the Larvilliers the Bottus inevitably even the Grossbirkes out of politeness, d'Eterville Louvois and Léglise Blinville the Simonots Frou-Frou Frédy Sagrin Leroy from Douves, Doctor Mottard the owner of the Colibri Monnier of course, Nippet Ducuze Monsieur Turina who else Doctor Vernet the manager of the Casino, Poussinet even he was there I don't know how

About fifty, we're a long way from the total

I tell you it's impossible there were loads of people I didn't know, friends of friends people from Douves some even who'd come from Vichy and a lady from London a friend of the Chastenoys my gentlemen had invited when they were over there, with two stuck-up boys you can't get away from it the English are not like us and then naturally a lot of visitors for the waters friends of the Duchess and of La Hem and holiday-makers from the Chasseur who'd never been to the house before even the manager Barbatti for example and his brother from the Trois-Abeilles, and the owner of the Mouton Gras

Talk about the party

At a quarter to eleven I left my cloakroom the show was to start at eleven o'clock we'd been given permission to watch, chairs had been put out for us on the right set back a bit

Didn't you say the people were invited from the village

Not before the fireworks which were at midnight, Lorduz had been paid to keep an eye on the main gate and midnight that weeded a crowd of them out for a start people go to bed early

Talk about the show

I forgot to say the orchestra had a spot of bother as they went up on the platform it collapsed with almost all the lanterns I didn't see anything of that they had to move their chairs to one side, it was only Raymond Pie who was able to stand on it right at the edge to conduct it made the overture a bit late starting

What orchestra was it

The Lyre as usual except for the Soupot boy who was ill they did without a flute

Go on

Yes they went on playing quite a time before the show, the actors from Douves who were at the Casino all ready for the season had come at eight o'clock to arrange their set, there was a bench in the middle of the drive and propped up against Jupiter a sort of round door in cardboard that they'd brought on their truck it was meant to represent a house, the lighting it was Chantre who'd done that with two little spotlights on the ground he'd linked up to the lamp at the entrance with long leads at least fifty yards buried under the gravel on either side of the lake, my gentlemen would have liked candles as well but we wouldn't have seen a thing so they started about twenty-past eleven, it was called *Les Foutreries d'Escarpin* a complicated story with the flunkey playing the fool all the time he wants his young master to get married and the father won't have it as far as I could understand he puts his spoke in the wheel, Escarpin runs rings round him and gets him into a sack to beat him when you can't hear anything it's not so funny, they had some nice costumes Escarpin with his big floppy hat and the girl like a lady of fashion it lasted till half-past twelve apparently to cut it short they didn't do it all, the guests were in the dark I couldn't make them out in the front row anyway there were my gentlemen and the Duchess and the Longuepies and Miette and Frédy I think, but it was very nice to see the big drive lit up every statue had lanterns hanging from it too, as soon as they'd finished while the people were clapping I went to my buffet in the courtyard with Cyrille he'd already started serving them whiskies before the show, must admit that's what people drink most nowadays all the rest stays in the decanters there's no getting away from it, the ladies all had low-cut dresses you'd never believe it Boubou for example at the back it went down as far as this and at the front La Hem she was no angel as Marthe used to say, the Duchess is so thin she's got nothing to show she had bracelets up to the elbows neither has Madame de Longuepie she was in black with her mangy bit of fur, Marthe made a comment to Riquet that she'd have been better in a woollen dress or something but Riquet said the gentry so as not to look new-rich are only too willing to dress up in mangy furs, then there was Frou-Frou with her it was her legs the slits in her dress right up high I agree her legs aren't bad like Dame Longuepie's but I mean to say, they say they're dressing for the evening they might as well call it undressing, it was the same with all the ladies except for three or four like Mademoiselle Lacruseille almost like a man except she had a skirt and a jacket like a dinner jacket with revers and a fancy little tie, and the old ladies like Lady Chastenoy buttoned up to the neck dripping with jewellery, if you could have counted it all up there'd have been enough to buy the whole estate or at least ten times the Château de Sirancy they all went off to the buffet we had our work cut out the two of us,

La Bottu didn't even greet us as my mother used to say the less you have to shout about the more you throw your weight about, the candlesticks were all mixed up with the glasses my table wasn't big enough it wasn't practical for serving and people nearly burnt themselves, they just walked round the lake drinking while the orchestra started up again, I could see Raymond Pie under the remaining lanterns beating time with his hands like birds flapping, then the musicians came for a drink they were allowed at our buffet and the guests congratulated them, Raymond was sweating in his tails too tight for him he's had them thirty years though he hasn't got much fatter his cuffs came down over his hands, I think my gentlemen gave him a good tip anyway they gave a hundred thousand francs to the Lyre and ten thousand to each musician twelve of them which makes

Go on

All this lasted nearly an hour the fireworks were put back Lorduz said our yokels were beginning to get impatient though they had something to drink too fifty bottles of white wine, they were allowed to go forward as far as the drive that comes into the courtyard but not beyond it, it seems they were making quite a din and at one moment Nénès trying to come up to the buffet went sprawling over the table about ten bottles got smashed on the paving stones I certainly saw some people turning round and Poussinet running, he wrote something in the *Echo* very kind for my gentlemen straightaway you see people like that are ready to change their tune when the occasion offers

Go on

At half-past the first rocket shot up in the sky a huge multicoloured star with little ones and golden balls and a second one silver with three large stars that burst separately and dropped down and a third one that was

Cut it short

A third one was the signal for the flares all in a row in front of the terrace along the river and behind them a glowing fountain three tiers one white one yellow one pink, and more rockets three or four together like chrysanthemums with green shooting stars which went even as far as Crachon I'd never seen anything like it it was like

Cut it short

Then there were the firecrackers that burst in the air, Madame Grossbirke stopped up her ears the young people enjoyed themselves no end it's the noise they like best they've got what they want in our day and age and they'll get even more by what people say, the village folk were beginning to cross beyond the drive Lorduz was frantic I told Cyrille to go and give him a hand, then more rockets and we had to wait for a moment my gentlemen were in a state the set-piece had been delivered at half-past eleven, three men who had had to shin up the scaffolding quick sharp Gérard told us it was just like a building site he couldn't do a thing nor could Chantre they had the rockets with Poulet and Luisot and *they* were frantic, big fireworks they were and when they all had to go off together anyway in the end we had the set-piece it was three catherine wheels spinning round in the air while the rockets went off with stars and fountains I've never seen anything like it, it cost my gentlemen three hundred thousand francs everyone was impressed, just to show you Georges Trapaz did pictures of fireworks right through the season which sold like hot cakes

Where was Marthe during the fireworks

At the kitchen buffet with the cleaning woman

And the chambermaid

With me and Cyrille she was meant to pass the sandwiches but there wasn't any point people preferred to come to the buffet, I sent her to the cloakroom

Go on

Then whisky again and champagne it was nearly a quarter-past one people were beginning to let themselves go in the park, Cyrille went back to Fifi in the orangery I was left all alone for almost an hour I could see people walking about in the main drive or going down to the boats the red lanterns swaying about before they went off on the river, then the early-to-beds went home it was about half-past two Dame Longuepie the Grossbirkes the Chastenoys the Bottus the Simonots the Ducreux

Did Madame de Longuepie go off alone

No her husband took her home but he came back later, Marthe came to keep me company while the cleaning woman and the chambermaid cleared up their buffet, the village folk had gone except for a few young ones I saw slinking about the garden they're always after a good thing I didn't say anything knowing my gentlemen they're quite fond of the unexpected at that hour of the night there's no-one left but the good-timers and the young ones everyone tries to amuse himself in his own way

What do you mean by that

I mean to amuse himself the way he likes and in that park just imagine all those people and the soft lights in the odd corners people meet up together I think there was plenty of that that night, I finished taking my glasses back about half-past three I didn't feel like sleep so I went down to the river there was no-one else there the buffet was deserted, I tidied up a bit and stayed there watching the boats in the distance, at one moment Hotcock turned up he asked me something he seemed anxious I saw Gérard go by too with someone else and on the bank on the left right on the edge of the water I thought I saw Mademoiselle Lacruseille

Alone

With a lady

Who

It may have been the negress

What negress

Boubou she came with Morgione

And Gérard who was he with when he went by
A boy from the village
What were they doing together
They'd just met I suppose
What do you mean by met
You're going to bring that up again
Didn't Gérard used to try and meet foreign women
In theory yes but as he used to say you can't always be thinking of your beefsteak
What was going on round the orangery
People were drinking and dancing
Was it still Cyrille who was there at the buffet with Fifi
Yes
Did anything unexpected happen where they were
As far as that goes yes the Duchess made a terrible scene with Morgione she wanted him but he was for Fifi you must admit it's funny
Wasn't Morgione Boubou's friend
So what
And you're not surprised he wanted Fifi
If that was meant to surprise you you wouldn't go far
And you find it normal this kind of reversal
This kind of what
This change of attitude
I don't understand the question
What did Morgione do
He walked off with Fifi giggling
And Poulet
What about Poulet
In whose arms did he end up that night
Not in yours anyway
Answer
I've no idea

And Cyrille and Luisot and your employers
I'm not in the habit of spying on people
That precious lot probably all finished up in the house
They slept until midday
In the house
Yes yes yes
Who was there
The regulars except for La Hem she'd left you'll never guess who with, d'Eterville she must have been pretty high
What do you mean by that
That she was drunk
Was the Duchess there too
Yes
Who with
I'm fed up with your questions
Answer
I've no idea I'd enough to do serving all my breakfasts
How many were there
Thirty
So all the beds were taken even in the loft
Not so many it's amazing what little room people take up when they're drunk
When did they depart
Some of them in the evening some of them the next day they all gave us a hand to clear up and put away, a real shambles it was everywhere it took Pompom a week to clean up the park but they were all very nice, on the whole they're the only sort of people who have any respect for servants
You said the opposite about your employers
They were my employers
What time did you get to bed
I didn't feel like sleeping I told you
What did you do till midday

It's obvious you're not used to housework
And what happened to the orchestra in all this
They went to play for the dancers near the orangery where there's level ground the old tennis court it's all it's good for now but they don't know how to play modern dances, Chantre started his record-player that he'd fixed up in case of need and he told them to go about three o'clock I think they went home
The actors too
The actors no they stayed on the young ones at least
Why haven't you mentioned the supper
I knew I was forgetting something, we served it about two o'clock but it wasn't a success Jean-Pierre only had about a dozen people, it was such a lovely night everyone was still walking about or dancing it was only after about four or five o'clock it was broad daylight when the lingerers ate some of it before going off to sleep but there was enough left to feed everyone the next day
Where was this supper served
In the drawing-room
Why didn't you mention it among the preparations
I forgot it was Jean-Pierre who saw about it but I said we'd moved the furniture it was for that too
And you say the invitations for a party of this scope were only sent off a week in advance
No it must have been more than that you're right
So Chantre and Gérard stayed on more than a week after Rivière's visit
That's it yes perhaps a fortnight
Why did you say a week
I made a mistake that's all my brain's still in a whirl just thinking about it all again
Don't you think there's another reason that puts your brain in a whirl
I can't see what

Rivière for example
What's he done now
How did he spend the night of the party
Same as everyone else, he stayed a long time with Cyrille in the orangery he was very much on form it appears then he went to bed
What time
I've no idea
Cyrille would know then
I'd be surprised if he noticed he had other fish to fry as they say
What was Rivière's attitude next day at noon
Attitude attitude that's the only word you can say what have attitudes got to do with me
Didn't he have something to say to your employers
Of course he did everyone did
What did he do when everyone was busy helping you out
He was wiping the dishes with Marthe if you want to know
And your employers
They were stacking the spare dishes in the cellar
Do you know the names of the actors who came to perform
There was Mademoiselle Lili whom I knew specially, one of the two old ones was called Ducroy the other one Auber and the young ones were Baronet and Grangier and the other girl very pretty is new to the company I've never seen her before, and Escarpin that was Baptiste Lepoquin the others
Didn't you say this Lili was also a friend of Morgione's
Yes she was there was even quite a story attached to it, Riquet kept us posted
Say what you know
A story just like the others plenty of water will have flowed under plenty of bridges before you'll see two people getting on together, the poor young lady according to Riquet Morgione had just dropped her she'd imagined it was serious she must have been

mad when you know Morgione, she wanted to pretend to be consoling herself with Lepoquin and they went out together and of course she wanted to come to the party my gentlemen hadn't invited her they always fall in with their friends, she moved heaven and earth to replace the lady who usually acts in *Les Foutreries* and she managed it knowing Morgione would be there in order to show herself off with Lepoquin that's women for you but they can't take the rap and then it's a disaster, she was very good in the play very sweet and then excited by the champagne she kissed Lepoquin on purpose while Morgione was watching her, still after excitement there's a reaction I saw her round three o'clock weeping like a fountain in a corner Lepoquin had gone off on his own and Morgione I said what he was doing, I'd have liked to go up to her and say something to her but is it up to me to get mixed up in it why was it she stayed on instead of going to bed drink only makes you do silly things, I saw her again about five o'clock she must have left at that time she wasn't there next day, Riquet told Pernette she'd swallowed some sleeping tablets to try and kill herself isn't it stupid, she slept for three days like Frou-Frou and then she had to get back into harness but it may be women need a big jolt to bring them down to earth, men don't get so upset in general I mean if they start drinking they rather tend to lose their taste for love affairs and that's a real consolation for them, not women that's why they swallow sleeping tablets to have done with it and if it doesn't work then they're cured

Who is this Ducroy

An old man who's been in the company for goodness knows how long he's the oldest member, they take him every year for the season they find him a small part two minutes even one year he brought on a chair and that was all, he never stops laughing bent almost double he's lost all his teeth he was drinking his champagne with the others who were pointing out his lovely silk scarf to everyone, I thought to myself it's rare to grow old like that above all your character changes young people turn away from you we know what's in store for us, he's a widower I think with a daughter somewhere in Africa

And Grangier

He always makes such a song and dance I watched him chatting to Madame Larvillier he forces his laughter out and lunges forward like when you hold your ribs, the chambermaid said he talked nothing but tommy-rot for example about Ducroy and superannuation it would be better if

And Baronet

He's a friend of Donéant's he hasn't been back from America long but I don't think he's any good or what would he be doing in Douves after New York, he's harum-scarum his wife was a Chapouillot a cousin of the sculptor he ditched her with two children when he left, now he drinks a lot according to Riquet he's meant to have taken up more or less with the new girl in the company

Who is Auber

My gentlemen used to know him in the old days he's in a home they thought they'd do something for him and they asked the theatre director to take him on, and so it worked out though he forgot all he had to say the prompter was there behind the door you could hear as much of him as the actor it seems but the old boy finished up all right lots of applause, Dame Longuepie kept him chin-wagging for ages afterwards to show how charitable she is

Which of the village boys did you see slipping through the garden after the fireworks

I didn't recognise them on the spot

And later

Next day there was the Pintonnat boy one of Mother Jacquot's nephews and young Génois a cousin of Miette's old friend they were probably the ones I saw

Do you know if anyone took Lorduz' place for the night in the Gendarmerie
Yes they'd sent some type from the police station
His name
I don't know
You say the river is navigable
I should say so almost as far as Rottard and in the other direction as far as Douves
What stops it being navigable right up to Rottard
The old mills at Siterne they're disinfected
Who is Perruchon
He hires out boats to the holiday-makers he's the one who set up the little bathing beach at Le Foliot before Crachon with sunshades and a refreshment-bar-cum-restaurant, it's very popular in summer with the young folk they've got a six-foot diving board and a raft
What's the lay-out of the riverside at your employers'
Like a little port with a jetty that checks the current for the boats, they've got a sailing boat and a speed boat they haul up into the boathouse nearby for the winter it's Chantre and Hottelier who use them most it doesn't amuse my gentlemen, there's also a little bathing beach where they used to ask me to take their aperitifs when they'd been bathing in very hot weather it's an amenity, we used to be allowed to go there in the afternoons but I don't like cold water neither does Marthe whereas the flunkey
You haven't mentioned the flunkey during the party, what was he doing
Back and forth between the buffets to keep them stocked up and changing the candles too but he didn't do much he seized his chance and was mostly invisible
And the secretary
He was with my gentlemen
Did he stay after the fireworks

You bet he didn't unsociable as he was
Do you know where he went
I saw him passing through the large dining-room he must have been going to his office
And Baptiste Lepoquin
Another actor what do you expect me to say about him they're always acting a part and turning everyone else's lives upside down
Details
Not much detail to tell according to Riquet he's continually ferreting out the gossip the more dirt he can find the merrier he is me and actors if you want my opinion we should never let them get mixed up in our lives nothing interests them but the figure they cut in public, they can make us laugh all right but when the play's over let them get on with it with their who's going to bed with who if you'll pardon the expression then they wouldn't take so many people in, they're a pest that lot how can you expect other people to resist them when they're always getting their exploits dinned into them they don't realise it's all window-dressing, how could they guess that actors act out their feelings like the ones written down for them in books, it's all put on the whole lot for ordinary folk and don't go telling me it's *their* fault they believe the moon's made of green cheese when the actors know only too well what the score is
You forget that in this case Lili too was an actress
Not a bit of it if only he hadn't dropped her and played his part through to the end they'd have finished the night together for that's what it is that's always getting them worked up that would have straightened everything out, I'm telling you what they get up to among themselves Marthe's not the one to be backward in coming forward she gets on her high goat about that when you talk to her about actors, the dregs or stinkers as she says
Why was Gérard furious after the party
You don't miss much do you

Answer
Riquet had pinched his little village-lad
They met up again next day
No Riquet had walked off with him
Where
I've no idea
How did you find out
Marthe heard Gérard talking about it to my gentlemen
Say something about the days following the party
Back to the old grindstone putting everything straight cleaning everything up it took us a good three days, I was short of goodness knows how much cutlery that we found scattered about over the next few days or didn't find at all people put things down anywhere, not to speak of the broken crockery the glasses the stains on the carpets and all the rest

And the mess in the bedrooms too

That always takes the biscuit that and the bathrooms

What for example

All I can say is men or women they've none of them got any shame

In detail

Certainly not

Were you alone with the ordinary staff to do this work

No there was still Jean-Pierre, Chantre and Gérard we couldn't count on them any more Santa Claus comes but once a year

Who is this Jean-Pierre

Cruchet

Why are you laughing

Because I was thinking what Cyrille told Marthe he saw

Explain

La Hem at the far end of the orangery making passes at d'Eterville he was half asleep and she was in a state, first she tried to unbutton him but she couldn't see straight she plunged her arm right down his trousers under the belt, somehow the way she went about it one of his braces snapped in d'Eterville's face and he woke up with a start

Anything else

The orchestra yes it had launched out on a tango they'd already drunk a good drop of champagne and while one of the violinists was eyeing a girl who was dancing he gave Mademoiselle Bourgeon a great jab in the neck with his bow one of the oldest women in the orchestra, she turned round and slapped his face I think that's funny

At what time did Cyrille leave his buffet

Somewhere about six o'clock he was so tired he left everything topsy turvy and went up to bed, I brought the glasses in myself and what was left of the bottles

Where was he sleeping

In the attic

In one of the two bedrooms

No in the right wing

There are bedrooms in the right wing

Extra servants' bedrooms from the time when my gentlemen had a larger staff

How many rooms

Two they each have two beds the extras were able to make do

Would you mind describing these bedrooms

The first one communicates with a small bathroom on the landing and with the second one but you can get to the second straight off the landing too, there's a tiny kitchen as well it all made one little apartment

You say your employers used to have a larger staff

Before my time when they still had some of their family I think and the kee and they had more staff

What were you going to say

Nothing

Answer
The keep was inhabited
What keep
That's what they used to call the old part behind
What old part, behind what
I can't make it any clearer, the part they don't live in any more behind the house that's the old castle with its towers and its freezing bedrooms in the winter, the Commune pays a part of the upkeep in exchange for the right to open it to visitors on Thursdays and Sundays from ten o'clock till four, the keepers live in three small rooms
Why have you kept quiet about all this
What was the good of complicating things for you I tell you they don't live in it any more it's historical and very uncomfortable there's no heating or water that's no good these days, my gentlemen have given up showing off they prefer a bit of comfort you can understand them imagine what expense it would be to modernify those old places, the guard-room alone is a hundred feet long and you can't go right to the top of the big tower any more the stairs have been walled up as a precaution
Describe this old part
There's a main building running longways a second one sticking forward in the middle and three round towers the big one and two little ones, there were three other big ones at one time part of the walls of one are still there where they've made the service staircase you know, it made a kind of square shape how can I explain without plans the old ones I mean that Ducreux got up to give an idea, you can see what's left shown in black and what was there before shown in a dotted red line a great horseshoe if you like the other way round, the Revolution knocked it all about
Is this part of the residence connected with the present-day one
Through the attic next to that little kitchen I told you about a

low door, in the old days it was connected to the large drawing-room by a door where the chimney-piece used to be
So when you go round the present house you're obliged to pass round this old part too
No that's the point at the corner there's a big archway which comes out on the south terrace
Who is the keeper
Noël Perrin his wife and their son who works in the town
What were your relations with them
It was as if they didn't exist they never asked anything of us neither did we of them, they looked after the keep the cleaning I mean and the visits that had been arranged with my gentlemen who seemed satisfied since they'd got rid of the previous keepers shortly before my arrival
You say responsibility for the upkeep of these buildings rests partly on the Commune
Yes in exchange for the right to visit them it was the Archaeological Society I think who suggested it but still most of the takings went to my gentlemen it was their property after all
Were there many visitors
I don't think so about twenty a week perhaps during the season, anyway we were no more aware of them than if it had been Timbuctoo, they'd arrive round the back along a little lane that came direct from the Route du Plateau it cuts straight across the meadows
The plans that Ducreux reconstructed where are they kept
In the bedroom of one of my gentlemen with an old print of the buildings all complete it was quite a place the Château de Broy I can tell you
Is this residence still called the Château de Broy
In the guide book yes but it's always been referred to as a house
Do you know who used to occupy the living quarters with the kitchenette in the attic in the old days

A family in service to Madame de Broy she never wanted to move into the modernified wing she died of pneumonia, her bedroom was fourteen feet high and something like fifty in length it's still furnished and so are three others and two drawing-rooms, it's the guard-room and the chapel are visited mostly there's a gilded altar and pictures Italian it appears that a museum in Paris is meant to have offered a good price for

How many rooms are there in that part of the castle

About twenty apart from the loft and the cellars I'm taking care this time

Do you know why your employers have let the Commune lay its hands as you might say on this part of the residence

Because it's what you might call national there was an assassination in the Middle Ages and the visit of a Queen of Spain or Novocordia, the Historical Minister practically forced my gentlemen to allow the visiting they weren't keen on it that's why the Archaeological Society suggested this arrangement with the Commune to cover the running costs and pay for a keeper, it's no more than my gentlemen spend out on other things but I tell you the main repairs are their responsibility like the roofing and the years when they had to pump out the cellars a subterranean lake that overflows because of the Manu in the spring

Who was Madame de Broy

Monsieur Jean's mother she lived there all her life with her children three or four, in her last years she only had him and a daughter who didn't want to move either the two of them had installed their servants in the little flat for the amenities, it seems my gentlemen had suggested modernifying at least the ground floor for them but they wouldn't have it the daughter died before the mother after a chill the same thing

Did Marthe know these ladies

Towards the end yes by that I mean she only ever saw them in the distance by accident they never came to the house Monsieur

Jean used to go and spend the evening it seems from time to time
  Do you think their refusal to live with him was due merely to their dislike of modern amenities
  Ask me another
  Say what you think
  According to Marthe they'd quarrelled the mother never could stand Monsieur Louis and the daughter did as her mother on principle, mind you Monsieur Louis' family was the same they'd stopped seeing him
  Who was this family
  Louis' I told you
  Their name
  Bohémond
  A local family
  As old as the Broys the Château de Siterne was theirs which was handed down to Monsieur Louis, money breeds money it's the same old story
  Who lives in this Château
  Tenants at the moment an ambassador or an American minister my gentlemen didn't visit them except to collect the cash a small fortune, six million a year I've been told
  Describe the interior of what you call the keep
  Our attic door leads into a small round bedroom in the old tower with a wooden floor there's nothing there, you go down five steps and you're on the third floor in another empty room very long with beams on the ceiling the walls are almost six feet thick, then another empty room with five windows looking out on the farm it's freezing cold in the winter fireplaces are all right when you're on top of them but to heat that area, then a third bedroom furnished this time they'd tried to insulate it against the cold by stuffing up all the cracks that's where the lady died poor woman no wonder the fireplace is at the far end, first of all on the left there's a large bed with blue silk curtains and a bedside table

that still smells and two big wing chairs covered in pink silk and little grey and green flowers grey or green little grey flowers, little flowers I mean there it starts all over again

What starts all over again

It all starts all over again the armchairs the little flowers the chests and the chamber-pots

Go on

What interest can it possibly be to you

Go on

Another twenty rooms and then there'll still be more and you'll tell me to describe them, and more and more kitchens servants tell-tale tittle-tattle secrets of the bedchamber families mile upon mile of streets and stairs and lumber-rooms and junk-shops of antique-dealers grocers butchers of skimping and scraping everywhere in our heads how dreary it all is always starting all over again why, all these dead people around us all these dead people we third degree to make them talk when will you have finished I haven't asked anything, am I always going to have to start again the evenings in the bistro in the street what how why

Pull yourself together, describe them

Empty rooms now that's not much improvement

You said there were six of them furnished

Six or seven or ten how do I know

Say the exact number

There's no number in my head I can't count

What do you mean

How can anyone count memories you're crazy and all this coming back all the time everything coming back we'll never be able to sleep again where have they gone to earth where, such a noise in the head such bell-ringing and whistling and cold draughts through the cracks where have they gone to rest it's my turn to ask you

Pull yourself together, go on, the lady's bedroom

Poor woman she was unhappy

The blue silk bed the pink silk wing chairs with little grey and green flowers the pink silk wing chairs with little grey and green flowers

A table for whist in tropical wood the four wicker chairs the little inlaid dressing-table the glass case her collection of cosmetic jars a whole battery of pins and curling tongs the little spirit stove the large wardrobe lined with calico, the toilet table with its enamelled jugs the oil lamp the big Venetian chandelier the panelled walls the portrait of a man in colonel's uniform of another in evening dress and another in Court regalia, the lady with the cornflowers the girl with the sparrow and that sweet musty smell which reminds you of a forest in autumn

Another room

A small drawing-room with a round table and three armchairs and a sociable for two where you twist round to talk and a mahogany bookcase where all the books are in mauve leather, portraits again and the chimney-piece in polished wood with delftware tiles and standing on it the head of a lady in a high wig and the little door concealed by a tapestry that leads to the chapel there's a dark corridor where the visitors scratch their initials it's always having to be scraped and repainted

Describe the chapel

It's in the north-east tower a round one with an altar of gilded wood that looks like a little church, with six columns below like a pillar table Moroccan style if you see what I mean and carved bearded figures they're the prophets, and the Table and the Tabernacle with two angels and a rose tree engraved on a door and its little pointed roof with open tracery like a bell-tower there are two candelabra on either side and a brocade altar cloth, over the altar a picture representing the Descent from the Cross almost all dark except for the body, on the left another Jesus in the Temple talking to the scribes and on the right the Flight into Egypt on a donkey which was damaged by one of the tourists my gentlemen got Monnier to restore it and charged it to the Commune as was only natural, all round there are the Stations of the Cross small pictures rather Swiss I find they're like the figures in the attic in bright colours, the ceiling is pale blue with stars painted on and to light it the two windows of grey stained-glass left and right

Whereabouts is the guard-room

On the ground floor on the farm side

How do you reach it from the third

Down the stairs

Describe how you go from the chapel to the guard-room

It depends whether you come by the staircase in the big tower or by the one in the corridor or by the one in the south-west tower

Describe the longest route

You go back through the small drawing-room and into an empty room that gives onto the staircase in the tower, you turn left through the door where everyone bangs his head and you're in the corridor which is thirty yards long, you go past the first empty room average size then past two large empty ones which look onto what used to be the main courtyard that's the part of the building that juts forward as I told you, and at the end of the corridor there's a staircase which goes down to the second and first floors and the ground floor, a corridor again which you follow in the opposite direction as far as the visitors' great hall next to Perrin's small flat and on the right a flight of five steps that leads into the guard-room it's not on the same level as the ground floor

Describe this guard-room

I never liked that sort of thing armour and shamemail and chestplates that's all there is all round the walls like a lot of hanged men with pikes and lances and bludgeons, the collection's the finest in the district all right but I tell you I wouldn't give you that for it, there's also some armour standing up like a man with helmet gloves and pointed shoes and two on stuffed horses life-size, these fellows have got wax faces under the helmet one has a big moustache that Perrin catches in the vizor every time he gives a demonstration it wouldn't occur to him to trim it a bit, at the other end there's a big table too where the guards used to eat covered in knife marks and in the show-case their pewter plates and the jugs and great big spoons, in the centre on the right a huge fireplace with the old spit for an ox on its three-legged braziers weighing a hundred kilos each, no-one ever lights a fire there the visitors' feet get frozen in the winter Perrin makes them climb up to the chapel it thaws them out, it's a vaulted ceiling with several ribs when the Manu overflows the water sometimes used to rise to the guard-room which means to say the cellars were completely under water but the foundations are so solid there's not even a crack it comes up through the ground, I mean to say sorry there's an opening in the left corner under the room what used to be a postern that led straight into the moat, try as they might to cement it up several times it gave way from below with the pressure of the water but they didn't dare cement the ground because then the walls might have given way with the real flood waters

How are the cellars dried out in the event of a flood

There's a big mechanical pump under the lean-to at the farm specially for it, the firemen used to come and get it working once even they had to bring their own, my gentlemen had considered with Ducreux a permanent pumping system but since the lands Crachon way have been sold to the chemical company it's not worth worrying about they're going to build something deep down and channel the flood waters out their way, my gentlemen will be safe where they are it's all some special modern technique

Did you sometimes happen to follow Perrin taking his visitors round

I only did it once

You say every time he used to catch the figure's moustache in the vizor, how do you know

When Marthe went it was the same and sometimes my gentlemen used to take their guests along to have a laugh over the moustache bit

How long has Perrin been keeper

I said he started about the same time as me a month or two before at the most

And during your whole stay you never had anything to do with him

It sometimes happened we'd take him a message from my gentlemen or at the start ask some favour of him but he wasn't very helpful and the penny soon dropped

Why had your employers got rid of the previous keeper

Because of some indiscretions as they say he'd committed

Such as

He'd pinched some pewter dishes and some things from the lady's bedroom and the large drawing-room and some books too to sell them off to Bouboule who hadn't yet found out who he was and didn't know the stuff came from my gentlemen's, mind you in the eyes of the law he hadn't any right to buy them for his shop

Tell about the other furnished rooms in the keep

Opposite the guard-room as that's where we'd got to the large drawing-room where there was still some furniture round the fireplace, a table with knobbly legs and some armchairs known as Voltaire's with the big picture at the back where you could hardly see a thing a real battle of the blacks, and three aquatic tapestries my gentlemen didn't know what to do with it wasn't a good idea to put them there one day a visitor stubbed out his cigarette slap on the thigh of a water spite, the windows look out on us to the left on what used to be the main courtyard right opposite and to the right on that screen of oaks

This main courtyard is that what you've been calling the east terrace

That's it yes

So the large meadow was beyond it

Yes

Didn't you say you used to beat the carpets in this large meadow

Yes I said that

Why didn't you do it in the derelict courtyard

Derelict it wasn't derelict Pompom kept it going it wasn't much use that's all but to beat carpets on those cobbles, they were worse than the ones in the other courtyard all bumps and hollows

The carriage-drive that leads to the garage does that go as far as this courtyard too

Only part of the way, there's a large piece of meadow in front it bends round and almost encloses the courtyard, on Ducreux' plan you can see it was once one wing of the building that enclosed it on the oaks side, now the meadow comes further in the big tower stands inside it

Didn't you say there was a moat

It's been filled up all the way round, the meadow goes up to the walls on the east and on the south it's the terrace

You said the south terrace had a row of oaks on the left but really it ends with the keep

It goes on further than the keep, it ends with the oaks later

Go on with your description of the other furnished rooms

The dining-room nothing nor the kitchen either, the visitors' hall there's nothing but rustic seats you have to go up to the first floor to find the Queen's bedroom as it's called, a room that takes up the whole front of the jutting-out part and not only the front it's sixty by sixty foot square just imagine it could only be used as a ballroom, the furniture there has been brought from just about everywhere a bed to take at least five with a canopy that's a real plum pudding smothered in pearls and pompoms I think it's

Miette who made it up I ask you, at its head there are two crowns joined by a heart and at the foot a sort of marmot tangled up in ribbons, the counterpane is the same brocade as the altar-cloth there's a gilded stool to climb up it didn't do to miss it if you got up during the night, left and right of the bed all along the wall between the windows there's a row of Spanish chairs with this marmot on the backs it's Blinville who dug them up near Biarritz where he was on holiday I remember eight or nine years ago now, the Queen's bedroom wasn't open to the public at first my gentlemen hummed and ha'ed for quite a while, there are four windows on either side of the bed the fifth is blocked right to the top by the tester the shutters are kept closed, between the left corner and the first window over the chairs there's the portrait of a yellow constipated-looking king all in black gazing at a crucifix in one hand with the other he's making the sign for *mea culpa* and in the background a door opens on a cloister, between the first window and the second a frightful midget in a crinoline her stumpy arms hanging down either side with a fan in one hand in the other a little bag like a bag of marbles, on her head she has a bonnet with pompoms and under one baggy eye a large beauty spot you could mistake for a third nostril her nose turns up till it almost meets her eyes beside her her little dog is begging on a cushion, between the second window and the bed two ladies in mantillas they're whispering in each other's ears while some fellow behind with his guitar is trying to climb a ladder under a window where his fiancée is holding her chin as much as to say will he won't he, those Spanish pictures is there anything uglier between the bed and the third window which is really the fourth another constipated type in baggy breeches he's thinking about Paradise you can see some saints in the clouds round the Good Lord who's beating time, between the fourth and the fifth windows two midgets and their chaperone unless it's their mother she looks a bit of a tartar one of the midgets is gnawing her doll the other one is sticking one hand in a little fur muff where there must be some sweets as she's got one in the other hand, between the fifth and the corner a young prince with albino rabbit's eyes his cheeks are all swollen probably with grenadine pips as he's pressing one against his belly and on the side table there's a small Holy Virgin who looks almost neckless in a dress like a cornet, I saw one like it at the cinema documentary it was a procession with cowls and saxophones the statue was wobbling about on a bier up above the male-voice choir, against the wall the courtyard side between the windows there are only wardrobes where on earth can they have found them they're worse than cathedral altar-pieces gilt all over smothered in a shower of little men and fruit and animals, they're crammed full up all six of them three rows of hanging space in each with a collection of all period dresses, Perrin is not allowed to open them people might touch anyway the doors are thermetically sealed against the dust, my gentlemen have only shown them to us once there are fashion experts that come from all over the place just for that and directors of museums you should see the masses of lace and embroidery and skirts it would take you a year to look at them properly, Mademoiselle Lacruseille told Marthe one of these dresses had been worn by the Du Barrique the day of her marriage with Henri Quatre a blue dress no it's not it's pink the blue one is

Cut it short

On the left wall so that's on our side before the first window over the marmot chairs there's a large picture of nuns at table are they eating or is it arguing there are only three or four plates and two pitchers for the lot they're doing penance, one is standing in the corner with a book and above her the crucifix with a fresh-picked palm-leaf it's probably Holy Week, between the first and second windows a dressing-table the same style as the wardrobes with two shelves between the table and the mirror you had to be a giant to see yourself, those Spanish items you can expect anything but common-sense it appears that country's coming back in fashion people are meant to be finding a taste for bulls and seguidillas but according to Mademoiselle Thonac it's only the cheapness that attracts the tourists, between the second and the third windows a commode-cum-whatnot-cum-console in five pieces all fretwork that goes up to the ceiling at the bottom there's

Cut it short

Between the third and the fourth

Is there anything in the centre of this room

A table twelve feet long and armchairs with steps up covered in tapestry, on the table a vase that's a real bathtub with a bouquet of gilded flowers all rubbish picked up round about and on the ceiling three chandeliers Bohemian like the one at Fontainebleau said to be the dearest in the world

The other furnished rooms

I've said them all, the guard-room the chapel the lady's bedroom the

What is there on the second floor

Nothing but empty rooms and the corridor doesn't follow the same plan as on the other floors it's divided into three passages, one that goes to the south-west tower going round what they used to call the smoking room the other one that turns off twice to the left to come back to the round bedroom and the third one that goes straight on to the large tower

You say there's also a loft above the third floor

Yes but very low you can only just stand upright

How do you get up to it

A ladder at the end of the corridor, you could get there it seems by the staircase of the big tower before it was walled off

So the keep buildings are one storey higher than the wing your employers live in

Yes

Which way did the keeper take the visitors up from the guard-room to the chapel

Up the staircase in the big tower

Describe this staircase

It's the same as our service staircase good to break your neck on but the visitors like it

Used you often to go to the keep

Instead of going out sometimes in the evening I'd take a candle and go and wander round I always used to finish up in the lady's bedroom, I'd put my candle on the table and in her little armchair I'd meditate on what she must have thought about all alone it was a rest for me in a sad sort of way I used to like that

Wasn't it the keeper who had the keys

Yes Thursdays and Sundays early in the morning he'd lock all the doors including ours till the last visit was over, then he'd open them again and we could go where we liked

There wasn't any electricity

No except at the keeper's, for one or two special occasions my gentlemen made us light the candles the chandeliers and the oil-lamps, at the all-night party for example from the garden you could see the lights on every floor even in Mon even at the top everywhere Marthe wrote down in her notebook that it was

Even where you say

Even right up to the top floor of the towers

You were going to say even in Monsieur

Even to the top of the towers

Was someone living there

I said it was a museum

Tell the truth, was someone living in one of those towers

Why are you laying another trap for me

Answer

He'd never have wanted me to say

Who

Monsieur Pierre he only wanted one thing to be left in peace
Who was Monsieur Pierre
A friend of my gentlemen's they're very fond of him though he never mixed with anyone he lives all alone in the south-west tower lonely as a hermit, he's an expert in astronomy he's got a big telescope up at the top there to observe the stars and he's forever writing things for astronogical societies and all those books in his library, yes an expert but as for coming to the house it was as if it was the end of the world still my gentlemen went on pressing him he refused except very occasionally, he only liked a few of my gentlemen's friends who used rather to go to his place to see him just as I did although he preferred not to be disturbed but there was always one advantage, I'd go and see him and he'd show me the sky through his telescope and the moon explaining it to me as best he could, if I'd been able to I'd have gone every evening it was such peace being up there alone with him, five minutes at noon even once a day wasn't enough I used to take him his luncheon in the downstairs room his library-cum-dining-room, in the evenings it was the flunkey
How many rooms did he dispose of
Two the one on the third floor and the one on the fourth both small and round that was enough for him and for his convenience he used to use the bathroom in the small flat I mentioned
What does he do for heating in the winter
An electric radiator in every room yes I know what you're going to ask there was electricity for him my gentlemen had made him have it and for his telescope it's essential but he used to like writing by oil-lamp best
You say he enjoyed the company of some of your employers' friends
Monsieur Rufus and Monsieur Carré and Fifi and one can't help wondering why

Did your employers treat him as a friend or as a guest they obliged by putting up

A friend I tell you a real one but who mustn't be disturbed he's been with them since the lady died he was one of her friends

Don't you consider it a serious piece of dishonesty on your part to have given the impression up till now that your employers were only two

No I tell you Monsieur Pierre didn't get mixed up in anything, when I say my gentlemen it's only them I mean not him only a few intimate friends used to call them the Holy Trinity but to be frank the only holy man is Monsieur Pierre

Do you know if he has any financial interest in the house, any capital

I wouldn't know about that, what I do know is that he bought the fields at Milledoux in two goes Crachon way and it extended the property quite a bit on that side twelve acres but I think it was a present he made my gentlemen he's only interested in the stars, oh if you only knew him it breaks my heart already to think I mentioned him he'd never forgive me

You say he practically never leaves his tower

No except for his walks to Milledoux that's his favourite place in fact

Do you know if he stayed indoors the night of the party

I caught sight of him at his window for a moment he must have been watching the fireworks from up there

Would Rufus or Carré or Fifi have gone up to see him that night I don't know

How old is Monsieur Pierre

About the same as my gentlemen round fifty-five

Why are you surprised he enjoyed Fifi's company

Fifi's not serious I thought you'd have realised that after what I said Monsieur Pierre is a saint yes a saint what could he have to say to her he used to call her his little Cancer that's a star several even, from where we are you see the sky is like this round and Cancer is over there, Monsieur Pierre showed me the Lyre too and the Boots and Berniece's Hair he knows everything I've seen his opuscrules as he calls them they're little books full of calculations, Marthe heard Rufus say he was one of the best amacher astronogists once seven years ago now in August the thirteenth to be exact he even went to England for a conference where he received a decoration and a prize, it was when he came back that he bought the other half of Milledoux

It's difficult to believe you after your changes of tack and your continual omissions

I don't care I don't care a damn I'm delighted even, all this rigmarole Mademoiselle's typing on her machine it's just as if it wasn't me saying it you're worming out my secrets we know what comes next there are some things you have to be alone to do which are only of interest to vicious people like you, yes I say vicious if I hadn't had to say them or if I'd said them carefully and taken my time they wouldn't have sounded the same instead now like this you're going to have something on my gentlemen or on the others or on me, it takes time to digest things and before they're digested they may do some harm if they're not understood you're tempted to condemn them at first when you've not had the experience that's how we are always in a hurry to form our ideas with bits and pieces only that way all our judgements are false, but with time anything can be digested nothing's really poisonous it's just this stupid speed that grinds away and gradually makes us like brutes let me have my say for a moment and get it off my chest, makes us like brutes that's it do you think I don't realise, I think about it all the time at the café you see someone do something straightaway you jump to conclusions we must be mad there are no conclusions except those we imagine at the moment or that we're determined to call conclusions, the true ones are nothing like them they get mixed up with everything else and that's life but it's a slow process and listen though I'm on my guard your questions still make me slip up, I still fall into the trap it does happen and give my opinion and draw conclusions in spite of knowing it's all tommy-rot except in a hundred years' time or never even that's what I think, anyone would think we were in a hurry to leave life behind well I'm not you understand, in spite of everything I'm not soon I'll be going back to my room and tomorrow to the bistro again which isn't always such fun but I'd like it to go on all the time and that's that

What did Monsieur Pierre think of the flunkey

I feel sorry for you

Answer

I feel sorry for you you'll go on to the bitter end with your fly-blown questions

Answer, what did he think of the flunkey

I'm not the one to have asked him but what I do know is that he never let him look through his telescope, the flunkey couldn't care less he just did his job and that's all

Why wasn't it you who waited on Monsieur Pierre in the evenings too

That was the way things were my gentlemen had made up their minds and I was busier before dinner than before luncheon

Didn't you say it took five minutes to serve him

Plus five minutes at least to go there plus five to come back to the kitchen that makes a quarter of an hour and you've been pestering me with your riddle-me-ree's

Would Marthe know whether the flunkey got on with Monsieur Pierre

What she does know is that the flunkey called him cranky

And the secretary

He never set foot in the tower Monsieur Pierre pointed that out to me

Do you think there might be reasons for his not doing that

What do you mean
Reasons for being afraid of Monsieur Pierre
That's like saying a fox is afraid of a rabbit
It could be important to know if Monsieur Pierre really never went into town or to the village, say exactly what you do know
I tell you he never left his room
Yet he made that trip to England
That's still not into town
Answer
I tell you he never went into town or to the village
And his walks
I repeat they were to Milledoux
He'd never go as far as Crachon
That would surprise me he didn't like meeting people but if he did he was within his rights
Are you sure he had no acquaintances at Crachon
Acquaintances at Crachon anyone can see you don't know that God-forsaken hole it's the dirtiest in the district the folk there wallow in the they wallow in it all year round
Were Rufus and Carré still at your employers' the day after the party
Why back to that now we've got somewhere else somewhere else now
Explain yourself
It's not possible to answer any more don't you understand something's happened, you can be as artful as you like we've gone past that stage now
What stage
In our heads it was in our heads before we began we've done what we could and here we are like Monsieur Pierre with a different sky overhead, we'd have to do fresh calculations to check up on yesterday's or else as it doesn't stop moving we'd still be in the same boat

Answer the question about Rufus and Carré

Look where we are in this room there's just us and that big bundle of papers that's what we've said, but if we'd said the opposite it would all come to the same you and I here at bottom what we're hoping for is to get out of the wood we've just got to find the way, and when we feel like going home if your typist hasn't passed out we'll put off the bit about my life till later my gentlemen that's for now, we can't always be lagging behind the truth won't stand for that it gets caught by surprise like a girl by the first man she sees, it pays no more attention to all-night parties and the rest than it does to Father Christmas

Do you mean that your answers are misleading

I mean I've lost interest if you'd questioned me at the time it would have made a difference

To the general picture or to the details

The general picture as for sorting out the details now

Answer

Ten years is that enough

The all-night party and Johann's trial didn't they take place last year

It all boils down to the same thing now a sloppy mess you don't know what to do with

You refuse to answer concerning Rufus and Carré

I don't refuse I say that my life is now

For the last time answer

For the last time and again for the last and again for the last yes Rufus was there and Carré had gone home

And the secretary

The secretary was there too

How did he behave the day after the party

As usual

Did he have breakfast with the others

Yes

Did he stay with them
No he went off to work
At what time
I don't remember
Roughly
Between two and three o'clock
Who was he with during the meal
With my gentlemen
Was Monsieur Pierre there
No more than usual
And Rivière
He went off the next day
Alone
With Chantre
Give details about his departure
What is there to say about that
Answer
It was shortly before midday my gentlemen had just got up they'd stayed up late the previous evening, Marthe had made a light lunch Chantre came to say good-bye to her I went with him to Rivière's car which had been left in the meadow for parking, my gentlemen in their dressing-gowns with Gérard were saying good-bye to Rivière, Pompom was still busy raking the drive on the other side Rivière gave him five thousand francs and he got in the car with Chantre it's an English make and they drove off and there you are
 Did Rivière give you and Marthe a tip
Five thousand too it wasn't too much for the trouble
And to the flunkey
The same it was too much and the same for the chambermaid
Where were Rivière and Chantre making for
I've no idea
Do you know if anyone might have seen them at Sirancy

Pernette

What did she see

Them I tell you

What were they doing

They were meant to have met the secretary driving through the square and stopped in front of the Cygne for a drink, Cyrille served them on the terrace

At what time had the secretary left the house

Round about ten probably

What to do

Jobs as usual

Did he spend long talking to Rivière and Chantre

I've no idea

Would Cyrille know

I didn't ask him

And Pernette

I've no idea

Did she see them go off again

Yes the secretary got back in the car and Rivière with Chantre got back in his they went off towards the town at least along Chavirat that's all she saw it started raining and she went home

Aren't you getting mixed up with the fortnight before when Rivière went off with Poulet after his visit

That's possible

Make an effort

Impossible

Are you sure he set off again with Chantre

Yes Marthe said they're going off somewhere on the spree again

Where did they most like to go on the spree

I've no idea you can go on that anywhere

Did the secretary come back for luncheon

Yes

Who was there at luncheon

My gentlemen and Gérard and the secretary and Mademoiselle Lacruseille, she came down very late she'd stayed on since the party on the advice of my gentlemen I think she was rather unhappy at the time she'd hit the bottle, she stayed on for the evening too she had a long talk with Marthe who showed her what she'd started writing about the party Mademoiselle Lacruseille said it was very good except for the names not properly spelt she corrected them for her, she even said if Marthe kept it up she'd be able to make a book with her reminiscences they'd call it Memoirs of a Cook Marthe didn't like that much she'd prefer Memoirs of a Lifetime it's more distinguished

What happened in the weeks that followed between your employers and the secretary which might have motivated his abrupt departure

I said I've no idea

Between him and the flunkey perhaps

Definitely not

When did the flunkey leave

A month later

For what reason

I don't know he gave notice

Did he complain about his duties

Not as far as I know

Didn't the secretary's departure come shortly after Johann's trial

It did

Mightn't Marthe have surprised some conversation between your employers which could have enlightened her on the reason for this departure

No nothing

And Monsieur Pierre

Monsieur Pierre is above gossip

Please say exactly how the present house is linked to the keep

A low door I told you
Externally
There's a square bit at the south-east corner of the house where the old tower used to be and the archway crosses it
So this part sticks out from the east front
Yes right at the end when the big tower was demolished it prolonged the façade and they were able to put a window on that side to balance the other one
When was this alteration carried out
I don't know some time ago
Didn't you say the fireplace in the drawing-room had been rebuilt in stone during your time
I did
Where was it before
In the same place
Didn't you say that the keep once used to communicate with the drawing-room by a door that was where this fireplace is
I did
At the time the fireplace was reconstructed were you aware of the existence of this door
You could still see where it was it had been walled up a long while
Are you sure of that
Of what
That it had been walled up a long while
That's what I'm telling you
Might it not on the contrary never have been walled up which would have justified during the reconstruction of the fireplace the arguments of your employers' friends concerning the removal of the fireplace, as the door must have been very inconvenient in the restricted space left for it against the window
Yes if you like
Answer

Perhaps
You admit this door still exists
Yes it does
Why did you say the opposite
Because
Is it more difficult to say that it existed than to pretend the fireplace had been put there instead
Yes
Why
It leads into an underground passage
And then
It goes as far as the quarry
How do you know
They say it does
Who
People, the district is full of underground passages to Vaguemort that's how misfortune strikes in the different houses I always told my gentlemen that
How did they answer you
That the passage stops at the keep but *I* know I know it goes further than that everywhere I tell you they're everywhere
Did you go down into this passage
Never in my life
Where does it come out in the keep
Near the guard-room
So it passes underneath the archway
Yes
How do you think it's dangerous
Mustn't talk about this any more at Nutre too there are underground passages everyone says so
Did Johann know of them
I've no idea I don't want to say any more about them misfortune will come into all our homes until we wall up those doors

Where exactly does the row of armchairs start that encircles the fireplace

Between the window and the fireplace I told you that's the truth the first armchair is bang in front of that cursed door

Did your employers or their friends pass through it to go to the keep

Never the stairs are too steep and there's mud in the passage they always used to go the top way when taking visitors

What did you mean by saying that some people in the region nowadays pretend to have forgotten the yarns that are told about them

I don't know if I said that now

You did say it, answer

Did I mean the secretary did I mean my gentlemen's friends really I don't remember

Why did you say Pompom was in a bad mood in the evening with his wife when this was mentioned before

Because it's true

Didn't they have their daughter Gabrielle to keep them company

When the time comes for you to see a daughter in our district keeping her parents company the sun will shine more than it does these days

Didn't you say she was a serious girl

That doesn't mean she's company for the old folk

Didn't you say she used to help Marthe in the house

I did

Was she away at the time of the all-night party

No she was there

Why didn't you mention her

Mention her how

Among Marthe's helpers, you said she only had Jeannette and the farmer's wife for the bulk of the preparations, then Loulou and the cleaning woman for the cooking

378

What are you going on about now
Answer
What am I meant to answer
Did Gabrielle also help Marthe for those few days
Yes she did the silver and cleaned out the cupboards in the basement where we packed the spare china away and scrubbed everything
Once again why didn't you say so
But Heavens above you're crazy
Answer
Because I forgot
Did Gabrielle know Johann
I don't know
Answer
What what what's this you're after I don't know I've no idea what does it matter whether she knew him or not he wasn't in the limelight at that time
You said her mother Jeannette did needlework for almost everyone, what did you mean by that
People from the town and the village who give her work
Who
I've no idea
Answer
I'm tired
Answer
Madame Larvillier and Madame de Ballaison and Madame Emmerand and Madame
Madame Emmerand
I no longer know what I'm saying fine state I'm in
Didn't you say your employers were often buying pictures they put in the loft
I did
Where exactly

In the three rooms

Why when you were describing these three rooms did you only mention four pictures two in the former dining-room and two in the second bedroom whereas you said the loft was full of them

Because I forgot

Were these pictures on the walls

Some of them the others were on the floor by that I mean propped against the walls especially in the dining-room between the sideboard and the painted wardrobe quite a stack of them and another on the left of the door

Is it true that apart from the small flat there were no other rooms in the attic you omitted to mention

Yes that's true

Why do you call these apartments a small flat when they cover the entire right wing and therefore the same surface as the large dining-room

In Heaven's name compared to the whole house

Didn't you say that when Cyrille came as an extra to your employers' he fixed things with his colleague at the café

Yes

Who is this colleague

Martin Hévrier he's still there now

Did he know your employers

By sight perhaps not otherwise

Do you know if Cyrille talked to him about them

It would surprise me he's not one for tittle-tattle

It is however beyond doubt that Martin knew it was for them Cyrille was working

Well that yes everyone

And Cyrille didn't experience any unpleasantness from this

Unpleasantness to be paid what he was paid

We mean no-one and this Martin in particular used to reproach him for going to work for your employers

Reproach someone for working
Are you sure Martin wasn't jealous of him
I don't know
Used Cyrille to compensate him for the extra hours he stood in for him
Martin didn't do any more instead of starting work at eight next day he didn't come till ten and that was that
And the boss was in agreement
Cyrille never told me he made any fuss there aren't so many customers early in the morning or late at night, one waiter on his own can easily cope with that from time to time
Didn't you say your employers used to entertain almost every evening
Yes
So Cyrille was on call there practically every evening
Not a bit of it to start with we didn't always need extras I told you then when we did need them it was Cruchet and Luisot we used to ask for I told you, it was only on special occasions that we used to take Poulet and Cyrille as well yes I'm sure I told you that
When does the fête take place at Sirancy
Generally the second Sunday in June
Tell about this fête
Couldn't we wait for a moment
Didn't you say you used to go into town to collect the drinks
Yes
Where
To the sole agent's for Loewenbräu and Sucrette for soft drinks
Who's he
Toupin's brother
Who's Toupin
The one-eyed man who begs on the bridge his brother's quarrelled with him

And this Brize you used to borrow the van from
He's in transport
Give details
He's in transport on his own account since he left the navy he's got this van he hardly uses any more it's broken-down half the time
Didn't you talk of some punch session where Longuepie seems to have cut a sorry figure
What a memory for trivialities
Answer
It was when he wanted to get divorced the week he spent with us, one day Marthe made some punch her own recipe and Longuepie came to have a cry in the kitchen he *was* in a state my gentlemen had to cart him off to bed
Who are the people your employers sold the land at Les Vernes to
Strangers I told you
Their name
I said I don't remember now
Whereabouts is this land at Les Vernes
Quite a way in the direction of Saint-Porvan
Who is Jacob Goldshitt
I told you a dealer in minxes one of Rufus' friends
Is he a friend of your employers
No
Did he never come to see them
Once perhaps or else it was one of his cousins I've forgotten
How would you have got to know he was his cousin
I think the flunkey knew him
Where, when
I don't remember I don't remember
Answer
You're doing it on purpose I won't answer

Did Marthe know him

Answer, did Marthe know him
No
What kind of familiarity was there between your employers and the flunkey
Joking with him and asking his opinion
Why wasn't Madame Rufus at the all-night party
She was
Why didn't you mention her as well as her husband
I forgot
Why when you first talked about the billiard room did you say it would have been better if your employers had cleared out this room and turned it into rooms for the servants, were you seriously thinking this or was it to pull the wool over our eyes and avoid speaking about the other rooms in the attic
If I said it I thought it
Don't you think it would have been more natural to gain more space by using the rooms in the attic or in the small flat
Natural or not natural servants take what they're given
Who was the small flat used for the bathroom apart
No-one
Didn't you say the extras had slept there the night of the party
So I did yes
So wouldn't you have found it more natural in view of its size that it should be used in ordinary times for you and the flunkey for example, as your small rooms were earmarked for the extras on special occasions
I repeat if we've got to start looking for what's natural or not you're nowhere near finishing and I've had enough anyone would think you no longer know what to ask me
How do you explain that among all the chambermaids who have passed through your employers' hands not one ever spoke

to you of what they heard at the door of the secretary's office
What a palaver and all for that
Answer
You asked me before
Answer again
I can't explain it better now than then
Didn't you say Marthe was sure they knew something
I told you you asked me before
And you don't suppose they mentioned it to Marthe who refused to give you any details
No reason why Marthe had no secrets if she thought the maids knew something it was precisely because they didn't say a word
So there was something compromising involved
What compromises some folk doesn't compromise others
What do you mean
That the chambermaids were too scared of getting the sack they earned good wages I've told you all this I've told you are we starting all over again
What was the flunkey's attitude to the chambermaids
He led them a dog's life
Did they respect him
They were scared stiff of him
Don't you agree this power he had over them was enough to make them hold their tongues
And what about me and Marthe
We're talking about the flunkey, is it possible they kept their mouths shut because of him
Possible
Did Marthe mention about the chambermaids being afraid of the flunkey
She could see for herself there was no need to say so
Is it possible to suppose they learnt far more about the secretary's conversations from the flunkey than from listening at the door

I've no idea

We're asking you if it's possible to suppose this

You can suppose what you like there's no charge

What advantage do you think the flunkey could have gained by systematically giving the chambermaids information about these conversations and forbidding them to talk about it

What any man can get from a silly woman

He had affairs with the chambermaids

Affairs I wouldn't know God knows what he did with them

What do you suspect, what did you catch them doing together

I tell you he used to lead them a dog's life when we were present anyway

And when you weren't

I've no idea

You never stumbled on any incident during the night

At night I sleep

You said that during the night Marthe used to disturb the chambermaids with her coming and going, but wasn't it just the reverse it was the chambermaids who disturbed Marthe

That did happen yes it was even according to Marthe always the chambermaids who made the most noise and that's what gave rise to their scenes

Did Marthe think the chambermaids were going to the flunkey's room or vice versa

In any case he didn't go to theirs Marthe would have known her bedroom's next door, she said she used to hear them going to the lavatory

What do you think they got up to there

Well I ask you

What we mean is do you think they were up to something else like plotting with the flunkey

It seems to me it would have been easier to do that in his room

Wasn't that next to yours

He knew I was deaf all right
What do you mean by what any man can get from a silly woman
A lot of things
What apart from bed
I don't know they might have known better than he did what was going on after listening at the door, perhaps he paid them for it perhaps *I* don't know
Say what you suppose
According to Marthe but it's always the same mania with her they used to report things to the police and so they wouldn't know too much my gentlemen wouldn't keep them on for long but I mean to say my gentlemen had the police in their pocket with all their contacts, no I think the flunkey might have been paying them to give him information and if they didn't play ball he'd threaten to send them packing
Didn't you say the flunkey was very familiar with your gentlemen and weren't you deploring the very fact that they confided in him to the point of asking his opinion
That's got nothing to do with the conversations in the secretary's room
What do you think these conversations were about
I told you I've no idea the income tax business perhaps
Didn't you say the flunkey was kept informed about these matters by the secretary who even entrusted him with certain calculations
That doesn't mean the secretary told him everything especially about the important clients
Who was employed as chambermaid when the secretary left
One called Félicie something-or-other
Young
In the thirties
How long had she been in service there
A week or two perhaps

Say what you know about her
Nothing except she had proper carpet-beater hands
Did she stay long after the secretary left
I don't remember
She wouldn't have left the same time as the flunkey
That's possible I don't remember
Could she have been the cause even indirectly of the secretary's departure
I've no idea
When you look back on it dispassionately in the café for example what do you suspect may have provoked the secretary's decision
If you think I bother about that you're mistaken it's ages since I racked my brains to find reasons for the things that happen to us we know how much is lost to us every day and that's enough, memory there was a time when I'd have given ten years of my life to have it back again and now I don't even care it leaves you where it found you you know less and less about things, a load of useless rubbish at first you try to retrieve a few bits and pieces then you give up you take things as they come and you daydream about memories you've got all wrong what you once wanted and what you didn't get, you remember all that for a long time and a day comes when you don't remember any more and that's the end you're ready for the other side, the dead you see they don't remember anything but isn't that normal you're so keen on normality isn't that so *you* tell *me*, that they don't remember a thing any more even us when you come to think of it all this hopscotch of days without rhyme or reason work time-off plans the house in the country the family for all it amounts to for all we've got out of it *we* forget it all too

Answer, say what your suspicions were at the time
I'm not playing any more you can see for yourself we're not getting anywhere I've told you before your questions you don't know how to ask them and perhaps you no what's the good

What were you going to say
Nothing just things I think about
Explain yourself
You don't understand what's the good
Answer
It's not by saying I want this or that that you get it but rather when you're looking for something else and suddenly what you wanted drops in your lap, I tell myself all I can do now is to do without the cart as I can't put the horse before it, it's difficult of course but you'll get there in the end what are you risking when there's no choice there's nothing to lose, but you've taken good care not to let me talk about that you've made up your mind it's all my eye
Go on
It's too late
What do you mean by your cart
Put the cart before the horse it seems clear enough to me everyone's the same and the result is my gentlemen's life-story in a thousand typewritten pages a proper inquisitory but the main question hasn't been answered it'd be good for a laugh if we weren't so tired, yes I often think so many people all so tired just to end up with empty heads you don't cut off the heads of dead men empty you hear me so we might as well get worked up over something else as it all comes to the same, but neither Monnard nor Martin nor Cyrille nor any of the others I still see now do any different they're all the same spreading their nets to catch the wind the blackbirds have found new vineyards
Who is Monnard
That's right keep it going
Answer
The boss of Le Cygne
What do you mean by spreading their nets
I don't know it just came to me

Answer

That's the impression it gives me

Clarify your impression

I tell you I don't know just think of the times I've seen them chatting to this one or that one or laughing or fuming or worrying their heads about tips and bonuses, and old Henriette at her cash desk's the same who wanted a car she got it and her fur-lined coat and her Sunday in the country, those are their nets they're expecting something different you can't tell me they're content with their lot or even Eugène or Blimbraz busy hoping all morning that Cyrille will forget the bill but if he did they'd think about tomorrow's or winning five francs at dominoes, that's what I mean by the wind they catch

Does Monnard work at the counter

In the mornings he sells the tobacco and when Martin's busy in the restaurant he's at the counter with Cyrille but in the afternoons he's not there often he's the type with ants in his pants always some job to do, old Henriette's constantly complaining about it

Where is the tobacco sold in relation to the table you sit at

At the far end right in the corner that separates the café from the restaurant

Describe Le Cygne once and for all

In the corner the tobacco and a large opening that leads into the restaurant where there's a seat that runs all round and tables, to the right facing the square and after the coat-hangers two this side of the door and two beyond, then against the wall with no a window one two three four five I think yes five tables, then opposite the door three and in the corner the staircase that goes up to the Monnards' flat and another table and a coat-hanger and in the café there's first starting from the restaurant on the right the tobacco as I said then the cash desk, then the passage between the cash desk and the counter then the curved counter with its zinc top and behind all the bottles and the cupboards and the fridge and the Italian coffee machine I used to prefer the perco, expressos leave a taste in your mouth and they don't do your stomach any good or a good filter why yes a good filter that's really something, then in the corner on the Town Hall side at the end of the counter the trap-door that goes down to the cellar it's most impractical because over that there's the door to the toilets which leads into Philippard's passage there's always someone getting stuck in that corner if it's not Cyrille it's a customer, so then the toilets then two tables and a coat-hanger then facing the square my table and a second one this side of the door and three beyond, another coat-hanger in the corner and against the end of the partition wall the fruit machine Monnard's just put in for the teenagers but they don't come much to Le Cygne I told you it was an attempt to attract them

Are there windows looking onto the square

Yes four two in the café two in the restaurant

And the restaurant has no light on the Chavirat side

You're forgetting the shoeshop that's on the corner it's the same house

Say again the name of this shop

Topiron

Didn't you say Monnard had never carried out any alterations in his establishment

Yes I said that

What's its general appearance

Its general appearance its general appearance well I suppose its appearance is that of a café without alterations there's some panelling painted brown with black mouldings, over the fruit machine a mirror where they write the price of the new wine and beside it almost hidden by the coat-hangers an old framed picture of a woman with poppies in her hair, above the bottles behind the counter old ceramic tiles representing Holland with its windmills and the natives skating in trousers baggy at the bottom, there used to be another it appears where the opening to the restaurant is long before Monnard's time and another that's still on the wall on the Chavirat side, snow-capped mountains and chalets with a horse-driven sledge passing through the fir trees that's where Cyrille puts the Christmas decorations as it's all in keeping, on the wall at the back there are some of Trapaz' pictures to be sold but they don't go at Le Cygne the ceilings are painted brown like the wall there's not even a crack after all this time builders were builders then

The lighting

Bracket lamps with three tulips if you see what I mean red and wavy all round and two white globes, one over the tobacco the other at the end of the counter they couldn't see there properly

What is Phillippard's passage

The entrance to Phillippard's house which adjoins I told you the toilets are at the end of the passage the customers can use them you get the key at the cash desk

Which flat in Phillippard's house are these toilets meant to be for

The ground floor one but it's not let Phillippard uses it for storage

Didn't you say the tenants on the third floor were trying to get rooms in the attic

I did

Wouldn't it be simpler for them to rent the ground floor as well if Phillippard cleared it for them

It looks as though it doesn't suit Phillippard

Why are these toilets locked if they're only used by the customers of Le Cygne

So they don't become too public with people if you give them an inch

Is there a telephone at Le Cygne

At the cash desk
Have you ever happened to use it
Oh me and the telephone but it has happened when I was still at my gentlemen's that they'd telephone to the Cygne to pass me some message they'd forgotten
Used your employers to consider you something of a drinker
Drinker drinker why don't you say drunkard, I was a well-trained servant don't you forget it I could have knocked spots off a few of the others
Who is Blimbraz
An old boy who used to be in contracting I told you for a long time he was a road-sweeper after his spot of trouble
And Eugène
He was once a concierge in the town now he's at his daughter's he won't make old bones, only yesterday I saw him all hunched up on his chair the longer you live the lower you stoop
And you say the secretary was a customer at Le Cygne
Customer the secretary I never said that
Didn't you say that at the time of his meeting with Rivière two days after the party he had a drink there with him and Chantre
That's not to say he was a customer it's Rivière who must have invited him he's not stuck-up he's at home everywhere but the secretary
He never went to Le Cygne apart from that day
Not so far as I know
Was he on bad terms with Cyrille
That would surprise me Cyrille's not on bad terms with anyone he's very good-natured
And you think the secretary would have felt it beneath him to call and say hello to Cyrille
I don't say that I say he wouldn't have gone for a drink
You admit he may have called at Le Cygne from time to time to pass on a message for example to Cyrille from your employers

I don't deny that
Might Cyrille remember certain occasions when the secretary could have called with this object
You'll have to ask him
Might he have mentioned it to you at the time
If you're asking me to remember that
You don't remember his ever telling you the secretary called shortly before the latter's departure
Good Heavens no besides I haven't seen him at my gentlemen's since then, at the café he can't tell me anything
Up to what time do you generally stay at the café
That depends if I've finished my paper I go for a bit of a walk about eleven o'clock otherwise I go home for lunch
You always have lunch with your landlords
Always unless Clothilde can't manage it in that case she gets my stew ready the day before and I warm it up in my room
Describe your room
It really looks as though we're getting to the end we're back in my room again we should never have left it
Answer
I don't want to that room don't you see
Didn't you keep a few souvenirs there
Some photos and the vase I had at my gentlemen's on my table
Photos of what, of whom
Photos
Answer
That's all
Photos of your folks
Photos of what no longer exists of what one wants to retain in one's heart and what's gone what need is there for photos of the café, or of the street that's what's taken their place that's how we're made
Do you intend to remain with your landlords

Do I intend to remain why of course I intend to remain
You seem to wish for something else
I think you've got that wrong
Describe your room
What again you won't have spared me anything
Describe it
It's on the second floor the bedroom of the son who went off I told you
The furniture
Clothilde moved the wardrobe down to the first floor and the big table she needed in the kitchen
What did she leave
The small table and the chair and the bed and the cupboard
How do you get to your room
Up the staircase
Inside or outside
Inside
So you go through your landlord's place
Yes
How many floors to the house
Two
How many rooms
You think you're still at my gentlemen's place
Answer
The kitchen and the dining-room downstairs and the toilets, two bedrooms on the first floor two on the second
Who uses the second bedroom on the first floor
One for her the other for him he can't sleep
No bathroom
No
Didn't you say there was water in your room
I did
Hot

Cold
Go on with the description of your room
That's all
Is it a good bed
Yes
How is it fitted up
Fitted up with what
Blankets and so on
One woollen blanket beige and a padded quilted coverlet
Colour
Red
And that's all
For the winter an eiderdown as well
Good one
Very heavy
The sheets
She changes them for me once a month
No pillow
One pillow and a bolster I slip under the bottom sheet
Go on
That's all
Nothing to decorate the room, no picture
Over the bed a sort of carpet a small blue one to protect the wall
Plain blue
There are cats on it
Go on
At the head of the bed a First Communion picture belonging to their son
What does it represent
The Child Jesus
What is he doing
In one hand he's holding his cross with the other pointing to Heaven

Go on
I'm tired
Whereabouts is the table
At the bottom of the bed
And the chair
So is that
Where is the lavatory basin
On the right as you go in
Beside the bed or the table
Beside the table
Describe this table
Wooden
And the chair
Cane
Where used the big table to be
Opposite next to the cupboard
What is there in place of it
Nothing
Where used the second wardrobe to be
Next to the bed
What is there in place of it
Nothing
Didn't you say you used to put your extra belongings in a cupboard in the corridor
I did
Where is it in relation to your room
Opposite
How wide is this corridor
Five feet
What do you put in your cupboard
My belongings
Specify
My clothes

Which ones
My dark brown suit and my black one
And your linen
As well
Specify
I can't go on
How many shirts
Six
Handkerchiefs
Twelve
Underclothes, pants
Four vests five pants
Socks
Seven pairs
Wool, cotton
I don't remember
Answer
Don't make me go on to the end
Do you wish for extra linen, more clothes, pocket-money
No
What do you wish for
I've stopped asking myself that question
Haven't you a favourite subject for your meditations
I perhaps yes
Such as
I you'll only think me pretentious
Answer
Monsieur Pierre and his stars that's it yes that's what goes best with the rest
What rest
The distances I mean that every day you need a little more we're bound to understand in the end
Understand what

The rest what one's forgotten sometimes I tell myself
Explain
Perhaps that's the answer that does the least harm
What answer
Understanding what one's forgotten
What
It seems so to me unless I'm talking nonsense and as for that
Have you seen Monsieur Pierre again
Never I wouldn't dare disturb him
You haven't thought out some way, by making use of Cyrille for example
Never I wouldn't dare disturb him
Does Cyrille carry on as an extra with your employers
Everything carries on till the day it's stopped
What way have you thought out
It's like the mariner lost at sea
What do you mean
There's a journalist who comes to question his son about what his hopes are
And so
All the son can say is leave me alone
Answer, have you envisaged some way of seeing Monsieur Pierre again
Never I wouldn't dare disturb him unless
Unless
As I dreamt one day one morning I was walking along my little lanes
Go on
I took one I didn't know before and there's Marie in a garden with our child and she says to me come in come in and I go into the kitchen where I find Monsieur Pierre
Go on

    He asked us to dinner we had all night long to talk about the
stars and another night and then another and
    And
    We were going to talk for a long time
    Go on
    I could hear everything I could hear everything I was telling
him all the names Cyrille came to shake me
    You were dreaming in the café
    I don't remember
    You'd fallen asleep in the café
    I don't remember
    Has it ever happened that you fall asleep in the café

    Answer, had you fallen asleep that day in the café
    I don't remember
    Answer

    Yes or no answer
    I'm tired

John F. Byrne French Literature Series

The John F. Byrne French Literature Series is made possible through a generous contribution by an anonymous individual. This contribution allows Dalkey Archive Press to publish one book per year in this series.

Born and raised in Chicago, John F. Byrne was an educator and critic who helped to found the *Review of Contemporary Fiction* and was also an editor for Dalkey Archive Press. Although his primary interest was Victorian literature, he spent much of his career teaching modern literature, especially such writers as James Joyce, Samuel Beckett, and Flann O'Brien. He died in 1998, but his influence on both the *Review* and Dalkey Archive Press will be lasting.

SELECTED DALKEY ARCHIVE PAPERBACKS

PIERRE ALBERT-BIROT, *Grabinoulor*.
YUZ ALESHKOVSKY, *Kangaroo*.
FELIPE ALFAU, *Chromos*.
  Locos.
  Sentimental Songs.
IVAN ÂNGELO, *The Celebration*.
ALAN ANSEN, *Contact Highs: Selected Poems 1957-1987*.
DAVID ANTIN, *Talking*.
DJUNA BARNES, *Ladies Almanack*.
  Ryder.
JOHN BARTH, *LETTERS*.
  Sabbatical.
ANDREI BITOV, *Pushkin House*.
LOUIS PAUL BOON, *Chapel Road*.
ROGER BOYLAN, *Killoyle*.
IGNÁCIO DE LOYOLA BRANDÃO, *Zero*.
CHRISTINE BROOKE-ROSE, *Amalgamemnon*.
BRIGID BROPHY, *In Transit*.
GERALD L. BRUNS,
  Modern Poetry and the Idea of Language.
GABRIELLE BURTON, *Heartbreak Hotel*.
MICHEL BUTOR,
  Portrait of the Artist as a Young Ape.
JULIETA CAMPOS, *The Fear of Losing Eurydice*.
ANNE CARSON, *Eros the Bittersweet*.
CAMILO JOSÉ CELA, *The Hive*.
LOUIS-FERDINAND CÉLINE, *Castle to Castle*.
  London Bridge.
  North.
  Rigadoon.
HUGO CHARTERIS, *The Tide Is Right*.
JEROME CHARYN, *The Tar Baby*.
MARC CHOLODENKO, *Mordechai Schamz*.
EMILY HOLMES COLEMAN, *The Shutter of Snow*.
ROBERT COOVER, *A Night at the Movies*.
STANLEY CRAWFORD, *Some Instructions to My Wife*.
ROBERT CREELEY, *Collected Prose*.
RENÉ CREVEL, *Putting My Foot in It*.
RALPH CUSACK, *Cadenza*.
SUSAN DAITCH, *L.C.*
  Storytown.
NIGEL DENNIS, *Cards of Identity*.
PETER DIMOCK,
  A Short Rhetoric for Leaving the Family.
ARIEL DORFMAN, *Konfidenz*.
COLEMAN DOWELL, *The Houses of Children*.
  Island People.
  Too Much Flesh and Jabez.
RIKKI DUCORNET, *The Complete Butcher's Tales*.
  The Fountains of Neptune.
  The Jade Cabinet.
  Phosphor in Dreamland.
  The Stain.
WILLIAM EASTLAKE, *The Bamboo Bed*.
  Castle Keep.
  Lyric of the Circle Heart.
STANLEY ELKIN, *A Bad Man*.
  Boswell: A Modern Comedy.
  Criers and Kibitzers, Kibitzers and Criers.
  The Dick Gibson Show.
  The Franchiser.
  George Mills.
  The MacGuffin.
  The Magic Kingdom.
  Mrs. Ted Bliss.
  The Rabbi of Lud.
  Van Gogh's Room at Arles.
ANNIE ERNAUX, *Cleaned Out*.
LAUREN FAIRBANKS, *Muzzle Thyself*.
  Sister Carrie.
LESLIE A. FIEDLER,
  Love and Death in the American Novel.
FORD MADOX FORD, *The March of Literature*.
CARLOS FUENTES, *Terra Nostra*.
JANICE GALLOWAY, *Foreign Parts*.
  The Trick Is to Keep Breathing.
WILLIAM H. GASS, *The Tunnel*.
  Willie Masters' Lonesome Wife.
ETIENNE GILSON, *The Arts of the Beautiful*.
  Forms and Substances in the Arts.
C. S. GISCOMBE, *Giscome Road*.
  Here.
DOUGLAS GLOVER, *Bad News of the Heart*.
KAREN ELIZABETH GORDON, *The Red Shoes*.
PATRICK GRAINVILLE, *The Cave of Heaven*.
HENRY GREEN, *Blindness*.
  Concluding.
  Doting.
  Nothing.
JIŘÍ GRUŠA, *The Questionnaire*.
JOHN HAWKES, *Whistlejacket*.
AIDAN HIGGINS, *Flotsam and Jetsam*.
ALDOUS HUXLEY, *Antic Hay*.
  Crome Yellow.
  Point Counter Point.
  Those Barren Leaves.
  Time Must Have a Stop.
GERT JONKE, *Geometric Regional Novel*.
JACQUES JOUET, *Mountain R.*
DANILO KIŠ, *Garden, Ashes*.
  A Tomb for Boris Davidovich.
TADEUSZ KONWICKI, *A Minor Apocalypse*.
  The Polish Complex.
ELAINE KRAF, *The Princess of 72nd Street*.
JIM KRUSOE, *Iceland*.
EWA KURYLUK, *Century 21*.
VIOLETTE LEDUC, *La Bâtarde*.
DEBORAH LEVY, *Billy and Girl*.
  Pillow Talk in Europe and Other Places.
JOSÉ LEZAMA LIMA, *Paradiso*.
OSMAN LINS, *Avalovara*.
  The Queen of the Prisons of Greece.
ALF MAC LOCHLAINN, *The Corpus in the Library*.
  Out of Focus.
RON LOEWINSOHN, *Magnetic Field(s)*.
D. KEITH MANO, *Take Five*.
BEN MARCUS, *The Age of Wire and String*.
WALLACE MARKFIELD, *Teitlebaum's Window*.
  To an Early Grave.
DAVID MARKSON, *Reader's Block*.
  Springer's Progress.
  Wittgenstein's Mistress.
CAROLE MASO, *AVA*.

FOR A FULL LIST OF PUBLICATIONS, VISIT:
www.dalkeyarchive.com

SELECTED DALKEY ARCHIVE PAPERBACKS

Ladislav Matejka and Krystyna Pomorska, eds.,
  Readings in Russian Poetics: Formalist and Structuralist Views.
Harry Mathews,
  The Case of the Persevering Maltese: Collected Essays.
  Cigarettes.
  The Conversions.
  The Human Country: New and Collected Stories.
  The Journalist.
  Singular Pleasures.
  The Sinking of the Odradek Stadium.
  Tlooth.
  20 Lines a Day.
Robert L. McLaughlin, ed.,
  Innovations: An Anthology of Modern & Contemporary Fiction.
Steven Millhauser, *The Barnum Museum.*
  In the Penny Arcade.
Ralph J. Mills, Jr., *Essays on Poetry.*
Olive Moore, *Spleen.*
Nicholas Mosley, *Accident.*
  Assassins.
  Catastrophe Practice.
  Children of Darkness and Light.
  The Hesperides Tree.
  Hopeful Monsters.
  Imago Bird.
  Impossible Object.
  Inventing God.
  Judith.
  Natalie Natalia.
  Serpent.
Warren F. Motte, Jr.,
  Fables of the Novel: French Fiction since 1990.
  Oulipo: A Primer of Potential Literature.
Yves Navarre, *Our Share of Time.*
Wilfrido D. Nolledo, *But for the Lovers.*
Flann O'Brien, *At Swim-Two-Birds.*
  At War.
  The Best of Myles.
  The Dalkey Archive.
  Further Cuttings.
  The Hard Life.
  The Poor Mouth.
  The Third Policeman.
Claude Ollier, *The Mise-en-Scène.*
Fernando del Paso, *Palinuro of Mexico.*
Robert Pinget, *The Inquisitory.*
Raymond Queneau, *The Last Days.*
  Odile.
  Pierrot Mon Ami.
  Saint Glinglin.
Ann Quin, *Berg.*
  Passages.
  Three.
  Tripticks.
Ishmael Reed, *The Free-Lance Pallbearers.*
  The Last Days of Louisiana Red.
  Reckless Eyeballing.
  The Terrible Threes.
  The Terrible Twos.
  Yellow Back Radio Broke-Down.
Julián Ríos, *Poundemonium.*
Augusto Roa Bastos, *I the Supreme.*
Jacques Roubaud, *The Great Fire of London.*
  Hortense in Exile.
  Hortense Is Abducted.
  The Plurality of Worlds of Lewis.
  The Princess Hoppy.
  Some Thing Black.
Leon S. Roudiez, *French Fiction Revisited.*
Luis Rafael Sánchez, *Macho Camacho's Beat.*
Severo Sarduy, *Cobra & Maitreya.*
Nathalie Sarraute, *Do You Hear Them?*
Arno Schmidt, *Collected Stories.*
  Nobodaddy's Children.
Christine Schutt, *Nightwork.*
Gail Scott, *My Paris.*
June Akers Seese,
  Is This What Other Women Feel Too?
  What Waiting Really Means.
Aurelie Sheehan, *Jack Kerouac Is Pregnant.*
Viktor Shklovsky, *Theory of Prose.*
  Third Factory.
  Zoo, or Letters Not about Love.
Josef Škvorecký,
  The Engineer of Human Souls.
Claude Simon, *The Invitation.*
Gilbert Sorrentino, *Aberration of Starlight.*
  Blue Pastoral.
  Crystal Vision.
  Imaginative Qualities of Actual Things.
  Mulligan Stew.
  Pack of Lies.
  The Sky Changes.
  Something Said.
  Splendide-Hôtel.
  Steelwork.
  Under the Shadow.
W. M. Spackman, *The Complete Fiction.*
Gertrude Stein, *Lucy Church Amiably.*
  The Making of Americans.
  A Novel of Thank You.
Piotr Szewc, *Annihilation.*
Esther Tusquets, *Stranded.*
Dubravka Ugresic, *Thank You for Not Reading.*
Luisa Valenzuela, *He Who Searches.*
Boris Vian, *Heartsnatcher.*
Paul West, *Words for a Deaf Daughter & Gala.*
Curtis White, *Memories of My Father Watching TV.*
  Monstrous Possibility.
  Requiem.
Diane Williams, *Excitability: Selected Stories.*
  Romancer Erector.
Douglas Woolf, *Wall to Wall.*
  Ya! & John-Juan.
Philip Wylie, *Generation of Vipers.*
Marguerite Young, *Angel in the Forest.*
  Miss MacIntosh, My Darling.
REYoung, *Unbabbling.*
Louis Zukofsky, *Collected Fiction.*
Scott Zwiren, *God Head.*

FOR A FULL LIST OF PUBLICATIONS, VISIT:
www.dalkeyarchive.com